VIOLENT
DELIGHTS

VIOLENT
DELIGHTS

HANNAH BOGGS

Library Congress Control Number: 2019909408

ISBN: 978-1-645-70830-8 (PB)
ISBN: 978-1-645-70334-1 (HB)
eISBN: 978-1-645-70333-4

To Brittani Buckley (a.k.a. Ms. Preschool),
who gave me my love of reading and
encouraged me to be more.

"These violent delights have violent ends ..."

~William Shakespeare

I

Tall pine trees swept past Odette's line of vision in massive green blurs. In between them were bits of the greying sky. A storm was approaching—she could feel the electricity.

It seemed that the car ride would never end, and that she would die on this long stretch of road, which honestly *could* happen. Odette didn't mention this because her mother, Pamela Sinclair, didn't like self-deprecating jokes. Especially nowadays.

Odette tore her eyes away from the trees and closed her eyes. She was in desperate need of rest, despite the fact that all she ever did was rest. Her back ached from not having moved since the last rest stop about three-and-a-half hours ago in a small town near the border of New Hampshire and Maine.

Her mother caught sight of this and, instantly, her eyebrows knit together in concern. "Honey, are you okay? Do we need to stop?"

The girl opened her eyes and looked into her mother's through the mirror. "I'm fine, just trying to find a way to pass the time."

The woman nodded and muttered a near inaudible "okay" and returned to her driving. Still, she snuck a few more glances through her mirrors at her daughter.

"We're almost there. Maybe about forty minutes or so."

The girl rolled her lips and said nothing. She jammed a finger under the band of her "special bracelet," hoping to cool the sweaty skin underneath.

The trees suddenly broke open and a city entered her eyesight. There were tall towers of glittering glass, apartments, stores, random art pieces, homes, and, most importantly, the hospital.

The reason they were moving in the first place.

Giant billboards advertised fishing and soda; a few advertised the children's hospital. She shuddered to think of all the extra tests that she might have to be put through in the future. All the extra *needles*.

The drive continued through the city and the Sinclairs passed many more opulent buildings, one was a private school—but it was a Saturday in the beginning of June, so they had already let out—a museum, and a mall, but her mother didn't stop. She only made a comment here and there about a building's exterior design or about pulling over to allow Odette to climb up front with her, which Odette refused politely. In fact, they drove straight through the bustling city and out until they were back into the woods.

Odette sighed, sinking back into her chair. Now all there was to look at were a few rundown houses. Depressing. She almost wished she had driven up with her father, but it would have been just as depressing if not more. *But,* she thought, *at least he laughs at my jokes ... sometimes.*

The trees did break again and revealed a small town of log cabins and more shabby houses. There was a giant water tower with the name *"Sunwick Grove"* painted in large, black letters. Only two miles later did the welcome sign greet her eyes.

"Welcome to Sunwick Grove, Maine, where anything is possible."

It would have been cute if the overhanging trees and ruggedness of the sign hadn't given it an ominous undertone.

"This place seems ... interesting." Odette craned her neck to see how far behind her father was.

"I think that it's charming! Oh look, Det!" her mother cried, pointing to a large billboard. On it were a boy and a girl dressed similarly to each other with similar features. "Those are the magic twins I had told you about."

"Come and see the Mages Twins in the Tent of Mystery. They're expecting you."

"Why, that's not vaguely terrifying at all, Mom."

Pamela chuckled and shook her head. "It does kind of sound like that, doesn't it? If you're feeling well enough on Monday, my work gave me two tickets to see the show."

Odette's eyes lit up, "Really?"

"I wouldn't offer if I didn't mean it. I know that these past two years have been rough and you've had to give up a lot of stuff you loved. If I can make you happy by taking you to see some kids pull a rabbit out of a hat, I will." Her mother winked at her through the mirror, like it was some big secret.

Many more billboards flew passed them, some of them advertising things like restaurants or local attractions, but most of them seemed to veer towards the Tent of Mystery and those magic twins. Odette stopped paying attention to them after they passed the fourth one as it had become a little annoying.

The car came to a stop and Odette realized that they had finally arrived. Even though every fiber of her wanted to jump out of the car and run around, she knew her mother would stop her. Something about her being too fragile.

Odette unbuckled herself and stepped out of the car gently. The air was muggy and thick and her hair had already begun to stick to the back of her neck but she smiled all the same.

She recognized the house from when her parents showed it to her in pictures. It was a smallish colonial style home, not very large but larger than the one they lived in back in Oregon. The nearest neighbor was nowhere in sight, which was kind of odd considering the smallness of the town.

Her mother handed her the keys and she gladly rushed up the porch to open the door.

The first thing that hit her was how it smelled. It was musty from being empty and it just didn't feel like a home yet. A cloud of dust plumed out and caught the light in a pretty, mystical way. It was completely void of furniture with wooden floors and arched entries and exits. The walls were a pale blue with white trim. It was hotter inside than it was outside but a breeze started to blow in from the opened door, chilling her sweaty skin.

Cautiously, Odette entered the home, her footsteps kicking up more dust.

How long has this place been empty? Odette wondered to herself.

It looked like the type of place that would have been used as a horror movie set, and she couldn't help but conjure up a strange-looking monster peeking at her through the window. As soon as she did, Odette squeezed her eyes shut and shivered, pushing that out of her mind as fast as she could.

She found the stairs and glanced behind herself to see if her mother would reprimand her for such a "dangerous" task but she was busy with her father. She took the moment to quietly run up the stairs and into the hall that it led to. At the end of it was a window seat, the only furnishing she had seen so far. The cushion was faded from being exposed to the sun but, other than that, it was in a good condition.

Odette turned to the first door she saw and opened it. There was a large window that made the room more spacious and a small closet that was on the opposite side. The walls were a dove grey, which she didn't mind at all. She smiled, walking the length of the room to get a feel of it. Her fingertips ran along the dust-coated walls, looking up and out and around to soak in all the details of it.

"Odette? Odette, where are you?" Her mother yelled from down below.

There was the pounding sound of feet on floor and her mother's head popped into the room that Odette currently occupied.

"Why are you up here? Your heart could have acted up and you could have fallen down those stairs. Please, next time, be careful!" Her mother exclaimed, her sandy brown hair falling out of the bun she had clipped it in.

The girl sighed, leaning against the window. "Today's a good day, Mom. I'm fine."

"But it can change in just a split second, honey, you know that. Just, *please*, tell me before you do anything like that again," her mother pleaded, walking into the room to hug her daughter.

Odette hugged her mother back but was secretly fuming in her mind. "Sorry." She wasn't sorry at all.

"The moving van won't be here until tomorrow, but we have sleeping bags and pillows and a change of clothes for the morning!" she pepped up, rubbing her daughter's arm for comfort. If it was for Odette or herself, she didn't know.

Odette timidly looked up into her mother's hazel eyes. "I think I like this room; can I have it?"

There were so many reasons why her mother would say no, starting with the fact that it wasn't on the ground floor. She searched her mother's face for a sign.

Nothing.

Not a single hint as to what was going on in her head. Then, Pamela frowned and rubbed her forehead, thinking it through.

Odette studied her mom's face. It had seemed to age immensely over the past two years, but she was still a beauty. She had frown lines around her mouth and her forehead was starting to crease deeply from always being knitted so close together. Her face barely had any color left in it but it was still way more than what Odette had.

She had become a shut-in of sorts, never went outside or to many events at all. For a while, the only activity she had was being able to go to and from school, but, eventually, that stopped as well. Odette, now very sensitive to the sunlight, couldn't spend very long in it at all and always had to wear sunglasses to protect herself from oncoming migraine.

"Well ..." her mother began. "I suppose. The master bedroom is downstairs and your father has already started putting our boxes in there. Or we could just move into one of the bedrooms up here to make sure you'll be okay ...." She continually drew out her words, making them sound unsure of what she was even saying.

Odette shook her head. "No, no, I'll be fine up here. I saw a bathroom across the hall, so if I get weak, I can just crawl to it. Besides, I need to be able to have my space and so do you guys."

Her mother scoffed and crossed her arms, her mood changing instantly to suspicion. "Why do you need your own space? Are you hiding something?"

"What? How did you even get that from what I was saying?" Odette could feel her face turning red. She had nothing to hide because she rarely went out. Besides, she didn't even know anyone in Sunwick Grove, aside from the Mages Twins and she hadn't even *met* them.

"You can hardly take care of yourself, Odette. I want you to be able to but I just don't think you're at that stage yet." Pamela was giving her daughter her mother-knows-best look, doe eyes and stern eyebrows and all.

Odette could feel her frustration bubbling over a manageable level. "Mom please!"

Her father's head poked through the open door and smiled at the two women but they didn't smile back.

"Hey, pumpkin. Nice room. You pick this one?" He asked, completely clueless to the argument the two women were about to get into.

Odette glanced at her mother and then to her father. "Yes ... please?"

He shrugged his shoulders. "Fine with me. You just sit tight while your mom and I bring your stuff up. We don't need you wearing yourself out." He gave her a wink and vanished at once.

Her mother gaped at and rushed after her father. "Jonah, I don't think–" her voice became more muffled as she went further and further through the house.

Odette smiled again, a sense of victory washed over her and she looked out her window again. There were trees; a particular one was close enough to her window that, should she want to, she could make a daring escape.

There was a flash of something in the foliage that made Odette jump. Her head whipped to the source of it but whatever it was had already vanished. She frowned, pressing her nose up against the glass. Whatever it was, it was about the size of her torso and had a silvery-blue sheen. Other than that, she wasn't able to discern what it *was*.

Odette snorted, backing up from the window. *It was probably a ghost or a demon or something like that.* The freaky monster that she had created in her mind popped up again when she closed her eyes and she dug her nails into her arms. The pain would help bring her back to reality. When she turned away from the window and walked out of the bedroom, she couldn't help but feel like she was being watched.

II

The plush pews did nothing for the aching in Odette's spine the next morning. She hadn't slept well last night, not by a long shot. The large window had seemed pretty during the day but, at night, it was terrifying. It certainly did not help that her overactive imagination just wouldn't stop creating horrid scenarios of what could be waiting for her out there.

Odette shifted again, holding the bodice of her all white sundress, discreetly fanning herself. The church that her mother had found, Lighthouse of Christ, obviously hadn't had an update in the last fifty years. The air conditioner was shot, the walls were crumbling, and it was mostly filled with old people who were probably alive when this place was built. But it was the closest place to their house, a ten-minute drive with light traffic.

Lighthouse of Christ got its name from the large lighthouse that was only three blocks away from the church. It looked out into the sea but it had been unoccupied for at least a decade and was now used for teenage hookups. She learned this through the gossipy old ladies who sat behind her, wearing floral hats and bright red lipstick.

She couldn't help but wince as the organ player began to play yet another hymn on his ancient instrument. It was loud and headache-inducing, causing her to wither slightly, shrinking back as the congregation rose to its feet.

Maybe if I faint I can get out of this mess, she wondered. But she knew that one of two things would happen. Either everyone would think that she had been touched by the Holy Spirit, or they would send her pitying looks and the *"I'll pray for you"* would start. So, Odette suffered in silence until the hour and a half was up.

Odette gathered her purse and walked down the aisle with her mother, her father following behind, when she was suddenly surrounded by the "good" parishioners. Inside, she was screaming bloody murder.

"We just wanted to welcome you to our church, it's so rare we see new faces," an old lady said.

Odette smiled politely but it was more of a bared teeth grimace.

"Aww, thank you. I'm Pamela Sinclair and this is my husband, Jonah, and our daughter, Odette," her mother placed a hand on her back, pushing her forward slightly.

"Nice to meet you," Odette murmured, shaking their frail hands. They were almost as thin as she was.

One of the old women who had sat behind her spoke up next. "I have a granddaughter who might be around your age. She comes sometimes, but that girl has so much going on these days. How old are you, dear?"

"I'm seventeen," Odette replied.

The women around her reeled, eyes wide and thin lips forming into "O." It was as though she had become an alien or one of those cryptids that Odette liked so much. An oddity.

"You're so skinny, sweetheart. Don't you eat?" One of them asked.

Odette faltered, her smile slowly sliding off her face. "Err—yes. It's a medical issue." She silently wished that her mother wouldn't elaborate, which was Pamela Sinclair's favorite thing to do when it came to her daughter's medical history.

Odette glanced her way and her mom kept her lips sealed.

Her mom, however, took her glance as a sign of weakness and wrapped her arm around her daughter to support her. Odette didn't fight it. "It was a pleasure meeting you all; I think I should be getting her home."

Odette gave them all a small nod and tried to walk as fast as she could with her mother half-carrying her.

As soon as they reached the threshold of the door, the summer heat hit her like a brick in the face, and she could feel the faint coming.

The dizziness set in and she stumbled backwards. She was ripped from her mother's grip by gravity, Pamela's nails scratching into her flesh and leaving long red marks, but that hardly bothered her. Her heart was pounding too fast, the bracelet on her arm beeping loudly.

Odette was on the ground before she knew it and the cloudy blue sky spun around her in a vortex of pain ... and she blacked out.

The first thing she saw when she came to was the popcorn ceiling above her. Her body was stiff but she had an electrical sort of energy coursing through her. Enough energy, she determined, that she could easily sit up and function like a normal person.

Her attention was brought to her dress next. The white had been tarnished by the mud that she had apparently landed in, and it had dried enough to make it uncomfortable. It was chalky and flaking now, and she couldn't help but wince.

She threw off the dress and slipped on another one, another white one but with purple butterflies.

Odette tip-toed out of her room, suddenly aware of the noises coming from the downstairs. The movers must have arrived. Two men who were rather brawny were carrying in the new couch that her parents had purchased for the new house. They maneuvered as carefully as they could around her parents, her father showing them where to put it.

"Mom?" Odette called out.

Her mother turned around quickly and a look of pity crossed her face. Odette hated that pitiful smile.

"Hi, sweetie. How are you feeling? You're up, so that's good." She came over and smoothed over Odette's hair in a comforting manner. "I was worried."

Her face remained passive as ever, only looking out the door at the trees. "Mom, do you think I can go for a walk—just a small one! I need to stretch my legs."

"I don't think that's a good idea. Besides, we're trying to move everything in right now and I can't have you walk by yourself."

"Please Mom. I won't even go that far. I'll take my phone and a bottle of water!"

Her mom gave an exasperated sigh. "No! I can't risk you fainting on your walk and not be able to call for help. You don't know the roads and someone could jump out and kidnap you or murder you or rape you!" She pinched the bridge of her nose.

Odette clenched her jaw and looked to the side; she felt tears welling up in her eyes. There was no point in arguing with her mother—this is something she learned after spending countless hours cooped up in her old room.

You wouldn't understand anyway, Mother.

"Fine, whatever. I'll just go lock myself in my room and contemplate my wonderful existence," she snapped.

Her voice was heavy and strained but she refused to cry. Sticking her head up with false pride, she walked down the hall but didn't go back up the stairs like she said she would. Instead, she walked to the back of the house where the kitchen was, nearly bare like everything else in the house.

There were snacks that littered the kitchen counter but none of them appealed to her.

In the back of the room there was a door with a small window covered by a gauzy white curtain that casted pretty shadows over the room.

A surge of defiance took over her and she made sure to grab a bottle of water (like she said she would) and opened the door.

The grass reached up to just under her knees, desperate for a mowing, and swayed with the humid summer air. Everything was very green, like a highly saturated photo, and it was near impossible to look at without squinting.

She looked over her shoulder once more and stepped outside. The warmth was never something she particularly enjoyed, but it was better than just being locked inside like a fictional princess.

Odette trudged through the grass and through the trees, so she would not be caught by her parents. She looked around her surroundings, taking in all the beauty that she beheld.

She never really liked the forest or nature in general before she was sick. It was filled with bugs and—ugh—*dirt*. Saying that she was a bit of a girly girl was an understatement. Now, things were different. When you spend so much time indoors, you can't help but want to be anywhere else, even with mosquitos and flies.

When she was a safe distance from the house, Odette exited the "safety" of the trees and onto the open road. It obviously wasn't traveled much except for those who lived in this area. The road was mainly dirt and gravel, which was annoying as the little rocks would get in her sandals.

She walked for less than ten minutes when she came across her (only) neighbor's house. Odette's eyes went wide. It wasn't a house, it was a mansion.

There was a large wrought iron gate, the metal mimicking twisting ivy and leaves and honeysuckles. No name had been welded into the bars, though. None that she could see anyway. The house itself was humongous, with a large wraparound driveway and a fountain in the center.

She had only ever seen places like this in pictures or on television, but being so close to it in real life was breathtaking. Ivy crawled up the dark stone walls but it was clearly a well taken care of house. Nothing looked out of place from the outside. There was a garden further down the way but it disappeared around the corner of the house and Odette couldn't see any more of it.

One car sat in the driveway, it looked very expensive. That made sense, though. Whoever lived in the mansion must make good money.

Something in one of the upstairs windows moved. Odette squinted to make out the person. It was hard to see anything with the sun beating down on her like it was, but she just knew that they were looking at her. Neither of them moved for several seconds.

It was that person who moved first. They disappeared behind the curtains and Odette felt herself sigh in relief. She didn't want to loiter any longer, though, and tore herself away from the house. She had to get back before her parents realized she was gone.

The back door was still open slightly, allowing her easier entry. Odette cautiously peeked through the door, sighing in relief upon discovering that it was empty. The movers still made a ruckus, bringing things in the house.

She knew she wasn't in the clear just yet, especially if either one of her parents had gone looking for her during the fifteen minutes she had been outside.

Odette sat down on the counter, chugged her water bottle, tossed it in the trash, and braced herself for a fit.

Her mom saw her and sighed, shaking her head. "We're almost done; they have to bring in the kitchen table and chairs but they'll be finished really soon. Then, if you want, we can look through town for a place to eat."

Odette bit her lip but the yelling didn't start. "Yeah, yeah, that's great. I'll just get freshened up." She walked up the stairs two steps at a time, just in case, and reached her room with her frail heart beating way too fast.

She noticed that her bed frame had been brought up the stairs along with her desk and a mirror. Her mattress had already been laid out and folded up sheets sat on top, waiting to be fitted. Odette didn't bother with this and went to the mirror, inspecting her sweaty face.

I'm surprised she didn't interrogate me, Odette thought to herself. *But who am I to question good luck when it comes my way?*

The diner that Pamela had chosen was not at all what Odette expected. She had pictured greasy tables, trash littering the floor, and a bathroom that you could catch an illness from. What she got was a quaint little '50s themed restaurant, very clean and, unlike the Lighthouse of Christ, actually had a lot of young people around.

Their waitress was a thirty-something woman with lively red hair. After placing their drinks on the table, she began to speak. "So, are you guys here for the Tent of Mystery?" she asked enthusiastically. She smiled at Odette but the girl was lost on its meaning.

"No, we just moved to town, actually," Pamela explained. "But my daughter and I will be seeing the show tomorrow evening for my work."

The woman, whose name was Patti, gasped. "Oh! It's wonderful to meet you guys. We are a pretty tight knit community and everyone gets to know everyone! You are both going to love the Mages' magic show, especially you, hehe." She winked teasingly at Odette again but she was still very much at a loss as to *why*.

"Are they really that good?" Odette asked. "I hadn't heard of them before we came here."

"Oh yes." Patti nodded along, suddenly serious. "The Mages Twins are amazing. Their tricks are just … just out of this world. They are what bring in so much money to Sunwick Grove, you know? And it isn't even the tourists that go and see them so often but the locals too. They're celebrities."

She held in a snort of disbelief, *Yeah right*.

Odette let her gaze shift from their waitress to the flyer advertising the twins' show behind her. She had seen similar papers on their drive to the restaurant, in alternating purple and blue. They all just read the same thing—"Tent of Mystery" and then the times and dates of their shows for the summer.

"Those twins, they have a pretty charmed life, I'll tell you that," Patti continued. "They just popped up out of nowhere several years back and became instant stars. They just have this quality about them. Everyone loves 'em …. Ah, anyway, what would you, guys, like to eat?"

III

"My office, apparently, gave us some good seats. I did some research on the show and read through their fan pages. These two have been doing their show for about five or six years. Everyone *loves* them because their magic is so realistic," Pamela explained.

Odette raised her eyebrows. "Wow, I guess we'll just have to see for ourselves, huh?"

After their dinner out, Odette had decided to look up the Mages twins to see what they were all about. They actually *were* celebrities despite what she had thought. The twins were widely known, they did tours throughout the USA, they had TV specials, and some people were even talking about a movie deal for them. How Odette had never heard of them seemed crazy.

Her mother pulled into the "parking lot," which is a large grassy lawn out the front of a large tent. There were *many* cars, so they parked near the back of the lot.

The Tent of Mystery reminded Odette of a circus tent. It reached three, maybe four, stories in height with silver fabric covering the most of it. The second tier had purple stripes running up its sides, and purple poles held it upright. At the very top was a purple pentagram that seemed to stare down everyone who passed by.

The smell of cotton candy and popcorn met Odette's nose, drawing her attention to a smaller tent that served the overpriced food. A ticket box office sat right beside it, and an old man sat there with a sly smirk on his face as he handed out tickets in exchange for the wads of cash the line of people handed to him. Odette reached the entrance of the tent and handed the man her ticket, then she slowly walked inside. She couldn't help her jaw dropping.

The décor inside was a reversed version of the exterior with a deep mauve color lining the walls and silver accents here and there. Rows upon rows of seats lay out before her with plush cushions and armrests. In the front of the room was the stage, currently hidden from view by the heavy silver curtains. Several spotlights whirled around the room in a hypnotizing manner; some were a soft lilac color while the others remained regular white lights.

An arm intertwined in with Odette's, making her jump. She looked over at her mother and breathed a heavy sigh of relief.

"Did I scare you?"

"Little bit," Odette admitted. She shook her head, calming her nerves. Her dark hair fell in her face but she swept it back with her hand and walked to their section of seats.

"Maybe I shouldn't have brought you," Odette heard her mother mutter.

She couldn't help but feel somewhat offended. "What is that supposed to mean, Mother?"

Her mom waved her hand, as though trying to clear the air physically. "I'm just worried. Yesterday, you fainted and now there are all of these lights. I just don't want you to faint on me again—or worse—have a seizure."

Odette shrugged, looking down at the program they had been handed. "I haven't even had a seizure, so there's no need to worry about that."

A hand was placed on her arm. "But they said that you could. It's just—we can't be too careful, Det. Please tell me if you feel the slightest bit woozy."

"I will." Odette probably wouldn't.

The lights began to flash, signaling the five-minute warning. People's already hushed whispers almost quieted down, their excitement tangible. Odette saw a few girls her age with signs in their hands but she couldn't figure out why.

It was getting quieter by the second until the lights started flashing again.

"Ladies and gentlemen," a female voice spoke, silencing everyone. "Welcome to the *Tent of Mystery!*"

The crowd began to clap eagerly. Odette looked around, searching for any sign that the two twins had actually appeared yet, but it was just the same dark tent. Still, she clapped along.

Then, the heavy curtains rose up with one sharp yank. Two twin figures stood there, tall and strong. The curious thing was that they weren't only twin in looks but in costumes, which mirrored one another in color and pattern, and in the twin jewels they wore in different spots of their clothing.

"My name is Greer," said the girl who spoke before waving her hands with a flourish.

"And I am Grayson," said the boy. He didn't do anything more than prowl the stage, his face passive.

The teenage girls Odette had seen earlier started screaming, waving their signs around like mad. Obviously, his fan girls. Odette had to admit he was very attractive ... but she wouldn't have gone as far as making a sign for him.

"And we are the Mages Twins!" They shouted in unison. Their arms flew upwards and dozens of doves appeared out of thin air. The birds only flew a few feet upwards before exploding into purple and silver confetti.

It was slightly macabre but stunning nonetheless. Odette gasped, applauding along with everyone else.

Their purple and silver attire enhanced their pale skin and dark hair. It made them look sharp—*Or maybe cruel would be the best word*, Odette thought even though they hadn't done anything mean. It was an unapproachable look that one couldn't help but, it was something they owned naturally.

"I think they are excited, brother dearest," Greer commented, resting her hands on her leotard-clad hips.

Grayson raised an eyebrow curiously, "Let's give them a night they won't forget, darling sister." He straightened the jewel on his neck before continuing. "For our first act, we are going to play with fire."

There was a collective "oooh."

"Something we were always told not to do, right? Now, fire symbolizes a lot of things but change is the most important one. At least … in my opinion. Fire can be a great companion if you know how to treat it right. It is a fickle being." He snapped his fingers and, suddenly, a flame appeared in his hand. It wasn't an ordinary one either, it was a blue flame. He flexed his fingers and the fire began to grow until it engulfed his whole hand.

"If you're going to control fire, you have to be like fire—no. You have to be more powerful than it. You have to show the fire that you are the one that is in control and that it will be doing your bidding, not the other way around," he explained. Grayson opened his mouth to say more but there was a loud and overly dramatic groan from Greer.

"Get to the point!" she exclaimed.

Grayson made a face, "Hmph. Perhaps it is you who must change."

He acted in the blink of an eye. There was fire in his hand, blue fire, and Odette didn't have time to wonder how it got there. He threw it fast at his sister, the flame streaking in the dark tent. Her entire body ignited in flames instantly; from head to toe, she was on fire. Odette clapped her hand over her mouth to hold in her scream. Greer didn't make a sound, only thrashed about on the stage, staggering back and forth. Others in the audience screamed or gasped, some stood on their feet but no one ran. Everyone was paralyzed, watching the horrid scene unfold.

Then, the blue flame that covered the magician's body flickered purple. It raged high, the blue being eaten away by a deep prune color, and then began to recede back into Greer's body, as if she were absorbing it.

The whole tent held their breath. What was left ... *was* Greer, not a pile of ash! She pushed her hair back in her blue headband and drew attention to her outfit, which had changed entirely. Her leotard, skirt, and tights were still there but now in reverse colors.

The two took a bow and everyone began to shout their praises. Everyone except for the Sinclairs who were shocked at what they had just seen. Odette couldn't believe that he had just lit his sister on fire! She just couldn't work out *how* he did it.

"Thank you, thank you!" Greer shouted. "Now, for our next act, we will need some volunteers." Her lips quirked up into a sly smile, winking at the whole room as she stepped off the stage.

The spot lights followed them as they split up down the aisles.

Odette couldn't help herself from leaning forward, interested as to what they might do next. It was like everyone in the audience had done the same thing, some of them subconsciously hoping that they would be picked while others were not so subtle about it.

Greer came down Odette's aisle, looking through the mass of people. She stopped at her row and cast a strange look. "Hello there," she greeted. "Would you care to join me on stage?"

Odette glanced around her to make sure she wasn't talking to anyone else. Greer extended a hand to her and she took it gently, her face igniting bright red. Everyone was staring at her.

At the same time, Grayson walked up the opposite aisle with an older man beside him.

"Can everyone give a round of applause to our brave volunteers?" Greer asked, showing off Odette and the other man.

Odette blushed and looked down at her flats, embarrassment rushing through her. She silently wondered if she chose the right sundress, hoping that her underwear isn't showing through because of the spotlights.

A hand came up and made contact with her chin, pulling her gaze up from her shoes. She had to keep tilting her head up to meet their eyes, but, judging by the clothes, it was Grayson.

Blue eyes met her heterochromatic ones and she momentarily lost breath. He was even prettier up close. It was unnatural.

"Are you with us, darling?" he asked, his pink lips mimicking that smirk his sister had given her before.

"I—uh—yes."

Grayson turned to the audience, "It looks like we have a shy one." This earned several chuckles.

"Now, dear, I think I should ask your name," he said. "But where would be the fun in that? I'm going to guess your name, my dear, in front of this very judgmental audience. Please don't laugh too hard if I get it wrong."

The crowd laughed and so did his sister.

Odette swallowed hard and gripped her fingers behind her back. "Okay."

The boy walked around her like a predator stalking its prey. "This is your first time at our show, yes?"

"Yeah." Odette mentally frowned. Compared to his other stuff, this was very boring so far.

"You're a dancer .... What was it? Ballet? Or ... you used to be a dancer and then you injured yourself. Am I correct?" he asked, his eyes narrowing playfully.

That made her falter. What an odd thing to guess. "Y-yes, that's right."

Grayson chuckled at her hesitation and gave his sister a knowing look. "Let's see ... I promised you that I would guess your name, I haven't forgotten but you're pretty fun. Forgive me if I try and draw this out," he cooed. "You don't have too many friends. You just moved here."

Odette nodded mutely, her face tinged pink.

Grayson hummed. "You've never been out on a real date, overprotective parents. Probably the reason that you've never had a boyfriend too."

Now she really frowned, pretty offended. Even if it was true, that kind of stuff didn't need to be announced to a group of strangers. That was just cruel.

"Oops, don't hate me, please. It's all part of the process," he "apologized."

The group of teenage girls snickered loudly and Odette couldn't help but shrink back.

"And now, for your name. It isn't one you hear a lot nowadays, it's something classy and elegant," he tapped his chin dramatically while sizing her up. He snapped his fingers like he understood a really hard question on a test. "I've got it! You are Odette, the Swan Queen."

Odette's jaw dropped, not actually expecting him to guess it. "Yeah, it is."

Grayson smiled at her but it wasn't a kind one. It was sinister and set her on edge. He reached out and tucked a strand of her hair behind her ear and, out of nowhere, produced a white rose.

She cautiously took it from him, careful not to prick her fingers on the sharp thorns. "Thank you."

"A pretty rose for a pretty girl," he responded. "Everyone, please give the lovely Odette a hand!"

He pressed his hand to the small of her back and helped her off the stage and back to her seat. Odette noticed that he didn't break contact with her body once, not until she sat back down in her chair with her rose in hand. He didn't say anything else or even look at her again once she sat back down. He strode back to the stage with confidence, his once bored look changed to one of cockiness.

The old man whom Grayson had previously brought up to the stage had been locked into a box where only his head and feet where visible. Greer stood behind him, making sure everything was secure.

"And now for one of the oldest tricks in the book! I will saw this man in half." Greer brandished a large and very *real* and *sharp*-looking saw.

Odette looked down at the rose and touched its delicate petals and looked back up to the stage at the boy. There was something very strange about him, strange but magnetic.

"Thank you for coming to our show!" Greer shouted

"We hope you all enjoyed it," Grayson added.

They held hands and rose them up over their heads. "GOODNIGHT!" they shouted in unison. They bowed and a plume of smoke exploded. When it cleared, the twins had vanished.

Odette saw her mother turn towards her from the corner of her eye. She met her mother's eyes with her own inquisitive look.

"Are you ready to go, Det?"

She nodded, grabbing her purse and walking out the tent with her mother beside her.

"That was exciting, wasn't it? Were you excited when you got to go on the stage?" Her mom probed, nudging her with her shoulder.

Odette blushed, twirling her rose. "I was scared. There were a lot of people looking at me."

"You looked scared. I thought you might have puked," she teased, sticking her tongue out at her daughter.

Well, Odette thought, *you're not wrong.*

"How do you think he did it?" Pamela asked.

She shrugged, "Magic probably."

The drive home was quiet; aside from Odette listening to her mom dictate her notes for her article about the twins' show.

Her father pulled in just as they did, just in from his work. He greeted his daughter with a tight hug and his wife with a kiss, asking how the show had gone. Pamela was happy to tell him all about it while Odette claimed she needed to go upstairs to rest a little.

She laid the rose on her vanity and changed out of her sundress into something more comfortable, taking her time to relax after her venture out.

Odette couldn't help it; she brought the rose up and smelled it, feeling the silky petals brush against her face. A small smile came to her lips, running her fingers over the petals. She needed a vase for it but she would wait.

Who was Grayson Mages? It sounded like a stage name honestly, and she wouldn't be surprised if she was right. She grabbed her phone and typed his name into the Instagram search bar. There were a lot of fan accounts made for him, most of them had a picture of Grayson in a flower crown with a colorful background, but she did find his personal account eventually. He had a few pictures on the account, not many "personal" ones, most were advertisements for his show. There was one from a party that he had attended but, other than that, it was empty.

Greer's account had much more content. There were pictures of her with her best friends at the mall, pictures of her during her show, pictures of her with famous people, pictures of her with her brother, and then some other miscellaneous photos of books or tea. All of them looked very professional and made her look even more glamorous.

They had quite the following and, even though Odette had never heard of them until recently, it seemed like everyone else in the world had. There had been a TV interview with them, someone wrote a book about them, there were some fanfiction, and even talks of them making a movie.

Odette set her phone down and decided that she should get a vase for her flower. She didn't want it to die any time soon. She chewed on her lip and worked on dodging all of the moving boxes that had yet to be unpacked.

She held the rose gently in one hand and held onto the stairway railing with the other. She was two steps away from the bottom when she heard voices, more than just her mother and father, and she was sure that it wasn't the TV.

Stepping off the stairs, she curiously glanced at the doorway to see who had come to visit so soon and almost didn't stop until her brain had processed who was standing at her door.

Greer and Grayson Mages.

Her mother was talking to them. And they were actually outside her house. It seemed far too bizarre, especially since she now knew how popular they were.

Greer's eyes moved past Pamela's face and landed on Odette. She had no time to hide. The magician smiled a genuine one unlike the mysterious one she had worn in the show. She seemed like a regular girl. "I remember you, you're Odette?"

Her mother looked between the three teens with a smile. "Det, I was just telling the twins how much we enjoyed their show."

Odette swallowed her nerves and stepped off onto the landing. "Yeah, it was really amazing. I'd never been to a magic show before," she admitted.

Like her, they had changed since the performance, yet they still matched color wise.

"We came over to greet the new neighbors. It's always good to make new friends in a new place," Greer said.

Pamela stepped back and allowed the twins inside, followed by a "Please excuse the mess."

Odette's eyes lit up, "You all must be in that big house down the road." It made sense to her now. She didn't miss how her parents gave her a questioning look, they didn't know about any big house. They hadn't driven down that way. *Oops.*

"You would be correct," Greer said.

Grayson remained quiet, his passive face studying the room around him and then focused on Odette. His eyes didn't rake up her like they did at the show, only remained on her face. It was just as unnerving and—somehow—as attractive as before.

He probably knows *he's gorgeous*, Odette thought bitterly.

Greer turned to her brother who broke his gaze from Odette. They just stared at one another.

Odette wondered if they had twin telepathy, conversing with one another in their heads. They reacted to one another like they had been speaking. It only lasted for a few seconds before they turned back to face Odette.

"We would like to invite you all to dinner tomorrow night," Grayson requested suddenly, though it sounded more like a demand.

Jonah, who was sitting on the couch, smiled, "That's very kind of you all. We don't want to intrude on your family time, though."

Greer laughed, "Oh no, Grandfather requested it himself. We adore new visitors, especially new neighbors. It is very ... rare that we get any new people in town." She winked at Odette and shot her brother a look.

"Yes, it's been a long time," Grayson added robotically.

Greer's heels clicked against the wooden floors as she crossed what little distance was left between herself and Odette. She took the girl's hands in her own and smiled, "I can tell that we're going to be such great friends already."

The girl towered over Odette like her brother; even without her heels, Greer would have had several inches over her.

"I hope so." *I don't really have any*, Odette left out.

Yes, the twins were strange. They had an intimidating, almost dangerous aura around them, but they were magnetic. They were probably going to be Odette's only contact with the outside world too.

"It was a pleasure getting to formally meet all of you. We look forward to seeing you tomorrow night, say ... six thirty?" Greer asked, turning away from Odette.

"Yes, that sounds perfect," her mother replied.

Greer quickly pulled Odette into a hug. She wasn't prepared for it and couldn't properly return it but Greer was gone as soon as she came.

Odette turned to Grayson, her lips forming the word *goodbye* when he grabbed her hand. Her eyebrows pinched together and she watched as he led her knuckles to his lips. Their eyes met. He was gone.

It hadn't lasted longer than a second but she blushed pink all the same. He had already moved on to shake hands with her father and kiss her mother's hand as well but she stayed paralyzed, running the scenario over and over in her mind. That ... really just happened?

The twins left her home but Odette remained firmly planted in her spot, looking at her hand and envisioning an invisible lip print. No one had ever kissed her hand before. No one had ever made her feel so *anxious* before. Then again, no one was quite like Grayson Mages and she hadn't even known him for that long.

His lips were warm ... and soft ...

"Odette, you're bleeding," Jonah pointed out.

The girl looked down, having forgotten that she still had the rose in her hand. At some point during the conversation, she had clenched that hand into a fist and the thorns had pierced her flesh in several different places.

She curled her hand again, the pain now beginning to set in. Odette hissed and went into the kitchen to clean herself up.

The rose's green stem was streaked with her blood but it contrasted with the white petals in an oddly pleasing way. Still, she had to clean it off so that it would remain pretty. She didn't even know what to do about her palm.

Odette dug around in the cardboard boxes and pulled out a skinny vase and filled it with some water, then lowered the flower inside.

She waved to her parents, claiming she was going to bed— even though she hadn't eaten dinner— and retreated into the sanctuary of her room.

She placed the vase on her vanity. It seemed rather pathetic, honestly, with her room in shambles. There was nothing she could do about that now, not tonight. Her parents would probably come up in thirty minutes and force her to eat something, so she figured that she had better lay down.

Odette laid down on her bed, her body needing rest. She had her eyes trained on the tree closest to her window. She blinked slowly, each time her eyes getting heavier until she was asleep.

When she opened her eyes next, it was pitch black in her room and the house was quiet. There, however, was a strange air to everything, a feeling that made Odette's throat constrict.

She remained laying as still as she could but her eyes ran rampant around the room. There were strange shapes, but she assured herself that these were just things like her boxes and a floppy hat or maybe a pile of clothes that she needed to put away.

A cold breeze blew across her and Odette froze up. It couldn't be the air conditioner because she expected to hear it roaring. She shifted onto her side and noticed her window open. How was it open?

A shudder racked her body. There was a small sound that came from the corner of the room, something that she knew she shouldn't worry over. All the same, her heart sped up. There in the corner were two glowing, electric blue eyes, staring back at her like two live wires.

Odette sat bolt upright, her covers pooling around her waist but the glowing eyes didn't as much as flinch. She scrambled to her side table to turn on her lamp. The yellow light flooded the room, illuminating every corner of it. The eyes—or the person they belonged to—weren't there anymore but the window remained open. The wind howled outside and the trees rustled, as if nature was laughing at her for being an idiot.

Odette rubbed her eyes. She needed more sleep, her mind was playing stupid tricks on her.

IV

The morning came and the events from the night had all but slipped her mind. It was deliberate; she began to read a random book by her bed to forget the image of those eyes. Odette had almost convinced herself that she had created them like she usually did with those horrible monsters in her dreams.

She became immersed in the book and didn't put it down until her mother came upstairs with her meds and a plate of waffles. Odette always referred to this as "the breakfast of invalids," her daily ritual.

"What are you going to wear tonight?" her mom asked, sitting on the foot of her bed.

Odette shrugged her shoulders and threw her head back to swallow the pills. "Nothing too flashy. One of my dresses."

Her mom nodded and looked around her daughter's room. She got up and dug through a box, pulling out different sundresses and laying them out.

"You don't have to get ready just yet. Take it easy this morning, okay?" her mom instructed, rummaging around some more. She pulled out one of Odette's notebooks and flipped through it briefly before setting it down again.

She had learned a long time ago that Pamela Sinclair wasn't really one for privacy, but it didn't bother her too much now; what did she have to hide? Certainly not a schedule of parties that she had to attend, like she would ever go to such a thing.

Odette nodded and chewed her waffle slowly. Truth be told, she felt a headache coming but she just hoped that the painkillers would kick in soon. "I know, Mom."

Eventually, her mom finished digging through her stuff—for what, Odette didn't know for sure. Drugs? All of the heavy duty stuff was downstairs and Odette hated taking them. Then her mom gave her a kiss on her forehead, then left the room.

Odette finished her food and pulled out her phone, looking for something to do. There was a notification from Instagram that *xxGreer.Magesxx* had followed her. She smiled and followed her back, something she hadn't done yesterday when she had been stalking her and her brother. Grayson had requested to follow her, too, but she waited before accepting his request and got out of bed to take care of herself.

The June sun shone the brightest it had since Odette had arrived in town, not blocked by clouds or fog. She took the time to sit down on the window seat in the hallway to admire the outdoors. The bench creaked underneath her as she shifted around to get the full view of everything.

She noticed something about the window that made her frown. She lifted the glass up, letting in a warm summer breeze, and pressed her slim hand on the screen. Did her window have a screen?

Odette rushed back into her room and threw open the window where she found the screen properly attached. They were meant to keep things out like spiders and leaves, so how could have someone possibly gotten into her room?

There was no conceivable way to pop it out of its place, at least not without brute force and making a lot of noise. That would have woken her up and her parents.

Did she really see someone or something in her room in the middle of the night, or was it all just a dream?

Her efforts to forget about the incident were demolished as a creeping fear blossomed. She couldn't tell her parents about this because they would brush it off, saying that it was a bad dream or a hallucination as a side effect from the meds.

A knock on her door frame scared her out of her thoughts. "Earth to Odette."

The girl whirled around, clutching her chest. Her heart was beating faster than it should have been, the little monitor giving a warning beep. "Ah! Geez, you scared me," Odette chuckled, running her hands through her hair. "What do you need?"

Her dad stepped into her room further, leaning against the wall opposite her. "Just checking in with my daughter."

"Oh."

"That boy yesterday, the Greg guy ..."

"Grayson," Odette corrected.

He chuckled, giving her a weird look. "Yeah whatever. You seemed to like him." Jonah raised his eyebrows, daring her to deny it.

She shook her head, "He's nice, yeah. But I think it's too soon to say if I 'like' him or not. He's just ... our neighbor, and a guy. His sister seems nice, though."

Jonah shrugged, "There are lots of 'just guys' out there, Det. Whatever you guys do, just be friends first."

"I don't even know him." Odette waved her hand flippantly. "We probably won't say two words tonight, you know?"

"Whatever, weirdo." He clapped his hands together and stepped through her doorway. "Just take care of yourself." And, with that, he left.

"Never!" she called after him. She could hear his chuckles echo from the stairs.

Odette waited until he was gone all the way before she returned to the window seat. As she sat down there was a strange creaking noise again. Odette stood again and felt around the bench when the top half of it lifted up.

A dust cloud rose up and Odette sneezed. When the haze cleared, there laid a dictionary.

Odette frowned, lifting it up out of the compartment. The yellow and dry pages cracked every now and then when she flipped through the pages. There was nothing special about it, which was a major letdown.

She went to put it back inside but saw something that caught her attention. Stuck between the side and the base was a piece of paper. All she could make out was that it was once white but was now slightly yellowed and dirty.

It would be no good to reach down there and pry the paper out, doing so could rip it and then she would never know what was written on there. She sat back on her heels and chewed on her bottom lip, her mind reeling with how she could get the paper up.

Odette went into her room, rummaging around her makeup bag until she pulled out a nail clipper. She pushed out the nail file on it and rushed back to where she had been and dug into the board. Maybe if she pushed it back enough, the paper would slip out easily.

What she did not expect was for there to be a secret compartment. She really hoped there might be but she didn't expect it. She felt like a super spy. A thin, square piece of wood came out, revealing a journal, some papers and photos.

There wasn't anything special about the journal, no distinguishing marks to reveal whose it might have been. It was brown leather and just barely held together by an elastic band. The journal was bulging and to the point where one wrong move would make everything explode.

Odette gently ran her hand over it, smoothing away the dust. She removed the elastic band and turned to the very first page.

There was a Polaroid picture taped up inside of a man and a woman in front of the house and then beside it, one of a teenage girl and two little siblings of undetermined gender standing in front of the house. It was worn and wrinkled and the two pictures took up most of the page. Below them were short descriptions of who was who.

Under the photo of the man and the woman, she put together that it must be the man's journal as it read "Me & Ava." The children's names were unreadable because of an ink smear. Odette turned the page and read the first entry.

"Today is our first day at the new house. Ava was car sick the whole way, but it could be the twenty-four hour bug that R. had yesterday.

The kids picked out their bedrooms and fought over who got what. Ava laid down on her sleeping bag and went to sleep early. I'm nervous about her, so I brought in a bucket in case she has to throw up again.

R. kept asking if she could leave the house to see the town. I told her no. She's been upstairs in her room listening to that junk she calls music since. The boys haven't stopped screaming once.

I hope this place will be good for us. R. will forgive me eventually about having to leave her deadbeat boyfriend behind."

The entry ended. Odette pursed her lips; did she want to read more? Sure. But something held her back. She sighed and closed the journal, then placed it back inside of the compartment but did not place the wooden cover over it. She shut the cushioned lid and went back into her room. There was still plenty of time until dinner but she had nothing better to do, so she started getting ready. Pulling out her hair straightener, she plugged it into the wall.

Unfortunately, six-twenty snuck up on Odette faster than she expected. She ran around her room, fluffing her hair up, and throwing around miscellaneous items in her way.

"MOM?!" Odette shouted.

Her mother appeared almost instantly. "What's wrong?"

"I laid out my shoes, the light blue ones that match this dress, and I can't find them," she ranted, picking up a box to see if they had somehow gotten in there.

Her mom held in a laugh and went to the other side of Odette's bed and picked up said pair of flats. They dangled from her fingers teasingly.

Odette snatched them from her mom's hand with a quick "thanks," then slipped them on. She hadn't been allowed to wear heels because of her mother's constant fear that she would get dizzy or faint and break her neck. Instead, she owned an impressive flats collection in nearly every color, pattern, and style.

She did a quick check of herself in the mirror to assure that she looked perfect. Not too dressy, not too casual, but distinctive and pleasing. The powder blue dress was one of her favorites but she rarely got to wear it out because she never went out. It had a small rose on the front center with a lacy hem. Her shoes matched the color perfectly.

"Are you ready?" her mother teased.

Odette turned from the mirror with a fake, confident smile. "Yeah."

She was not ready.

The Sinclairs piled into Pamela's minivan and drove down the wooded path. It took less than three minutes but it was better to drive anyway because they would most certainly leave after the moon had risen.

The gates had been opened, allowing Jonah easy passage inside. He pulled his wife's minivan around the driveway and parked it next to the very expensive sports car. Odette cringed hard, both inside and out, but she refused to say anything.

They walked up the chalky white steps to the front door, which stretched well above their heads. The knocker was an ugly looking face but Odette couldn't make out if it was an animal of some kind or a human. It had fangs that seemed to wrap around the giant brass hoop, its eyes sharp and with slits instead of pupils.

Her father rang the doorbell and Odette thought that the knocker's face seemed to twist up in offense. The door was answered a few seconds later by a man dressed rather well. He was on the chubbier side but looked like he could have been a football player earlier in his life.

"Are you the Sinclairs?" the man inquired, studying each of them. His eyes seemed kind, not harsh and calculating like Grayson's.

Her father cleared his throat, "Err—yes, we are. I'm Jonah and this is my wife, Pamela, and our daughter, Odette." He waved his hand in front of both women as he spoke.

The man's face brightened up a little more and he stepped aside to let them in. "Wonderful to meet you all. I'm Zeke Rivet. I am Mr. Mages' caretaker but I really just help around with everyone in the family," he explained. "Follow me, they will be excited to know that you're here."

Odette crossed her middle and pointer fingers behind her back, holding in her nerves. She had thought the outside of the house had been magnificent; the inside really showed it off.

There was a grand staircase that led up to who-knows-where, with a deep magenta carpeting covering it. The walls were lined famous and expensive paintings along with floor-to-ceiling windows. Everything seemed so dark and foreboding, it made Odette shiver.

Zeke led them through a pair of double doors and into a room that appeared to be a drawing room of sorts, like in a Jane Austen novel. The room had a long, purple velvet couch where an old man sat on. She recognized him as the man in the ticket booth from the show.

His face was stony and wrinkled but not as horrible as it should be. He looked like he might have been only ten years older than her father, but she knew that was probably incorrect. His grey hair had dark roots and he had kind, dark brown eyes. He really didn't look a thing like his grandchildren.

Behind him, Greer sat on a fancy armchair and Grayson stood with his back to them all. He didn't turn around until his grandfather started talking.

The old man, upon seeing his guests, grinned crookedly and the resemblance to his grandson came out. "Ah! Welcome to our home! It is such a pleasure to meet you all. I am Jethro Mages." He stood up and came to shake their hands. He started with her father, gripping his hand and shaking it vigorously. It was the type of handshake that used both hands, entrapping her father's between his own sunspotted ones.

"You must be Miss Odette," Jethro said, kissing the back of her hand. "I have heard much about you." He winked playfully and Odette didn't know if she should laugh it off or feel embarrassed. After all, it had only been one day, what could he have possibly been told?

"And you must be Odette's older sister!" he joked, holding Pamela's hand close to him.

Odette was almost immediately pulled away from her family by Greer. "I'm so excited to see you again, dear," she mused. She tucked Odette's hand in the crook of her elbow, escorting her to where her brother was standing.

"It's nice to see you again too," Odette replied, feeling like she was really in a regency era novel. "Hey, Grayson."

Grayson spread his lips in a thin smile, "Hello, Odette. How was your day?"

Odette shrugged, "Pretty normal. I read a lot because I didn't have much else to do."

"What kind of books do you like to read?" Greer asked, not releasing Odette's arm.

She pursed her lips, "I like classical literature. Like *The Picture of Dorian Grey* and *Mystery of Udolpho*."

The twins nodded in sync with each other, watching her with slight fascination. Odette couldn't help but feel like a new toy or something of the kind. Their eyes didn't leave her for a second, but maybe they were just curious about her.

"You should see our library," Grayson commented offhand, adjusting his dark blue button up.

There was a gleam that caught Odette's eye on his lapel. She didn't recognize it completely at first because it blended in so much, but she eventually recognized the oval shape of the amulet he wore at the show. The jewel was swirly, hypnotizing her, drawing her in.

"Grandfather, would you mind if we took Odette to the library, at least until the food is ready?" Grayson asked politely, although there was a demanding undertone to it.

Jethro, however, wasn't bothered by his grandson's attitude. "Go ahead kids, we can talk grown up stuff this way." He seemed like a very cheerful man, if it wasn't for that similar mischievous glint in his eyes that the twins had during their shows.

Odette looked to her parents, waiting for their outburst about how she needed to be near them at all times, *blah blah blah* ... but they didn't even look at her as they began their conversation with the older Mages. Not even a flicker of eye movement.

A swell of pride rose within Odette's chest and it was hard to contain a smile. Greer gently tugged her along but it didn't bother her. Grayson stayed behind the two of them, only walking in front to open the doors like a true gentleman.

The library was only a room away from the drawing room and it, too, showed the excess of wealth that the Mages' possessed. A rich mahogany covered the walls and the floors were carpeted by a crimson plush. Large and long shelves lined the walls with multicolored books, adding a pop of color to the room. A couch and two armchairs were placed in front of a live fire. Over the mantle there hung a painting of the twins and Jethro, all looking especially menacing.

I am *in a Jane Austen novel,* Odette thought to herself.

"That is a beautiful portrait," Odette said quietly, slipping away from Greer to admire it even more.

Greer followed close behind. "Yes, it was done about six months ago. We needed to have an updated one considering the last time we had been painted was over six years ago," she explained.

Odette's eyes raked over every inch of it. The eyes were by far the most prominent part of it. They were almost electrifyingly alive, standing out against their thick, dark lashes and pale skin. There was something smudged over Grayson's lip but she couldn't tell what it was.

"I hate that picture," Grayson grunted. He had gracefully flung himself onto one of the couches, one leg dangling off the side while the other was propped up on the cushions.

"Why?" Odette turned around to look at him curiously.

The boy's nose twitched in an almost like a snarl but he calmed his facade. "The stupid man actually painted the scar I have on my lip. At the time, it was still fresh so it was red. I didn't think he would actually do it."

She frowned, not knowing what to say.

"Its ancient history now but I'm still very ... annoyed by it." He glared at the painting but finally let his gaze drop back to Odette, his gaze softening from stern to something like indifferent.

Greer perched herself on one of the arms of the couch and gazed at Odette with leisure. "Tell us something about yourself, dear. Why did you move to Sunwick?"

Odette winced. She hated telling people "why."

"My health. I have a lot of things wrong with me but my heart is the worst. I have this thing called an 'atrial septal defect,' which is just a fancy way of saying that I have this hole in my heart. It's actually pretty small and they tried to fix it when I was a baby but ... it didn't really heal."

"That's horrible," Greer said.

"It isn't so bad," Odette added quickly. "I just can't do anything that would make my heart rate go above normal. That's usually when most of the problems start."

Grayson leaned forward on his elbows. "But you were a dancer, weren't you?"

"I made it work. After dealing with it for so many years, I just began to disregard my symptoms and flare-ups. I couldn't let that stop me. It all changed a couple years ago. I was getting worse but it wasn't just my heart. I was on stage when it happened. I just sort of ... collapsed, right in the middle of my solo. People thought it was part of the dance but my coaches and my parents knew better." Odette rubbed her arms, feeling the ghosts of needles pricking her veins.

"The doctors said that it would happen a lot more if I continued. I would have these bad headaches and dizzy spells and I just couldn't get out of bed, like I was paralyzed or something. My hands, legs, and feet would swell up too and, sometimes, turn blue. My parents withdrew me from ballet and from school within a couple of weeks after the accident. I've just ... never gone back to normal since."

Someone laid their hand on her shoulder and she jumped. Odette barely had to turn her head to see him. He must have snuck up on her while she was reliving her painful memories. His hand slid from her shoulder to her hand, picking it up and bringing it closer to his eyes. She thought he might kiss it again but he stopped with her hand well away from his lips.

"So, is this your heart monitor then?" He motioned at the bracelet on her arm that looked a lot like a smart watch.

Odette nodded, peering over him to make sure that it was at a normal rate. She didn't need him to know that he made her feel nervous.

He gave her one of his crooked smiles and turned his attention on her arm once more. "What's this?"

Odette glanced at where his eyes were focused and mentally sighed in relief, it wasn't anything embarrassing. "My birthmark."

"It looks like a crown."

She couldn't stop the smile that came and giggled a little. "That's what my mom says."

Grayson brushed his thumb over it lightly and wet his bottom lip. "I guess that makes you a princess."

Before she could answer, there was a knock on the door. All heads turned towards it.

"Enter," Grayson called out monotonously, his slightly cheerful mood gone.

The door slowly opened and a head with wild, silver hair peeked through. At first, Odette believed that it was Jethro but the fire's light made his hair shine enough to assure her that it wasn't. The hair was like molten silver, shimmering like liquid and dazzling her. She didn't catch what his face looked like as the head was bent and the door covered a great deal of it.

Despite the warmth of the room due to the fireplace, Odette became cold. A chill settled over everything and the twins lost their "welcoming" mood.

Grayson clenched his jaw, his entire body going rigid. "Thorn, why are you out of your room?" His voice was cold and sharp.

"Mr. Mages requests ... requests that y-you join th-them for ... for dinner now," the man, Thorn, stated. His voice was strained and raw, almost coming out in a whining tone.

Greer was the next one to speak, "And he couldn't have sent Zeke or anyone else?"

"We have a guest, Thorn. Three of them," informed Grayson, his eyes narrowing.

The man faltered, unsure if he should leave or fulfill his duty. Before he could turn around and leave, Odette stepped towards him with a friendly smile.

"Hello, I'm Odette." She only had a foot or so between the two of them and stuck her hand out for him to shake.

The man kept his head down. "H-Hello, miss."

He didn't take her hand at all but she wasn't deterred. She stuck it out farther for him to take. He finally took it. She tried not to react when their skin touched but he was freezing. The man barely held onto her for more than a second before he let go.

"Are you a relative of Grayson and Greer or do you work for them?" she asked, recovering from her shock.

Again, Thorn hesitated before speaking. "I-I assist with the ... with the shows, miss." He kept his head bowed the entire time, she couldn't see anything. Odette was going to ask more but she couldn't.

Grayson cleared his throat and Thorn quickly put a distance between himself and the girl. "I think we should be going to dinner now."

He appeared beside her quicker than she anticipated and placed a hand on the small of her back, sending warmth all throughout her body.

"Sister?"

"Right behind you, brother."

Odette looked back to say goodbye to Thorn but he had ran off somewhere. She hoped that he didn't think she was weird or rude.

"Don't worry about him, he's a bit shy," Grayson whispered in her ear.

She swallowed hard and weakly nodded her head and allowed Greer to loop her arm with hers again. The twins had sandwiched her in between them, giving her no room to escape.

V

"So, how has the town been treating you?" Dr. Noel Short asked her newest patient.

It took everything in Odette to keep her eye from twitching. She didn't want to be in the heavily perfumed office and she couldn't believe that her mother had sent her to a psychologist in the first place.

"Your pediatrician thought that it would be a good idea, especially with you being in a new state. We just want to help you, Det," those being the words of her mother that very morning.

Yeah right, Odette wanted to have it out with her mother then and there, but there had been no room to argue the situation. It was better to just go rather than fight it until she was forced.

"Fine, I think," she finally responded. "I haven't really gotten out all that much yet to really explore it all."

Dr. Short wrote something down on her notepad. The sound of the pen scratching against the paper irritated Odette, but she didn't try to look to see what it said. No, she tried to keep her expression as cool and collected as she could.

The woman couldn't have been older than thirty-five and wore smudged eyeliner that was a little too heavy around the bottom of her eyes. The room and the doctor were very eclectic and looked like they had begun to bleed into one another. Rich crimsons, vibrant teals, and burnt amber covered the room in paint and in fabric. It was almost enough to be blinding.

She finished whatever she was writing down and gave Odette a meaningful look, "What do you think of your new house? Is it bigger than your old one?"

"It's bigger ... I like my room. It gives me a nice view of the trees and it's a lot more spacious than my old one. I've been trying to unpack everything but it seems like there are more boxes than I remember," Odette added with a laugh. She was finding it hard to look at the woman as she talked, she didn't like that Dr. Noel wouldn't look away from her either.

"Have you met your neighbors?"

She nodded her head. "Yeah, they even invited us to dinner a few nights ago."

Dr. Short pursed her lips, her eyes smiling. Odette felt like the doctor was treating her more like a wild animal, one which had an unpredictable nature. It was unsettling.

"Were they nice? Did they have any children your age?" Her pen was poised and ready on the sheet of paper, Odette noticed.

"Actually, yes they did. Two of them, just a little older than me. They were nice and I think the girl considers me as a friend," Odette told her, toying with the mustard yellow pillow in her lap. "Her brother, I don't know what he thinks. He seems nice too. It would be nice to have some friends here, seeing as I won't really make any at my school."

This made the doctor frown. "Why would you think that, Odette?"

"Probably because I'm homeschooled."

Dr. Short hesitated, her brown eyes narrowing slightly. A tiny giggle escaped her, followed by an almost inaudible snort. Odette laughed a little as well, happy that she could lighten the overly critical atmosphere.

"Well then," Dr. Short began to compose herself once more. "Tell me more about yourself and what you did before you moved to Maine. You mentioned that you were a ballerina, yes?" She flipped back through her notes to make sure that she had that right. "Do you miss it?"

Odette looked away from the therapist and focused on one of her many elephant decorations in the room. *Dancing*—a sore subject. Odette sucked her lip into her mouth and bit into it, fighting against the tightness in her chest.

"Sometimes, but I know that I probably shouldn't have been doing it anyway. I was always at risk of making myself worse or ending up in the hospital," she answered.

Dr. Short's eyebrows pinched together and she wrote something down. "And ... what if you were suddenly healed? Would you go back then?"

Odette couldn't hide her snort of dissatisfaction, "If the hole in my heart suddenly closed up? I don't know, I think that I've missed that mark. There really is no point in thinking about it."

More writing. Odette could practically hear *pessimist* with every scratch.

"But, if I was, I wouldn't," she replied seriously. "It's my last year and I never wanted to be a professional dancer. I didn't see myself doing it past college, or even in college. I think I would just ... go somewhere, like Europe, and sightsee."

Odette really wished that there was a clock in the room with them, not just the watch on Dr. Short's wrist that was too far away to read. Her legs ached with the desire to get out but she refused to tap her foot or shake her leg.

"You mentioned college; do you have any idea what you would like to do after you graduate?"

"Not really." Odette's face twisted up. "Well ... I've considered some things but they're still up in the air. I've been more focused on my health than much of anything else in recent years."

Dr. Short cocked her head to the side before speaking. "Have you thought about doing something medical? After all, you are around it a lot."

Odette shook her head "no" firmly. "No. I don't like it *because* I'm around it a lot."

Odette could see the shadows of the trees through her eyelids. The sun was harsh but she didn't care at the moment. She felt so refreshed, especially when the wind would pick up, blowing her hair across her face. For now, she could relax. No doctors, no one worrying about her ... not yet anyway. Soon, it would be too hot for her to be outside and Odette knew her mom would be on her instantly.

Beside her, her phone buzzed, drawing her attention away from the fresh air. She didn't know who would be messaging her, it couldn't be her mother. Pamela would just come outside if she needed her.

Shielding her eyes, she squinted to see a name—Greer. *"Hey, I wanted to know if you were allowed to come and sleepover tonight. Text me back as soon as you can."*

A sleepover. Odette hadn't had a sleepover since before the "accident." She sprung to her feet and *carefully* sprinted back inside to where her mother sat, typing away on her laptop.

"Hello, Mommy," Odette said, kissing her mother on the cheek. She sat beside her mother with her arms around the older woman.

Her mother paused her typing and looked at her daughter suspiciously. "What do you want? You only do the 'mommy' thing if you're aggravated or want something and you think I'll say no."

Odette scoffed. "That's not true. I call you 'mother' when I'm aggravated but that's beside the point," she took a deep breath before continuing. "Greer Mages invited me to her house for a sleepover tonight … can I go?"

She shut her eyes and silently wished for her mother to say *yes.*

Pamela chewed on the inside of her cheek as she thought it over, leaving her daughter even more nervous. "You'll have to set an alarm for when to take your meds, I can pack them up for you in separate bags along with some Tylenol or Aleve. Make sure you pack enough clothes and a pillow ... oh, and don't forget your toothbrush."

Odette's eyes popped open. "You're saying I can go?"

Her mom laughed, shaking her head. "Yes, I'm saying you can go. I'm not heartless. I still need you to be responsible, so you can take everything you need to take. They live just down the road so, should anything happen, I can be there quickly."

Odette squealed, tackling her mother in a hug. "Oh, thank you, thank you, thank you! I love you, Mom! I'm going to start packing right now!" She kissed her mom on the head and climbed the stairs to her room with a speed that her mother reprimanded her for.

She texted Greer back, letting her know that she could go and asked if Greer needed anything for her to pick up. She couldn't believe that she was finally getting to be somewhat normal again.

The day couldn't pass fast enough, so Odette took naps and read to save her strength for whatever the night would bring. From somewhat knowing Greer, she figured that they would be doing some pretty crazy things. Greer didn't seem like the "silly" type who would play hide-and-seek in her mansion; she seemed like the type of girl who would take you to a party and somehow induct you into a cult.

By six, Odette insisted on walking over to the Mages' house by herself. She lost that argument and her mother hopped into the car and drove her there, even though it was pretty pointless. Again, the gates had been left open for Greer's guests to arrive. She didn't specify how many people would be there but Odette assumed there would be a lot.

She was wrong. Only two cars had parked in the Mages' driveway and, while multiple people could have arrived in them, something told her that this was a more "intimate" gathering.

"Know your limits, Det. If you have to rest, just tell them. I'm sure they'll understand," said her mom.

Odette smiled, kissing her mom's cheek. "I will." A complete lie.

The front doors were just as intimidating as they were last time, the ugly knocker staring her down. She eyed it as she pressed the doorbell, hoping it wouldn't do anything weird. The door was opened a moment later by Zeke, dressed just as fancy as last time.

"Hey, Odette," he greeted, stepping aside. "I'm assuming you're here for Greer's sleepover?"

"Yes, I am."

Zeke nodded and started walking. "Follow me then."

The further they went into the house, the more noise that Odette heard. There was shouting but not in an angry way. It was a girl shouting and lots of giggling.

They passed one of the first open doors that Odette had seen and there sat Grayson, reading something while frowning. Their footsteps must have disturbed him because his concentration broke away from the novel a second later. His eyes snapped to hers instantly and he smirked. A second later, she passed by him completely, the wall cutting off their stare.

Odette shook her head, turning back around. She wasn't there to see him anyway; she was here to see her sort-of-friend, Greer. The sound of footsteps behind her made Odette feel a mix of panic and excitement as Grayson jogged to catch up with her and Zeke.

"I can take her from here, Zeke," Grayson stated, looking at her.

Zeke pursed his lips, looking between him and Odette. Finally, he sighed and shrugged his shoulders. "If you insist." He backed away and then disappeared around a corner.

"Hey," she greeted.

"Hello, princess. How are you feeling this evening?"

Odette smiled. "Great, I've been resting up all day, so that I would have enough energy for this evening." *He called me princess*, she thought, a light pink dusting her cheeks.

"I'm glad to hear that, if you're hanging out with Greer, then you'll need it." He adjusted the sleeves of his button up and a reflection caught her eye. It was his gem stone. Did he ever take that thing off?

He looked good, she noted, although he looked good on every other time she had seen him. This time, he was disheveled but in a cute way. His hair hadn't been gelled back like it always was, leaving it in a floppy brown wave. Another thing she noticed was that they were completely alone.

If she hadn't been nervous before, she was now.

Trying to break the sudden tension, Odette had to think of something fast. "Uh, it must be awful for you to have to deal with your sister's friends coming over to hang out and do girly stuff," she joked.

Grayson only shrugged, pressing his hand in the small of her back, but he wasn't walking or escorting her. He was just ... touching her. "It's not as bad as you would think. The house *is* big enough that I can avoid you all without you knowing it."

Odette laughed nervously, tucking a strand of hair behind her ear. "Do you do that often?"

"If I feel like it."

The conversation stopped and Odette held her breath. Being near him was making it hard to breathe. He was just so intimidatingly beautiful but something inside of her was screaming for her to run away from him.

"Which way to the party?" she asked suddenly.

Grayson nodded his head in its general direction and the walking finally began again. His fingers pressed into her back, tapping imaginary codes and making it stiflingly hot in the cotton sundress she wore.

They turned a few more corners and up a flight of stairs before reaching the correct room.

Grayson knocked on the door and Greer answered it.

"Grays? And Odette! Finally! I was beginning to think you fell in a ditch or something. Come in and meet the girls."

Greer tore her away from Grayson and into the very purple room. It ranged from a deep prunish color to the palest of lilacs. Two other girls were in the room too, one laying on the bed and the other on the floor.

"You can leave now, brother," Greer commented and, with a flick of her hand, the door slammed shut. "Girls, this is Odette Sinclair, she moved into the house down the street. Odette, this is Bonnie and Nadia."

Bonnie was a curvy girl with deep auburn hair and had a smattering of freckles on her nose. She looked up from her position on the floor and waved politely.

Nadia was a small girl with large doe eyes and bluish, black hair. She had a deep tan to her skin and pretty hazel eyes; she wore all green, strangely enough, but she made it work. Her smile was more reserved and she flicked her dark hair over her shoulder.

"It's nice to meet you," Nadia said in a quiet voice.

Greer placed both hands on Odette's shoulders and led her over to her vanity, then sat Odette down in front of it. "Are you ready for your makeover?"

"We're going to make you look so hot," Bonnie added, standing up to be next to Greer.

"Okay."

Greer looked over her shoulder at Nadia. "Nadi, can you pick out something appropriate for Odette to wear?"

Odette furrowed her eyebrows but said nothing. She was actually really excited about this but there seemed to be another plot to this besides a makeover.

Bonnie and Nadia chatted avidly while Nadia showcased different clothing choices to her. Greer took out a comb and started to run it through Odette's hair in long, gentle strokes.

"You know, Odette," Greer murmured in a sweet, calm voice. "You could be a Mages sibling, you have the hair for it ... and the eyes, well, *eye*. It doesn't hurt that you're pretty either."

Odette's face turned red. "Oh ... thank you."

Greer, however, continued on, maybe she hadn't heard what Odette was saying at all. "But my brother wouldn't like being related to you."

This caught the other girls' attention.

"W-why?"

Greer paused mid-brush and smirked, looking more like her brother in that moment. "Why? Because he *likes* you, darling. He thinks about you all the time, it's so distracting."

"Oooh, Graysie's got a crush," Bonnie sang.

Nadia remained passive, "Does he really?"

Odette ignored the two girls and looked Greer in the eyes through the mirror. "Why are you telling me this?"

Greer continued her brushing and shrugged her shoulders. "Because I approve of you, you're not like the other girls he's liked before. And because you like him back." She paused yet again to meet Odette's eyes in the mirror. "Don't try to deny it either."

"I seriously doubt your brother has a crush on me. I'm sure that there are many other girls in this town—or anywhere—that he would like much better." Odette started chewing on her lip and playing with her fingers. *Did he really like me? Could he?*

It seemed almost obvious when she thought about it but, at the same time, it didn't. He could just like making her feel flustered.

"You'd be surprised."

She twisted a piece of Odette's hair back and pinned it, then started to apply makeup to Odette's face. They didn't talk anymore during this time. Odette wasn't bothered by this; her mind was going a thousand miles a minute.

Next thing she knew, she was pulled from the chair and passed off to Nadia and Bonnie, who handed her a bundle of clothes and shoved her behind a glittery purple changing screen.

The outfit they had given her was most definitely something of Greer's because it looked like the clothes Greer owned. They were form-fitting and eye-catching and *very* short. The skirt did not cover much of anything on her legs, and the shirt clung to her like a second skin. Odette timidly stepped out from the screen a moment later, tugging on the hem of her skirt.

"You look great." Bonnie said, dabbing lipstick on her lips. She rolled them together and blotted, fixing herself in the mirror.

"You look wonderful, dear," Greer cooed, slipping on a pair of her bright teal heels. "I think you need a boy's opinion, though." She threw Odette a pair of flats from her closet and motioned for her to put them on.

Greer grabbed Odette's phone and handed it to her and shoved her out of the bedroom and into the hallway. Nadia lounged against the opposite wall, fluffing her stick straight hair with her fingertips.

"Grayson?! Where are you?!" Greer called out into the house.

Grayson's faint reply echoed up to where the girls were standing. "The library!"

Odette knew that this was most definitely a bad idea. Greer grabbed onto her hand and sprinted down the hallway to the grand staircase and back through the maze of hallways that Odette had only been through once before. Even though she was in heels, Greer never stumbled once during their sprint. The same could not be said for Odette.

The other girls either didn't run with them or got lost somewhere. Both of those choices seemed logical to Odette. They had most likely been here so many times that they didn't need to run to get to where they were going, or they just didn't want to come. Greer certainly didn't care at the moment.

"Brother, we need your opinion on something," Greer cooed just outside of the library's doors.

Grayson sighed exasperatedly, "I have told you before, I am no longer giving you insight to the inner workings of the male mind. I learned my lesson when we were thirteen."

The wooden door opened up further, the deep red carpet being the first thing Odette saw walking in. He had the fireplace lit even though it was sweltering that evening. Grayson was lounging on the couch, a book in one hand while the other dangled off the back of the couch.

Odette looked down, she really didn't want to bother him.

Greer laughed mockingly, pulling the other girl inside the room even further. "As if I need you to know what goes on in a guy's head. No, I need you to tell Odette how she looks."

Her twin's head shot up at the mention of the name, eyes meeting Odette's. The room fell quiet except for the crackling of the fire and Odette's heavy breathing. He looked at her, Odette thought, like she was the only thing in the room. To him, his sister melted away into the background of the house, just another piece of decor.

He let his eyes fall from hers to drop lower and lower, picking apart her outfit. Odette felt exposed under his gaze.

"And where are you going dressed like that?" he asked, his voice strained.

Odette opened her mouth but she actually had no idea where they were going. She didn't even know they were going anywhere. She just thought this was some odd ploy to get Grayson to "confess" to her like in all those romance books.

"Out," Greer replied haughtily.

Grayson scoffed and smiled sarcastically. "Oh, *out*, okay. I thought you wanted my opinion of her outfit and 'out' doesn't give me any specifics."

Greer tossed her long hair, "The only 'specifics' you need to know is that there will be boys."

His jaw flexed ever so slightly. "Oh," Grayson all but spat. He checked her out again and looked back at his book. "The boys won't stay away from you."

Odette glanced at Greer, giving her an *"are we done here"* look, but Greer wasn't paying attention.

"Would you?" Greer questioned, tilting her head to the side.

"Would I what?"

"Would you be able to stay away from her?"

Odette nearly screamed at Greer.

What is she doing? Is she TRYING to embarrass me? Does she want me to go home and cry into my pillow for the rest of my life? Never show my face again? Please, don't answer. Please pretend you didn't hear her, she begged in her mind, squeezing her eyes shut.

Grayson took a deep breath and Odette flinched mentally, waiting to be berated. "I wouldn't let her go."

What?

She opened her eyes to Greer's smirking face. "Come on, Det, we can't leave Bonnie and Nadia for much longer."

Odette didn't know what to do. Should she say bye to Grayson? Should she thank him? What should she be doing that wouldn't make her feel or look like an idiot?

Greer linked their arms and Odette had to take long strides to keep up with her steps. "You need to trust me next time."

They walked out the front door and down the steps to where a very expensive purple car was idling. Bonnie and Nadia were already seated in the back of the car, watching them with expectant eyes.

Odette opened and closed her mouth several times, words not seeming to want to come out of her mouth. Finally, she turned to Greer, her eyebrows furrowed. "Where are we going?"

"To the mall, that'll be the first place Grays will look for us."

Odette made a face. "Why would he come to the mall to look for us?"

The three girls laughed at her, sharing looks with one another.

"What?"

"Seriously? Odette, he's not letting you out of his sight dressed like that. Now, we're going out to make him jealous."

VI

O dette was sure of one thing—her mother would kill her if she figured out what she was doing right now.

Greer's expensive sports car peeled out of the driveway at a high speed, slamming her back against the leather seats with enough force to knock the breath out of her. She was breaking the speed limit ten times over, and Odette had to hold down her skirt to keep from flashing anyone. Worst of all was that they had to drive *past* her house in order to get to the main road. She prayed that her parents weren't looking out the window.

The girls in the back cackled with glee, throwing their arms up in the air. They would make high pitched squeals every time they made a sharp turn or ran a stop sign.

Odette hadn't really noticed until that moment that they were all dressed up for a night on the town. She also noticed that there was a lack of cops everywhere. She just really, really hoped that they wouldn't end up in a ditch somewhere.

"Calm down, Det, I can hear your worry from here!" Greer shouted over the wind.

Odette crossed her arms over her chest, holding down her top. "S-sorry! I've just never been in a car with someone who disregards traffic laws!"

"Then you've had a pretty boring life!"

Odette laughed nervously, watching through one of the mirrors as the town grew smaller and smaller. They passed the *"Now Leaving Sunwick Grove, Maine"* sign, and soon it was a mere blip in the blurring trees.

Greer took one hand off the wheel and turned on her radio and cranked it up loud. Some synthesized pop music blared out, nearly giving Odette a heart attack. Bonnie and Nadia started screaming about how this was their favorite song. Odette really didn't know how the other girl hadn't wrecked with all of their squawking.

It wasn't very long until the high-rise buildings and neon lights greeted them in all their glory. The streets were bustling with people but did Greer slow down?

No. The car whizzed past them all and people started cursing at her for nearly hitting them. She did, however, stop for the first time at a red light to allow a group of teens to cross.

"Aren't you worried that you're going to get pulled over?" Odette thought out loud. She started to smooth her hair down into what it had looked like before. It was pretty hopeless but she could honestly say she had the authentic windblown look.

Greer shrugged, pulling out some of her blood red lipstick and dabbing it on her lips. "I'm very persuasive."

Bonnie and Nadia giggled at this, probably an inside joke between them.

Odette turned her head and the car roared back to life and turned into a parking lot. Greer beat a beat-up sedan with a tired man driving two teens for the closest spot to the entrance of the mall. He glared at the car of girls as he pulled away to search for another spot.

"I think we got here in plenty of time, girls, don't you think so?" Greer asked, gracefully stepping out of the car. "Now, the order of business is to pick up dresses for the gala next week. I hate to say it but, Nadia, you really need to update your closet. That little black dress only lasts for so long."

Nadia rolled her eyes and groaned. "I know, but I only get so much for my allowance *plus* summer job. Thankfully I got a bonus for working later because *someone*," she pointed to Bonnie, "was late picking me up for, like, a month."

"In my defense, I thought you told me to pick you up at eight," Bonnie explained.

"What gala?" Odette asked.

Greer linked their arms together and they started to walk towards the mall's entrance. "We throw a gala every summer just for the fun of it. We invite people to come from all over the USA and you, my darling, have scored yourself an invite."

"Oh!" Odette raised her eyebrows. "That's very thoughtful but I didn't bring any money with me."

Greer only laughed. Odette didn't like it when she laughed at her, she felt self-conscious or like she had done something wrong.

"I'm going to get you your dress, silly. Think of it as your welcome to Sunwick Grove present."

The mall wasn't the largest that Odette had ever been in but there were a lot of name-brand and high-end stores. That surprised her. Greer and the girls made a beeline for one store that looked like it cost more than Odette's hospital bills. It had wall-to-wall gowns of all colors and styles. The shop's female staff pounced on the four of them instantly, knowing exactly who Greer was and how much she was willing to pay.

The girls decided that Odette would be the first "victim" and pushed her at one of the grabby shop ladies. She was shoved into Dressing Room 3 and left alone for several minutes. When the woman came back, she had seven different floor-length dresses. There were two purple dresses, one lighter than the other; two silver dresses; two classic black dresses; and a white dress, all in varying styles.

With each new dress she put on, Bonnie, Nadia, and Greer demanded for her to come out, so they could rate how she looked on them. By the fourth dress, she was yet to receive a positive review. It wasn't necessarily her, it was the dresses. She didn't look good in any of them—or, that was what they claimed.

"This is your first gala, Odette, we want to make sure you look your best," Greer explained after the fourth one.

Odette trusted her judgment, she had to.

The last dress she was put into was the white dress with the sweetheart neckline. It was much longer than she had expected, but she couldn't tell if that was because she didn't wear heels or if it was because she was too short. The straps were a little too long but she found a way to shorten them enough to fit her properly. She did love it, though. Odette liked how her dark hair looked against it; she imagined she was Snow White on her wedding day.

The saleswoman quickly clipped Odette's hair up in a sloppy swirl, but it helped show off her neck and collarbone. She felt like a ballerina again, dressed in her white leotard and ready to go on stage.

Odette gathered the skirt up in her fists and walked out of the dressing room again. The girls silenced their chattering, ready to critique the gown and the girl wearing it.

"You look so pretty!" Nadia gushed, cupping her cheek.

Greer nodded her head. "We can definitely work with this. I do have a request, though ..." She stood from her seat, her heels clicking on the tiled floor. She gathered the skirt in her own hands as well. "How do you feel about high heels of your own?"

"We have some high heels in the back, what color would you like?" The saleswoman piped up.

The female twin pursed her lips. "Silver, size five. Not too high, please."

The saleswoman walked away to the back of the store and through a white door labeled "Employees only."

Odette sighed, rubbing the back of her neck. "I've never actually had the chance to wear heels," she admitted. She waited for the other girls to laugh in their condescending way, or in pity. She waited to feel even more embarrassed than she already felt.

She lowered her eyes and took a breath to calm herself down. The ridicule never came.

"Well," Greer began. "Now you get the chance to."

Odette tilted her head and stared at her reflection in the mirror behind Greer. She smiled lightly; she thought that she looked pretty. Something blue glinted in the other girl's hair under the fluorescent lighting.

She observed Greer's royal blue headband. Come to think of it, Odette hadn't seen her in a picture or in real life without it.. The jewel on the side of it matched her brother's perfectly.

Greer raised her eyebrow, "What is it?"

"Sorry, I was just looking at your headband. It's really pretty, where did you get it?" Odette tilted her head to get a better look..

Greer reached her hand up and lightly touched her headband's jewel. She looked right through Odette, deep in thought. She didn't speak but her blue eyes twinkled with mischief. "Deals with demons get you places, darling."

Odette was taken aback but laughed anyway. "What?"

It was then that the saleswoman came from the back with an armful of shoeboxes that piled just over her head. She laid them down on the plush ottoman where she had previously sat.

"Here are a few different shoes for you to try on, miss. Need anything else?"

Greer flashed the woman a charming smile and gently shooed her away. She pulled out one shoe from each box and fit them on Odette's feet.

Greer had narrowed them down to three different pairs of high heels when a new customer came through the door.

The perky sales woman jumped out from behind the register to greet whoever it was. "Hi, can I help you with something?"

"No, I'm just here to find someone."

Odette's head whipped up and towards the distinctly male voice.

"What did I tell you?" Greer sang, patting Odette's shoulder. She bent down and picked up the strappy heels studded with small gems. "These are the ones. Get changed and I'll get everything ready at the register."

Greer helped Odette out of the heels and shoved her into a dressing room.

"But don't you guys have to pick out your dresses?" Odette half shouted. She had been stuffed into multiple different sparkling and restricting dresses, *then* paraded in front of those girls. She had assumed that they would, at least, be doing the same.

Greer made a *pft* sound and rolled her eyes. "We already picked out ours. We've had our eyes on them for months, just had to pick them up. You, however, are new to this. Do you need help getting out of the dress?"

Greer didn't wait and unzipped the back of Odette's dress, then forcefully closed the door. And, just in time, it seemed, a new set of footsteps approached the dressing area just as Odette stumbled into the mirror that was screwed into the wall.

"Brother," she heard Greer say.

Odette made it a fast change, slipping back into her borrowed clothes. The white dress laid in a heap on the small stool in the corner. She didn't want to even think about the price of it or the shoes. This store didn't exactly scream "inexpensive" to her.

Her flats slipped onto her feet easily and she exited the dressing room. Odette wasn't watching where she was going and ran straight into Grayson's back.

"*Oof!*" she grunted, stumbling backwards.

Grayson remained unfazed and smirked down at her. "Having trouble, Odette?"

She forced a grin and clutched the dress to her chest protectively. "I'm fine."

Greer, seeming to materialize out of nowhere, plucked the dress from her arms and vanished to the front of the store with the other girls.

Grayson smoothed his hair back. He had changed his clothes, wearing a regular T-shirt and a jacket over it. Stupidly attractive but not the smartest thing to wear in the summertime.

"Did you find what you all were looking for?" he asked.

Odette shrugged, "I think so. Greer kept going on and on about how she wanted me to look perfect for your gala next week."

She clutched her fingers behind her back, looking anywhere but the pretty boy in front of her. He was very close to her, closer than she had ever been to him ever. She could feel his body heat and smell his cologne.

He raised a hand and tucked a stray strand of hair behind her ear. Odette jumped and her heart momentarily stopped. "I'm sure you'll look beautiful," he whispered.

"I sure hope so," Odette joked, taking a mini step back.

The boy noticed this and raised an eyebrow. "You know that it is a masked gala?"

"Oh cool. It'll be hard for you to find me then." Odette lightly punched his arm, cringing internally at how awkward she sounded. Why couldn't she sound cool and collected like she wanted to?

Before she could retract her fist, Grayson caught it swiftly and lifted it higher to his lips. "I will be able to find you. Even if you hid, I would track you down with ease."

Odette needed a way out, "Um ... hey, Greer's done."

She stepped around Grayson, staring at the floor the entire time, and speed-walked until she caught up with the other girls. Bonnie, Nadia, and Greer were already close to the exit but it didn't seem like they would be slowing down for her anytime soon. Well, it was Greer's plan to have Grayson come and ... what? See her?

Odette had almost caught up with them when she felt the warmth of Grayson's palm against her lower back. Her breath stuttered and she almost made a misstep, looking to the side to see just how close he had come.

"Hey, now, princess. Don't just leave me all alone in a dress store. That is one of the worst places to get mobbed by fangirls, you know?" Grayson said in her ear. He had an almost smile on but it really didn't reach his eyes.

"Well, I wouldn't want that," she laughed. "But my ride is Greer and I really need to catch up with her."

He shrugged, his large strides becoming smaller and smaller until the two of them were barely advancing at all. "We're all going the same place. No need to rush, I'm sure she would understand."

"But," Odette interjected, "I wouldn't want her to think I was ditching her. Even if she did want ..." she stopped herself before she said too much. She didn't want to make herself look like an idiot in front of him.

She hadn't realized it but he had been leading her off to the side, so that they wouldn't be in anyone's way. They weren't even moving anymore.

"Even if she did want what?" he asked quietly.

Even though they were in a very public place, Odette could almost let herself imagine that it was just the two of them, just for one second. There was this urge to spill to him her silly crush that probably everyone had on him. How could they not, especially when he would look at them like that.

"Um ..." Odette started to formulate the words in her mind.

Grayson's hand on her back tightened for a second in an almost pleading way, and she looked at him questioningly.

"Um ... are you Grayson Mages?" asked someone. The mood broke and Odette turned her head to see a girl around her age staring up at Grayson like he was her god.

His hand slipped away from her back, her skin tingling where it had once rested, and he gave the girl a heart-stopping smile. "Yes I am. What's your name, gorgeous?"

Odette knew that it would be best to just move away. This was his job and she was getting too caught up in the moment beforehand. She caught sight of both Bonnie and Nadia who weren't too far away. Greer was also busy with one of her fanboys, so Odette decided to join the other girls.

"Hey," she said.

"Don't worry," Bonnie assured her out of nowhere. "These won't take long ... and they rarely mean anything." She nodded in Grayson's direction, who was taking a picture with his arm around the girl.

Odette shook her head, "I wasn't even thinking of it that way." She watched as the girl hugged him in thanks. "Besides, we aren't together."

Once they returned to the mansion, the girls all wanted to go to bed. Odette had figured that they would want to stay up to talk about boys or gossip but that wasn't the case. Makeup wipes were passed out, they changed into their sleepwear, and then laid down in their respective spots.

She closed her eyes and drew her blanket up to her chin. Even if it was summertime, the Mages' house was very cold. It made sense to her now why they had that fireplace lit in the library.

Nadia was the first to fall asleep but Bonnie followed only a few seconds later. Bonnie snored and Odette got a full blast of it in her ear because she was right next to her. She doubted that she would be able to go to sleep anytime soon.

Eventually, Odette had relaxed enough to doze off. She felt weightless as she floated off until everything around her quieted down. It didn't last very long.

Odette's eyes shot open, met with the endless blackness of the room. It took a couple of seconds until her eyes did adjust to everything. Around her, the girls slept on. She needed to get up, she was thirsty.

The girl took care to not make much noise when she got up, maneuvering carefully around the girls' overnight bags and other trinkets of Greer's. Greer's door wasn't shut all the way and Odette was lucky that it didn't make a loud creaking noise.

Odette peered into the hallway and looked both ways. She had no idea where the kitchen was and there was no way she would wake up the girls just to ask.

Maybe I can find a bathroom and just drink out of the faucet, Odette thought.

She padded down the hallway and squinted. Every now and then, she could make something out from the light of the moon but she found it difficult to even locate another room. Maybe it was because she was still so sleepy.

The hallway seemed to change with each step she took. Then, she ran into a wall.

Odette landed not-so-gracefully on her back. Where had the wall come from?

Maybe I wasn't paying attention. She sighed, pushing herself back up to her feet. She was ready to go back to Greer's room when she paused. To her right, was a door. *Finally.*

Odette turned the handle, hoping that it would be a bathroom. It wasn't. Instead, she had stumbled upon a dimly lit stairwell. It was narrow and steep with no railings, and might have been a servant's stairwell at one point. If it had been, then it should lead to the kitchen.

Despite her overwhelming desire to go down there, Odette hesitated. It was creepy and she didn't like the horror vibes she was getting from the house. Normally, this voice would have stopped her. Normally.

Hesitation gone, Odette held onto the wall for support and descended the stairwell. She took her time with each step and made sure that she wouldn't trip and fall to her death. The further down she went, the more sounds greeted her ears.

Noises from someone. She stepped off the last stair when a loud scream caused her to let out a yelp. She pressed her hands to her chest and poked her head through the opening of the arch way. There was no light in the chamber. What light had spilled into it revealed a cement wall, far from the glamorous interior upstairs.

The noises, however, were much clearer now. Someone was whimpering like a child. A sniffle here and a hiccup there, but mainly a soft whining sound.

"He-hello?" Odette whispered. *Great, now I'm that person in the horror movie.* "Are you hurt?" she asked a little louder.

Whoever had been making noises suddenly stopped. A warning bell went off in her head but her feet moved without her thinking about it. She had now abandoned the safety of the light but was thankful that her eyes adjusted once more. The wall to her right, the one that had only just been illuminated, had spaces and breaks in them. It was like a prison.

Something shuffled inside the bars and Odette walked towards it. "Hello?"

"Y-you-you sh-shouldn't be here," the voice warbled, thick with tears.

She tilted her head but didn't get close to the bars. Something was shining inside the "cage." It wasn't blue, so it wasn't Grayson and it obviously wasn't Greer as she was asleep upstairs. The more Odette squinted, the more she could see— she could now figure out the small window just above whoever was in the cage.

"I'm sorry. I was looking for the kitchen. Are you hurt?" She knelt down, the cold cement floor pressing uncomfortably to her bare knees.

The person jerked farther inside the cage. "You n-ne-need to g-g-oo!" The person, probably male, started crying again.

"Why are you in bars? Has someone hurt you?" She inched closer slowly.

"*Please!*" he whined.

Why would the Mages' have someone in a cage? Did he put himself in there deliberately? Did he hurt himself? Did they hurt him? Why would they hurt him? Was this some kind of trap?

"Please m-m-miss, you need to-to lea-leave now!" he hiccupped.

Odette frowned. "What's your name?"

He was quiet.

If he wouldn't answer, she might as well tell him something to make him more comfortable. "I'm Odette Sinclair, I just moved to town."

"I-I need you to *leave! Why won't you leave?!*"

"Did someone here hurt you?" she asked quietly again.

"STOP!"

Odette gasped. A strange energy surrounded her and several invisible bonds wrapped around her wrists, ankles, and neck. It threw her backwards with a force so strong that she hit the wall behind her almost instantly. Her head connected with it hard, and the next thing she knew she was sprawled out on the floor. Spots danced in her vision as she gasped for air. Her skin burned from where she was bound but she didn't worry about that. She couldn't really think of much aside from the throbbing pain in her skull.

"I-I didn't ... didn't mean to-to do that!" he wailed, his breath labored.

Odette pushed herself upright, everything moving in slow motion. Her limbs were shaking with extra effort and her head spun. "Hm?"

"I'm-I'm so sorry! I got scared and ... and angry and I hu-hurt you, I didn't mean to!" The man or boy was shaking with fear. Despite his exclamations, he was whispering so to not attract attention.

Odette didn't respond. She wasn't sure if she was going to throw up yet or not. Whatever had caused her to hit the wall, that brute force, it burned her flesh. Her head ached from the impact and everything in her mind was moving slowly around her, her limbs feeling like jelly.

There was more shuffling and scuffing going on in the cage. She turned her head, despite her body screaming in pain, and came face-to-face with a man with silver hair. She had met him the last time she was here.

"Thorn?"

Seeing his face in the dim light sufficiently horrified her. His face was pale but some areas were more grey and black, which she pieced together as blood. Only one dark bluish black bruised eye was visible through his shining hair. His cheek marred with old scars, some more fresh than others.

Her daze had melted away with the harsh reality. Her trembling hand came up to cup her mouth, she didn't know whether it was to scream or to keep the horrid stench out. "Oh my God, what happened to you?"

Thorn's lip trembled and he covered his face with his hand. "N-nothing."

Odette crawled forward and grabbed his shirt, holding him from escaping. The man whimpered and flinched, still trying to tug away from her.

"This is not 'nothing,' Thorn. This is ... sadistic."

"Please miss, y-you need to leave be-before you g-get hurt-hurt too." He tore himself from her grasp and scrambled back into the shadows.

Odette's hand remained outstretched through the prison bars, maybe hoping he'd come back so that she could examine his face again. She slowly let it drop and pressed her face to the bars. "By 'leave' ... you don't just mean this room, do you?"

Thorn didn't speak again. He didn't have the chance to. The room lit up as glowing silver chains appeared on Thorn's neck, arms, and legs. He cried out in pain. A sharp hissing sound met her ears, accompanied by the scent of burning hair. She could only assume in was coming from those horrid chains.

"You shouldn't be here, princess."

Odette whipped her head around and pressed herself up against the metal bars. Grayson stood directly behind her, his face void of emotion. The jewel was held tightly in his hand and, with every squeeze, Thorn screamed louder.

Now she felt even sicker. How could he be acting so calm?

"You're a monster," Odette whispered, her voice thick with fear.

Grayson quirked an eyebrow but his face remained as passive as ever. "Am I? Has this good-for-nothing been poisoning your mind with his lies?"

Thorn's screams no longer sounded human but like a wounded animal. It gurgled and pierced her ears like millions of knives. He seemed to be trying to speak but his words were warped and incomplete.

"You're the real monster here," Odette spat, scooting away from Grayson. "You're certifiable!"

Grayson humorlessly laughed and yanked Odette up by her hair. He slammed her up against the prison bars and held her by her throat. He didn't actually choke her but he squeezed lightly letting her know that he *could* at any second. He was displaying the power he had over her.

"Oh Odette, you know nothing. You're so innocent and naive, it's adorable." He leaned down and ran his nose along the junction of her neck and shoulder in a faux loving manner. "That's why I'm going to keep you. You're mine, princess! My princess."

And then he was kissing her. He practically head-butted her into the bars and tore at her lips with his teeth. Odette thrashed around, kicking and shoving, but nothing loosened his grip.

The amulet around his throat pulsed. She could feel a power lodge itself in her throat. The taste of iron filled her mouth but she didn't have time to place where it came from. Grayson slammed her head against the bars again, silencing her cries, and all the fight drained out of her. There was no use now.

Then, she woke up.

VII

O dette shot up from where she laid, clutching her blanket to her chest. She panted heavily, looking around the completely purple room. There were three pairs of eyes on her, all in varying degrees of concern. She wasn't hurt, nor was she bleeding, but she was *terrified*.

"Odette? Are you okay?" Greer asked. She slid away from her nest of pillows and laid a hand on her shoulder.

Odette jerked away, fear in her eyes. "I ..." she began. "I think I need to leave."

She gave no further explanation. She gathered her belongings and sprinted out of the room. She found the stairs with ease and flew down the steps, threw the front door open, and ran down the path to the road.

It didn't matter that she was still in her pajamas or that she had on flats over her fuzzy socks. It didn't matter if the whole thing had been a dream. It didn't matter that she felt a fainting spell coming, that didn't stop her from how fast she was running. And it most certainly didn't matter that it was seven o'clock in the morning, five hours before her mom said she would pick her up.

Her hair slashed at her face as the wind picked up. Every knot in a tree had eyes. Every bird was chirping her name tauntingly. The clouds were dark and angry looking. Odette glanced over her shoulder, nothing was behind her. Nothing she could see.

Paranoia chewed at her. She wouldn't be safe until she was home. Odette pounded on the front door, knowing that, if her parents weren't already up, they would be now. The house came alive, lights turned on, and she heard the panicked talk of her mother and father.

Her breathing was frantic and silent tears fell from her eyes. She couldn't turn them off or stop them even if she wanted to. She spun around, making sure that she wasn't followed, before she beat on her front door again.

The door swung open and Odette looked up to see that it was her father, dressed and ready for work. "Det? What's wrong?"

Odette opened her mouth but a small voice spoke inside her head. *Don't tell them about the dream. They will think you're crazy.*

They're going to think I'm crazy anyway, Odette though in reply.

The alarm on her heart monitor was blaring. Again, she opened her mouth, only to fall down in an unconscious heap on her front porch.

Odette was certain that she had been dreaming of something when she woke up but she couldn't think of what it was. No, it wasn't that terrifying nightmare she had at Greer's. She could still recall bits and pieces of that dream but even those were fading. This one was different but she couldn't figure out how.

Eventually, she gave up trying to remember and busied herself with something else. She glanced down at her portable monitor. There was a little heart pulsing on the upper right hand corner along with her actual heart rate displayed in large print beside it. She was stable for the moment as it stayed at eighty-four beats per minute.

Odette placed the ice pack beside her and sat up. Her joints protested against this and her head throbbed. It was going to be a bad day.

The TV was on downstairs. Her mother was probably watching her comedy movies, which she did when something went wrong with Odette's health. It took her mind off of the horrid reality that she lived in. Odette didn't mind, she would watch them with her to make her mother happy.

Right now, Odette didn't feel like facing her parents and their endless barrage of questions. Instead, she walked around her room and picked up different things that might amuse her. No book caught her attention and she had no energy to doodle and she didn't even want to look at her phone. She had no doubt that the twins had messaged her, asking what was wrong.

Nothing was wrong—she was *fine*.

Lightning flashed and illuminated the window seat in the hallway. Odette took that as a sign and followed her gut. When she came to the old window seat, she gently lifted the lid and pulled out the journal she found, along with some other photographs and loose-leaf papers. They seemed to be pretty ordinary but there was something thrilling about looking into someone else's life. She settled back on her bed and flipped the journal open to the second entry and began to read.

> *"The logging company is laying off workers. Might be next. Ava says I'm too important, but that's what every wife says to her husband.*
>
> *R. met another boy today. Didn't like him. She's too young for boys. Ava doesn't agree. She says fifteen-year-old girls need dating experience. I was a fifteen-year-old boy once. Don't want them anywhere near her.*
>
> *Boys are giving their mother grief about going to see this magic show. It was advertised the other day. Twins. Not much younger than R. Trying to find a day to take them. Looks like fun."*

Odette skimmed the next few pages of the man's journal. It was mostly him talking about average, everyday things with very short descriptions. A handful of them mention this "R.'s" dating habits and teenage mood swings. There were some things taped up inside, like business cards and a Sunwick Grove postcard.

She flipped a few more pages and came across ticket stubs for the Mages' magic show. Odette ran her finger over them and turned her attention to the writing beside the tickets.

"Took the kids to see the magic show. I was impressed. They were very good for being twelve. R. was called up to be an assistant. The boy flirted with her. I laughed. He's too young for her.

They put R. in a box and shoved swords in it. I didn't like it. The trick could have gone wrong and killed her. When they opened the box, R. was gone. The crowd was really excited. The girl closed the door and reopened it, and R. came stumbling out. She didn't look like herself.

When she came back, I asked if she was okay. She didn't answer. I'm worried."

The next entry was much shorter.

"R. went out and got a job. The Tent of Mystery. The boy walked her home."

A photograph of a girl had been hastily taped inside the book. It was blurry and there was a finger blocking the top half corner, which covered her face. She wore a purple button up and a pair of black ripped jeans along with a little black tie.

On the next page, there was a photo of the girl, "R.," in a booth, serving food. She looked furious as she handed an unknown customer a bag of popcorn. Her hair was tied into a loose ponytail and her shirt had wrinkles in it.

"That boy follows R. everywhere she goes. Still walks her home. Sometimes walks her to the Tent. Found her diary and saw his name

mentioned, so I read it. Says that he hardly leaves her alone and only leaves when he has to. Told her multiple times that he's going to get her a new position inside the Tent as a tech person or something. She thinks he has a crush on her. I don't like him. Not just a dad thing. He's dangerous. I can feel it. Too smug and flirtatious for a normal twelve-year-old boy.

We were invited to their house for dinner. Wanted to refuse. Ava accepted. That boy was smirking.

Update: Turns out they live down the street. Didn't know that. R. was quiet all day and locked herself in her room. Worried. Dinner was fine. The grandfather seemed just as shady. The girl was nice. The boy seemed too nice. Must know I don't like him. R. chatted with him and his sister, nothing else happens. When we were leaving, the boy kissed R.'s hand."

Odette pursed her lips. This family, presumably the ones who lived there first, was connected to the Mages twins. An ugly nauseous feeling twisted in her gut but she forced herself to keeping reading.

When she flipped the page, the date read that it was the next month. That was a large jump in time for this guy. Taped inside was a picture of the inside of a journal. She had to bring the book close to her to make out the words on the page.

"He won't leave me alone. I'm really scared, to be honest. He's ... everywhere. I've been moved inside and promoted to 'backstage manager' even though all I do is stand there with a headset and a clipboard with copy paper. I doodle during most of the shows.

Grays is a nice boy. He was a nice boy. Maybe he still is. He is always watching EVEN during the show, which is totally weird. I've been telling my friends about it. Ian thinks that he's just having his first crush and not to worry. Kalum is weary of him. Bree is on Kalum's side, especially since our sleepover. I didn't tell Mom and Dad about what happened.

When I go to sleep at night, I dream of these eyes watching me. They're his eyes. I don't know. Maybe I just need to tell him I'm not into him like that.

Anyway, Westley is taking me out tomorrow. I think I'm going to—"

The photo didn't show the rest of the sentence but the father's journal picked up right after.

"I knew it. I KNEW that kid was messing with her. She's paranoid now. Doesn't help that she's keeping more things from us now. Ava is starting to worry as well. R. really isn't herself. Very jumpy. Won't watch scary movies anymore.

Happy she's found friends her own age. Going to keep a closer eye on this boy."

"Oh good, you're up!"

Odette screamed. She slapped her hand over her mouth, cutting it short.

"Geez, I'm sorry. I thought you heard me coming up," Pamela apologized. She turned on the light in Odette's room and walked in to sit next to her daughter. "Det, I've told you about keeping the light on while you read."

Odette sighed and laid the journal aside facedown. "Yeah, I know."

"So," her mother began, "do you want to talk about what happened today?"

She winced, tugging on her pointer finger. "Um ... I just had this really bad dream and it scared me. I can't remember why I ran, I just did."

Her mom gave her a pitying look and pulled her into a hug. She stroked her hair in a way that she thought was soothing but Odette winced with every touch. "Oh sweetie. I'm so sorry. Do you want to talk about it?"

Odette hesitated. "I—uh—don't remember what it was about."

"That's good, I guess. While you were out, your friend, Greer, stopped by with a dress and some shoes for you to wear at a gala next Friday?"

She nodded her head, a knot forming in the pit her stomach. "Yeah," she said quietly. "It's supposed to be a big deal. She gave me a dress and shoes to borrow. I just forgot them on the way out the door."

Odette knew that if her Mom found out that Greer had bought those for her, she would demand that for them to be taken back to the mall.

"Aww, that sounds like so much fun. I'm excited for you. Do you want to come downstairs with me and watch some movies? *Clueless* is next on the list," her mother nudged her with her shoulder. "I have extra buttery popcorn."

"Yeah, that sounds great. I'll be down in a minute; I want to change my clothes."

Her mom winked at her and left the room without another question.

Odette sighed with relief and took the journal and placed it on her bookshelf. It was hidden in plain sight. The photographs and papers were stuck inside her pillowcase and inside a boot that wouldn't be worn for a while. She wouldn't want anyone finding those.

VIII

It was exactly the same every night since she ran away from the Mages' home. She would go to sleep and dream the same dream. Odette was on stage, waiting for the lights to turn on. She was in her pose, holding her breath. Her hair was pulled tight against her skull in a bun and her face shimmered with the amount of makeup and sweat she had accumulated. The curtain rose and the music started.

Her movements were jerky and robotic; she wasn't in control of her body. Every leap, every turn, every time she rose up *en pointe,* something was pulling her and twisting her. The invisible strings around her wrists turned into thick ropes. She was bleeding but her masters didn't care. She was nothing but a puppet, a doll for amusement. If she broke now, there was no telling how harsh her end would be. Odette would look up at the sky and see those cruel masters. Greer and Grayson holding her and controlling her. Her life was quite literally in their hands.

The strings pulled her until the skin on her wrists were raw and then gone altogether. Blood beaded up from the wounds, trickling down to stain her beautiful costume. She grew exhausted but they pulled and yanked for her to dance for their audience. She was only for entertainment. Odette continued to dance until she died, and all the world laughed.

It frightened her every time.

Odette didn't leave the house much. Leaving brought the risk of running into the twins. They had done nothing to her, nothing she could actually prove, but a deep-seeded fear had taken root. She only asked to leave the house once to go to the bookstore in the city. Her mother agreed to drive her, knowing that her daughter needed the activity. Pamela, however, wasn't pleased to see why they had gone to the bookstore.

Odette had found many books on things such as dream interpretation, the uses of crystals and other magical gems, and supernatural beings. She paid for them with her own money. That was her only saving grace that day. Odette devoured those books, scouring their pages and learning all they had to offer.

In the papers that had been found with the journal, the man suspected the twins of witchcraft. It was old fashioned but his theories made sense. He had diagrams, written out notes, and other types of things that went along with his crazy theories; but the man had no proof. His scribbles were as good as fiction.

Unfortunately, as her days of self-exile had grown, so was the threat of the gala. It loomed over her head like the ever-changing dark clouds over Sunwick Grove. Odette's mother had gone out and bought a plain mask and a bunch of faux jewels. She used her glue gun and years of arts and craft experience to create a gorgeous mask for her daughter to wear. Odette had it propped up against the vase that held Grayson's ever living rose. It was a shrine of fear. She had drawn out the quote *"What doesn't kill you makes you stronger"* and taped it above them. Pamela didn't get it.

She had decided to immerse herself in her examination of the journal, in hopes of possibly gaining evidence that she wasn't completely crazy. There were many ordinary entries that she had to read through but they always included some update of how "R. wasn't herself" or how "R. was becoming paranoid." Nothing overly hard-hitting until she stumbled into an entry towards the end of the journal.

> *"R. is missing. It's been three days and her friends haven't heard from her either. The police are out looking but they're missing the obvious! Mages is the one who did it, I know it. Went to ask if they had seen my daughter, the bumbling idiot that is the old man's caretaker didn't know anything. Asked him to ask the kids and the old man. Said he would. Don't believe him.*
>
> *Ava is frantic. Drives the kids to school late and picks 'em up early. She cries a lot, especially at night. Boys don't know what to do. Last night they came to our room and slept with us because they were scared. I'm scared too. Don't know what that boy has done to her.*
>
> *Last place she was at work. Mages swears that the last he saw of her was her walking back home. Saw a car following her but thought it was*

her friends. Said that she didn't want him to walk her home this time.

Collecting evidence from anyone I can. One old man shares my thoughts. He is supposed to be crazy, so it doesn't make him a very credible source. Only one who believes me that the twins are evil. Says we can get to talk more about why tomorrow. Says I'm not ready."

Inside, there was another picture of R. She was laughing at the camera and it was summertime. Her hair showed purple highlights and she had on a heavy eyeliner. There was a black beanie on her head and a ripped up band T-shirt. The picture had been printed on a paper and, in big bolded words on the top, it read—"HAVE YOU SEEN ME?"

"I met with my friend today. Not sure what I expected but what he told me wasn't it. Said that the twins have magic powers. Said that the blue jewels they wear are connected to some kind of voodoo-witchcraft-demon. Surprisingly, I believed him. Nobody knew them before last year, suddenly they are famous. From now on, this journal will be my field journal. Will research and learn everything I can. This has everything to do with my R."

From there, Odette found several conspiracies and chicken scratch sentences about magic and demons. He had pasted in photographs of pages from books, pictures of strange happenings in the woods, and images of amulets and talismans.

There was a whole ten pages dedicated to the Mages twins, more specifically, Grayson. It was a strange collage of their youth taken from shows mostly. Their jewels were in every shot.

In the books she bought, Odette skimmed and underlined things that pertained to the journal or added further to the research that this man had been doing. He just couldn't find out where was the source of their power. Odette thought that she might have an idea.

Odette shot up in her bed in cold sweat, running her fingers through her hair. She turned on her lamp and pulled out her own journal and books. Recording her dream, even if it was a recurring one, helped her pick out new things each time.

The book she had bought on interpreting dreams already held creases in its spine. Her tongue darted out to wet her lips and she furrowed her eyebrows. The task, no matter how necessary it was for her mental health, was becoming tedious.

Across the room, her phone buzzed. Odette stood from the bed and tiptoed over to where it was being charged. The familiar username of Greer Mages lit up her screen. *"I know it's late but I would like to have you come over early tomorrow so we can get ready together."*

Odette didn't bother to respond right now. She would need to ask her mother and she didn't want her to know that she was awake at this hour. She didn't want to give her another reason to worry.

Morning came quicker than Odette had expected and so did the dread of the gala. She thought that, if she wasn't so terrified, it could be fun. That was going to be a stretch anyhow.

Her mother was thrilled with the idea of Odette going over to get ready with Greer. Pamela made sure to give Odette her medication, so she wouldn't randomly drop during the gala but she also gave her daughter strict rules to follow.

Odette had to sit down most of the time. As long as she was careful, she was allowed to dance if the opportunity arose. She had to drink water. No taking off her heart monitor. Phone on at all times. But the worst rule of all was that she had to stick with either Greer or Grayson the entire time. The girl debated on feigning sudden illness but she knew better. Being confined in her room while sick provided very little entertainment as her mother sat with her the entire time and forbade watching TV or playing on her phone until she had slept for a long time.

So, the Mages' mansion it was.

Pamela insisted on driving Odette over there so she wouldn't get too tired out. Odette had no problem with this. The most surprising thing was the sheer number of people who were already at the mansion. They weren't guests either but caterers, servers, and decorators. They swarmed around the courtyard, hardly paying attention to anyone. Due to this, Pamela couldn't pull the car into their driveway.

"Do you need me to walk you in?" she asked.

Odette shook her head no and kissed her mother on the cheek. "Bye. I'll text you!"

She mustered up her courage and weaved her way through the swarm of people. She gripped the bag that the dress was in tightly, shrinking herself to fit through the small spaces that these people left for movement.

At the door stood Zeke. He pointed people to different directions and nearly shouted to be heard.

"Hi, Zeke," Odette greeted.

The man paused his shouting to smile. "Hey, dude. Greer told me you'd be coming by. Need help getting to her?"

"No need," a familiar voice said. Greer came into view, her heels clicking against the marble flooring. "I was waiting for her anyway. Come darling."

Odette said goodbye to Zeke but he was already back in business mode.

"How are you feeling this evening, Odette?" Greer asked. She peeked over her shoulder at her with a raised eyebrow.

"Pretty good. I'm nervous."

Greer patted her head affectionately. "You shouldn't be. Since I have decided to take you under my wing, you'll go to these type of events all the time."

Odette furrowed her eyebrows, unsure of how to respond. "Oh?"

"I've always wanted a little sister, Odette. Someone else to depend on and talk to ... Girl things, you know? Grayson can only understand so much and he can be so insensitive to my feelings." She pushed open her bedroom door. "You, however ... you understand me. We are more alike than you would believe. Sit down at the vanity, darling. Did you pack some of your makeup? A mask?"

"Yes," Odette confirmed. "I have it in my bag."

She took a moment to observe the room. It had changed since last week. Purple was still the main focus but there were black tapestries that hung on the wall now, with silver detail images of stars and pentagrams. In the corner, there was a whole section with candles burning. They had melted enough to make wax icicles, the drippings landed in a bowl of water on the floor.

Another thing that she had not noticed was the ginormous glass cage with a large albino snake. Odette's eyes widened and she scooted away, as it was practically right beside her. "Y-you have a snake?"

Greer looked up from her pilfering and at the animal. "Oh yes. That's Squiggles. I got him when I was twelve and just haven't had the heart to change his name. Don't worry, he can't get out of his cage, he's a good boy."

Squiggles looked like he wanted to kill Odette.

Greer finished going through Odette's bag and pulled out everything she wanted. She strutted back over to the other girl and flicked her wrist. An unlit candle in front of her came to life, its flame tall and strong.

"Whoa!"

She smirked, "I'm a magician, darling, what do you expect?"

Greer began to brush Odette's hair with an eerie calmness. The candle light was the only thing lighting the room but the amount she had in her room was a fire hazard.

A thought wormed its way into Odette's mind. "Greer?"

She hummed, not speaking.

"Did you know the people who lived in the house before me?"

Greer's eyes flashed and she gave a harsh yank through Odette's hair—on purpose or an accident, Odette wasn't sure. They stared at one another through the mirror and Greer sighed.

"Yes. The girl there was Grays' first crush. Her name was Romy, I think. Why?" she asked. The brushing lost its calming gentle strokes.

Odette shrugged. "I was curious. The pace had been abandoned for a while. I did some cleaning and found a ... a poster of some missing girl."

Greer pursed her lip and looked away. Her eyebrows pinched together and she brought a hand up to push her hair back, even though it was already in the headband.

"Romy was a few years older than Grays and myself. She was nice, helped out at the tent. Grays was practically in love with her but she didn't like him back." Her voice was a dreamlike whisper and she wore a funny smile on her lips. Odette regretted asking. "She made friends with the 'cool' people, a bunch of scene kids who thought that self-harm was cool, you know the type. They would go out partying and hang out in the graveyard.

"Romy lost this 'spark' she had, according to Grays. She became more and more withdrawn and secretive. I think that she had been planning to run away and kill herself. She had become very depressed all of a sudden, no one knew why. One day, after work, Grays wanted to help walk her home. Her idiot father wouldn't give her a car or bike so it took forever for her to get back. She just vanished. Her father blamed us, everyone knew it. The police looked around everywhere but couldn't find her."

Greer's fingers combed Odette's hair out of her face, scraping her scalp uncomfortably. Greer had the strangest expression on her face and her blue eyes glowed in the candle light.

"Soon after, her brothers killed themselves. Their mother couldn't take it and went next. The father became a shut-in, associating himself with a crazy, homeless man. They discussed conspiracy theories and other research crap that drove him insane. Maybe a month after his wife's death, he killed himself. It wasn't until a year later that they found Romy's ... remains.

"The police said it was gruesome. No one released any pictures but there was a report. They said that animals found her body. You can imagine what happened there ..."

Odette's eyes widened. She thought that she might get sick. "Oh my—that-that's horrible."

Greer hummed. "Grayson was devastated but he moved on. Found a new crush." She wove some strands of Odette's hair together in an intricate braid-like headband. "Unfortunately for him, she also died."

"W-what?"

"Car crash. Her parents were these hippies and they were moving away to California to protest something in Hollywood. I think that they were almost there when this car ran a red light and plowed into them. I didn't like her very much but she still didn't deserve it."

Odette was visibly shaking now. She clenched her fists tight, hoping that the pain from how her nails dug into her palms would take away this deep-rooted fear inside of her.

"Sometimes I wonder if Grays and I are cursed," Greer mused. "In the past, it always seemed like people would get hurt around us. It's why we don't make many friends."

She placed her hands on Odette's shoulders and shot her a wan smile. "I want you to be careful, Odette. Grayson really likes you and you are the first girl that I have ever approved of. Even if you aren't dating him yet. In time, you'll learn our secrets." The blue jewel sparkled for a moment.

Greer's face lit up and the dark atmosphere vanished. "There, your hair is finished! Do you need to do anything before we do makeup? Bathroom? I have water in here. Do you need an outlet for your charger?"

Odette blinked, her friend's change in mood startling her. "The bathroom please?"

Greer led her out into the hall and pointed to the door across from her own. Odette pinched her eyebrows together and thanked Greer nonetheless.

Once inside, she gripped both sides of the sink and sighed heavily. She turned the faucet on and splashed cold water on her face. She wasn't sure as to why. In the back of her mind she knew that this was the closest to drowning she would get. She had learned what happened to R., or Romy. There was no satisfaction. Maybe the girl's father was just insane. But that still didn't sit well with her; something *was* wrong with them.

"Are you alright, princess?"

Odette jolted up, "GEEZ!"

Behind her, lounging against the wall, was Grayson. He sported a crisp, white button up and an untied bowtie and a smirk had placed itself on his lips.

"*Why are you in here?!*" Odette exclaimed. She hadn't even heard the door open, or was he in here before she was? No, she didn't see him when she walked in. He must have come in.

Grayson *clicked* his tongue. "I do live here."

"No! Why are you in the ... the bathroom with *me*?"

"I heard the sound of your mental screaming and fear," Grayson said. He stepped forward and placed his finger underneath her chin.

Odette backed up into the sink. "I'm sorry?"

Grayson did not elaborate. "Tonight, at the party, Greer and I are doing a small performance. She was going to ask you to be our 'brave volunteer,' but she obviously hasn't, so I will. Are you willing?"

Odette would be more willing if he wasn't leering over her. "Yeah sure. So long as it doesn't kill me," she joked.

His blue eyes glimmered with mystery. He, at some point, had laced his fingers with her own and gave her hand a squeeze. "How could I slay such a beautiful princess?"

Grayson leaned in closer and, for a second, she thought he was going to kiss her. At the last second, he pulled all the way back and exited the bathroom without so much as a "goodbye" or an "I'm sorry."

Odette scoffed, her skin tingling not only from what could have been but also because he was a strange jerk.

"What were you two doing?" Greer teased as Odette came back to her room.

"I have no idea what you mean."

Greer made a face as she swiped purple eye shadow over her eyelids. "Don't play dumb, darling. My room is right across the hallway. I saw him leave."

"Then you must have heard me screaming at him for sneaking up on me too." Odette perched herself on Greer's bed and pulled out her phone to text her mom that she hadn't died yet.

"You two will be dating by the end of the night." Greer paused and added quietly, "That's how it always happens."

Odette blanched, "Probably not. He asked me to help out with one of your tricks you'll perform tonight."

"You said yes?"

"Yeah." *It would be rude not to.* "What does your mask look like?"

Greer pointed over on her nightstand with the incense sticks. There was a silver mask that was probably made of real silver. There was a swirling, silver stick that was attached for Greer to hold it up. It looked heavy. Odette wondered if her arm would get tired.

"It's pretty."

"Isn't it? Grandfather bought it especially for this occasion." Greer's primping didn't stop for a second. She grabbed a tube of dark purple lipstick and rolled it onto her pouting lips. "He says that it came from Italy but I'm pretty sure he got it illegally from one of his old prison buddies."

Oh boy.

"Come, Odette, I'm finished with my makeup. You need to do yours. We can't have you looking all blotchy."

Greer pretty much left her alone after that. She had gotten up and went out of the room to get something. When she came back, her hair was no longer held back by the headband but had been pulled back in a bun. On her neck, the blue jewel had been attached to a silver chain and hung down to her stomach.

Odette was only acknowledged by Greer when the latter told her to wear red lipstick instead of pink. The quiet added to Odette's anxiety about the party.

Noises from downstairs became louder, and soon the hundreds of people stopped running around the courtyard and vanished inside the house. The girls helped each other into their dresses and adjusted their masks.

"Don't worry, darling," Greer reassured Odette. "Tonight will be memorable."

IX

The entire mansion had been transformed. In the entrance hall, the grand staircase had ivy wrapped around its railing while glittering, leafless trees and moss-covered pillars adorned the walls. It was an enchanted forest.

In the actual ballroom, candles had been lit and provided the light for everyone to see. It was nearly dusk and its orange glow was let in through the floor-to-ceiling windows. The candles were held up by the decorative branches, wax pouring over them and growing longer and longer till it nearly touched the floor.

Odette strolled around the halls, admiring everything that the gala had to offer. Greer and Grayson had to greet the guests as they came in but she felt out of place behind her friend, so she wandered away. She had broken one of her mother's rules already and the gala hadn't really begun yet.

Another thing that she found enjoyable were the masks everyone wore. Many were just the simple black or white masks but some were more creative. There were masks with beaks and antenna, some were butterfly-shaped, some were cat-like. They ranged from soft pink to an ugly vibrant green. One guest with an elephant mask had rainbow paisley patterns all over it. Odette had no doubt that these masks were just as expensive as Greer's.

"Hello."

She turned her head and regarded a man in a gold rabbit mask. "Hi."

"You're new in town, aren't you?" He leaned against the wall she was leaning on.

"What makes you say that?"

He shrugged, "I haven't seen you before."

"We're at a masked ball, you don't know who I am," Odette laughed.

"I know," he chuckled too. "That's why I'm trying to get to know you."

She shook her head, "I think that defeats the purpose of this gala."

"No, it doesn't. The point of a masquerade is to guess who the person is, and possibly get to know them. I'm Claude." *Claude* stuck his hand out for Odette to take.

"You're not supposed to tell me your name!" Odette exclaimed, very flustered.

"Why not?"

Odette stuttered, "Because ... because it's not how this works."

"You're the only one making this proper, you know that, right? Everyone else here pretty much knows who is who. This is just a snobby display of wealth," Claude reached down and took

Odette's hand in his, tired of waiting for her to take it. "So, how about that name, doll?"

Odette pursed her lips. If everyone else here already knew everyone else, what was the point of the masks? The Mages' didn't really seem like the people who do things "just for the heck of it."

She sighed, "My name is–"

"Princess! There you are. I told you I would find you," Grayson said. He sauntered up beside Odette and scooped up her free hand, planting a swift kiss on it. "Oh, and you've made a friend?"

Claude laughed nervously, staring at his shoes. "Yes, we've been talking about what is and isn't proper to do at a masquerade."

"Hmm, sounds boring. I'm going to be taking her away now, goodbye." Grayson tugged Odette's hand and she finally freed her hand from the other man.

"Bye!" she called out.

Claude chuckled, "Bye *princess*."

Grayson glowered and made sure to hold onto Odette tight. He linked their arms together, his other hand placed on top of hers. A strange feeling went through her. Anxiety, yes, but also ... attraction.

Odette knew that Grayson was good looking, it was really hard to deny that fact. She had noticed it the first time they met. It could be described as heavenly but something dark lurked under the surface. There, in his eyes, underneath the fake pleasantness, laid a devil.

"Penny for your thoughts?" Grayson mused. He quirked an eyebrow and smiled crookedly.

Odette wondered if he ever actually smiled. "Just taking it all in. Also, trying not to fall. It's been a while since I had to walk in high heels."

"Don't worry about that, I'm here to catch you," he said, giving her arm a reassuring squeeze.

She smiled, mentally thanking him. "When are you all doing your thing?"

He chuckled, shaking his head. "Our 'thing'? We'll perform in about thirty minutes. Again, don't worry. You project your thoughts so loud, anyone can hear them."

What was that supposed to mean?

He led her into another room where people were dancing. An orchestra had been set up on the far side but it was hard to see them with all the couples. It was a swirl of colors as dresses fanned out and grotesque masks stared down other grotesque masks. On the walls, faux gargoyles sat on top of pillars with candles on their heads. It was a beautiful nightmare.

"Care to dance, princess?"

Odette sucked in a deep breath, not tearing her eyes off of everyone. "I can't dance."

"You were a ballerina," Grayson deadpanned.

Odette laughed humorlessly. "Doesn't mean I can ballroom dance. Those are two very different things," she informed him.

The boy rolled his eyes. "Well, it isn't rocket science. Plus, you would have an excellent partner."

"You can dance?" She narrowed her eyes.

"I'm not incompetent."

Odette didn't have time to come up with a reply. Grayson spun her out of his hold and into a form similar to everyone else's. She was very aware of the fact that he had a hand on her waist and that it was almost too warm for her to handle.

Grayson leaned down so that his mouth was right next to her ear. "Relax," he whispered.

If anything, that made her even more tense. "I can't relax because, any second now, I'm going to step on your toes," she hissed.

The boy huffed and pulled her in closer. He would instruct her every now and then to step back or to step to the right or left, keeping the moves relatively simple. When she had somewhat gotten the hang of it, Grayson danced them around the room, weaving in and out of the other masked couples.

A few people greeted him, obviously recognizing the host of the gala. Grayson kept those interactions as brief as possible. Odette didn't really notice, she focused on not puking or passing out.

He wasn't lying when he told her that he could dance. Grayson was twirling her, dancing them in literal circles around the others in the room. The orchestra started playing a new song and Grayson's movements changed to match the rhythm.

"How did you learn? I mean, who taught you?" Odette asked. She figured, if he was going to hold her hostage, she might as well make it less awkward.

Grayson stared at her through is midnight blue mask, eyes trailing all over her face. "After my sister and I gained more and more fame, we needed to reinvent ourselves. We needed to learn how to act like people who had money. Grandfather enrolled us, he wasn't very happy about having to *spend* money on something like this but it helped keeping up appearances. The more galas and parties we threw, the more attention we bring and the more money we earn."

His hand slid from her hip to her lower back and he waltzed them in a circular motion to avoid a rather large man and his drink. She had to force herself even closer too, practically hugging his neck while he twirled the two of them away.

"Oh cool," Odette said. "Do you know where Greer is now?"

He nodded his head towards the arched doorway. "Waiting on the two of us, princess."

She looked over her shoulder but found herself being twirled, once again, and nearly freed herself from his grasp. They were right in front of Greer, side by side. Grayson swiftly took her arm with his and faced his sister with a forced smile.

"Sister dear."

"Brother," she chided. "I hope you haven't made our friend sick."

Odette swayed slightly, leaning into Grayson for support. "I'll be okay," she assured.

Greer pursed her lips, her face twisting up ever so slightly. "Come, let's get you some water before the show." She shot her brother a discreet glare, which he paid no mind to.

Odette hated to admit it but having someone to lean on and hold onto helped with her walking. It also helped that he smelled good. She pressed herself further into his arm to avoid people who had no regard for personal space.

In the dining room, Greer handed her friend a glass full of water, the liquid sloshing against the sides. "Drink up."

She sipped it gently, the glass bumping up on her mask. Odette tipped her head back and downed the rest of it. "Thanks."

"Just making sure that you don't drop dead, darling," Greer cooed. She patted Odette's head with false affection.

Odette flinched away, unconsciously moving behind Grayson to escape Greer. Everything started to sway, or maybe that was just her. This wouldn't happen, not here and not now. She wouldn't allow it.

"Princess?" Grayson's face dropped.

Odette had a difficult time looking up at him, her limbs were jelly-like and her vision swimming. "I'm fine." This wasn't going to happen.

She tried her breathing techniques that one of the doctors had taught her. Sometimes it stopped the oncoming disaster that was a part of her life.

"Are you okay to walk or do you need me to carry you?" He winked at her, his blue eyes glowing in the candle light.

A wave of calm and normalcy washed over her, shivers going through her. All of the sluggish thoughts and unclear surroundings came into focus. That hadn't happened to her before.

"No, I can walk. I'm good now, I promise," she said earnestly.

The twins shared a look but it was brief, and soon the trio was on the move again. Passersby paid them no mind, a surprise to Odette as they had been so excited to see the brother and sister all night.

They opened a door that led through the back of the ballroom. A stage had been set up with deep purple curtains shielding them from view. Night had fallen and more candles were lit, some of them lining the front of the pop-up stage.

"You'll wait up front in the audience until we call you up," Grayson explained. He escorted her to where the rest of the party milled about.

"I probably should have asked before," Odette began. "But what exactly are you going to have me do? Nothing that will, like, humiliate me?"

Grayson cupped her cheek, "Have faith in me, princess."

If it weren't for the fact that she was still wary of him, she would feel flustered that he was holding her face like that. "That didn't answer my question."

He smirked and gently pushed her away and back into the party. Grayson vanished into the shadows, his shimmering jewel was the only evidence that he hadn't actually gone anywhere.

Odette sighed and moved back a few steps. Her feet were starting to ache from standing too long and the dancing. Was she having fun? It was difficult to tell, even for her. It wasn't the horror show she had imagined deep down but the night was still young.

Suddenly, Odette started to stumble forward when a person in the crowd bumped into her. Trembling hands caught her and pulled her back up, setting her right again.

"Thank y–"

"You have t-to be careful, miss," the young man whispered.

Odette only saw the flash of liquid silver-colored hair before he practically threw himself into the crowd and away from her. She had hardly begun to think about the man when Jethro stepped onto the stage, taking her attention away.

"Welcome, everyone, and thank you for coming this evening. So far, our masked gala has been a success. But we can make it better," Jethro paused for dramatic effect, his eyes glinting under his mask. "Ladies and gentlemen, I present to you, The Mages Twins!"

The crowd had gathered around the stage during Jethro's brief introduction. They cheered as Jethro disappeared behind a cloud of smoke but, other than that, they remained in a trancelike state. Odette couldn't help but step closer to the stage.

"What a lovely sight you all are," Greer mused, the crowd parting to reveal her lounging on a chair. Her mask was off—there was no use for it now. "I hope you're ready for the show?"

This cued the applause. Greer's smile widened. She stood from the cloth-covered chair and wiped off imaginary dust from her dress.

Greer cleared her throat and dramatically bowed to everyone. "For my first act I will–"

"Where's Grayson?!" A girl in the back shouted.

Greer's movement halted and she furrowed her perfectly penciled eyebrows. "Hmm? Where is that brother of mine?" She dramatically gasped as though an idea popped into her head.

She grasped the rich purple fabric covering the chair and ripped it off ... to reveal a boring wooden chair. Odette half expected for Grayson to pop out from behind the thing but there was no way to hide behind it.

Greer whirled the fabric around and—as though by magic—Grayson appeared out of thin air, with the fabric fastened around his shoulders. He, too, was maskless.

Their crowd burst into another bout of applause and shouting adoration. At least, the people in attendance weren't as rowdy as their usual crowd.

"Thank you, sister," Grayson winked at her and gracefully bowed to the audience. "For our first act, we are going to pull a rabbit out of a top hat. It's a classic for a reason."

Grayson reached up and plucked a top hat out of the air and brought it down with a twirl of his fingers. Beside him, his sister did something similar as she pulled a "magic wand" out from somewhere on her person.

"I want you all to see that this hat is, indeed, empty," stated Grayson. He flipped the top hat's insides towards the crowd, pointing at them for an extended amount of time. Once he was done, he flipped it back over so that the bottom was facing the ceiling, holding it out for Greer.

She swirled the wand over the brim of the top hat, shooting a wink at the crowd.

They said no magic words or phrases, only let the stick run slowly on the hat. Greer would occasionally tap it on the sides or reverse the motion of it.

"Now, I'm going to reach my hand inside of this *very empty* hat, and pull out a bunny rabbit!" Grayson declared.

More chuckles came from the guests. Odette chewed on her inner cheek and watched with bated breath.

Grayson hammily reached inside of the hat like he said and pulled out a ... white snake. Squiggles. A few women screamed when Squiggles raised his pale head and stared out. His tongue flicked out menacingly. Odette shrank back as the snake's cold eyes looked directly at her.

"Err—technical difficulties, folks," Greer teased. She gently took Squiggles into her arms and let him back inside the top hat. "Let's try again!"

She ran the plastic wand over the rim of the top hat while Grayson yawned theatrically. He reached his hand back inside in an exaggerated fashion until his arm nearly disappeared inside.

What happened next frightened Odette. An invisible hand clamped onto her right wrist like a vice and her world went dark. She hadn't passed out, she knew that much. It was as if the walls shrunk in size, turning them black, and the people vanished. Her free arm was pressed tightly against her torso and she was seemingly being pulled through a tube. Odette couldn't open her mouth to scream. She was just frozen with fear. Finally, her eyes were greeted by the light. Odette wondered if that was a new side effect of her *little problem* but she was proven wrong. Instead of standing in the front row, she was now facing the audience and half of her body was inside of the hat. The people watched in awe as the twins pulled a human girl out of an accessory.

"Ladies and gentlemen, please give a round of applause for our lovely assistant, Miss Odette Sinclair!" Grayson exclaimed. He gently grabbed her hand and helped her out of the hat, which was now placed on the old chair.

Odette's breathing was ragged and she was positive her hair was a mess. "How did you do that?" she breathed.

The boy winked at her and sat her down on the rickety chair. His hand was entwined with her own, the heat of his palm seeping into her skin. Unsettled by everything, she allowed him to maneuver her like a puppet.

"Now our next trick will allow you all to marvel at the susceptibility of the human mind," Grayson proclaimed. He began to strut about the stage. "Hypnotism is a fine art, one that I'm sure everyone here is aware of. It requires not only the magician's excellent talent but also the trust of the subject."

She stiffened. *Hypnotism?!* She really should have asked them to specify what she would be used for in their show. It was too late now. Grayson and Greer approached her with false, flashy smiles and confident posture. Odette wasn't certain if she was frightened of them or what they would make her do.

"Are you ready, my lovely assistant?" Grayson asked.

Odette glanced around the room at the eager faces of the crowd and back to Grayson's devilish one. "I—uh—yes?"

He smirked and slipped off the jewel that held the cape together and wound a cord around it. Perfect. Now, Odette, I want you to look at my amulet. I want you to gaze into it deeply and allow yourself to get lost in the color. Don't look around, don't look at my face or my shirt, only the amulet. I want you to focus on my voice as well. Let the party fade into the background until it is completely gone. It is just you and I, Odette."

His words lulled her into a state of calm. Her heartbeat slowed down and her eyes were trained on the enticing blue gem. It twinkled and winked at her dangerously. She could feel her body not only start to droop but also lean even closer to him.

Grayson continued to speak to her and draw her in, even though she couldn't hear him. She was too far gone in this trance. His voice was loud so that the audience could hear him but, in her mind, it was a whisper. His low voice surrounded her with a warmth and seduced her into a sleep.

Your mind is mine.
Words swirled around her unconscious mind.
Your mind is under MY control.
Odette couldn't fight it even if she wanted to.
Only you and I now.
You must obey me now, do you understand, Odette?
Yes.

X

Odette's body was slumped over in the chair and the audience waited with baited breath to see what would happen next. The brother shot his sister a sly glance, one not meant for the others to see. The corner of the sister's mouth twitched slightly but did not move otherwise.

"What should we make our poor, unsuspecting assistant do?" Greer asked the people. They murmured amongst one another but no one was brave enough to speak up. "Do you have any ideas, brother?" She tilted her head in a coy manner.

Grayson discreetly ran the pad of his thumb over Odette's jaw, observing her peaceful face. "I have a few. Our first 'test' will be an entertaining one, if I say so myself."

He adjusted the girl so she faced the audience before he continued. "Odette, you are now completely under my control. When I tell you to do something, you will. What I want you to do is to believe that you are as light as the air. When you wake up, gravity will no longer have any hold on you because you are as light as a feather." He paused and everyone waited with baited breath. "Wake up!"

Odette's eyes opened but only halfway through. She appeared to be like she was only semiconscious. Greer waved her hand in front of the girl's face but Odette didn't react to anything.

Grayson cleared his throat, "Now, Odette, remember you weigh absolutely nothing. I want you to climb on the very top of this chair and stand there. It shouldn't be hard for you, right?"

She stood up off the chair and gathered her skirt into her hands before standing in the seat. Her right leg lifted and pushed her weight onto the back of the chair before doing the same with her left. The chair shook beneath her but Odette didn't flinch. She wasn't afraid.

The crowd gasped, some of them holding in a scream of fear.

"Oh, come on now, we can make this more interesting," Greer cooed. She used that moment to step off the stage and, when she returned, she was pulling a large box full of spikes. She left the box a few feet in front of the balancing girl.

Grayson tapped his chin, "Hm, perhaps you *are* right." With a snap of his fingers, the box doubled in length and the spikes grew longer. "Odette, I want you to jump off the chair and into the box."

Someone in the back began to shout, "You're going to kill her!" but none of them paid attention to that person at all.

Odette suddenly flung herself off the chair. The crowd watched in horror as she descended onto the spikes, the whole thing seeming to go in slow motion ... until they realized it was, somewhat, in slow motion. Her fall had been slowed to the point where she wasn't even falling anymore but suspended in midair.

"You're no fun, brother, drop her!" Greer whined playfully.

The male magician sighed, dropping his hands. "Fine."

Odette began falling once more, and, when she hit the spikes, they exploded into feathers. The feathers flew up in the air in miniature clouds, falling back down around the girl slowly. Grayson took her hand and helped her up, out of the mess, and they were met with loud applause.

As soon as she had sat back down, Grayson commanded for her to *sleep* once more and her body went limp. She could vaguely make out Grayson's voice, the only thing she could hear at all. He seemed to be thanking the crowd before he went quiet again in her mind.

"We aren't finished yet with the darling Odette Sinclair," Greer stated, circling the chair that held the unconscious girl.

"For our next hypnosis trick," Grayson picked up where his sister left off. "I shall make Miss Sinclair believe that she is totally *enamored* by me."

There were several gasps and whispers in the audience as many of Grayson's fangirls were not at all pleased by this.

"*Tsk, tsk,* brother," teased Greer, but she smirked as she spoke. The female magician rested her arm on the back of the wooden chair, intrigued with how the trick would turn out.

Grayson winked. "You are no longer as light as a feather, Odette. When I tell you to wake up, you will be deeply in love with me." His words were much quieter than what he had spoken before. In fact, none of the audience heard a word of what he said. "Wake up!"

Odette's head lifted up instantly, all looks of fear and confusion wiped from her features. Instead, her eyes locked onto the boy beside her. They were glossed over but conveyed such a deep emotion of love, it was startling. Greer was even surprised at the end result.

The brunet extended his hand to the girl who gladly accepted. Her gaze never strayed from his eyes, and everything melted away. There was a faint pink blush on her cheeks from being so close to him. It was dizzying how she couldn't think of anything else besides him; her senses filled up to the brim with Grayson Mages.

"Tell me, princess, how do you feel about me?" he asked. His fingers gently squeezed her own in a caring gesture.

Odette shivered, her blush darkening. "I ... I am in love you, Grayson. Completely and wholly in love with you," she confessed. Her mouth moved on its own and the words poured out without a second thought.

Deep in the recesses of her mind, Odette was mortified by what she had said. Not because she didn't mean them—she didn't but that didn't mean that she couldn't—but because it was for show.

"Really?" he whispered. He moved from being in front of her to being directly behind her, his other hand entwining with her free one.

"Really," she confirmed.

Grayson hummed. "And what would you do if I said I loved you back?"

Odette's heart fluttered and her face broke into a wide grin. "I would be the happiest girl on the planet," she giggled.

"Would you kiss me?" Grayson asked, moving his head to be closer her ear.

The crowd, meanwhile, was just as captivated by the performance. Some of them would chuckle every now and then but most of them were quiet. It was slightly awkward to watch but they couldn't look away.

Odette turned her head to the side, their faces only centimeters apart. She was finding it hard to function with him being so close to her, her nerves acting up. In her chest, her heart began pumping harder and violently.

"I would."

Grayson's lips were barely a hair's breadth away, his flesh *just* brushing against her own. It was enough to make her heat up and to make her stop breathing entirely ....

But before it could become a full kiss, Grayson backed away, releasing one of her hands. He continued to step back until their hands were connected only by their brushing fingertips.

"And what would you do if I said that I *didn't* love you?"

Those words caused her daze to come crashing down, the warm and fuzzy feelings dissipating into the icy tendrils of dread. The butterflies in her stomach dropped dead. Odette was pretty sure she could hear the sound of her heart shattering into nothing.

"If ... if you—?" she couldn't even finish the sentence without feeling like she would break down.

"Yes," Grayson smiled sadistically. "If I said that I did not love you."

Tears were welling up in her eyes, the stupid mask that she wore was actually useful to hide how broken she really was.

"Then ... I might as well die." The words slipped out of her mouth easily, like when she professed her love to him.

Deep inside, she knew that this was all part of the act, that she wasn't actually in love with him, and that his words don't mean anything. She, however, couldn't stop showing the face of a jilted woman as she nearly broke down on stage.

The male seemed pleased with the response—the crowd gasped at how sincere her words sounded—and crossed the stage, so he was beside her once more. "Thank you for your honesty. Now *sleep*," he commanded.

Odette's body crumpled. She dropped to the floor but Grayson caught her at the last second, cradling her in his arms delicately. He gazed at her peaceful face, annoyed that the mask was obstructing it from him. A quick yank of the ribbon and the mask fell free and off her face, tumbling down onto the floor. A stray tear, leftover from her "heartbreak," fell down her face and held his attention for a moment longer.

His arms snaked around her waist and under her legs, carrying her back over to the chair that she once sat on. Greer eyed him knowingly but he didn't meet her gaze. His sole focus was on the girl in his arms.

"It is time to awaken our assistant," Greer said loudly, stepping in front of her brother and Odette.

Grayson took one last look before snapping back to reality. "When I say the word, Odette will awaken and return to just how she was when she came up on the stage." Grayson ordered her to wake up and her eyes fluttered open instantly. She looked to Greer first, eyebrows furrowed in confusion.

The other girl helped her up from the chair and presented her to the crowd. "Please give a hand for our brave assistant!"

Odette was startled by how loud the audience cheered for her. She smiled, embarrassed from the attention she was receiving. Grayson came up beside her, taking her other hand with his, and bringing it up for a kiss.

"You didn't make me do anything embarrassing, right?" she muttered.

Grayson chuckled. "I wouldn't call it embarrassing. Entertaining, yes. Slightly endearing."

Odette didn't like that answer at all.

"Come with me," Grayson murmured in her ear.

Odette turned around to face him, she had been over at the punch table sipping on her water. "Where are you taking me?"

The boy shook his head. "You'll find out."

He led her through the throngs of people, heading up the grand staircase in the entry hall, and up a few more flights of stairs. Odette was breathing heavily, one hand holding her skirt up, so she wouldn't trip over it while the other was held tight within Grayson's grasp. She wished that she could just kick off her high heels but it was nearly impossible to do so as the boy was not slowing down anytime soon.

Finally, Grayson pulled her close to him, stopping in front of a large window. He smiled slyly at her and pushed it open, crawling onto the roof.

"Come on," he urged, waving her on. He patted the space beside him, like that would entice her more.

"There are several reasons why I should not go out on the roof with you," Odette said. "Starting with the fact that it will probably ruin my dress."

Grayson rolled his eyes and shrugged off his suit jacket, laying it on the area beside him. "There, one problem solved."

"I faint at the worst of times," Odette sighed.

"I will have my arm around you the entire time. I was looking for an excuse to do it anyway."

She laughed, still shaking her head. "My parents would kill me—"

"Well, then, they better not find out. I won't tell them." He raised his eyebrows, waiting for her to come up with another excuse.

Odette chewed on the inside of her cheek, glancing down the long hallway behind her. No one to stop her, no one to witness what was about to take place. She sighed, bending over so that she could fit through the window. She didn't need to look up to see how smug Grayson was looking.

"If I die ... " she warned, pointing a finger at him.

"Completely on me, I'll admit it. I'll feel so guilty that I'll turn myself in to rot behind bars, leaving my grandfather and sister to go bankrupt." Grayson scooted closer to where Odette had perched herself, wrapping his arm around her, and pulling her in close like he said he would.

She shuddered, her mind at war with itself. She knew that she should run away, that she was stupid to have come out on a roof with a boy who practically screamed danger. She had been warned in a dream and by his own sister to be careful, not to mention the nightmare that she had at the sleepover ...and yet, the gushy, hormonal side of her was freaking out because she was stargazing with the most beautiful boy she had ever seen in her life. He had his arm around her and his body heat was chasing off any chill that tried to come her way. Plus, he had never actually hurt her.

"Do you see those stars right there? That is the constellation *Draco,* which happens to be my middle name," he told her, pointing up at the sky.

Odette followed the pattern of stars with her eyes. "That's a beautiful thing to be named after. The stars." With her face upturned, she couldn't look at him but she could feel him. She could feel him shifting to get closer to her. Even though it was warm outside, she was shivering from the leftover chill of the mansion. Or, that was what she told herself.

"You need to relax," Grayson whispered in her ear, making her jump. "You're so tense. I don't bite, you know? Unless you *want* me to ..."

"I'm sorry," Odette murmured, turning away. She didn't want him to see how flustered she was.

Grayson sighed, the hand around her torso tracing circles into the fabric. "Why are you so intimidated by me?"

Odette met his gaze.

"You're always ready to run away when you are close to me. It confuses me. Don't you like me?"

"I-I'm not." Odette stuttered quietly.

Grayson's eyes hardened. "I could always make you tell me how you feel." His voice got deeper when he said that. His forehead was pressed against hers and she was practically pinned to the house.

"Maybe it's 'cause you say things like that," Odette hinted.

The intensity in his eyes vanished and was replaced by amusement. *"Maybe.* You're so strange, Odette. You're so ... innocent and naive. It's refreshing. I just hate seeing you so frightened of me." His eyes switched between Odette's.

She swallowed hard and willed herself to look away. His eyes were hypnotic, just enough to make her paralyze.

"And, yet, despite your obvious fear, you followed me without question. You allowed me to convince you to join me out here on the roof even though it's putting your health at risk. You trust me enough to take care of you ..."

And part of me is regretting it.

"I hardly know you, Grayson. Even so, you and Greer are my only friends here," Odette admitted. "I haven't ever had any boyfriends of any kind and I don't want to screw up anything. Besides ... I-I ..."

Grayson leaned in closer. "You what?" He was so close to her that he could easily kiss her. His lips were a distraction and Odette didn't like that. Everything about his stupid face was a distraction to her.

"I ..." Odette hesitated, "don't know how to feel around you." With the admission out into the universe, she felt lighter somehow. And, at the same time, chained to the boy beside her.

The silence between them was stifling. Grayson's constant eye contact made her feel odd, like he was peering into her soul. A cool breeze blew ruffled both of their hair, some of his tickling her temples.

"How do you feel about me?" His hand on her waist slid across to where she was resting her hand. He ran his thumb across her knuckles, soothing her.

Odette finally looked away from his blue orbs, focusing on how his hand caressed her own. It was extremely dark out now, the light from the party spilling out in yellow squares on the ground below. The moon hardly shed any light at all, just enough to lit up his profile.

She felt compelled to tell him the truth. "Afraid. Nervous. And ... sometimes ... warm."

His hand abandoned hers and skimmed across her jawline. "Good."

In an instant, his lips were flushed with her own. Odette's breathing stuttered, her eyes widening. Grayson, however, had his eyes closed. His hand cupped her cheek, drawing her in closer. She blushed a horrid shade of red, the heat crawled all the way up to the tips of her ears.

Grayson pulled back just enough, so their lips weren't touching as much, his eyes still closed. "Just relax, Odette. Give in to it."

And he kissed her again.

This time, Odette closed her eyes and did as he instructed. She gave in.

XI

"Hey, Det, I have a surprise for you!" Jonah sang from the front door.

Odette laid her book on the couch and then approached the open threshold. "Yeah?"

Pamela giggled over whatever the surprise was. She was right in front of Jonah, blocking Odette's line of sight of whatever was in his hands. There were small noises that sounded like squeaks coming from her father's hands. The girl fought the urge to rise up on her toes to see what it was—if she did that, they would hide the thing from her.

"What is it?" Odette asked, glancing between her mom and her dad. She had a suspicion but she didn't want to get her hopes up.

Pamela finally stepped aside and Odette squinted. At first glance, she saw nothing. That was until *nothing* moved, making her gasp. A small gray and white kitten that had blended in with her father's shirt lifted its small head and *meowed* at her.

Odette threw her hand over her mouth, so her squeal wouldn't scare the small thing. "Oh my God! *Can we keep it?! Are we keeping it?!*" She rushed to her father's side and scooped the fuzz ball from his arms and cradled it to her chest.

"That's why it's a surprise," her dad chuckled. "There was a guy at my work who brought in a box full of them. This little girl was the runt of the litter and I know how much you've always wanted one ..."

The teenage girl was just barely paying attention to her father as she cooed over the fluffy kitten. It certainly was small even for a kitten. It was a girl and it had big eyes—one blue and one brown, like herself—that stared back at her.

"Since you will be home a lot, this kitten will be your responsibility. Now, your mom and I will help out a little but you have to clean the cat box and feed her. You have to brush her and keep her clean too; we don't need fleas. I bought some stuff at the store ..."

Odette continued to pat and scratch behind her little kitten's ears. The cat just purred, closing its eyes and relaxing into her hold. In her mind, she was already going through many different names that might suit the little animal.

"Hmmm," Odette hummed. "I think you'll be Runt."

Pamela frowned. "You're naming the cat 'Runt'?"

"Why not?" Odette shrugged. "It isn't set in stone but I like it a lot. She's so small and she was the runt of the litter. It just makes sense to me."

Her mother didn't let up the unhappy face. "Why don't you think on the name for a while?"

Odette laughed and went back inside, hearing her mother and father bicker about the name choice. She decided to forget about her book and just head straight up to her room with the new kitten. Fur was sticking to her shirt but she didn't mind at the moment.

"You like the name Runt, don't you?" she muttered to the cat.

The small animal only blinked at her slowly.

"Hm, I'm going to take that as 'you'll think about it.'"

Runt had curled up on Odette's chest when there was a knock on the door. Odette perked up slightly but didn't move too much to disturb the animal. The low rumble of voices was all she could pick up on, no distinguishing words, but she still wondered who would be visiting.

Then there were footsteps on the stairs and her heart leaped. Whoever it was, they were coming to see her. And there were only two people she knew who would come over.

Her mother's caramel hair came into view. "Odette, Grayson's here to see you." As if she couldn't see his towering figure behind her. Pamela winked at her daughter, making her blush even harder.

"Hey," she greeted.

Her mother stepped aside and allowed the older boy to walk inside.

"Hello."

Pamela waved to get her daughter's attention, mouthing at the younger girl to leave the door open. Odette's eyes widened in horror at her mom even thinking like that, cursing the older woman for making her even more nervous now.

"Oh, uh ... look what my dad got me from work! Isn't she cute?!" Odette exclaimed, scooping the kitten in her hands.

Grayson sat down at her desk, eyeing the animal warily. "Not as cute as you are," he teased.

The girl snorted, rolling her eyes. "Whatever. How are you? How's the show?" She sat Runt down on her lap, turning her attention back to her *"maybe-boyfriend."*

"I've been restless, actually. One of the reasons I came to see you. I need to see you again," he smirked to himself. "Because I cannot get you out of my head."

Odette inhaled. "Wow. You're ... honest. And I probably look like a tomato ..."

"I like it." Grayson cocked his head to the side. "I want to take you out on a date."

Even Runt reacted to his words, popping her head up from her curled up position.

Odette couldn't stop the smile. "A date?" So many scenarios flew through her mind about where he would take her, how she would screw it up, and how that would be the last time they would ever speak to each other.

"There is a production of *Swan Lake* being put on in the city; I thought of you immediately. Something like fate telling me to go on and ask you out." He reached into the pocket of his dress pants and pulled out a colorful flyer that advertised the ballet.

"I would love to go," she whispered. "And this is going to sound lame but I have to ask my parents first." She cringed, looking down so she wouldn't have to see his reaction.

Grayson chuckled. In a second, he was kneeling in front of her with a finger under her chin, making her look up at him. "What kind of gentleman would I be if I didn't ask your parents? I need to know what to do if something happens to you, don't I?" He ghosted his thumb over her bottom lip. "Besides, your father has to threaten me. How else will he know that I'll be on my best behavior?"

Odette stopped breathing for a second. She was almost certain that he would kiss her again. He was looking at her like he did at the gala, his eyes peering into her soul and making her feel so exposed. He was so close to her that she could almost feel his lips ... until Runt meowed, making them break apart.

She giggled at her cat's actions, scratching behind her ears. Grayson, however, glared at the gray fluff ball. Runt stared back at him with unblinking eyes, almost challenging him.

"If you want, I can go downstairs with you," Odette said, looking up from the cat. "I just have to clean myself of the fur." She blushed, feeling so unkempt next to him. She wasn't even wearing makeup and she was certain that she not only looked like a slob but smelled like one.

Odette sat Runt on the floor and the cat scampered off to a small pile of old towels that were her temporary bed. The girl dusted herself off, trying to ignore the feeling of his eyes on her the whole time.

"You never did talk about the show?" Odette said, digging around in one of her boxes for a lint roller.

Grayson sat back down on the vanity chair, leaning back casually. "It's going. Greer and I have come up with a few new tricks. Grandfather is the one who forces practice every day, even though it is unnecessary." He eyed the rose that he gave her at one of his shows, his fingers tracing over its petals lightly.

Odette scoffed lightly. "Practice does make perfect but you both are already pretty perfect. It's unbelievable." She discreetly sprayed some perfume on, glancing back to make sure he didn't notice.

The boy hummed lightly, his attention moving to some photos she had in her room. Most of them were old dance photos in her costumes and heavy makeup. "You look so tiny in this picture," he commented.

Odette turned around completely, running her fingers through her hair. She acknowledged the photo and nodded. "That was ... fifth grade, I believe. I was a doll."

"Yes you are," he winked at her teasingly.

Odette fought her embarrassment. "Shut up, not like that. It was a group dance and we were the figurines slash dolls in music boxes. I was new to *demi-pointe* and I kinda sucked."

"And what is this one?" He gestured to a photo in which she was much older. It was the last dance picture on the wall.

"That's that *Swan Lake* solo I had, I was fifteen. The picture was actually taken after the accident on stage because we don't take dance pictures until much later in the year. You can faintly see the bruise I have in the junction of my arm from the IV." Odette pointed it out, circling the area.

Grayson examined it again. "You still look beautiful."

"I never said I didn't," Odette joked, sticking her tongue out. "It was so awkward taking that photo. I had been out for a few months by that time and I was having trouble getting into the poses because I hadn't used those muscles in so long."

The boy hummed.

Odette became acutely aware of how close they had gotten again. She tilted her head to the side and admired his profile.

"You're staring," Grayson said.

"You do it all the time." She leaned in and pressed a small kiss to the corner of his mouth and moved away with a small smirk. She picked up her phone and knelt down to pat Runt's head. "I'll be back."

Grayson's hand wrapped around her bicep and pulled her upright. He spun her around so she was facing him, his face blank. She was pinned to the wall, the hand on her arm now holding her wrist up above her head.

"If you're going to kiss me, do it right," he warned.

All at once, his entire weight was pressed against her, nearly smothering her in the kiss. His lips connected with hers roughly, her teeth pressing against the inside of her mouth harshly. Her eyes remained wide open but so was his, staring down at her darkly.

Odette thought her heart was going to beat out of her chest. She was, quite literally, trembling but not in fear. It was from how sudden he had approached her and just *kissed* her. When he finally did pull away, his lips were quirked up in a small smirk. The only sign that he had just been kissed was his reddened lips; he wasn't even blushing or breathing hard. Odette wondered if this boy was even human.

"You're such a cute tomato. You might want to calm down, though, as we are still going downstairs to your parents. You wouldn't want them to get the wrong idea now, would you?" Grayson's voice was even and full of sarcasm.

Odette gaped. He was impossible but she really didn't want him any other way. She slid out of his grasp and checked her face in the mirror. The blush had crawled all the way up to her ears. It wasn't fair that he could affect her like that. There wasn't much that she could do for herself besides breathe, and she knew that, if she took too long, her mother would wonder why they were so quiet and embarrass her even further.

She examined Grayson from the mirror while he was distracted. He was dressed downish, as much as she had ever seen him be. He sported a white polo shirt and dress pants and, on his dress pants, his amulet was discreetly fashioned.

Odette frowned. "Do you always wear that?"

His eyebrows jumped high. "Wear what?"

"That blue jewel. I've never seen you without it. Not even your sister takes hers off." Odette smiled softly. "Funny."

Grayson shrugged and pulled his lips into a pout. "I think that I would look weird without it on, don't you?"

"I guess." She finally turned around.

"Are you ready?"

"Yeah."

Grayson took her by the hand and kissed it gently, his eyes sparkling with mischief. Odette didn't bother to reprimand him. If she did, she would only be fooling herself. His affection was something she wanted, Odette could admit that to herself now.

XII

"*You're going on a date with my brother,*" Greer said as soon as Odette picked up the phone. "*What did I tell you?*"

Odette laughed. She threw another dress onto her bed, adding to the small mound that was already there. "You were right."

"*Did he kiss you?*"

She stayed quiet. A grin threatened to spread on her lips, so she bit down hard; but, unfortunately, it seemed that her silence was an answer in itself.

"*He did!*" Greer insisted. "*Was this the first one?*"

"Well ..."

Greer shifted across the line. "*When?*"

Odette leaned against her bedroom wall, looking out the window. "You're his sister, isn't this weird to talk about?"

Greer groaned, "*Just tell me, Det.*"

That was all the coaxing she needed. "Okay. It was at the gala. Before I left, he took me up to the roof and we started talking ..."

"*And ...*"

"And what do you think? We kissed ... twice."

"*No!*"

"Yes," Odette giggled.

Greer sighed. "*That's too perfect, darling. I couldn't be more happy .... What are you doing now?*"

"I am picking out my dress for this evening," Odette grunted and dug deeper into her closet. She balanced the phone between her ear and shoulder, half holding her breath. The phone was dangerously close to slipping.

"*Do you need help?*"

"No, actually, I think I'm good. Unlike a gala, I've actually been to a ballet before. The only thing I'm worried about is ... the date part." Odette's heart plummeted just thinking about it.

"*Why?*"

Odette sighed. "Because I've never been on one. I'm afraid that I'll do something embarrassing or say something stupid. You and Grayson are the only people I really know here and, if I mess this up, then it will be a disaster." She rubbed her forehead with her free hand, easing a worry-induced headache.

"*I wouldn't worry your pretty little head on it. Everyone's nervous when they go on their first date. Grayson isn't an exception. Nothing will go wrong. Grayson will do everything in his power to make the night ... magical.*"

Odette smiled, though she knew her friend couldn't see it. She stopped her rifling for a moment and leaned against her closet doors. It was hard to imagine Grayson Mages getting nervous over anything, but he was only human.

"Thanks, Greer. You're the best."

Grayson arrived at the Sinclair's at five thirty, spending a few minutes downstairs talking with Jonah and Pamela while Odette finished getting dressed. Her nerves got the better of her, making her hands shake no matter how hard she squeezed them. She just hoped he wouldn't notice.

Odette gave herself a once-over in the mirror, approving of the dress and the shoes. Her jewelry? A pair of pearl earrings and her silver heart monitor.

She was halfway down the stairs when she got a good look at Grayson for the first time. He had dressed up; his blue amulet glinted on the lapel of his jacket.

He met her half way. "You look beautiful."

She smiled. "So do you."

Pamela and Jonah didn't linger any longer than necessary after giving them both some instructions, what they could and couldn't do as well as the curfew. Odette did catch her mother drag her father off by his collar, saying something along the lines of "she'll be fine."

Grayson opened the front door for her and her eyes landed on his car. It was a sleek midnight blue sports car that looked like a similar model of his sister's. She wasn't all that surprised.

He opened the passenger door for her and helped her in before getting inside himself. Anxiety crackled within her. It was really happening and she had no backup, no one to rescue her if she said or did the wrong thing. She could totally screw herself over with this guy and lose him and her only friend—who also happened to be her neighbors. Odette was beginning to regret her decision.

The silence between them was killing her but Grayson didn't seem perturbed. In fact, he seemed *happy*.

She blurted out the first thing that came to mind. "Have you seen *Swan Lake* before?"

Grayson smiled. "I have, actually, but it's been a while. I liked it; the ending is my favorite."

Odette laughed incredulously. "You *liked* it when they committed suicide?"

"I thought that it was poetic. They loved each other so much and they knew that they couldn't be together, so they jump off a cliff. It foils Von Rothbart's plans and ties everything together." He glanced at her every few seconds while he spoke, gauging her reaction.

Odette couldn't stop shaking her head. "It's tragic, that's what it is. And slightly flawed. Yes, the idea of love at first sight is romantic but the prince fell in love with a swan. I question his sanity."

He clicked his tongue but he didn't disagree. "Then what is your favorite ballet, Miss Sinclair?"

"I never said this wasn't my favorite, but it would probably be *Romeo and Juliet*."

Grayson snorted, startling Odette. She'd never heard him make that noise before. "Oh right, the *other* ballet where the love interests kill themselves? That's totally different."

"I like Tchaikovsky. I have to like *Swan Lake* or else I would be a traitor to my name," she explained, resting her hand beside his.

The brunet smirked, shaking his head. "Nobody would want that." He laced their fingers together slowly, taking his time in order to fluster the girl.

Odette turned her head to the side, hating how he could get a rise out of her so easily. She did set herself up for it, though. She liked holding his hand; it was comfortable and gave her butterflies at the same time.

She came to the conclusion that, if she had to pick a Mages to drive her somewhere, she would choose Grayson. He, unlike his sister, obeyed traffic laws and didn't have a band of screaming girls in the back. Well, she's glad he didn't, that would be weird. But, at the same time, if that situation ever came about, she would just walk because being near Grayson Mages is enough to make it hard to breathe.

The city lights came into their line of sight. He took a turn that she hadn't been through before and went down a very nice-looking street. Many couples were walking; all of them were dressed up in semi-formal attire. There were a few children; most of them were six-year-old little girls in sparkling dresses with tulle skirts.

He drove past the giant theatre; the lights were lit up on the marquee, advertising the ballet in its large black letters. There were black marble columns with golden flecks out front and a plush red carpet that led to the inside. The line of well-dressed people was only just starting to form.

Grayson pulled the car up to a valet but he paid more attention to her than the male. "Are you ready to go?"

Odette grabbed her purse and opened the door, her date appearing beside her in seconds with his arm extended. She took it bashfully and thanked him.

"Have I told you yet tonight how beautiful you look?" he whispered in her ear, staring down the valet boy threateningly.

She blushed, biting the inside of her lip. "Thank you."

He pressed a chaste kiss to her cheek and led the way to the ticket booth. There weren't many people in front of them, which was good. Odette was slightly surprised because it was the evening performance, which was what most people would attend.

Grayson kept a tight hold on her the whole time they were in the line. He had a sour look on his face, one that bordered on emotionless, and it worried Odette.

"Hey, are you okay?" she asked him quietly.

His face softened when he looked down at her. "I'm fine. There are a lot of people looking at you."

Odette laughed. "They're probably looking at you, Mr. Celebrity." She poked his chest gently and stuck her tongue out.

"No," he chuckled. "They're looking at you because you're gorgeous. They want to have you on their arms but they can't because you're mine." His voice dropped down several octaves when he said that and what was supposed to sound like cute jealousy just sounded ... creepy.

Odette glanced behind her but she saw no one watching them. "Yeah ... I guess they were too late."

Thankfully, he didn't push the subject anymore for the remainder of their wait. Once they got inside, the cool air of the theatre embraced them. Odette liked the change in temperature as the outside was becoming uncomfortable.

"Come this way, we're up in the boxes," Grayson said monotonously.

For most of the walk, the aisle was only an incline. When the stairs did start, Grayson insisted on walking behind her just in case she would fall. Odette assured him that she would be okay but he wasn't moving anytime soon. The stairs up were rather narrow, made even more so by the two handrails on the walls. Everything, as far as the eye could see, was varying shades of red—the carpet, the walls, the railings, the drapes, the wood that peeked through.

Grayson's arm looped around her waist and gently pulled her into the last box that they came to. He pushed the heavy crimson curtains aside and ushered her inside of their private viewing box. There were only two plush chairs but the space was relatively open and wide. He pulled the curtains close and settled into the seat beside Odette, taking her hand in his.

"Are you excited?" He was grinning a genuine grin unlike the smirks he wore so often. It was the type of smile that made others want to smile too.

Odette nodded her head, looking into his eyes so he knew she was genuine. "I am. I haven't been to a ballet in years. This is honestly so perfect, thank you."

"The date has hardly begun; you shouldn't thank me yet, princess."

Odette played with the end of her dress, admiring the decor of the theatre. When she had been a dancer, she had been up in a box seat but never to watch. It was usually during dress rehearsals when she and a few other girls would explore the area and watch the other acts from above.

There was a flash that drew her attention back to the boy next to her. She blinked repeatedly, surprised. "What did you do?"

"I took a picture of you, obviously." He was typing something on his phone, not looking up at her.

The girl scoffed. "Well, can I see it?"

"No."

"No?"

"That's correct." He turned the phone off, putting it away.

Odette was miffed. "Well, why not?"

"Because, if I show it to you, you'll say that it looks horrible and demand that I delete it," he shook his head, laughing to himself. "Besides, you will see it. You and all three-point-five million followers I have on Instagram—"

Odette didn't even let him finish his sentence as she tore open her purse. Her phone was the biggest thing in there but she still fumbled with it, her nerves getting the best of her.

"Oh, you jerk," she mumbled, glaring at him.

The social media app took forever to load; it was like it knew the urgency of the situation and wanted to make her die. She didn't really know why she hated the idea of him putting up a picture of her; maybe because she hated the attention, as strange as it sounded.

His page came up finally, loading the newest picture that he had tagged her in. Odette hated to admit it but it wasn't as bad as she thought it would be. It was just her looking over the front of the box. She did stand out against the all red background but he had cropped out the ugly "EXIT" sign above her head.

Odette glanced up from her phone at him, not missing the smug look on his face. "At least you know how to take a decent picture. I might have killed you if it was horrible."

Grayson said nothing, only motioned for her to come closer to him. He wrapped an arm around her shoulders and kissed her forehead. "Do you want the program?" He handed her the booklet and they flipped through it together.

The lights flashed and the curtains rose. As soon as the theatre darkened, Grayson squeezed Odette closer to his side. The dancers came out on the stage and the party scene began.

"Who is your favorite character?" Grayson whispered.

Odette turned her head to the side but kept her eyes on the stage. "Von Rothbart or Odile. I like the villains."

"Really?!" he whisper-shouted. "That surprises me."

"I like the villains because they are the ones that make the story. What about you?" she asked, settling her elbows on the arm rest.

Grayson had a funny smile on his face. "You'll laugh."

"I promise I won't ... much." Odette grinned, waiting for him to answer.

"Okay ... I like Odette," he admitted.

Odette feigned a gasp. "Wow, I wasn't expecting *that*."

"It's true. My favorite character is the Swan Queen. She is the lead after all but she is also the most graceful of all of the dancers. And, now, I have a new reason to like her." Grayson turned away from the dancers, watching her face.

Odette hummed. She leaned her head down on his shoulder and didn't say anything else for the rest of the act. She didn't make a show of it but she noticed that the boy was watching her more than he did the actual performance. Many thoughts of why came to mind, such as he might not actually enjoy watching it. She couldn't blame him there if he didn't. It wasn't until the prima ballerina who played Odette in the ballet came out on the stage that Grayson roused her attention again.

"I bet you could do a much better job than her."

Odette snorted, lifting her head from his shoulder. "You've never seen me dance, and I can promise you that I never looked like that. I could hardly do three turns perfectly, and this girl is doing a million pirouettes."

"You doubt yourself too much. Besides, I know two very loving parents of yours who would willingly show anyone the recordings of your dances."

Even in the dark, Odette could make out that he had just winked at her.

"You put too much pressure on the old me, you would be disappointed," she warned.

"I could never be disappointed in you." He said it with such confidence that she didn't dare point out the fact that he hardly even knew her. It made her feel good, though, knowing that he felt like that. Even if it would only be for a short while.

The music from the orchestra pit was coming to an end, heralding the end of the second act. Everyone clapped politely and intermission started.

"So ... how was it?" Grayson asked as they walked to his car.

Odette smiled, pressing in closer to his arm. "It was great. I loved every second of it."

The boy hummed, "I'm glad you did. Are you hungry? I can't send you home without feeding you, that would just be rude." He tipped the valet who pulled his car back around, opening Odette's door for her.

"Honestly? Only a little, I ate a little something before we left but ..." she trailed off. "Are you?"

"I could eat something small," he replied. "Let's drive around a little bit and tell me if something catches your eye."

Pulling out of the parking lot, Grayson had one arm resting on the back of her seat and the other on the wheel. He didn't even spare a glance at the people who stopped and pointed at him at stop lights. Even at the ballet, people recognized who he was and gawked.

"Are you okay? You're kind of staring off into space," Grayson pointed out.

Odette blinked a few times, turning red in embarrassment. "Sorry. Yeah, I'm fine, just thinking." She tucked some strands of hair behind her ear and looked away from him. "How about there? They have good fries." She pointed out a fast-food restaurant that they were coming up on.

"Whatever you want, princess."

There weren't many people at the small restaurant; most of them were teenagers or druggies. The person working the register was a squat-looking woman in her late thirties who seemed like she hated her life. As soon as they walked in the door, the woman struggled to hide her displeasure of having to serve another customer so late, but that all melted away when she saw Odette's date.

Grayson's impassive face turned into a pleasant smile. He sauntered up to the woman like he would on stage and used his most charming voice while ordering a hamburger and curly fries with two cola drinks. It was almost comical and Odette hid her growing smile behind her hand. The employee ate it up, her dull eyes brightening considerably.

"I'm actually a big fan of your show. Do you think I could have your autograph?" she asked timidly.

"That would be no trouble at all." He winked and, with a wave of his hand, a pen appeared.

The woman, so flustered, scrambled for something for him to sign. She picked up one of the paper to-go bags and handed it to him. He made quick work of signing the bag, and when he offered the woman his card to pay for the order, she declined it.

"It's on the house, Mr. Mages," she insisted.

Grayson protested but she held up her hands, saying that her decision was final. "Thank you, you are a very sweet lady."

Food came soon enough and the two of them settled down in a corner booth, eating their food relatively quietly.

"That was nice of you," Odette said suddenly. "Signing that autograph for her."

Grayson shrugged, finishing his food. "It's part of the job. If I didn't do it, we would lose fans and people would stop coming to shows. Less people at shows means less money and the next thing you know we're bankrupt. It's better to put on that flashy show than risk it all."

Odette slightly frowned; he made sense but he also sounded like he just didn't care. She knew that the show had to have a lot of acting in it, and it must tire him out having to act like that all the time, but didn't he genuinely appreciate his fans?

Her thoughts were halted abruptly when she felt him caress her face. His thumb ran across her cheekbone with a feather-light touch, the heat of his palm radiating off of him. She wondered if he was going to speak, say anything instead of just watching her. It seemed like all he ever did was watch, gauging her reactions to him and reading her like an open book.

"How long have you been interested in magic?" Odette asked, tentatively bringing her hand up to cup his own.

He looked surprised. Grayson was probably asked this question more than he was asked if he was single, so what made it so different when she asked. He straightened his back and cleared his throat.

"Several years now, when I was much younger, I was good at sleight of hand magic. I learned it at the school I attended from an older kid," he chuckled to himself, lost in a memory. "I used to get picked on a lot. My *darling* sister was always the stronger one out of the two of us, and, if that wasn't enough, I was poor, small, and scrawny. One day, this kid—I think he was probably twelve at the time and I was eight—taught me how to use my smallness. He gave me a book of magic tricks and I learned everything in that book.

"The kid, he moved away not long after and he was the only person I could really count as a friend back then. I was upset but I had had enough of being picked on. I would break into my bully's lockers or take things from their desks and I would hide them or plant them in other places. I got my revenge on them for beating me up." Grayson retracted his hand and looked out the window. "My sister was never really interested in magic; she called me a nerd for knowing all about it.

"Then ... our parents died. We only had each other. She got into this really dark place and I followed after. Our grandfather saw us as an opportunity to make some money from before he died. Greer and I used magic as a way to escape—a coping method—and, when we were twelve, we had our first show. The rest is history."

Odette swallowed hard. She hadn't expected that kind of answer ... *at all*. But then again, he was the "dark-and-tortured" type, so it wasn't all completely out of the blue.

"I'm sorry ... I didn't know," her voice was far too quiet, but he heard her. "At least you had your sister."

"Yes," he said sharply. "At least *she* was there."

She inhaled deeply, placing her empty fry carton on their tray. She didn't want to press him more or open any wounds. "You all do such a good job with your show, I thought that you must have been doing it for a very long time."

Grayson smirked but it didn't reach his eyes. "You're cute, princess. Don't think too much into all of that." His words were bitter and cold, like he was spitting poison at her.

Had she made him upset? His agitation was almost palpable, probably from having to relieve such a memory in front of her.

"Grays—" before she could finish, he stood up abruptly, taking the trash with him and dumping it. Odette stayed seated. What had she said? She tried to replay the conversation in her mind but there was nothing she could come up with. It must have been a particularly painful memory. She noticed Grayson waiting for her by the door now, impatiently.

What is the deal with him? She stood up roughly and stormed past him. True, she asked a question about his past but she never expected him to react like that.

And he didn't have to take it out on her.

Odette made sure she stayed a few feet ahead of him as she walked back to his car, having to half-sprint to stay in front of his long legs. Rationally, she knew that she shouldn't be too upset with him. After all, he really didn't do anything wrong. She was overreacting, she realized.

She was about to turn around when she saw the cold barrel of a gun pointed an inch from her nose. Her breath caught and she tried to stumble back but another person who was not her date wrapped his hands around her biceps, holding her in place.

"HEY!" Grayson barked, crossing the distance to where Odette was in a matter of seconds.

Seemingly appearing out of nowhere, three more thugs surrounded them. Odette was too scared to even breathe, her heart beating far faster than it should, but Grayson remained confident and *pissed*.

"Oh, is this your boyfriend?" the man with the gun sneered. He looked like he was only a year or two older than Grayson himself but the tattoos and bloodshot eyes and yellow teeth made him seem older.

"Let her go and I might let you live," Grayson seethed, stepping forward. Long gone was his foul mood ... no, he was angry now. Two of the thugs grabbed his arms, stopping him. Grayson's eyes were burning with a fire that Odette had never seen before and she felt scared.

Or … maybe she had seen that look of anger before … but in a dream. A nightmare.

The gunman laughed, his yellow teeth on display. "That's cute. Hand over your cash, pretty boy, or we *take* the girl." Once again, the gun was on her, pointing at her abdomen.

"Stop it, please," she begged the men. She raised her hands to show she had nothing on her.

"I'll be takin' this." The guy behind her snatched her left hand. He roughly yanked her wrist to take the monitor off of her.

Odette tried to fight him, but he ripped the monitor off her, leaving a red mark in its wake before pocketing it.

"N-no, please, I need that—"

"*Shut it!*"

Her heart was beating too fast. Odette could feel her head becoming lighter, she couldn't control her breathing no matter how hard she tried. Not with the gunman pushing the weapon right against her stomach. If they didn't get out of this soon, she would be deadweight.

"Haha, you're funny, girly," the gunman said, getting so close to her that the barrel of the gun was now touching her. His breath stunk and his nose skimmed over her cheekbone. "Tell lover boy to *give us his money* or you won't like what happens."

Grayson roared, tearing an arm free from the skinny thug behind him. One of the men screamed. There was a gunshot. Odette did something that she hadn't done in years—she prayed.

Please, God, don't let him get hurt!

Her vision faded and her legs gave out. She dropped forward into the thug's arms. She could hear the sound of a person being knocked to the ground and a shout of pain. Someone began to scream but the sound started to fade away the deeper Odette fell into unconsciousness. The last thing she could feel was a splitting pain in her head before she felt nothing at all anymore.

XIII

W hen she came to, the street lamps were swirling above her in a blurred dance. She knew that she was still in the parking lot; things, however, seemed different. Maybe it was because she was so disoriented. Her eyes focused on Grayson's face, shrouded by shadows, cradling her head.

"Odette!" he exclaimed, his arms wrapping around her torso awkwardly. "I was so worried about you. I am so sorry."

She blinked several times, her head throbbed but not in the normal way it did after she fainted. She pressed her hand to her head, hissing when her fingers made contact with the area that hurt the most. Pulling her hand away, she saw her that fingers were bloodied. The girl frowned, blinking rapidly to make sure that it wasn't her imagination.

"Are you okay?" she whispered, trying to pull herself out of her daze.

Grayson's lips twitched. "You're the one who fainted and you're asking me if I'm okay?" His body shook as he laughed but the concern was still there.

"Yeah," she grunted, trying to sit upright. Nauseating dizziness hit her so she resumed laying down. "I don't remember much." Odette swallowed down the rising bile. Her surroundings continued to spin even when she closed her eyes.

"You're bleeding," Grayson noticed, panic filling him. "I should have killed them all. They touched you and pointed a gun at you. They made you *bleed!*"

Odette reached for his hand, lacing their fingers together. He hissed, all but jerked away. Odette let her eyes travel down his arm. In the dark, it was hard to see but she could make out a dark stain that was growing on his jacket. He had been bleeding for some time too as the blood had also gotten on her dress.

"Oh ... my God," Odette was trembling and bile rose up in her throat again. "W-we need to get you to a hospital."

"I'll be fine," Grayson insisted. His face remained passive as he looked down at the wound. He showed no signs of it even hurting him.

"You were s-shot!" Odette forced herself to the side, ignoring the dizziness that was nearly blinding her. She dug her fingers into the crumbling black top and used a nearby car to help herself stand up. "Y-you shouldn't drive. M-my phone, where's my phone?" she stuttered, holding her head in her hands.

Grayson scoffed and stood up, handing her purse over in the process. "Stop stuttering. I *can* drive, and the only reason we are going to the hospital is because you might have a concussion."

He wrapped his good arm around her waist and helped her into his car, his face obviously paler than it had been before.

"Grayson, you're losing a lot of blood," Odette cried, her stomach churning. "We should call the police too."

He slammed his door shut, starting the car up with his left hand. "The police won't be able to do anything," he said through gritted teeth.

"B-but—" Odette protested.

Grayson shot her a look that told her to shut up. "The police won't be able to track down those men. They didn't do anything to us—"

"That guy shot you!" Tears were rolling down her cheeks now. She could clearly see the wound now under the streetlamp. She couldn't look away if she wanted to.

"They won't be able to do what I can." He sped out of the lot and started weaving through traffic. He was erratic now; the look in his eyes was one between anger and insanity.

In a very perverse way, Odette liked how protective he was of her, but he couldn't put his health on the line when he was obviously worse off than she was.

The lights of passing buildings were starting to get too much for her. Odette's stomach lurched and she closed her eyes. "Pull over."

"What?" Grayson looked at her incredulously.

She could feel it in her throat... on the back of her tongue.

It was climbing up higher. "Pull over!"

He jerked the wheel, cutting off several cars, and Odette ripped off her seat belt. She didn't even get to open the car door before she puked. Half of her body hung out of the car as she retched, her head pounding even more. It was gross and she never wanted to show her face to Grayson again. Coherent thought, however, was very far away and a dizziness settled over her once again. She couldn't think, she only felt.

Behind her, Grayson cursed. She could hear him moving stuff around in the car and she felt a hand on her lower back moments later. "It's okay. Are you finished?"

Odette grunted, trying to push herself back up but she lacked the upper body strength at the moment. Grayson helped her as best he could, his phone resting in between his shoulder and his ear. Whoever he called finally picked up. Odette couldn't make out much of what he said as he was talking too fast for her brain to process at the moment. Her head was hurting even worse now and she just wanted to close her eyes and go to sleep.

"Hang on—no, no, princess. Keep your eyes open. Odette, hey!" Grayson shook her shoulder.

Odette whined. "I'm tired."

"No, you can't sleep now." He wasn't getting anywhere with her. "Greer, just do what I said. I have to go." He hung up and drove off to the hospital.

It was torture; every time she tried to close her eyes, he would shake her. Couldn't he see how bad she was feeling? Grayson wasn't doing much better, despite what he said. He was blinking a lot, his eyelids drooping, but he remained alert. The blood was pooling on his expensive leather seats and, every time they would make a turn, it would seep into the fabric of Odette's dress even more.

She was vaguely aware of her phone ringing in her purse; she had even attempted to open it up but her fingers wouldn't work right. She was too dizzy anyway.

"Grayson ..." Odette mumbled, her fingers digging into the edge of his jacket. She slumped against him involuntarily, both of them wincing as their wounded areas were touched. Her trembling hands came around his injury and she squeezed it.

He jerked, the car swerving. "What are you—?!"

"Aren't you supposed to ... put pressure on wounds?" she slurred. "'T-to stop the bleeding?"

She could tell that he really didn't like being this vulnerable, showing that he was in pain or needing help. He grimaced but he didn't resist any more.

He sped into a parking lot of the hospital, parking haphazardly near the entrance. Grayson forced himself out of the car and had to half-carry Odette inside. The pair did not stop for cars that drove through, which earned them several honks, but neither of them really paid any mind to it. They stumbled inside, the clinical smell hitting them in the face full force.

The lobby was rather busy with families and the farther they walked in, the more attention they drew. It looked worse than it really was because of the bloodstained dress Odette was wearing. Someone got up and flagged down a few of the nurses.

Odette didn't like the smell of the ER. Being in there made her afraid—afraid of the pain from needles and the feeling of being numbed by drugs. All the same, she forced herself away from Grayson when the time came; trusting that he would be fine and that she would be okay.

☆☆☆

It felt like hours before she saw someone who wasn't a part of the hospital staff. They had done a few tests on her, determining that she did indeed have a concussion, and asked her many questions that were hard to answer in her current state. She had managed to tell them enough about her preexisting conditions as well, so there she laid in the hospital bed, EKGs sticking out on various places of her chest along with an IV drip supplied with morphine.

Her mother was the first one to come through the door. Her hair was a mess, her face pale but her eyes were red. She was dressed in pajamas and tennis shoes; a large emergency tote bag tucked under her arm for nights that had to be spent in the hospital. Her father came in next, looking haggard.

"Mom," Odette murmured, blinking slowly. "Daddy."

They rushed to her side, her father holding her hand with his warm one. She was very cold here but the nurses had been kind enough to give her extra blankets.

"How are you feeling, sweetie?" Pamela asked. She was trying not to cry in front of her, Odette knew that.

"I've been better. Have you heard anything about Grayson?" She had to fight to keep her eyes open, she needed answers.

"I don't know, sweetie. We just got here and we only asked about you."

Odette sighed, shutting her eyes for a second. "He lost a lot of blood. I'm worried."

She looked over to where the nurses had folded her blooded dress. The bright red was now beginning to look more like a rusty brown. Revulsion rolled in her stomach and she looked away before she made herself puke again.

"You should rest. I'm sure we'll know more in the morning," Pamela assured her, stroking her arm lightly.

Odette looked down at her blanket, one hand playing with the rough fabric. Her purse was most likely still in Grayson's car and she wondered if he even brought it inside with him. Probably not, it wasn't like either of them were thinking clearly.

Someone knocked on the door and all of the Sinclairs looked up. Greer smiled sadly, her head poking through the door. "Is it okay to come and visit?"

"Of course, Greer," Her father said. "You don't have to ask."

The brunette shut the door again softly, walking over to Odette's side. "Are you hurting terribly?"

"The medicine is helping." Odette moved her legs over so her friend could sit down.

"Grays is still getting stitches but they haven't told us how many. He won't be able to write anything for a while but the bullet didn't do anything too bad. He heals fast, so don't worry about him too much," Greer said with teasing tone.

"If it wasn't for him ... I don't know what would have happened. I think he scared the thugs off, I wasn't much help," Odette admitted. "He was very brave and I hate that he got hurt."

Greer shook her head. "They threatened you, he told me that over the phone. I'm not surprised that he did what he did." She clasped her hand around Odette's in a reassuring manner and Odette couldn't help but notice that Greer's hand was colder than hers.

"He acted like the bullet didn't even bother him," Odette said. "It was crazy; he just ... drove us here like it was nothing. He was more concerned about me bleeding than him." She was looking off into the space, her eyes unfocused as blurred memories flashed through her mind.

Greer wet her lips, gently patting her friend's hand. "I'll leave you to get some sleep. I'm glad you're safe now." She said goodbye to Odette's parents before quietly slipping back out of the room.

Odette could feel her eyelids sinking down further and further, but it was several minutes after they were closed that she realized how tired she actually was. Sleep came easily. Unfortunately, it didn't last very long. The doctor came back an hour and a half later when her IV drip was nearly all gone and told them that they were cleared to leave. The nurse came in a few minutes after that and took out the needle that was still in her arm.

They placed Odette in a wheelchair and she used one hand to keep her head propped up. Her eyes were too heavy to keep open fully, but she did catch sight of the Mages family.

Greer was in her brother's room, her feet propped up on the hospital bed while she played on her phone. Grayson was asleep, looking very much like a corpse, so much so that Odette panicked for a moment but she managed to calm herself down ... or the morphine did. In the lobby, Jethro stood by the coffee machine with another man and Zeke.

Pamela greeted them quietly but it was a very short encounter. Jethro's eyes darted over to Odette, filled with sorrow. He gave her a small, crooked grin. Odette was too tired to do anything else but barely nod her head. She glanced at the man standing with the other two just as she was being wheeled out the front doors, recognizing him from somewhere.

Odette watched the clouded sky with fascination. There had been storms all week long since the start of her unofficial "house arrest." Runt slept peacefully in her lap; her tiny little body purring happily with the warmth that her owner provided. There was a large crack of lightning that splintered into two different branches. Thunder followed behind several seconds later with a horrendous boom, one that shook the house.

The wind was howling, the trees bending under it. Shadows danced across her bedroom floor, shadows that had begun to haunt her dreams. She felt stupid being afraid of the shapes that trees made at nighttime. When it was daytime, like it was now, she could laugh at herself, but, at night, the trees looked like human figures.

Odette was now so scared to go to sleep that she had her cat come up on the bed with her.

"Odette!" her mother called from downstairs.

The girl sighed, setting her kitten down on her little cat bed, and went downstairs. "Yeah?"

Her mother wasn't in the living room but her laptop was. The article she was working on was still pulled up, her tea resting on its coaster. The next place to check would be the kitchen.

Odette rounded the corner and saw her mother by the sink, phone in hand. She looked up from what she was doing and at the girl. "You need to take your medicine."

"Oh."

Odette hid her displeasure of having to take yet another pill to help quell her concussion symptoms. It was a rather large pill too and, if it lingered on her tongue for a second too long, the most horrendous taste would coat her mouth for the next hour. Opening up the bottle, Pamela laid out the absurdly large medication while Odette poured herself some grape juice. She held her breath as she took a swig of the liquid and threw the pill inside her mouth. It was hard to swallow, so she chugged the rest of the juice to wash it all the way down. She wiped the corner of her mouth with the back of her hand, excess juice staining her skin. Her mother's face displayed her disgust and she handed her daughter a napkin.

"Your dad will be home any minute now. I hope he beats the rain," Pamela said absentmindedly. She turned her attention to the window of the backdoor, watching the swirling gray clouds. More lightning flashed. The electricity made the hair on Odette's arms stand on end and she could feel it coursing through her— either that or the medicine was kicking in and she was feeling loopy.

"Yeah."

The sound of little claws pattering across the wooden floor caught Odette's attention. Runt wondered mindlessly towards her food bowl. She was very small compared to the bowl Odette had given her but it was cute. She smiled lightly.

The backdoor opened up, startling both Odette and her mother. Her father stood there, looking tired from work but lively enough to greet his wife and daughter. "I had to pull around back, so I could get this stuff in here easier. Can you help?" he asked his wife.

Pamela walked outside, hurrying after him. Odette furrowed her eyebrows but she came forward and held open the door as they carried in several medium-sized boxes. She assumed that they were some kind of new kitchen appliances.

Odette looked up at the sky; she could smell the rain that was about to come. Her parents came in, holding one box together, when a small gray blur darted through their legs. It took a moment to register the feeling of fur against her skin but, when she did, she felt her stomach drop. She gasped, abandoning the door.

"Runt! Come back!" she cried.

The kitten didn't listen. She continued to zip forward through the grass and towards the woods.

"Runt, no!"

Odette lunged, but she didn't want to accidentally crush her cat. Her bare feet ran over the dirt and slick grass, twigs, and rocks were jabbing at her. She was panicked and didn't care about that; her kitten could get lost and hurt. It was about to rain too and—for some reason—that seemed like the absolutely worst thing in the world. Odette could hear her parents shouting after her too but she couldn't be bothered by them right now.

Runt darted to the left and Odette nearly smacked into a tree because of this. "Cat, come back right now!"

The kitten was going in a zigzag pattern now and Odette was almost certain that she was running in a circle. Her lungs burned from not being used this much in a while, her feet stinging. She knew that, if anyone was watching her, they would think she was a mad woman with her messy hair and overly wrinkled shirt.

Runt started to slow down but Odette didn't. She ran full force into a low hanging branch with a very loud *OOF*. The teen girl fell backwards, the branch collapsing on top of her ... until she realized that branches didn't have flesh.

Odette screamed loudly, pushing the person off of her. Her kitten meandered over towards the person, hissing loudly. It wasn't until she got a good look at the other person that her screaming got worse.

It was a corpse.

XIV

O dette scrambled backwards, breathing heavily. The sky was getting darker now and she could feel a raindrop land on her shoulder. The body landed on her facedown but now half of the face was revealed to her. He had obviously been dead for some time as the man hardly looked human anymore.

She was petrified, screaming and crying, shaking so unbelievably hard. She wanted to scoop up her kitten and run but she was too frightened. His face was inhuman, distorted from the lack of oxygen and from death. The eyes—*oh, the eyes*—were still open and discolored. Rationally, Odette knew that he couldn't see her, he was long gone, but, at the same time, it was like he could.

Odette finally kicked the man off of her legs and drew her body into a tight ball. Her heart was beating so impossibly fast that she wondered if she would faint again. She reached over the man and picked up her kitten, practically crushing her into her chest. Runt's claws dug into the flesh of her shoulder but, at the moment, she didn't mind the pain.

Where am I?! Odette couldn't help but notice that the woods around her all looked the same.

The rain picked up and Odette used her hair as a curtain for the poor cat. She tucked her inside of her shirt, mostly for her comfort. She felt so strange; she was cold but hot at the same time. The raindrops were warm, splattering all over the exposed skin of her arms.

Quit staring at me, she begged the lifeless man in her mind. Using the tree behind her, she rose up to her feet. Her legs quaked beneath her.

"Mom!" she screamed, hoping that she was nearby. The wind blew through the trees, rustling them. They were laughing at her.

"Dad!"

Lightning crashed and she spun around in a circle. Was that way the way she came from? Or that way? The dead man was taunting her now with his dull eyes.

"Anybody?!" Her screams were drowned out by the thunderclap. She fell back against a tree, sobbing. She couldn't help but look at her *other companion*, now soiled from the mud.

He wasn't wearing anything special—a pair of ratty jeans and a T-shirt. His blond hair was limp and dull, sprinkled with bits of leaves and dirt. Odette wondered if he killed himself out here. She had heard of people getting dressed up for their last days on earth but he looked like he didn't care. He looked scared. She wondered if he had a family who missed him. Now, as she looked at him, the revulsion died down little-by-little; he couldn't have been too much older than Grayson.

"MOM!" she screamed again.

There was no answer, only the howling in the wind that sounded too much like her name.

A hand clasped down on her shoulder and Odette screamed bloody murder once again. She whirled around, slapping a hand over her mouth. Grayson.

He was soaked, his dark hair matted down on his forehead. Rivulets of water ran down his cheeks and forehead, dripping from the ends of his hair. He was looking at her with so much concern.

Odette opened and closed her mouth but her voice refused to work. *Why was he here? How did he find me? He's here to save me. Everything will be fine now.*

The boy pulled her into his chest, hugging her tightly. Runt squirmed around inside her shirt, meowing to be let go. Odette continued to shake in his arms, crying hard. She was so afraid and here he was, her knight in shining armor.

He pulled away, still holding onto her like she would drop any minute. He looked over her shoulder and saw what had spooked her so much, his face darkening.

"Did you find him?" he asked, having to yell over the noise of rain.

Odette nodded her head rapidly, too hysterical to actually do much else other than clutch onto him and cry her eyes out.

"Let's get you home."

It surprised her how easily Grayson could navigate the woods but he had lived in Sunwick longer than she had. Odette wanted to ask about his arm, how he was feeling, but she couldn't speak. She was frozen, one hand holding onto him, the other holding Runt.

Her backdoor came into view and they could see the lights were on inside and the door was ajar. Grayson held it open for her and she walked in, seeing her parents almost instantly. They were sitting at the kitchen table, holding hands and not talking.

Jonah jumped up upon seeing his daughter. "Are you okay?"

"You were gone for a long time, you shouldn't have done that. Runt is an animal, she would have been able to find shelter through the storm and been safe," Pamela lectured.

Odette just stared at the ground, her eyes wide. Hiccupping sobs left her mouth, the feeling of that body laying on top of her, that deadweight crushing her, burned into her mind. She had nearly forgotten about Grayson being there until his hand connected to the small of her back. It was a pitiful source of comfort and not even doing that good of a job as all she could imagine was that it was the dead body touching her.

"Odette," Pamela said, trying to gain her attention. "What's wrong?"

Jonah walked out of the room, coming back a second later with two towels. Odette just allowed hers to be draped around her. She was trying to think, trying to find her words.

"We need to call the police," she mumbled.

Grayson frowned but ushered her to sit down.

"What? Why?" her mother asked.

"I found Odette in the woods after I had heard a scream outside," Grayson started. "She was huddled up against a tree, shaking. She found a dead body."

Both of her parents sucked in a deep breath, Pamela covering her mouth with her hand. Jonah reached for his cell phone and punched in 911.

The police arrive almost forty minutes later, which was strange for how small the town was. The rain had died down to a drizzle but the thunder and lightning had gone away completely. Grayson stayed by Odette's side the whole time, much to her mother's displeasure. He didn't say much, only held her in his arms on her living room couch while they both watched TV.

When the police did arrive, it was two cops—one short and one tall. They both had the same horseshoe mustaches; the taller one's was darker while the shorter one's was a graying red. They looked very peeved by the fact that they had been called out to do something, but, when they caught sight of Grayson, their attitudes changed.

"Okay and where did you say that this happened again?" the smaller cop, Sheriff Landry, asked.

Odette released her bottom lip from her teeth. "In the woods. I-I don't know where exactly."

"About a two-minute walk from their back door, Sheriff. It looked like the guy had hung himself," Grayson added. His arm was still resting protectively around her, giving her a reassuring squeeze on the shoulder every now and then.

Landry nodded, writing down in his little notebook. "And you found him how exactly?"

Odette shuddered, looking down at her hands. "My cat ran off through the woods when I ran straight into the body. I hit it so hard that the ... the rope that was on the tree ..." she turned her head to the side, gathering her bearings. "It made the rope snap off of the branch and he fell on top of me. I didn't know what it was at first."

Landry nodded his head. Odette could see his Adam's apple bobbing as he swallowed hard. "Did you recognize him? Do you know this man?"

Odette frowned, shaking her head. "I don't think so. I haven't been around town too much, so I'm not familiar with the locals."

"Grayson?" Landry asked.

Grayson shook his head, "The guy was from out of town. Maybe from the city? It was dark, but he didn't look like any of the college students around here."

The sheriff nodded, slapping his hands on his thighs. He stood up from the armchair beside the couch, "Thanks kids. I'm sorry you had to see something like that, Miss Sinclair." He motioned for his deputy to follow him out of the door.

"How are you feeling?" Grayson asked quietly, turning Odette's attention to him.

"I'm ... I'm okay." *A lie.* "I'll be okay. It wasn't me who was, well, you know." Odette cringed, resting her hand on his arm gently. "Besides, you saved me before I went crazy. How are you feeling?"

Grayson's blank expression turned sour. "I'm not the one who just body slammed a dead person, princess. I'm fine."

"No, you dork, I meant your arm." She inched out of his arms, the cold blast of the air conditioner making her shiver.

He knew what she meant the first time; she could see it in the twitch of his eye. "I'm fine. I have painkillers for when I'm not fine. It's nothing." An obvious lie.

Odette scoffed, resisting the urge to roll her eyes. "Dude, a bullet wound is not nothing. Bleeding out in your car is not nothing. Seriously, you got really hurt and yet it's 'nothing.'"

Grayson's eyes darted around the room, checking to see if any of the cops had come back inside. It was strange to see him so agitated. "It is nothing, princess. My pain is nothing compared to yours, don't you understand?"

"What?"

Grayson grabbed both of her hands, holding them like she would try and tear them away from him any second. "I would gladly endure any amount of pain if it meant that you didn't have to feel any. You're too pure; you shouldn't have to experience the pain of this world. I will gladly take a bullet for you any day."

His words stirred feelings inside Odette but most of them weren't good. If it wasn't the tightening of his hands around hers, it was that deranged look on his face. He looked completely unhinged.

"Oh," she whispered.

His blue eyes glimmered in the soft light of the lamp. He released one of her hands, which she quickly placed behind her but his hand came up to cup her cheek.

He caressed her skin, taking some of her damp hair between his fingers and twisting it around. "Do you know how beautiful you are?"

Odette didn't know how to respond to that. She took a small, calming breath. She was just being paranoid. Today had set her nerves on the fritz.

"You're scared." Grayson released her hair and pulled her in close to him. It was a little hard to breathe in this position, her face squashed against his shirt, so she fought to turn her head. His hand was rubbing her head in what was supposed to be a soothing manner but Odette had never seen this as soothing.

"Don't worry," Grayson said, kissing the top of her head. "Nothing can hurt you while I'm here with you."

Odette believed him. She relaxed her muscles and pulled herself in closer, wrapping her arms around his lower torso.

"Good girl."

Dr. Noel Short's visit had been scheduled not long after. The therapist was—to say the very least—mortified by what her patient had to say.

"I'm sorry?" she blinked several times, processing the words that had just left her patient's mouth.

Odette wondered if that was considered being professional. "It has been a really bad week," she said simply.

"You slammed into the corpse of a suicide victim? His body landed on you?" Her eyes were as wide as Odette's had been when it had happened.

The younger girl flinched, recalling the memories. The body and its weight.

"Yes," she said in a tight voice. "And ... and every time that I close my eyes or just *think* about it for too long, it's like I can see it—*him*—again. Hanging from my ceiling fan or from the banister. Sometimes it's not even hanging, it's—*he's*—in a heap on the floor."

Dr. Short was visibly disturbed but she fought to keep herself professional. "Has this been affecting your sleep?"

The girl dug her nails into her skin. "I don't sleep well anyway," Odette admitted. "I always have these ... nightmares, I guess, of someone in my bedroom. This has just added to it. But I've been coping. Grayson's been—"

"Grayson?" she cut in. "Who is Grayson?"

Odette rubbed her arms. Hadn't she mentioned him last time? Maybe she didn't by name. Still, Dr. Short acted like she struck gold.

"He's my boyfriend and he's my neighbor that I had mentioned during the last session. But, he's been helping. He's been checking up on me and comforting me," she replied.

"You wouldn't mean Grayson *Mages* would you?" Dr. Short asked, twirling her pen in between her fingers.

Her eyebrows shot up. That was quite the leap to make, she was sure that there was more than one Grayson in the area, but she couldn't blame the doctor for asking. "Actually yes."

Dr. Short made a noise, which Odette deemed as strange. Wasn't her job just to sit there silently and *judge silently*, not out loud? Her face, however, did not reveal her feelings to her patient, nor did her body language.

"Why?" Odette finally asked.

"Nothing, I was just asking. You two must have clicked fast, it's hardly been a month." Dr. Short looked down in her notebook, hesitating. "He always seems to get a new girl every year; it's tragic what happened with the last one."

I shouldn't ask, Odette thought, *She shouldn't even be bringing this up. She's being paid to listen to my problems, not make me jealous about his exes ... or pity them.*

"His sister has told me a little bit about their past," she informed the woman. "So far, Grayson has gone out of his way to protect me from any harm. He was the one who found me in the woods after I ran into the suicide victim."

Dr. Short didn't make any comment, only wrote away in her notebook.

"Brunch?" Pamela asked incredulously.

Odette rolled her eyes. "Yes, Mom, *brunch*. We've had it a thousand times."

The girl's mother raised her hands in defense. "I know but the way you said it made it sound so fancy. '*Greer invited me to brunch.*'"

"How does that sound fancy?" Odette laughed, pulling herself to sit on the countertop.

"It sounds like something that you hear in a soap opera," her mother explained. "But do you think that you could handle it? After the events of the past week?" She eyed her daughter carefully.

Odette knew that she had to show no weakness in front of her mother if she wanted to do this. She was beginning to go stir crazy in this house and her night terrors only got worse after finding the body in the woods.

"Of course I can. I'm pretty sure that's why she invited me over anyway. To get a sense of normalcy. She's invited her two other friends too, so it's not like it's just going to be us." Odette swung her legs playfully, waiting for her mother to speak.

Pamela was quiet, typing on her computer. She stopped and rubbed her nose as though she was battling with something that was truly a matter of life and death. "I don't know, Det. I love that you have friends and—*heck*—even a boyfriend, but maybe some separation from them would be good."

Odette felt as though her mother had just slapped her. "Excuse me?"

"You have been the best I think that I have seen you in years but you've also had some pretty serious things happen to you. You were held up and that boy got shot. There was a dead body in our actual backyard. Even though it's good to have friends to comfort you in times like this, it's also good to have some '*you time*' too."

Odette scoffed, pushing herself off of the countertop. Runt ran around her feet, rubbing up on her ankles and meowing for attention but she couldn't be bothered at the moment. "Isn't '*me time*' all I ever have?"

She started to walk off, making it through the threshold of the kitchen door when her mother called after her. "Odette, don't walk away from me. We are having a discussion."

"I think I need to go to my room before we have an unnecessary argument, Mother," Odette spat.

She stormed up the stairs, clenching her hands into fists. Her nails bit into the flesh of her palms, the pain easing the raging fire that was building up inside of her. She couldn't *believe* her mother! The woman who said that she didn't have enough social interaction didn't want her to go see her friends. It wasn't like she even saw them every day, maybe once a week.

Odette flopped onto her bed, angry tears threatening to spill over. She just wanted to see her friends and to get out of this God-awful house. Sharp taps on the side of her window made Odette sit straight up. Her heart leapt up into her throat but she soon calmed down when she saw who was there. She rushed over to her window, heaving it open. "What are you doing up here?!" she whisper-shouted at the boy.

Grayson smirked, leaning his weight against the side of the house. It was a little hard to see him through the screen but he seemed unfazed. "Can't I visit my princess?"

"You're going to get yourself killed, I swear. How are you even doing this right now? There's no way you can get through this window, you know that, right?" Odette ran a hand through her hair, looking as far as she could to see just what he was standing on.

"Princess-of-little-faith, you're ruining my romantic gesture," he teased. His confident smirk was making her more uneasy as time passed.

"You're going to have to go through the front door, you know that, right? Besides, my parents would never let me have a boy in my room. Your plan is very, very flawed and could get me grounded," she whispered, glancing over her shoulder. She knew it was only a matter of time before her mom came upstairs to try and patch things up.

Grayson chuckled, the sound making Odette's heart flutter—but she would never admit it. "My intentions are pure."

"Anyone who wants to sneak through a window does not have pure intentions."

His eyebrow shot up. "Oh my, princess, you're the one who's making this—"

"Shut up," she snapped. He snickered but stayed quiet. "I'm serious, you can't come through the window, Romeo. The screen will make a noise if I try to remove it and alert my mother of your presence."

He made a hammy gesture but it was unclear exactly what he did. "Good thing I'm a magician."

Odette wanted to make a very sarcastic remark, something like, "I don't think pulling a bunny out of a hat will help you in this situation," but the comment died in her throat.

Grayson wiggled his fingers at the screen, winking at her. It was entirely to show for whom he really was, but he did stuff like this for a living. All the same, she laughed a little. It wasn't until she saw the physical signs of the screen moving that she started paying attention to what he was doing.

Despite his obviously overdramatic moves, she could see him concentrating. Out of habit, she looked for his amulet. He always wore it, so where had he placed it this time? It was overcast that morning, so the sun wouldn't be shining off of it ....

The amulet sat on the cuff of his long-sleeved shirt. It seemed to pulsate, sending out a dull glow of blue with every tug of the invisible rope in Grayson's hands. Eventually, the protective screen rested in his hands and he slung his legs inside, one at a time.

"You may applaud any time," he commented, smoothing down his wavy hair.

Odette gaped, shaking her head. "You're ... amazing. How?"

He waved his hand, stepping closer to her. "It's just magic." He entwined their fingers, smirking down at her stupefied face. He leaned in and pressed a quick kiss to her lips, making her more stunned than before.

"Hi," she said quietly.

Grayson wet his lips. "Hello."

He was about to move in to kiss her again, Odette could sense it. He was unnaturally warm today but that didn't bother her. She liked that he was warm because he could hold her close and make her feel safe. His breath fanned over her lips when there was a small meow that stole her attention away.

Grayson grunted, "The cat is back."

Runt darted into the room, swirling around her owner's legs playfully. When the kitten did look up to regard the visitor, they both almost glared at each other.

Odette sighed, releasing Grayson's hands. She nudged the kitten away, giving her gentle pets in return for having to neglect her for a little longer. "Stay there," she mumbled.

Runt meowed with displeasure, stumbling forward. Odette didn't look back, turning her attention to the boy instead.

"So ... um ... why are you here exactly?" she asked sheepishly. She wished that he would try and kiss her again but she wouldn't say anything for the time being.

Grayson turned away from something he had been looking at and back to her. "Do I need a reason to want to see you?"

Odette blushed, rubbing her arm. "No, I guess you don't."

"Are you going to Greer's brunch tomorrow?" He leaned against her vanity, crossing his arms casually.

"I don't know yet," Odette murmured. "Mom hasn't really made up her mind yet."

She could tell that Grayson knew there was more to the story; he always seemed to know. It was the face that he made, the one that her mom made sometimes when she caught her in a lie. His lips were pursed lightly, eyebrows rose, and head tilted back. She felt guilty.

"I'd like to," Odette added, almost too fast. "But she might have something else planned."

Grayson's expression didn't change for several seconds. Odette began to wonder if she had actually said something wrong and replayed her words in her head. She couldn't find any fault with them, and then she came to the conclusion that something else was bothering him.

Almost as if he had been suddenly unthawed, he sighed, his shoulders sagging and his hand running through his hair. "You could always sneak out if you're worried about not being able to go."

Odette snorted, laughing so loud that she probably caught her mother's attention downstairs. "That's very funny."

"Is it?"

"I could never sneak out of my house, like, ever. My parents are helicopters; they are constantly in my business and around me. Even if I had the opportunity to get out, I would have *maybe* ten minutes before they notice that I'm too quiet," Odette informed him. "And that's not all, they'll freak out and think the worst of the situation. They'll think that I ran off to kill myself or that I've been kidnapped or that I'm fifty miles away off the side of the road, passed out. It would be even worse if they found out

I snuck out to see my boyfriend and they'll probably try to ship me off to a convent."

Grayson rolled his eyes. "That's an exaggeration."

Odette threw her hands up in the air, wanting to scream in frustration. "It's really not. They wouldn't let us see each other again and do everything in their power to make sure we had zero contact."

She pinched the bridge of her nose, closing her eyes. Grayson's face darkened significantly. She took a deep breath, the angry fire inside of her dying down.

"The moral of the story is that there will be *zero* sneaking out, okay?" Odette was much calmer now, her voice much gentler. "I'll just have to hope for the best. Besides, it's not like I won't have other chances to see you two." She laughed softly, turning back to the boy.

The first thing that she noticed was how tight he was holding the edge of her desk. His knuckles were white and his hands shook. "You can't leave me."

His tone was so deep that it didn't even sound like him talking. The trembling from his hands spread to his arms and his shoulders until his whole body was shaking.

"Oh my God, Grayson, are you okay?" Odette asked. She reached out to touch his arm but his hand snatched hers so fast that it was there before she could blink. His grip was too hard and she could feel her bones grinding together. "Y-you're hurting me."

"I mean it," he rasped. "You can't leave me."

That same deranged look that she had seen the other day was back. His eyes were darker than normal and unusually dull despite the tears that glittered in them.

Odette wrenched her hand back but it only pulled him closer to her. "Let go of my hand, you're hurting me," she said again in a firmer voice.

Automatically, his hand released hers. "I'm sorry," but he didn't sound like it. He sounded far away. The strange craziness had yet to leave his features. "Your pain is beautiful ... but I could never hurt you or make you bleed ..."

"Excuse you?" Odette choked out. Her stomach was twisting up in knots. The room was suddenly too cold and too small for her liking.

Grayson blinked a few times and the dark shadow over his face vanished. He tilted his head, frowning, almost like he couldn't understand why she was so terrified. The heat that radiated off of him only made her uncomfortable now. It was reaching out to her and trying to suffocate her. Like he hadn't been the one who had almost broken her hand.

"Step back," Odette commanded. Her hands twitched with the desire to push him back but she didn't want to risk him crushing her again. Her palm was pulsing uncomfortably.

This really puzzled him. "What?"

His blue eyes softened, losing the insanity that plagued them, but it really didn't matter.

"I told you to step back." She kept her voice level, her eyes narrowed.

She could actually see the sadness settling over his face. No— it wasn't sadness, it was heartbreak. Odette's heartstrings tugged but her resolution was stronger than some stupid doe eyes. She almost wanted to tell him that they had only been out on one date; they had only known each other for a little over a month.

"I think you should go. I don't really want to see you anymore." Her voice was strong, her words like a poison. "Or ever."

"Odette—" he started, his hand coming up to cup her face.

Odette flinched, swiveling her head away. "You can use the window since it seems convenient."

Grayson was at a loss for words. He stumbled back like she had slapped him—which Odette was tempted to do—and reached for the window. He ducked through it just as gracefully as he had the first time before he dropped out of sight.

Odette went over and slammed the window shut, glaring at the screen that laid abandoned on the floor beside her. She kicked it under her bed, the noise startling Runt from her nap.

XV

At Lighthouse of Christ, it seemed that every person there heard of what happened to Odette, specifically, her being in the hospital after the date with Grayson. Their concern was sweet but that wasn't the main focus. They wanted the gossip. How her relationship with the great celebrity Grayson Mages was going. Odette was surprised at how, each time she came to this church, it got more and more uncomfortable.

"My granddaughter saw a picture of Grayson on that smartphone of hers and she said that he had a girl with him!" exclaimed one lady, Ida, who had grabbed ahold of Odette. "I said, 'who is it' and she said that she didn't know, but I recognized your picture, yes I did. You looked so pretty and he looked so handsome. I was so devastated to hear that the date ended with the both of you in the hospital and all these rumors going around about what happened.

"And then I hear from Anne Landry, the sheriff's mother who is my next-door neighbor, that a young girl has found a dead body in her backyard. I was mortified and I asked her what the name of the young lady was and imagine my surprise when I learned that it was you again. Poor girl, you can't seem to catch a break, can you?"

Odette smiled, *You have no idea.* She opened her mouth to try and excuse herself but it seemed like *Ms. Ida* wasn't done talking yet and held her there with her wrinkly hand.

"So, how are you and Grayson? He's a very nice boy, yes, yes. How did you two meet? Is he good to you?" Ida asked, her beady brown eyes glittering greedily for all of the gossip.

Where the heck is my mother?! Odette screamed in her mind.

"U-um, well, we met at one of their magic shows ... but the Mages family is actually our next-door neighbors, so that's how we formally met. I'm friends with his sister and he and I just got closer." *Until he tried to break my wrist yesterday, but, other than that, we are peachy. Real husband material.*

Odette turned her head to the side, craning her neck to see if she spotted either of her parents. Unfortunately for her, neither of them were in the sanctuary, but a lot of other older women were and they all stared at Odette like vultures. They all wanted to console her but they also wanted to know about her "boyfriend." Maybe she should just tell them all that they aren't technically together at the moment and hope that they lose interest.

A flash of silver caught her attention in the sea of silver-haired grandmothers. Instead of this one showing age, this silver hair was like a halo of liquid metal. She was surprised no one else had looked at this person.

"Excuse me, please. I have to go find my parents," Odette said suddenly. She smiled as sweetly as she could and spun on her heel, following the shiny-headed person.

She exited through the arched door of the church, the muggy summer air hitting her full force. She squinted against the sun, looking around the parking lot for the mystery parishioner. She recognized him; the guy had been popping up lately but she couldn't put her finger on how she knew him. It was very irritating.

A cold hand wrapped around her upper bicep, pulling her behind a wall. Odette squeaked, ready to kick whoever it was in between the legs. She whirled around and came face-to-face with the hair of the guy she was looking for.

"You!" she cried. "Who are you?! I know that we must have met before."

"I-it doesn't m-matter, m-miss," the man stuttered.

Odette frowned and shrugged his hands off of her. She crossed her arms over her chest and glared at the guy. "Well, you can't just pull me into a random corner without telling me who you are. Can I see your face?"

Just talking to someone's hair was off the wall. Not to mention, a little rude.

"NO!"

A strong wave of déjà vu washed over her. Odette bent forward and squinted. She tried to make out his features through his bowed head and thick strands of hair. "Pine? No, that's not even close," she murmured to herself. "T-Toren? Thorn! Thorn, that's your name, right? You help with the Mages' shows?"

The man's shoulders tensed. "Y-yes m-miss."

"I think I've had a dream about you before," Odette thought out loud. "Sorry, that probably sounds weird. Why are you here?"

Thorn hesitated before he talked. "Y-you're in g-g-grave d-danger, miss. Yo-you need t-to leave Sunwick Grove b-before i-it's too late."

The hot breeze brought goose bumps to Odette's arms. A strange reaction but she was certain that it was caused by his words rather than the wind.

"I'm sorry?" Odette laughed nervously at his vague warning. "I can't just pack up and leave, you know that, right? I'm still a minor and I wouldn't go anywhere without my parents. I don't even have any money."

Thorn looked up as much as he could, his whole demeanor agitated and uncomfortable. "M-miss—"

"I'm not in any danger either," Odette added. "Except the danger of more hospital bills."

"There-there is n-not much th-that can b-be done for you now, miss," Thorn stated. "I-I just ho-hope you can s-survive i-it."

Odette pinched her eyebrows together. She glanced behind her, surveying the area before she spoke again. "What are you warning me from?"

The churchyard had gone unusually quiet despite the number of cars still present outside. Most parishioners, Odette reflected, liked to talk outside when the service was over. It was cooler out in the open than it was inside the stuffy building, so what were they all still doing in there?

She turned her attention back to the man in front of her who seemed to be near tears. Odette stepped back a fraction, surprised. Thorn sounded like he was one wrong word away from crying the whole time they were talking, but actually watching his shoulders shake and hearing the whimpers startled her.

"Hey, are you okay?"

Thorn shook harder, whimpering like a dog. "I-I-I can't s-s-*say!*"

"If you can't say then why did you bother coming to warn me at all?" She was beginning to become fed up with the man but she would give him the benefit of the doubt. Odette reached out to give him a reassuring pat on the arm but the man recoiled. "Did Grayson send you to scare me?"

"N-no, miss, m-my m-masters have no-no idea that I-I'm here," he sobbed. "M-master G-Grayson came h-home s-so *a-angry* and-and *sad* yesterday. He still w-won't leave his room."

Odette frowned. "Well, that was his own fault. If you know what happened and have come here with some convoluted plan to get me to run back into his arms, it won't work. If there's any danger around here, it's probably him."

Thorn whimpered again, the sound high-pitched and grating against her eardrums.

"Odette?"

The girl whirled around a little too fast and saw her parents walking out of the doors of the church. For some reason, she was worried about them seeing Thorn. She wanted to turn around and tell him to leave like she was keeping him like some big secret, but she wasn't, and Thorn was just another person that she was talking to. Her mother would probably be thankful that she was talking to someone else besides the Mages.

Pamela smiled, her eye darting between her daughter and the fleeing man. "Who was that?"

Odette looked back and was surprised that Thorn was gone. "Oh, he was just someone who wanted to know how I was doing."

"Oh. What was his name?"

"Didn't catch it. He had a stutter and it was a little hard to understand him." Odette smiled slightly and walked towards where they had their car parked.

In the car, Odette sat in the back seat and played with the seat belt that ran across her chest. Her father started the car and looked up at her through the mirror. "Have you heard from Greer lately?"

Out of the corner of her eye, Odette could see her mother's face in the mirror. She remained passive but Odette knew that her mom wouldn't rat her out if she lied. After all, Odette really wasn't feeling like going to see the Mages anyway. And yet, Odette couldn't make herself come up with a story. "Um, I have. She has a brunch thing going on today but I don't know if I'm up to it." It wasn't a complete lie, being inside of that church had drained her of her energy. She didn't feel like having to go into the mansion where *he* lived and run the risk of seeing *him,* but Greer was her friend and she couldn't avoid her forever.

Jonah's face hardened. "C'mon Odette, not this. These are your friends. Do you not want to be friends with them anymore, is that it?"

"What? No! That's not it at all, Dad. I'm really tired and I don't think I can do it. I'll still have plenty of opportunities to see her after this," Odette insisted. The car was starting to feel too hot for her and the scrutinizing glare from her father wasn't helping matters.

"You're not going to have any friends if you keep ditching them."

Odette wanted to snort. *Keep? When have I avoided them up until now?!* "I'm not avoiding her and I haven't avoided her. Pushing me to go isn't going to make me gain the energy to go, nor is it going to make me want to."

"Too bad." With that, he slammed his foot on the gas and sped off in the direction of the Mages' mansion. Her father quite literally kicked her to the curb once they reached their destination. He didn't bother pulling in the wide open wrought iron gates, but idled *just* outside of them. Her mother offered her no assistance out of this situation even though she herself wanted to avoid it and watched as Odette was forced out of the car.

"Enjoy yourself. Text us when you're done." Jonah's words were final and brought angry tears to her eyes.

Odette gritted her teeth and walked with her head held high through the gates, not looking back at either of her parents. In her head, she had some more *colorful* names for them but she refrained from showing more anger than she already was. After all, it would be kind of rude to show up to Greer's house saying, "Hi, my stupid parents made me come. How are you? I'm starved. Please keep your brothers at least three floors away from me."

The ugly knocker seemed to sympathize with her today but she still didn't bother to use it. "Don't worry," she murmured. "When I grow an extra two feet, I'll use you."

The knocker laughed silently at her joke.

Moments later, the front door was opened by Zeke. He was very surprised to see her standing there. "Hey, dude! How are you feeling?"

"I'm okay." A lie. "It's nice to see you again, Zeke."

"Yeah, you too. Are you here for Grayson?" he asked.

Odette made a face and Zeke winced; obviously, he knew of his bad mood too.

"Ah, not really. Greer. She invited me to a brunch thing. I wasn't sure if I was coming until today ..."

Odette rocked back and forth on her feet, suddenly very aware of how much of a mess she probably looked like. Her sundress was clinging to her uncomfortably and her hair was too frizzy to be considered cute, but she shouldn't be worried about that. She should be worried about leaving as soon as possible.

Zeke smiled but she could tell it was a nervous one. "Sure thing. I'll take you right to her."

He *finally* stepped aside and let her into their gloriously air conditioned home. She sighed quietly and ran her fingers through her hair to make herself more presentable. The hallways were almost familiar to her, but she couldn't get the feeling out of her that they were always growing and changing like a labyrinth. Some of the decor had changed but they were mostly subtle things like the color and type of flowers.

Most of the heavy wooden doors were closed as they passed by them but Odette tried to keep her attention forward in any case. She didn't want to be looking around and accidentally see him lounging on a couch, reading.

Her hand still hurt and was a light shade of green. She could even make out where his fingers had been on one side. Thankfully, her mother and father hadn't noticed anything. If they did, she'd probably tell them she got it when she had almost been shot.

Zeke led her past the dining room that she had eaten in when she first came to the Mages' house, and through another seemingly never-ending hallway. At the very end of it, the sound of girls' voices were becoming clearer by the second. He stood by the door where the voices were coming from and rapt on it a few times.

Greer opened the door with a glare. "Yes?" she hissed.

Zeke didn't even blink. "Miss Odette is here."

The brunette finally noticed Odette who was standing slightly behind Zeke. Her glare let up instantly and she smiled, her hands snatching up Odette's quickly. Odette tried not to wince as she pressed onto the bruise.

"Odette! I'm so happy to see you." Greer hugged her, forcing Odette's face into her shoulder.

"I'm sorry I couldn't tell you if I was coming sooner. I didn't know if I could myself." Odette was released from the other girl and pulled into the room. The room was what she guessed was called a sunroom. It was nearly all glass and it looked out at a small garden. There were small green plants that hang around over them, but the main features were the three long couches that ran the length of the room. A table had been set up with an array of sweet breakfast-like foods and what she assumed was orange juice in fancy glasses, but, knowing Greer, it could have been a mimosa.

Bonnie and Nadia were lounging on one couch, a small plate with a single croissant resting on each of their lap. They were watching her with an expression that could only be described as predatory. It was the same look those women at the church were giving her. They wanted to know about Grayson.

Odette smiled at them politely. "Hey, guys."

Greer must have done something behind her back because they stared down at their plates rather sheepishly. Bonnie busied herself by picking her French pastry and nibbling on it, not even looking at her friend.

"Come over here, you must be hungry," Greer said. She loaded Odette's plate up with an assortment of the foods that were there, some of which Odette knew she wouldn't eat but she didn't want to say anything.

Greer practically shoved Odette onto an unoccupied couch and the food was placed into her hands in a hurry.

"Drink?" she offered.

"No thanks."

Greer perched herself on the edge of the same couch she was on, smiling at her. "So, how have you been?"

Heavily medicated. "Pretty good. The concussion is going away."

"Grayson—" Bonnie started but she was cut off by a sharp jab in the stomach by Nadia. The red head coughed and sputtered but flushed as she realized her error.

"It's okay," Odette said. She turned to Greer. "How's his injury?" *Not that I actually care.*

Greer had a funny look on her face. "He's healing. Grays has always had a high tolerance for pain, so it doesn't bother him much. You wouldn't believe all of the get-well-soon cards and bears that have been sent to the house by his fangirls. It's nauseating."

Odette tilted her head, she wondered if Greer was trying to make her feel jealous. "They care about him," she said simply.

Greer laughed. "They care about his pretty face. They care about getting noticed."

Odette shrugged, chewing on a grape. She didn't have any more to say on the subject.

"Is he still locked up in his room?" Nadia asked. She flipped her dark hair over her shoulder and looked like she was ready to sprint up to his room if given the chance.

"Psssh, you make it sound like it wasn't voluntary," Greer said, sipping her still questionable orange drink. "Yes, he is. But I won't be surprised if he comes out for a five-minute break. After all, his favorite person in the world is here."

With that, Nadia visibly wilted. Odette wished she had one of Greer's drinks now. She put a cheese cube in her mouth and chewed on it angrily. It wasn't her fault that Grayson acted so ... *weird!* She didn't even know what to call it—extremely possessive, maybe? Abusive? That seemed too harsh, but ...

"Don't sweat it, Odette, we are your friends. We won't let him near you if you don't want to be," Greer reassured her but there was a mocking undertone to her voice. All the same, Greer didn't look like she was teasing her. Her smile was sincere but she had seen how Grayson had so easily faked being nice.

"Thanks."

Greer wasn't Grayson. She wouldn't do anything like that.

"He wouldn't tell me anything when he came home," she explained. "So, I don't know what's going on between you two but you can talk to us. We'll listen and help if you need us to. Or, if you don't want to talk, then that's fine too. I just want you to be happy."

Odette just wanted her to drop the subject. "We just ... I don't even know. It's complicated."

Bonnie leaned forward on her elbows, her plate was crushed underneath the weight but she paid little mind to it. "Complicated how?"

"Odette doesn't have to tell us if she doesn't want to," Greer cut in. "It could be that she's just not ready or that she doesn't want to burden us with her problems."

"You wouldn't be burdening us," Bonnie replied. Her elbow was now coated in butter and her croissant had a large hole in it.

Odette toyed with her fingers, her face stuck in a grimace. "It's really nothing I want to get into today."

Bonnie sniffed indignity and shriveled up like her friend. They both almost seemed like twins with their matching expressions and the similar colors of their dresses. Greer didn't care about her friends' change in attitude, though, and acted like nothing was wrong.

"I think it's almost time for our games, girls."

The "games" were never explained to Odette even though she asked. Greer only laughed, her headband twinkling in the sunlight while she shook her head.

"It's nothing to worry about," she said. "Only simple party games. It'll be fun."

It would be even more fun if the games were explained.
Odette had only eaten a fourth of what was on her plate, but she
wasn't questioned by the other girls weather she was finished or
not. They all seemed eager to start whatever Greer had planned,
which only made her more anxious.

"So, what are we playing?" Odette asked for what felt like the
hundredth time.

Greer motioned for Bonnie and Nadia to take away the
empty cups and plates before she answered. "Just a little game
of *truth or dare.*"

Odette's nose scrunched up. "Isn't that a little … juvenile?"
she asked.

"Maybe," Greer said, amused. "But we play it in a more
extreme way. No petty tricks or truths. After all, we're all big
girls here, aren't we?"

Odette shrunk back. The way Greer said that sent unpleasant
chills down her spine. These dares—or truths, for that matter—
could be anything.

Nadia sat down beside her and laid a comforting hand on her
shoulder. "Don't worry, we'll start out easy for you."

It wasn't all that comforting, if Odette was being honest with
herself.

Greer started the game and she chose Bonnie as her victim.
Bonnie picked truth and had to tell the group about her first
kiss. For the moment, Odette was rather calm because nothing
seemed too extreme.

They pretty much avoided Odette altogether, except for
Nadia who wanted to know if she and Grayson had kissed. Nadia
had been rather disappointed to find out that the answer to that

question was "yes" but Odette had made up for it by adding in details. Apparently, Nadia appreciated it and Odette was happy to be of service.

Greer had been dared to steal a fifty from her grandfather who was, apparently, sleeping upstairs in his room. She came back a little less than ten minutes later with a very crisp-looking dollar bill in her fist and a smug look on her face.

Bonnie had been dared to strip down to her underwear and run the length of the house. Odette had expected her to say no but instead got a dress in the face before hearing the sound of Bonnie running out of the room at top speed.

"What happens if you don't do the dare? Are there any consequences?" Odette asked. The girls had their noses pressed up against the glass and were waiting for a half-naked Bonnie to run past them at any second.

"That's up to the person who gives the dare," replied Greer. "But everyone does theirs."

Nadia had been dared by Bonnie—several turns after her run—to go upstairs to Grayson's room and confess her feelings to Grayson. The girl looked so afraid and she couldn't help but fearfully look to Odette like she would be upset with her.

"Nadia, you don't have to if you don't want to. That just sounds mean," Odette quickly interjected.

This didn't help Nadia at all as she turned a faint shade of green. Bonnie snickered, saying something about payback for her dare but this was nowhere close. Greer did nothing to help.

Nadia finally did stand up on two shaky legs, reminding Odette of a baby deer, and walked out of the room. It was quiet, too quiet, and Odette could hear her heart thumping loudly.

"How will we know if she does it or not?" Bonnie asked.

Greer shrugged, still acting unperturbed. "It's your own fault you didn't think about asking for proof."

Bonnie cursed and the three girls waited for what seemed like hours for the other girl to come back. When the door finally did open, Nadia wasn't green anymore. She actually looked calm, which tipped off the darer that something wasn't right.

"You didn't actually go to him, did you?" Bonnie questioned, poking the shorter girl in the chest.

Nadia blushed but she shook her head. "No, I did. I knocked on his door and he told me to go away. He said he didn't want to be involved in any of our games."

The turns kept going and going until Greer turned to Odette. "Truth or dare?"

It was an obvious choice, Odette was going to keep everything safe and choose *truth*. However, when she opened her mouth to say it, all that came out was, "Dare."

Her own voice sounded foreign in her ears but she didn't feel like correcting herself. She didn't think the girls would let her anyway.

The other girls *ooh*ed, smiling deviously. Their dares had been pretty bad but it had only been those two doing the daring. Greer hadn't shown how "extreme" she could make the game and Odette had a feeling she would find out.

"Follow me."

Never the good words you want to hear when you're being dared.

Odette stood obediently, smoothing out her sundress as she did so. Bonnie and Nadia were elbowing each other and stood up too. They stayed out of Odette's direct line of sight but she could hear them giggling and whispering. Greer led them out of the sunroom and down the winding halls until they were back by the front door. She continued walking and didn't look back once, her heels clicking haughtily against the floor.

The next room that they came across actually shocked Odette. She thought to herself that she shouldn't be too surprised considering they were wealthy; still, she had never seen anyone actually have an indoor pool before. It wasn't in use at the moment, Odette realized as she walked inside. The pool cover was pulled taut over the pool and to the sides, but it was a clear plastic that allowed the girls to see the water underneath. The cover was stretched so tight that it looked like a trampoline and she could see where the hooks were straining to hold it.

"What do you want me to do?" Odette asked quietly but her voice still echoed throughout the room.

Greer watched her slyly. "I want you to walk across the pool cover."

It suddenly felt like the air had been sucked from the room. "What? Are you kidding? No! Greer, people die from doing things like that." Her hands started to shake just from the thought of being forced onto the cover.

"Oh please. Do you think that I would let you die? It's perfectly safe." Greer stepped closer to the edge of the pool, the toe of her strappy stiletto teasing the flap of the plastic.

"I'm s-serious, that thing won't hold my weight and I'll sink. The cover will come up around me and suffocate me." She was sure that the girls could see her trembling by now. Odette didn't care about the game, what the girls would think of her, or what her father would say—she wanted to go *home*.

Instead of answering her or telling her that it was a joke and that wasn't her dare, Greer came to stand beside her. She looked her up and down for a minute, deep in thought. "I'm pretty sure you're lighter than me. Watch this."

She practically leapt onto the plastic cover, her back straight and chin up. Odette actually screamed, reaching her arm out. She knew that, any second, one of the ends that held the cover down would come flying off and Greer would sink ... or the heel of her stiletto would pop a hole in it.

"Greer no! Get off, you'll hurt yourself!" Her voice was shrill and the echo made it sound even higher pitched than it was.

Still, the girl didn't look back. She walked down the length of the pool with confidence, like it was a runway. Odette became certain at that moment that those amulets must be magic, or else that girl would have been swallowed up by the plastic already. It must have been some kind of crazy trust exercise to see if Odette could hang out with them, like a hazing or something.

Greer hopped off of the pool cover—safely—on the opposite side. She didn't look panicked in the slightest, so she must have known that nothing was going to happen. If she said that, then Odette should believe it too. Greer hadn't led her astray yet.

"Well?" Greer called, placing her hand on her hip.

Odette's heart was beating even harder and she could feel it in her legs. She swallowed hard, her mouth dry from fright. The edge of the water was teasing her, splashing up on the concrete.

Tentatively, Odette placed one flat-clad foot on the cover. It did not feel sturdy at all, but this was about trust, right? *Like a bizarre girl mafia and Greer was the Don.* Her other foot was on the cover now and she stumbled forward, her arms outstretched.

She tried to think of this as nothing but another ballet exercise, something that required her to use her core and balance. She couldn't look down, she was shaky enough as it was. Odette watched the ceiling, pursing her lips to make her feel like she was closer to it than the water.

She took a moment to glance at Greer, noticing that she was about halfway across the pool by that point, when she felt that she was a sinking like a rock.

Odette barely had time to scream before she was sucked downwards, her arms flailing. She grasped at the air, hoping that something would magically appear to save her from her fate. The plastic closed around her like a vice, suctioning to her limbs, and blocking her leg's frantic kicking. She screamed and screamed, panicking more than she should have been. Odette had remembered that, if something like this were to ever happen to her, she shouldn't be panicking in order to conserve her air or something like that. Obviously, she didn't listen to logic. She was in a cocoon of her worst fear, the plastic becoming tighter and tighter as the seconds passed.

A strange thought wormed its way inside her mind while she thrashed around in her prison. She thought that it should be dark, like nighttime. Instead, it was too bright and her eyes were wide open. She could see through the clear plastic and into the light blue water. She could make out the figures of the panicked girls above her ... at least she thought they were panicked. It could have just been the ripples of the water. Odette could feel the telltale signs of a fainting spell coming—the abnormally hard heartbeat, lightheadedness, and the weakness in her muscles.

NO! HELP ME, PLEASE!

Her body stopped its movements despite her inward protests. She could feel how drained she was, how much energy it took to fight, and yet she was still full of adrenaline. She was trapped, she concluded, in her own body and couldn't stop it when her eyes closed.

The plastic had completely wrapped itself around her to the point where she didn't know where it stopped and where her body began. It ghosted over her skin in some areas and, in others, it was tighter than a noose. *Noose*—the image of the dead man flashed into her mind and she understood that she would be like him soon. There was no stopping the inevitable.

Odette's vision turned black but she was still somewhat aware of everything around her, like the water rushing into her lungs. While her body started to convulse lightly, she could feel her consciousness dying out. Everything was on fire, which was such an odd thing to feel while dying in water. Her lungs burned, her throat burned, her eyes burned, but she only sank and sank until she hit the bottom of the pool.

XVI

Odette's eyes burned and she hadn't even opened them yet. Contrary to what happened with most people, she remembered exactly what happened the last time she was awake. She could still feel the water surrounding her and the plastic hindering her movements. Her body jerked violently, arms pulling against the plastic, and her legs flailing. She gasped, expecting to inhale more water from the pool like before, only to find out that she could actually *breathe*. Her eyes flew open and she came face-to-face with a scratchy white blanket. She wasn't under water but being covered made her panic, so she kicked the blanket off of her as fast as she could.

"Odette! Hey, hey, it's okay! You're okay!" It was a masculine voice coming from her right. A voice she really didn't want to hear.

She turned around, eyes blazing, to see Grayson. "Where am I? Where are my parents?" Her voice was scratchy and thick with tears that had yet to fall.

Grayson put his hands up in defense, picking up one of the blankets that she had just kicked off. He laid it on the bed, not on her, though, before he responded. "You're okay now. I got you to a hospital. Your parents just stepped out of the room. I'll get them now, if you would like me to."

Grayson started to rise up slowly, almost like he thought Odette was a wild animal and, if he made any sudden movement, she would attack him. She hated being looked at like that. She had enough of it from everyone in her life; she didn't need him doing it too.

Odette didn't answer, she only frowned. She wondered why they had left her alone with him of all people ... but then again, they probably still thought they were dating like the rest of the world did.

"You look like crap," Odette rasped. She grabbed the blanket with numb fingers and handed it to him. "Take it. You need to sleep."

Grayson accepted the blanket and sank back down in the rickety hospital chair. He really *did* look like crap, the worst that she had ever seen him. He had dark circles under his eyes and his hair was an absolute mess. His clothes were rumpled and he smelled like chlorine and something else that was probably just teenage boy body odor.

"Why are you here?" she finally asked, looking away from him.

She noticed the IV and that the area they had stuck the needle in was hurting, probably from her freak-out when she woke up. There was even a little blood. She looked away from it, adjusting her hospital gown. It was the kind that opened in the front so that they could put multiple electrodes on her chest.

Grayson played with the end of the blanket, his eyebrow deeply furrowed. "Do you remember what happened?"

Odette tensed up, drawing her knees in closer. She hated how cold it was in the ER. "Yes."

"I pulled you out of the water," he murmured. "That was the worst moment of my life, Odette, do you know that? Seeing you so helpless...I was terrified that I wouldn't be able to..."

The girl glanced at him from the side of her eye. He was crying. She picked at her hospital gown awkwardly, not knowing if she should say something to comfort him or not. Did she need to? He wasn't the one who was drowning. Maybe a "thank you" would be enough.

Grayson looked up, his cheeks shining from his tears. He looked so innocent and like a little boy, not the dark male who had nearly broke her hand. "Why...why would you play with Greer?" he sniffed, wiping his tears.

"I don't know what you mean by that. She's my friend."

Grayson shook his head vigorously. "No, no she's not. Greer has these sadistic tendencies—"

"*Sadistic tendencies?*" Odette echoed. "What is that supposed to mean, Grayson?! You're telling me that this wasn't an accident? That she meant for me to fail?"

"Any other day, I would have said 'no', she wouldn't kill you. She likes you—or she *did*. But then again, she knows that you and I..." his jaw flexed as he cut himself off. "So, she might have changed her mind...I should have protected you better."

Odette couldn't move, it was like she was in the water again. She could not believe what she was hearing—almost like it wasn't English. She could hear the words and the sounds he was making but they didn't make sense. How could she believe him?

She, however, could recall the look on Greer's face before she sank into the water. That cold, stony glare. It had hardly seemed important in the moment, not when she was thinking that her life was about to end.

"So, she tried to kill me?" Her voice was far away and the hospital was suddenly too cold for her liking. She was afraid, she was very afraid. "She tried to kill me because I ended it with you."

"Odette—" Grayson started but he didn't finish. He couldn't think of what to say.

Odette's mind felt as though it had been wiped clean. Her insides twisted up with nausea. Her mouth tasted like a swimming pool; that was the clearest thought she had and it wasn't helping. She knew it was only the calm before the storm as this rising, unsettling panic was proving to be too much. Another clear thought pushed through the sea of muddy blankness and that was, if it wasn't for Grayson, she probably would have been dead.

She could have died....

A choked sob left her mouth. The girl wasted no time and flung her arms around him. His neck was cold but, still, she buried her face deeper in it. The day had started out with her fearing him but now she knew that she needed him in order for her to be safe. She needed comfort.

Grayson moved himself to the edge of the hospital bed and allowed her to cry on him. He stroked her hair calmingly, wrapping the discarded blanket around her again. He whispered words of comfort in her ear, which she greatly appreciated.

"What did you tell my parents?" Odette muttered in his ear.

Grayson shook his head. "I only told them about when I got there. Greer hasn't talked to them, so they will ask you about it." He pressed a kiss to her forehead, wiping away her tears. "Will you tell them?"

Odette laughed bitterly. "How can I? I'll lie. It's what will be best for all of us."

There was no way around it. Any other way would be unsavory for everyone involved. She would have to tell them about Grayson sneaking into her room and having his mini freak-out, resulting in her bruised hand. Even if she did lie about that part, it would only add to the pile of lies. She would run the risk of ruining the Mages forever, or Greer would just try again.

"Are you sure?" Grayson searched her eyes for any sign of doubt but he found none. "And...what about...us?"

Odette smirked without humor, *Yes, what indeed.* She knew that it would be smart to have nothing to do with him and his family to avoid something like this again. It would also be smart to take him back for the protection he could provide. Did she have feelings for him?

Yes.

That, however, could just be her strung out emotions talking. He hurt her but he saved her from his sadistic sister. This was the second time that he had taken her to the hospital and, even though that may not be a good thing, he would do it.

She cupped his cheek with her hand and brought his face close. She could feel his heart beating fast through his chest, but it was comforting. For some reason, she liked knowing that he could be flustered too. He inhaled sharply before their lips connected, his hair tickling her face.

Grayson pulled away after a few seconds, his nose nudging hers. "Don't just take me back because you think it's the safe thing to do. I won't be used. Besides ... you would be miserable."

"I'm not," Odette whispered. "I like how I feel around you. I like that you'll always protect me and how I always feel warm next to you. You saved me today and I can never thank you enough."

Grayson shook his head a little. "No, I should have been there any way. I shouldn't have let the two of you get close in the first place. I just thought that you would be different—"

The door opened up at that moment and he stopped himself. Pamela and Jonah just stared at their daughter for several seconds, trying to process that she really was awake. It was when Grayson moved off her bed that their hesitation seemed to break and they rushed to her side.

"Oh sweetheart," Pamela was crying. Her eyes were red and puffy and she didn't bother hiding it this time.

"How did this happen?" Jonah asked. He grabbed Odette's hand and held it tightly. "Please, do you remember at all?"

Odette nodded, swallowing hard. She looked down at her lap—to her parents, it probably looked like she was gathering strength to tell the story, but she was trying to think of a believable lie.

"Greer was showing us the indoor pool. I walked a little too close to the edge and ... well, I had been feeling pretty weak all day. The food helped a little but I got very dizzy and I fell into the pool. I tried to get out but it was pretty impossible and I fainted." She glanced up at Grayson, who was his stoic-faced self.

Jonah's face dropped and his shoulders hunched over. He pulled his daughter's hand closer and kissed the back of it. Odette frowned as her skin began to feel wet until she understood that it was her dad's tears.

"I'm sorry," he murmured. "It's all my fault. I shouldn't have forced you to go. You told me that you weren't feeling well ... my mistake could have gotten you killed."

Guilt ate at her insides but Odette pushed passed that. "It's okay, Dad. You didn't mean to, you thought you were doing what was right." The words were making her sick. She didn't want her dad to think that this was because of him.

"No Odette." His voice was shaking and he finally looked up at her. She had never seen her father cry before. It disturbed her more than any dead body ever could.

"It's not your fault," her tongue felt heavy. "It's this weak body of mine. Don't blame yourself. Besides, it's because of Grayson that I'm here at all."

Grayson met her eyes, his face blank but his eyes still shining with some of the tears from earlier. He wouldn't let them fall.

"We can never thank you enough, Grayson," her mother said. She gave him a tight smile and motioned for him to come closer to her. The boy did so cautiously and was overly surprised when Pamela pulled him into a bone-crushing hug. His arms were plastered to his sides like he didn't know exactly what to do, but he recovered from his shock and hugged the older woman back.

"If you don't mind, could you tell me what happened when you pulled me out?" Odette asked.

Grayson sat himself on the end of her bed, his gaze not wavering from her. "I had trouble getting you out of the cover at first but, after pushing a lot of it away, I could get to your hand. You had stopped moving for a little while," he winced while admitting that. "Even though I had you, getting you out was hard because your legs were caught up in the plastic. It wasn't much of a problem in the actual water but, when I was trying to pull you out, it was weighing you down.

"The other girls weren't much help because they were ... frightened. I did get Nadia to help get you untangled, though. I gave you CPR, my sister and I had taken a class on it in our last year of high school and I'm actually glad now that I took it." He smiled a little before his face turned somber once again. "You took so long to wake up. I was about to just throw you in my car and speed to the hospital when you finally started to cough up water.

"You just ... you didn't wake up. I was scared that something else might have happened because your heartbeat was faint, so I took off without talking to anyone else. I called your parents once we got here."

Odette nodded, "Thank you."

"I'm just happy that you're safe."

If her parents weren't there, she might have kissed him again. She wanted him to hold her again so she wouldn't feel so vulnerable like always. But they were there on either side of her and watching both of them with hawk-like gazes. Grayson leaned down and picked up the other blanket that she had kicked off earlier, covering her legs with it.

"Does your grandfather know that you're here?" Jonah asked, helping him cover Odette up.

Grayson hummed. "He does. He only wishes for Odette to recover as soon as possible."

"Good, we wouldn't want him to worry too much."

"Actually, I think I will make a quick run home to grab Odette's things that she left," Grayson said. "Zeke messaged me that he found her things in the room the girls were having brunch in."

"Oh, thank you." Odette had completely forgotten about her things.

Grayson took a couple steps forward but he stopped as Jonah was blocking most of the way. "Of course. I'll see you in a little bit."

Odette had been released from the hospital a few hours later and she didn't miss the questioning glances that the doctors and nurses sent her way as she left. They had come in after she woke up and asked her a series of questions that boiled down to *"Are you being abused at home?"* She was glad to be out of there. The sight of her home had never been more welcome. Her phone was held tightly in one hand, hot from the constant use of it. After Grayson came back with her belongings, he had to leave again but he was constantly texting her to make sure that she was fine. She sent him silly hospital bed selfies and, in return, he sent her a photo of him at rehearsal. He was "levitating" the phone when he took it. Odette didn't tell him but she saved it because it was cute. She called him a dork after that and he had to leave or else Greer would throw a fit.

Odette went up to her room and flopped onto her bed, inhaling the musty scent of it. She had acquired a thin sheen of sweat just from being outside and in the car. It was nearing the hottest days of the summer, apparently, and their air conditioner was weak.

"Hey, Runt." Odette scooted to the edge of her bed and reached down to pet the sleeping kitten. The cat raised her little head and looked at the girl with her big blue and brown eyes. "How are you, kitty?"

The cat mewled, rubbing her head against her hand.

"I'm sorry I left you alone all day. I didn't mean to. I didn't want to either." Odette frowned and scooped the cat up so that she could hold her.

Runt cocked her head to the side, as if asking what was wrong.

"It's nothing now. Everything has gone back to normal ... I hope. I'm giving Grayson a second chance."

Runt meowed in protest, her claws digging into Odette's flesh.

"Ouch! Hey! You don't do that. What do you know anyway, cat? Huh?"

No reply.

"That's right. He saved me, okay? He protected me from something that could have been a lot worse. You could have never seen me again, kitty. Mom and Dad might have gotten rid of you too." She gave her cat a pointed look, which Runt seemed to return. Odette sighed, scratching the little pet behind the ears. "I'll let you stay up on this bed while I get cleaned up if you promise you won't hurt yourself."

Runt didn't answer but Odette didn't expect her to. She laid the kitten to the side gently and dug around in her drawers before she left the room. Runt didn't watch her go like she normally would but instead watched the window with careful eyes.

XVII

Quiet taps on her window woke Odette up from her sleep. Her heart leap up into her throat and she didn't open her eyes at first. If she opened her eyes, it would be real.

The tapping came again and she held in a whimper. In her mind, she conjured up a creature that had large eyes and a wide mouth that was stretched into a grin. Its sharp teeth would be on display, gleaming in the moonlight as it watched her sleep. The humanoid features would only scare her more as it slipped through her window and next to her bed where it would watch, so only the eyes were visible. She could practically hear it breathing, *Oh God!*

"Odette!" The monster had Grayson's voice!

No, you idiot, she said in her mind with one eye peeking open. *That* is *Grayson*.

Odette sat bolt upright—not her best idea—and stumbled over to her bedroom door, so that she could close it slightly. She went to the window next and shoved it open.

"What the heck, Grayson?!" she whisper-shouted. "I have no idea what time it is but I can tell you that it is late enough that I refuse to interact with you."

"Love you too." He ducked his head inside and pressed a kiss to her cheek.

Odette didn't want to move over, her mind replaying scenes from the last time he snuck through her window, but she didn't want him to fall either.

"What are you doing here? My parents will kill you if they find out you're here. Like, I'm pretty sure my father will murder you and then pass you off to my mother, so she can revive you and kill you again." Odette had to squint to see him.

Grayson shrugged. "Good, they're protective of you. Every princess should be heavily guarded." He glanced around the room. "You sleep with the door open?"

"Overprotective parents. You said that was a good thing." Odette jabbed a finger on his chest but it ended up being his stomach. "Now, why are you here?"

"I was worried about you," he said. His hands rested on her shoulders and he brought her into a hug. She could feel his thumbs rubbing soothing circles into her skin; they were slightly rough but not uncomfortable. "I couldn't sleep and I needed to know that you were safe."

"I'm not safe from nineteen-year-old boys crawling through my window at ungodly hours of the night. You know, you nearly gave me a heart attack," Odette told him. "I thought I was about to get eaten by a monster."

Grayson chuckled, pulling away from the hug. "You're still scared of the boogeyman?"

She could see his blue eyes glittering with amusement from the moonlight. "I'm scared of a lot of things, like what will happen when my father comes upstairs cause he feels like something's wrong," she warned, edging him closer to the window where he came from in the first place.

"Really?"

Odette nodded. "And also clowns and being stuck in a coffin. Heights are iffy."

"What about bugs?" Grayson asked teasingly.

She shuddered sarcastically, "Give me nightmares, why don't you?"

Grayson's fingers left her shoulders, trailing down her arms until he reached her fingers. He wove them together with his own, so that they were palm-to-palm with each other. Odette realized that, for the first time, she was the warmer one of the two of them. Even with the thick summer heat, Grayson felt like he had stepped out of a freezer. It was a wonder he wasn't shivering.

"It's a beautiful night tonight," he said calmly, pulling her closer to him. Odette's head rested on his chest and she listened to the sound of his heart beating.

"You can see the stars out here. It's nice," she commented. Odette was about to ask about something trivial, like how his rehearsal went or when his next show was, but she didn't get to.

Grayson knelt to her level and kissed her lips. His aim was a little off and he only got about half of her mouth, but she wasn't about to complain to him. It was a feverish kiss that knocked the air out of her lungs and she just stood there and accepted it.

He pulled away reluctantly, his forehead resting against hers. "I'm sorry, I just … you're beautiful. I needed to make sure I wasn't dreaming this."

Odette wanted to tease him, say something like, "You dream of me often?" but she didn't think that she had the energy to. Technically speaking, she dreamt of him often too but she didn't think he would like her kind of dreams.

So, instead she said, "Are you okay?"

"I have this … fear of losing you. My past is full of people I cared about dying and I can't let you be the next one." His eyes were dark, almost like the time before but, for the time being, he seemed calm.

Odette tilted her head and swallowed hard. "You know that I can't promise anything, right?" She brought their entwined hands up and kissed the back of his. "My heart, the condition I have, I'm always at risk if I'm not careful."

"I could never let anything take you from me. Not death, not a person, and not some illness," Grayson said in a deep voice. "I won't allow anyone else to be taken from me, not when that person is you."

He obviously wasn't feeling well, Odette rationalized. "Okay." She didn't bother to shush him either as she could still hear her father snoring downstairs. "I believe you."

Runt trotted over to the pair, her eyes gleaming in the dark. She meowed and it was loud like she was trying to alert everyone in the house that Grayson was there.

"Runt, hush!" Odette hissed, nearly jumping out of her skin. Even with Grayson with her, she was terrified of the dark and what could lurk inside.

The cat made a noise, rubbing against her owner's bare ankles. She stepped on Grayson's feet, bumping him with her butt, and whipping him with her tail. She mewled again, a little softer this time.

"Shh! Go back to sleep, it's not wake-up time yet."

Runt headbutted her, as if to taunt the girl further, before she curled up on Odette's foot and purred happily.

Odette was seething. "Runt, you turd."

"Cat," Grayson spat. He glared at the animal, his hand twitching. Almost as soon as his aggravation started, he turned his attention back to Odette. "Don't worry about her, she won't bother us."

"Her meows could wake up my parents—" Odette glanced behind her at the nearly shut door.

Grayson released her hand and cupped her jaw, pushing her face to look back at him. "Don't worry and stay quiet."

He kissed her again with the same frenzy as before but Odette was a little more reluctant to return it. The risk of getting caught was too great; even if they weren't really doing anything bad, her parents' minds would jump to conclusions.

She forced herself to turn her head to the side and his lip grazed her cheek. He sighed, burying his face in her hair. She could feel a defeat in his body language.

"Come by tomorrow at a reasonable hour," she instructed. "Maybe we can go somewhere."

Grayson snickered quietly, "Are you asking me on a date?"

"I said maybe, Mages. Now, out the window." Odette stepped out from under Runt, ensuring she wouldn't hurt the cat, and closer to him. She pushed against his chest, urging him to walk backwards. Odette prayed that he wouldn't trip over a miscellaneous item in her room and cause a commotion, but he made it to the window ledge without incident.

The boy had half of his body out the window, straddling the ledge. "How about a kiss goodbye?" He winked and Odette hated that it made her blush.

"Just because you're technically outside does not mean we are in the clear yet, dummy." She rolled her eyes at his overly puckered lips and swung down to give him a quick kiss, but his hand caught her by the back of her neck and held her there.

The night breeze blew through her window and chilled Odette's superheated skin. It was unfair how warm he made her. His fingers wove through her messy bed hair, angling her head just right. He smirked into the kiss, lingering a moment longer, before he released her and dropped down into the darkness.

Odette lingered by the window in a sort of daze and she squinted to see if she could see him down in the yard at all … there was nothing. It was like he vanished.

What felt like minutes later, Odette's eyes opened to see the sunlight filtering through her window. It was still partially open from hours before and she cringed at the thought of bugs crawling in while she was sleeping. At the time, that hadn't occurred to her.

Odette yawned and stretched her arms high above her, her joints popping loudly. It felt good, but she was too stiff in reality. After a bit more stretching, she let out a satisfied sigh and ran a hand through her messy hair.

Her eyes landed on her cat next, curled up in her little bed. "Hey, Runt." She leaned down and gave the fur ball a little head scratch. "I hope you slept well."

Runt didn't look up at her and stayed curled up. It disturbed Odette greatly.

"C'mon, talk to me. *Meow*," she giggled to herself. "Kitty, I'm not going to stop annoying you until you talk to me," she sang, poking her cat again.

The kitten's head moved and she sighed, but it was only a loll to the side because of how hard she poked her. Her eyes were only half open but there wasn't any sign of consciousness. Odette scrambled to get out of her bed, falling with a loud thud. The fact that she could have given her parents a heart attack was very far from her mind. She was almost afraid to touch the small kitten again. She didn't know exactly what to think.

"Runt, please wake up," Odette begged. Her vision was blurring over with tears but she knew she was just being silly. Her cat was fine. She was just playing a game and being lazy because cats were like that, right? "Kitty? Please?"

The loud thumping of footsteps of her parents didn't bother her. She scooped the cat up in her arms and held back a sob. The small kitten wasn't moving at all. There was no purring and there were no small movements as she breathed. Runt had gone cold. Odette held her close to her chest and allowed her tears to fall, not daring to make a sound. She rocked herself back and forth in a ball on the floor. A hand was laid on her shoulder and Odette jumped, a whimper tearing from her throat. She held onto her cat tighter.

"Oh baby, what's wrong?" her mother asked in a sweet voice. How could she be so calm at a time like this?

Odette parted her lips but a strangled sob came out. "Runt!" She held the small animal out in her shaking hands.

Her mother obviously didn't understand as she could see nothing wrong right away with the kitten. That was Odette's problem too. Pamela looked between the cat and her daughter's distraught appearance. It must have dawned on her that Runt wasn't moving and laying far too still even for such a calm kitten. Normally, Runt would greet even her, always up and always alert. Pamela gaped, turning to her husband for help. Jonah stood in the doorway, still and very grim. The two of them had eventually pried the dead cat from Odette's iron hold. Jonah had laid Runt in a fabric bag that his wife used for washing lingerie and dug a hole in the backyard. Pamela was not happy about having to give that up to bury a cat, but she got over it fast.

Odette watched the whole time, red-eyed and teary. Her body shook with sadness, her arms perpetually wrapped around her torso to hold herself together. She spent what felt like hours outside, staring at the freshly overturned dirt where her beloved pet laid. She hadn't had her long but she loved her. She found comfort in her. It made no sense that she would just die, unless she had been sick the whole time. Her father never did take her to a vet; they never thought about it.

"Odette?"

She looked away from the ground, seeing the boy that she cared for. He looked classy as always; the distraught version of him that she saw the day before was now long gone. Worry was plastered over his face.

"Your mother told me," he said carefully.

Odette could feel her throat tighten again and she threw her arms around him. In the back of her mind, she felt bad that she was probably ruining his shirt but that only made her more upset. She held fistfuls of his shirt, crushing him into her.

"I-I don't understand!" she cried. "She was fine last night, nothing was wrong with her. *You even saw her.*" Most of what she said was muffled by his chest but he heard her.

"I'm sorry," he whispered to her, stroking her hair.

Odette pulled back, her sobs turning to sniffles. "I just can't help thinking that it was my fault somehow. I wasn't caring for her enough. I just wish I had given her more affection. More attention. I wish that I just could have given her *more.*"

"Giving her more affection wouldn't have stopped this from happening. It's obvious that something was wrong with her." He tucked some hair behind her ears so that he could look at her easily. "I think I should get you inside now, these thoughts will only make you feel worse."

She didn't have the strength to argue with him. She spared the grave one more glance before following him indoors, clinging to him with her frail arms. Grayson took her to the living room and pulled her to sit down with him. He situated them both so that her head stayed tucked under his chin and she curled up on his chest.

"When you feel up for it," he said, lacing their fingers together. "We can go wherever you want to." He traced patterns, letters, and words into the back of her hand with this thumb. His other one rested on her elbow not on her hip, as Jonah was practically staring him down from the other side of the room.

Odette hummed but didn't answer him outright. For that moment, all she wanted was to be held.

XVIII

T here were only three people who ever visited the Sinclair's
home—Grayson, Greer, and the mail carrier named Enid.
So, when there was a knock on the door early in the morning,
Odette expected to see two of the three as she never expected to
see Greer at her house—at least not voluntarily—ever again. It
was, however, none of the three.

"Nadia?" Odette stepped back. Seeing her on her front porch
was alien to Odette. Nadia was never without the others, which
meant they could be nearby. That left a bad taste in her mouth.
Odette tightened her hold on the door knob.

As if she knew what was in Odette's mind, the girl reached
out fervently to stop the door. "Please. I need to speak with you.
It's important."

Odette shifted her jaw and kept her voice low, "Why should
I? Was my life not important?"

Nadia hung her head, her thick black hair forming a curtain around her face. "I know. That's why ... that's why I came to talk with you. Please, let me in. If they find out I've been here ..."

Guilt nagged at Odette. She risked one more glance over her shoulder to make sure neither of her parents were nearby, and reluctantly widened the door for Nadia to enter. "What do you want?"

Nadia shifted from foot to foot and gnawed on her lower lip. She, too, looked about the room with a questionable gaze. "Will we not be disturbed here?"

"I don't know. I still don't trust you." It was the truth.

They both were silent for what felt like too long, just staring at the floor, avoiding one another's eyes as best they could. Odette wanted to demand to know why Nadia had come. As she was Greer's crony, it only made her more of an untrustworthy opponent.

"I came to apologize," Nadia whispered, "I had no idea that Greer would go as far as to ... you know. Bonnie didn't either."

"But you stood by and watched as it happened."

"We thought she was just going to scare you, that's all. Not drown you. And ..."

Odette frowned, not liking her silence. "And *what*?"

Nadia sat down on the arm of the couch and rubbed her neck. When she gathered the courage to speak again, her voice was hushed and her eyes glassy. "Bonnie and I were worried. Greer never had any more than three friends—two that she always keeps with her and the third is always an object of ridicule. That's how it's always been. No one says no to Greer."

Odette could feel heat rising on her face and she clenched her fists tight. "So, why were you worried? Obviously, *I* was the object of ridicule."

"So did we!" Nadia exclaimed, too enthused by Odette's agreement. "But ... Greer had never acted the way she had with you with anyone else before. That was what made us worry. No one has ever been allowed to date Grayson that was in her friend circle. Bonnie and I used to joke with her that she should set one of us up with him, no offense or anything, but all she would do was glare. And then you came along and, suddenly, she was pushing the two of you together. I thought maybe I was being replaced."

Nadia pinched her lips together and looked at Odette earnestly. "I'm not jealous.... Maybe I was in the beginning, but it's different now. I'm *afraid* for you. I think you've gotten in over your head. You don't want to have Greer as an enemy." She glanced over her shoulder. "I need to go now. Any longer and they'll know I've been here."

Odette gaped and attempted to block her exit. "Wait! You can't just say stuff like that and leave," Odette protested. "If you know Greer is dangerous, then you need to take care of yourself. Get out from under her thumb or whatever you have to do."

Nadia shook her head rapidly and pushed past her. "I know too much, Greer would never allow it, but you can. Stay away from Greer. And Grayson, for that matter. They both have more secrets and issues than anyone I've ever known—and I don't even know half of them. They can tear any sane person to shreds. It's best to leave with some of yourself still intact." And, without allowing Odette to get another word in, she left.

☆☆☆

"I thought I was the one who was supposed to pick the date," Odette stated wryly.

Grayson leaned against his car casually, a pair of sunglasses resting on his face, glinting in the sunlight. "You can pick the next one. I want to show you a place I'm pretty sure you haven't been to."

"How can you be so sure?" she teased him, pushing up the sleeves of her sweater. "I might have."

Uncertainty crossed his face but there was that small crease of worry in his brow. "I would be very concerned if you had. It's kind of a place couples go to together."

"You're taking me to a *make out spot*? Geez, Mages!" She swatted at his arm, laughing nervously.

"Not like that," he looked uncomfortable but he did it to himself. "It's a nice spot and I thought you would like the drive. Get a break from being inside so much."

Odette chewed on her lip, glancing back inside. "I'll ask," she said quietly, hiding her embarrassment by digging her fingernails in her palms.

Her mother was sitting on the couch with her laptop open, typing away. "Hey, sweetie. What does your boyfriend want that he can't come inside for?"

"He wanted to take me on a drive to one of the diners in town, maybe do some sightseeing. Can I?" She couldn't believe how much of an idiot she felt like, having to ask her mother while he was right outside.

Pamela sighed, pinching the bridge of her nose with her fingers. "Just please make sure that he has you home by ten o'clock. Preferably before but ..."

Odette's face broke out into a grin, "Thank you, Mom!" she ran up next to her and pulled her into a tight hug.

"Promise me one thing—that you won't end up in the emergency room again. It always seems like something bad happens when ..." Pamela stopped herself before she started something with her daughter. "Just be safe."

The girl nodded her head slowly. She understood what her mother was saying but she knew that Grayson would protect her. "Of course, Mom." She hugged her one last time before she went back outside where her beau was waiting so patiently. He quirked an eyebrow, asking silently if she could come. Odette closed the front door and skipped over to him, kissing his cheek. "Let's go."

The car pulled out of her front yard seconds later. Grayson had one hand on the wheel and the other holding hers. She noticed how clingy he had become since the "incident." It was like he couldn't function without her but she thought that most boyfriends must act like this.

Odette laid her head back and watched the trees whiz past them. It was relaxing, a moment where she could really breathe.

"What are you smiling about?" Grayson asked suddenly. He squeezed her hand gently, glancing at her every few seconds.

"I didn't know that I was. I guess it would be you."

They were in town now, Odette had never seen so many people around. Most of them were looking over at Grayson's car too.

He chuckled, shaking his head. "You're cute."

Grayson had to stop for pedestrians. Unfortunately, the pedestrians were Greer and her best friends. It was a staring contest, full of ice and mirth.

Seeing them reminded Odette of her conversation that very morning with Nadia. She was a good actress. The girl wore a mask of indifference when staring at Odette and Grayson, tapping her lime green nails against her slushy.

They can tear any sane person to shreds. It's best to leave with some of yourself still intact.

Odette forced herself to look away, her heart thumping wildly in her chest. Surely, Nadia's words weren't true. She must have been trying to scare Odette away. Then again, Nadia had known the Mages longer. How much longer, Odette didn't know, but she assumed it must have been a while.

"I won't let anything happen to you," Grayson said. He pulled her closer to him and Odette could feel his sister's glare intensify.

"I know."

"She's been rather tame ... but then again, I've avoided her as much as I could." He accelerated and they were speeding through the town once more. Then he added, "That isn't new, though."

Odette tilted her head. "I had thought you two got along?"

"Not in recent years. We don't necessarily hate each other ... we just wish we weren't family," he said and left it at that.

The town was now getting smaller and there were only a few businesses that dotted the area until they were almost all gone. Odette could see the beginnings of the sea too. There weren't as many trees but there were more shrubs and rocks and a giant lighthouse. Even from far away, she could see that it looked pretty rundown. It wasn't in use anymore, not for many years now. Ivy crawled up the side of it, covering some of the porch as well. She could see evidence, as they drove closer, of where the police had once had this place taped off to prohibit visitors.

Grayson parked his car as close to the lighthouse as he could, smirking the whole time. He hopped out of the car and opened up her door like a true gentleman, helping her out.

"Come on, you'll love it here." He half-dragged her towards the stairs, his excitement getting the better of him.

"We aren't going to run into other people, are we?" Odette checked around the bushes for things like bicycles or human beings.

Grayson snorted. "Do you see any other cars? We're here alone, princess."

"Not everyone is as brazen as you, Mages. They could have walked here or hidden their ride." Odette tucked her hair behind her ear, standing on her tiptoes to peer around the area. It was extremely windy at the lighthouse but it was a nice and cool breeze that countered the blazing sun. She let go of his hand and walked out by herself, deciding that she wanted to explore this place some more. It was hauntingly beautiful, a place that was full of ghosts, probably. Odette ran her hand along the metal railing, looking down at the sand-colored rocks and the way the water splashed up against them.

Grayson came up behind her, resting his chin on her shoulder. "I knew that you would like it here. It's beautiful and it's quiet. It's almost like another dimension."

I'm pretty sure this place is infested with ghosts. "You're right, I do like it here. I like the charm it has." Odette turned her head to give him affection but Grayson was laughing too hard.

Odette frowned; she didn't know what was so funny. Had she said something? She didn't think so. Was there something on her face? Did she make a face?

"Oh, princess, you amuse me." Grayson's hands were on her hips and he turned her around from the sea so she would face him.

"What did I do?" She laughed a little too, only because she didn't know what else to do.

Grayson smoothed her hair back—it kept flying forward and getting in her face—kissing her lightly. "Your thoughts. Don't worry about it, though."

She let him kiss her, deeper than he had kissed her before but she didn't put much effort in it. She was thinking about what he said. *My thoughts are amusing?*

If anything, this added to her idea that the twins had actual magic. How was that possible, though? Obviously, their amulets had something to do with it, unless that was all for show but Odette didn't think so. It was very rare—if ever—that she had seen them without those things.

"Stop thinking so much…. You're miles away when you should be right here." His fingers were woven in her hair and they controlled how close the two of them could get and if she could pull away.

Odette shook her head. "I'm sorry, I'm just having a hard time concentrating on one thing lately."

"It's because you're stressed," Grayson murmured. He pressed a kiss to her temple. "I brought you here so you wouldn't be stuck in your house moping." He kissed her cheekbone. "Away from the cat." Her nose. "Away from my place and people who can harm you." Her cheeks.

Odette was bright red and only a small part of it was because of the heat of the sun. "You need to stop being so sweet or I won't be able to handle it."

"Relax and think only of me," he slipped his sunglasses off. "I am all you need."

There was a heavy pause between the two of them. Odette fully expected to see the dark intensity on him again but he didn't have it. He was still him, watching her lovingly. His warmth was all-consuming and she was certain that it was about to tear through her if he kept looking at her like that. Odette cleared her throat, her hands resting comfortably on his chest. "You're all I have," she assured him. She could feel with her fingertips how his heartbeat picked up. Grayson had a small smile playing at the corner of his lips, but before it could bloom any bigger, he crushed her into him.

Odette had to twist and push against him in order to free her arms from his painful hold. They rested comfortably over his shoulders, playing with the ends of his thick brown hair. He kissed her like he would lose her. It was breathtaking and soul-crushing all at once. Odette didn't know where the sudden passion came from but it was stifling. And, strangely, she didn't care. The numb hole in her chest needed to be filled by something—Grayson seemed perfectly happy to do that.

He pulled away once he had his fill, his chest heaving with every deep breath that he took. A dark shadow fell across his face from the setting sun. No words passed between them. None were needed. After all, he knew everything that would have been said anyway.

Grayson coaxed Odette into his chest and she relaxed there in his arms, knowing that she was safe.

Odette was half asleep as Grayson drove her home. He had her nestled up against his side, his arm wrapped protectively around her shoulders. It was about forty-five minutes before ten but he didn't want to give Odette's parents reason to worry. There wasn't a lot to do at the lighthouse anyway.

Grayson had told her about a tour that he and Greer were doing in January. It was supposed to take them further into the Midwest than where they usually went, and he was just ready to get it over with.

"You don't like being a magician?" Odette was somewhat shocked. He had always seemed so dedicated to what he did.

"I don't like being a *performer*," he corrected.

They arrived at her house faster than she expected. Grayson tensed beneath her as they drew even closer. There was another car parked outside and it was one that she had been in before. It had just been a while.

"I'm coming in with you," Grayson ordered.

They got out of the car and Odette eyed the other Mages' car. She felt like it was a trap and that, any second, it would explode or something. Was she there because of Nadia? Surely, she hadn't found out about it.

Odette opened up the front door, anxiety eating away at her stomach. What if Greer was going in for the final kill because of Nadia's warning? Was she waiting for her? What if she had her parents tied up? Oh God, what if she killed her parents and she was there to kill her too?!

Greer was sitting on one of the couches, smiling at something Jonah was saying. Pamela was beside her husband, laughing. For some reason this scenario made Odette even more uneasy.

"You're home!" cheered her mother. "Hello, Grayson; I trust you treated my daughter right?"

Grayson smiled kindly. "Of course."

How can he be so calm when I feel like I'm about to lose my lunch?!

"Good to see you, Mr. Sinclair," Grayson greeted, walking over to shake her father's hand. "Greer, what are you doing here?"

Greer giggled even though it sounded like she was mildly offended. "I hadn't seen Odette since the accident that happened under my watch. I feel horrible and I was hoping to come here and make sure everything was going well. I had wanted to see Odette but I was surprised to see you two going out on a date." She waved it off, wiggling her shoulders a little. "All the same, I had to see my favorite Sinclairs. You all are just so warm and welcoming that you make me feel like I'm your daughter too."

Odette held in a sneer of disgust. She was so *fake*. Greer acted as if she were on stage, putting on the show of a good-mannered girl for her parents. It wouldn't fool Odette.

However, her parents actually bought the act. They melted, their eyes softening and their shoulders sagging.

"That is so nice of you to say, sweetie," Pamela fawned. "Gosh, I think I'm going to cry." It was true, her face was turning red and her eyes glittered with happy tears.

Greer ignored that and turned around in her seat to acknowledge Odette. "I also came here to invite you to a summer pool party we are holding at our house in two weeks."

Odette stiffened and Grayson reached for her hand.

"I ... know it may seem a little inappropriate considering what has happened, but you don't have to swim! You can just stay by the poolside or even spend time inside. Grayson usually does that and I'm sure that he would be more than happy to entertain you in some way."

Jonah coughed and Odette turned red. She released Grayson's hand quickly, hiding hers behind her back, and, this time she didn't hide her glare at the girl.

"Thank you," she said in a tight voice. "I'll try my best to go."

I want to slap you as hard as I can, Odette thought to herself.

Being anywhere near that girl and water didn't sound like a good idea to her. It felt too much like Greer was plotting. Even in the low light of the living room, Odette could see how dark Greer's eyes were.

"It's late, sister, we should go so we won't be a bother to the Sinclairs anymore." He didn't glare at Greer like Odette had but his anger was pretty clear in his voice.

The female twin nodded reluctantly. "We wouldn't want Grandfather to worry." She stood up from her seat and embraced Pamela and Jonah affectionately. "Thank you for having me in your home."

"Anytime," said Jonah.

Greer sauntered past her brother, not sparing him a glance. She was focused fully on Odette who wanted to be anywhere but there. The older girl wrapped her arms around Odette tightly. It reminded her of the plastic of the pool cover, cold and suffocating.

"It was wonderful to see you again, Odette. I missed you."

Odette hummed, patting her lower back. The girl sounded sort of sincere, but she didn't care.

Greer released her, her smile turning sour. *I guess she wasn't received as well as she thought she would be. That's what you get for trying to drown people.*

Grayson came to her side a second later. She assumed he just got through hugging her mother too because he smelled a little like her. He grabbed her hand and kissed the back of it.

"I'll see you soon."

"Yes, soon." She squeezed his fingers and finally let him go.

The twins both glanced back at the family one more time before they left. The house was quiet and Odette went to sit with her parents.

They received her well, wrapping their arms around her lovingly. Odette smiled at them, feeling some kind of talk coming.

"Det," Pamela started. She looked at her mom, paying as much attention as she could, as tired as she was. "We don't want you to go to that party."

XIX

O dette breathed a sigh of relief. "I understand. I was a little nervous about going there anyway."

Maybe her parents had seen through Greer's act. Odette couldn't have been sure but she knew that they weren't dumb. Maybe they had seen that she was putting both Odette and Grayson on edge with her being there, or that she was being a little too sweet?

"Let me try to rephrase," Pamela said. "We don't really want you to spend as much time as you do now with those twins."

She thought wrong. That was not good. Odette blinked several times and sat up a little straighter. "Is this about that comment that Greer made? 'Cause I think she was just poking fun. You guys know I haven't—"

"It isn't about that," Jonah interrupted. "But ... thank you for clarifying."

"Then why?" She looked between both of her parents. "You are the ones who said that you wanted me to have friends. To *be* as normal as I could be. Why are you doing this now?"

Pamela laid a hand on her daughter's knee. "It's because we're worried. It just seems like any time you are with them, something bad happens. Twice already, you've ended up going to the emergency room for things that shouldn't have happened."

"On my first date with Grayson we were held up and I fainted. That was my illness. When I went over to Greer's, I wasn't feeling well and I accidentally fell in the pool," Odette was furious. "Those, *both times*, were caused by what's going on in my stupid body! It isn't their fault. And, both times, Grayson was there to save me. He even took a bullet for me!"

Both of them were quiet but Odette knew that this argument was far from over. It was one of those that left a bad taste in everyone's mouth, one that hung over everyone's head like an ugly storm cloud.

"All your life, since you were little, I've told you that I would take a bullet for you," Jonah said, "and I always wanted the boy you were meant to be with to do the same. Grayson has done that, but it doesn't mean that he is the one, Det. He seems like a good guy but you don't have to spend every single second with him. It isn't like you guys are getting married."

Pamela nodded along. "We don't want you to become one of those girls who abandon their friends for her boyfriend, even if it is Greer. I just think that maybe you should take this week to yourself. Start there. It doesn't mean that you can't talk to them on the phone either. Maybe the three of us could do something together this week."

They cared about her, Odette couldn't get mad at them about that. All the same, this was a punch to the gut. She swallowed thickly and nodded her head.

"Yeah, I guess so."

Her parents didn't talk to her much longer and told her to go upstairs to get some sleep. Odette was like a zombie and she rubbed her eyes roughly in an attempt to stay awake longer. She pushed the door open sleepily, about to launch herself onto her bed, when something caught her eye.

Odette yelped, "*Grayson, what are you doing in here?!*" She quickly pulled the door shut to ensure he wouldn't be seen.

The boy was standing over by her bookshelf and he didn't seem fazed at all by her reaction. "I wanted to make sure that Greer hadn't done anything to your house. I didn't need you to 'accidentally' miss a step and break your neck."

Odette glanced behind her, hoping that her parents couldn't hear anything. "Well, I haven't yet. Thank you, though ... but I think you should—"

"You seem tense."

"Yes, I'm tense. My boyfriend snuck through my window *yet again* and my parents are awake down stairs, meaning they could come up any minute." Odette put her hands on his chest and pushed him towards the window.

"No, it's not that. It's something else." He cupped her cheek, brushing his thumb across her skin. "You know you can tell me anything, right?"

Odette shook her head and looked down at her feet. "Now just isn't a good time. I'm sorry."

From the stairs, she began to hear the loud footsteps of her father. Odette had to act fast but she was practically frozen in place. Instead of just pushing him back out the window and trusting he would be safe, Odette shoved him in her closet and shut the doors as the door to her room opened.

"Are you okay?" Jonah asked, looking between her and the closet.

Odette nodded and scratched the back of her head, "Yep, just looking for pajamas."

Her dad looked even more confused. "Even though you don't keep them in there?"

"Just ... wanted to see if there were any T-shirts. Laundry. Not a whole lot of choices." She walked away from the closet doors. It took everything in her not to glance over her shoulder to make sure that Grayson was staying put.

"You women are strange," Jonah commented. "Get some good sleep."

Odette played with the hem of her shorts. "Is there a reason you came up here?"

"Not really," he said. "Well, I actually thought I heard voices but that could probably be the whole me-being-an-old-man thing."

"Yep, yeah it could. I was talking to myself. You might have heard me."

"Maybe? Night." And he left. He didn't close the door either.

Odette sighed and closed it like before and went back to the closet doors. Grayson was turned around, his back muscles taught through his shirt. He didn't move to face her or do anything really other than stay perfectly still.

"He's gone," Odette said simply.

Grayson glanced at her, turning back around to face her. In his hands, the journal she had found in the old window seat.

Odd, she hadn't left it in her closet.

"What's this?" He had it opened, so he was obviously reading it. It was some kind of test.

"It's a journal from one of the previous house owners. I didn't get very far in it so I don't know what all is in it." A lie. Odette had read that whole thing.

Grayson shook his head and looked at the pages with disgust. "You don't need to read this. This man ... he didn't have a very good opinion of me."

Before she could say anything about throwing it out, Grayson acted. The hand holding the journal erupted into blue flames, engulfing the book in one go. Odette's eyes grew and she stammered out a protest of putting the fire out for fear of it burning the house down. However, as soon as the flames touched the leather bound book, it dissolved into ash, then the ash dissolved into nothing.

It took less than a minute for the journal to be nothing more.

Odette knew better than to react. She tilted her head upwards to look at Grayson's face, which was passive. He dusted his hands off, even though there was nothing on them, and sniffed.

"You are very precious to me, Odette. Don't forget it."

He didn't gather her up in his arms like she expected him to do, and he didn't give her a heart-stopping kiss. He leaned over and pressed his lips on her hair line. It was a lingering kiss, bittersweet like him. He stepped away and slipped out of the window without another word.

Odette glanced over to her bookshelf and saw an empty space where she was certain the journal had once sat in. So, how did it get in the closet?

Odette wanted to confront Grayson about his strange behavior the next day but she couldn't. She woke up pale, cold, and sweaty and puked outside of her trashcan before she was able to call out to her parents. The rest of the day was a feverish haze, going in and out of consciousness and not being able to keep anything down. She overheard her mother telling her father that she had a high fever, which explained why she felt like a furnace. Her hands and feet kept swelling up and turning a light shade of blue but it wasn't anything that hadn't happened before.

Everything ached and her head swam with dizziness and in a fog of uncertainty. She couldn't tell what time it was, much less how much time had passed since she had last been awake. Her body—after dispelling anything that it could via her mouth— would heat up to an unbearable level with sweat pumping out of every inch of her skin. Ten minutes later, she would be freezing and her teeth chattering while her body shook to keep itself warm.

It was a vicious cycle.

The next day wasn't much better but she was able to keep down a bagel for almost three hours before she had another bout with the trash can. Her dizziness hadn't died down and the room was either too warm from her constant retching or too cold because of her sweat. Her room smelled like something died in it. She hadn't stayed awake for much of that day either.

Pamela stayed with her during the night even though Odette had protested. She knew that this was just a bug that she must have caught and she didn't want her mother to catch it either, but Pamela didn't listen. It didn't help that Odette fell asleep halfway through her own lecture. What she did remember was waking up in the middle of the night. Her mother was asleep at the edge of her bed and it looked very uncomfortable. She would have given her some of her pillows but they had been contaminated by her so it would only make things worse.

"Grayson?" Odette rasped, she wasn't sure if she was imagining him or not.

The boy was in the corner of her room, standing and watching her. He didn't even react to her calling out to him. Odette rubbed her eyes. He was gone. Was that a hallucination? It must have been, after all, Grayson wouldn't just come into her room and not do anything.

Her attention shifted to her mother, who was waking up. "Are you okay, sweetie?"

Truth be told, not really. She was too hot in the sheets and she could feel the need to dry heave rising up inside of her. "I think I just had a strange dream."

Pamela placed the back of her hand on Odette's head. Her hands were pretty warm but Odette was warmer. "Do you want some water?"

"Yes please."

Pamela left the room and went down the stairs quietly. The house was pretty quiet aside from a few creaks and the small clanking noises from the kitchen. Odette shivered, wrapping her arms around her torso. Her window was open.

"I've missed you," Grayson admitted over the phone.

Odette laughed at him, running a hand through her hair. "It's been—what? Four days? We have been apart for longer."

"It's different now," he said.

"How so?"

Odette pulled her knees to her chest while she waited for his answer. She could hear him sigh and some random background noises.

"Because it is. You're mine now and I miss you. I'm allowed to miss my girlfriend, especially when she's you."

"If you must." Odette laughed a little to herself. "How are your rehearsals going?"

Grayson grunted. *"Same as always. Greer's taking on the role of a dictator. Everything has to be her way, the things we say, and the way we act. It's tiring. I would much rather be with you, watching some horror movie and having you hide your face in my arm the whole time."*

"Jokes on you 'cause I actually like horror movies!" Odette laughed mockingly into the phone. That didn't bode well for her as, seconds later, she dissolved into a coughing fit.

He gave her a moment to collect herself before he started talking again. *"I doubt that. What's your favorite?"*

She pursed her lips. *"Sleepy Hollow."*

Grayson chortled. *"That is the weakest horror movie out there!"*

"Whatever. I like it, it's a great movie." Odette crossed an arm over her chest in defense even though he couldn't see her.

"I should be over there with you. Not only would I be helping you feel better, but I would educate you on horror films." She could hear the longing in his voice and she knew that, if she told him "yes," he would be over in an instant.

Odette grimaced. "I don't think that's a good idea. I'm almost better, though. I don't want you to get sick and my mom would turn you away at the door if you came in."

"And what about the window?"

"Then I would turn you away," Odette said. "I'll be better soon and we'll get together as soon as we can."

Grayson was quiet. She could hear him moving around in his room. *"I guess. Get well soon. Please."*

"I'll try. I've got to go; I'll talk to you later."

He mumbled out a quiet bye and hung up. Odette leaned her head back on the couch her eyes burning with the need to sleep.

Pamela entered the living room, carrying a tray of food. Odette longed to eat something but her stomach didn't want anything at all.

"Do you think you can eat something?" she asked.

Odette eyed some of the salty food. She grabbed a buttered piece of bread and tore it into pieces, popping one of them into her mouth and chewing slowly.

"What did Grayson say?" she asked.

"He was asking how I was feeling, he wants to come over and help ... I told him he shouldn't. Not yet." Odette didn't want to talk about him to her mom, she didn't like him so there was no point. She smoothed the blanket that covered her and her swollen calves, biting back her cringe of disgust.

Pamela sat down on the other side of the couch and nodded. "He seems like he can be a sweet boy. It's a shame that he and his sister don't have any parents."

Odette gagged and dropped her food, taking off to the nearest bathroom or trash can. At least she didn't have to talk about him with her mom anymore.

"So, do you want to go somewhere today? I could take you out to eat at one of the local diners. I know that you still haven't been around town all that much and it could be fun? I know I said that you could choose the next date but ..." Grayson drew out the last word.

Odette inhaled sharply. This was getting tedious. "I'm sorry, I can't today. My mom actually wants to take us out as a family. Maybe on Monday or something like that?"

Her fever had finally broke in the middle of the night, but she was still very weak. She hadn't kept food down for almost five days now and her stomach was trying to murder itself. She missed him too. But, she has also made a promise to her parents.

He was quiet for a long while and Odette could practically hear the cogs working in his mind. The white noise coming in over the speaker felt like knives to her eardrums.

"Odette, have I done something?"

Her eyes widened, "NO! God no. You haven't done anything ... I'm just busy today and it takes me a while to recover from these things. I don't want you to have to see me like that."

"I don't care about things like that! You're always beautiful to me even if you are weak or frail at the moment. You just seem like you're avoiding me and constantly making excuses as to why you can't see me."

She wished he was in front of her so she could see his emotion; she was so clueless right now. "I-I'm not. Are you angry?" Odette hated that she stuttered. He would obviously know something was wrong now. She just prayed that he wouldn't ask.

He took his time before he answered yet again. Odette could hear his ragged breathing through the phone. *"No,"* he said eventually. *"I'm not. I'm upset. I don't know what to think, honestly. There's something that you aren't telling me and I can't help but think the worst. Is there another guy?"*

She laughed. He wasn't being serious was he? This guy was probably the world's most gorgeous nineteen-year-old and he was worried that his sickly, homebound girlfriend had found someone else?

"No. There isn't, and, even if there was, I wouldn't just ghost you. That's awful." Odette pressed her head against the cool wall. It was sunny again today, the kind of sunny that made you wonder if you were going to melt if you put on a short-sleeved shirt.

"Then what is it? Are you tired of me? Did Greer threaten you?"

"Why would Greer threaten me not to talk to you? I thought she wanted me to be with you?"

Grayson huffed, *"This is beside the point, but she has done it before. I'm serious, Odette, what is it?"*

Would it be good to tell him? She didn't want him to take it the wrong way, and she didn't want to make things awkward between him and her parents. She chewed on her lip and chose her words carefully, looking around the room to make sure she didn't see her mother or father.

"My ... parents ... they think that it would be good for me to have some me time. A break from constantly being with you guys. They got a little concerned because of the pool incident ... and when I got the concussion," Odette admitted. "They're just a little protective sometimes and they thought this was best."

"Oh."

"It isn't forever!" Odette rushed. "They really don't want me to go to Greer's party, though. Have some time to myself. But we can meet back up soon!" She pinched the bridge of her nose, a headache building up. "I'm sorry."

"It isn't your doing. It's theirs. You don't have to be sorry." He had no inflection in his voice, he just sounded blank.

Odette hated this. "Are you okay?"

"I will be. Don't worry. I have to go now."

She nodded her head. "Yeah, okay. Bye—"

But he had already hung up the phone.

XX

On the day of the infamous pool party, Pamela and Jonah took Odette out for pizza. It was a small place in town that was too cold and served their pizzas a little too hot, but the Sinclairs didn't mind all that much.

Odette had hardly heard anything from Grayson since their phone conversation, which had been almost a full week now. She was worried, picking up her phone and checking it every two seconds in case he had messaged. She had tried to and he would respond, but only with one or two words.

The bell at the diner door tinkled and drew her away from her upsetting thoughts. Zeke was there along with Greer who looked like she wished she was with anyone else.

"Oh hey, dude!" Zeke called over cheerfully.

"Zeke, hey." Odette stood up from her seat and went over to great the two of them even if Greer was her least favorite person in the world. "Hi, Greer."

The female twin hugged Odette tightly. "I'm glad to see that you're up and doing great, Grayson has been so worried about you. He's actually been very depressed this past week because of it. I hope you come to the party; you'll be able to cheer him up. Or Nadia, maybe. Or someone else, so long as they have a feminine touch."

Odette took half a step back. Was she really insinuating what she thought she was? No, she was just doing it to get under her skin. Grayson wouldn't betray her.

"I'll try my best."

Greer smirked. "That's right, because you have to listen to what Mommy and Daddy say like the good little girl you are."

She had had enough. "Greer, do we have a problem? 'Cause if we do, don't just insult me, say it to my face like a woman." Odette crossed her arms over her chest, narrowing her eyes.

The girl looked surprised for half of a second, her lips parting slightly. Greer being Greer, however, recovered from it quickly and smiled slyly. "No problem. I hope I see you later. For Grayson's sake."

Odette couldn't believe that was the same girl who had been so excited for Grayson to ask her on a date. The same girl who had dressed her up and paraded her in front of her brother in order to get her to come and chase them down.

Zeke, apparently, had gathered the pizzas in the time it took for Greer to verbally assault Odette, so the two were out the door just as quick as they came in.

"Are you okay, sweetie?" her mother asked, coming over to her side.

Odette didn't particularly care if she had heard what Greer said. It was over with anyway. "Mom, I need to go to the Mages today. It's important."

The argument with her parents lasted the whole way home but she won by saying that she was concerned about Grayson. Odette told them half of what Greer had told her, which had gotten her all fired up and ready to pick a fight with her if the occasion should arise. Her parents didn't say anything but their faces showed their skepticism of their daughter beating that girl in a fight.

Odette didn't text Grayson to tell him she was going. She wanted him to be surprised. Plus, if there was even the smallest chance that Grayson would cheat on her, she would catch him. She, however, really doubted it.

Her dad volunteered to drive her over to the Mages' residence once she changed and had everything she needed.

"I know this isn't what you guys wanted," Odette stated, "but thank you."

Pamela gave her daughter a kiss on the cheek before she left. "I hope everything works out."

"Let's get going," said Jonah.

He led his daughter out the front door and started up the car. Even though it was a short ride to their neighbor's house, Odette was already too hot. She regretted wearing her zip up hoodie.

The gates were open and there were *many* cars inside. Odette was shocked; she didn't know Greer had that many friends. *Probably fake ones, though.*

"Thanks, Dad." Odette kissed his cheek and slid out of the car. Jonah pointed his finger at her. "Be safe. I mean it."

"Of course. I'll see you later."

Jonah didn't pull out of the driveway until Odette was at the front door. She knocked and squared her shoulders. She could do this; she was only there for her boyfriend anyway. It would be an added bonus if she could shove his sister into the deep end.

Zeke opened the door—as expected by this point. "Oh hey. Fun seeing you two times in a day. You want me to take you to the backyard?"

"Actually," Odette said with an embarrassed smile. "Could you take me to Grayson? Unless he's already there."

The man chuckled, nodding his head. "Yeah, totally. Maybe you can cheer him up. The guy's been really down lately. I think he's been worried about you. You're feeling better, right?"

"Yeah, it was just a bad virus. I tend to hold on to sickness a little longer than most people." Odette tugged on the sleeves of her hoodie, the chill of the mansion seeping into her skin.

"Sorry to hear about that, dude."

Zeke led her up what felt like a hundred flights of stairs. She held onto the railing, breathing as quietly through her nose as she could. Any second now, her lungs would explode.

They went past Greer's room, which was oddly quiet. She was probably already outside anyway. She looked away quickly, that room giving her a bad feeling. At the end of the hall, there was a room with a light on. Zeke stopped at this one, glancing back at Odette to make sure she was okay. He knocked on the door a few times.

"*What is it?*" Grayson snapped from the other side of the door.

Zeke didn't take offense to it. "I have someone who is here to see you."

"*Tell them to go away.*"

Zeke opened his mouth but Odette put her hand on his arm to stop him. "Mages, is that how you greet your girlfriend?"

She could actually hear him tripping over himself to get to the door. It swung open seconds later and a semi-haggard Grayson was staring at her with wide eyes. She yanked him down to her level, disregarding Zeke, and planted a kiss on his lips.

"Surprise, babe."

"You didn't tell me you were coming." Grayson sounded shaken up. He was still standing by his door, pacing.

Odette was sitting down at his desk, trying to look as casual as possible. "Did you not want me to?"

"No—hey, it's not like that and you know it. I thought you were still being kept from me." He ruffled his hair awkwardly. It was odd to see him so flustered. He was always so calm and put together but, in here, he looked like any other teenage boy.

Odette glanced at the deep purple cape that was draped over a hanger. "I ran into your sister at the pizza place in town. Fair warning, I may fight her if she provokes me *again*."

Grayson didn't outwardly doubt Odette but it was obvious in the half second before he processed her words.

"What did she do?" He was by her side in an instant. He knelt to the floor and grabbed her hands. "Are you okay?"

"I'm fine. She was just ... I don't want to say 'threatening,' but she was warning me that, if I didn't show up tonight, someone else would make a move on you ... *in a way* ..."

His concern melted away to something akin to annoyance. "And you believed her? If you hadn't told me it was you, I wouldn't have even let you inside. What makes you think that any other girl would be able to get in?"

"Because it was Greer who told me," Odette fired back. "And despite what you may say about you two not wanting to be family, she still knows you 'cause she's your sister."

Before Odette knew it, he was kissing her. Grayson was rising up from his knees, so he could lean over her even more, pressing her against the back of the chair. She released his hands and locked them around his neck automatically. It was a painful kiss, their noses were bumping against one another roughly, but it didn't matter.

Odette pulled back, her mouth tasting like iron even though she knew she wasn't bleeding. "Was that your way of telling me to 'shut up'?"

"More or less," he replied. "You think too much and you worry too much. But I am thankful that Greer convinced you to find a way to break out of your house. I was going crazy. Being kept away from you is like a nightmare."

The girl giggled, shaking her head. "You're so dramatic. Are you sure you weren't meant to be a performer?"

"You mock my pain." He placed a hand over his heart. "I mean what I say. I was ready to run to you and steal you out of that house. Now that you're here, I don't think I'll let you go."

"You don't have to." Odette kissed his cheek, standing up from his chair.

"And don't think that I'm letting you go down there. I don't want those other boys to see you in your swimsuit," he ordered.

Odette snickered to herself, her hand skimming over his cape. "If I don't go down there then you don't get to see it either."

Grayson's eyebrows furrowed and he blinked. It was several seconds later that he pouted. "Fine. Only after it gets dark, though. And you'll stay by my side the whole time. I don't want those idiots to get grabby."

"Look, I'm you!" Odette beamed, disregarding his words. She had his cape on her shoulders now and she struck a dramatic pose that he would do. "It smells like you too."

Although he was agitated that she was changing the subject, Grayson smiled at her. "You look better in it than me."

"That's a lie if I've ever heard one. No one looks better than you in a cape." She smoothed out the ends of it to make sure that it was laying on her correctly.

"Except you."

Odette played with the ties, making sure they sat properly on her shoulders. "Will you be my lovely assistant?" She winked at him playfully and extended her hand to him.

"Okay then." Grayson took her hand and twirled her around and, when she stopped, she was facing the mirror with her back against his chest. He placed his palm on the back of her hand

and lifted her hand so she was palm up. Grayson looked into her eyes through the mirror and moved, so his mouth was near her ear. "Concentrate."

Odette nodded dutifully, her eyes flicking between his and her open palm. Eventually, he looked away and only focused on their hands. She took his cue and did the same, holding her breath.

Warmth circled around hers, not the warmth that she was used to from Grayson's body heat though. Blue and silver wisps rose from his palm and wove over hers. It never actually touched her skin like it did Grayson's. It took her several seconds to realize that it was actually *fire*.

She was caught between yanking her hand away in fear and staying completely still. Odette didn't want to mess up his trick and hurt him.

"It's beautiful," she said hoarsely.

Grayson's nose nudged against her. "Don't be afraid of it. I won't let it hurt you. Just trust me."

"I do."

The flame grew larger and it swayed back and forth teasingly. Odette had the strange desire to touch it but she resisted. Even if it was magic fire, fire still burned.

Grayson's fingers twitched against hers and the fire receded back into his hand. Her skin was a light shade of pink from being so close to the heat, but it didn't hurt. It was actually a nice change to the mansion's cold atmosphere.

"What else can you do?" she asked curiously.

The hand that was on the bottom of hers came up, so he was holding it. Her first thought was, *Great, an excuse to be cheesy,* but soon she felt something inside of her palm. Something that most definitely wasn't a part of Grayson.

He pulled his hand away to reveal the head of a blue rose. It bloomed right before her eyes, the petals tickling her skin with their softness. When Odette looked closer, she could see that the tips of the rose were purple and they almost seemed to sparkle in the light.

"Wow," was all she could say.

Grayson smirked, a breathy chuckle leaving his lips. "I'm glad that you like it."

"Thank you," she said. Odette held it close to her chest and turned her head to look at him.

"Anything for my princess." He kissed her slowly, trying to make up for the rough treatment earlier. "You're my princess, remember that."

☆☆☆

Neither of them were very keen on actually joining the party but Grayson had to, at least for a little bit, because of keeping appearances. He was more than happy to just have Odette locked up in his room while he stood in a corner for five minutes, and even told her so, but Odette insisted on coming down.

"Why do you guys have two pools?" she asked him.

"My sister and I were in swimming for a while. In the colder months, when we couldn't use the outdoor one, we used the indoor one." He shrugged his shoulders, holding her hand firmly. "You don't plan on getting in, do you?"

Odette made a face. "I'd rather not be an easier target for being drowned again."

"She can't do anything if I'm by your side," he assured.

He was actually wearing shorts for once, which was strange for Odette. They were a mauve color and he wore a grey T-shirt over that. His amulet was on a leather cord and he wore it like a necklace. He looked very uncomfortable and he didn't bother to cover it up. His pout was enough to dampen Odette's mood.

"I don't like these things," he said out of nowhere. "Too many people, people our age that is. Screaming girls. People who want pictures."

Odette nodded in understanding. "So, Greer invites random fans?"

"No. She invites 'friends' and other people who give me a headache. If we invited random fans to our house, they would never leave." He shuddered in disgust.

Grayson led her down the main stairs and then behind them where the door to the backyard was apparently. Odette's eyebrows shot up when the door opened, the noise alarming her.

Music was playing at a loud enough level but the people there were screaming. It was an infestation of fake tans and neon bathing suits. Even in the fading light, it was pretty blinding.

Greer was—as expected—in the middle of all the action. Her bikini matched Grayson's swim trunks and her hair was pulled up into a bun. Nadia and Bonnie flanked both of her sides and they were surrounded by a fourth of the guests.

Beside her, Odette could hear Grayson swearing about something or another while he looked in the opposite direction.

His hand tightened around her fingers, so she squeezed back to give him comfort.

"Let's go over here." He tugged her over to a less populated area of the lawn. There were a few guys with their phones out, chatting about whatever. One girl was crying while her best friend consoled her.

"What is this party for anyway?" Odette asked, looking around the yard. She didn't think that there were even this many teenagers in Sunwick Grove. Some of them must have been from out of town.

"Our birthday," Grayson admitted.

Odette spun around and pointed an accusatory finger at him. "It's your birthday and you didn't tell me!"

"No, our birthday was at the end of May. We had to keep canceling the party, so here we are." He huffed. "It isn't that big of a deal."

"I wish you would have told me. I could have gotten you something."

He shook his head slightly. "I don't want anything."

"Too bad, life isn't fair." Odette stuck out her tongue. But, really, what could she get the boy who had everything?

Grayson had a strange look on his face. "I would want you to stay with me forever."

Her face began to heat up. She wanted to say that it was too soon to be thinking about forever, that anything could happen in the future ... but he made her feel all warm and fuzzy inside when he said that. Forever with Grayson? Realistically ...

No, I don't want to be realistic right now. I just want to enjoy right now.

"Yeah ... me too," she said softly. She wouldn't have been surprised if he didn't hear her over the loud music and the shouting but he did. She could tell by the way that his face brightened, even in the dark.

"Brother!" Greer sang, catching both of their attention. She had a parade of people behind her but either she didn't notice them or she didn't care. "There you are! And ... Odette. You, brother, have a lot of people to greet. It's your party too."

"I think Zeke greeted them for me." Grayson pulled Odette closer to his side by her hip.

The action didn't go unnoticed by Greer. She scanned them both, her eyes cold. "You two look cozy."

Grayson wasn't amused. "She *is* my girlfriend, sister."

The crowd of people started whispering. Didn't they already know that Grayson had a girlfriend? He hadn't been very discreet, not when he started putting stuff on his social media. Maybe the fans were in denial about it. Odette received a few ugly looks from the girls.

"Well, don't just stand there and mope in a corner. Join the party." Greer wasn't giving him much room to refuse. Everyone knew he was outside now and she was dragging him away. Grayson wouldn't let go of Odette, so she was forced to go with them.

Greer was not a fan of that. She took her brother on a lap around the pool, which happened to be the size of a large lake. They said hello to *everyone* it seemed and, with each person, Grayson's hand became tighter and tighter.

They had almost completed a full circle, or rectangle, around the pool when Odette felt something wedge itself between her ankles. She stumbled forward, her had yanking free from Grayson's, and she tumbled towards the hard ground.

A pair of hands caught her. "Are you okay, doll?"

She looked up to see a guy with short blond hair. Not Grayson. "Um, yeah, I think so. Thanks—" her sentence died in her throat when a familiar hand landed on her hip. She was instantly jerked away from the male and into her protective boyfriend's arms.

"She's fine." Grayson answered, his tone dark. He glared at the man—who was most likely older than him and yet obviously intimidated—until he backed away and left them alone. "Who did he think he was?"

"He helped me. I was falling," she scoffed, crossing her arms over her chest.

Grayson rolled his eyes. "No, he's been watching you all night, princess. The guy thought he had a shot, so he took it."

Sure, she thought sarcastically. *That's some sound logic.*

He glared at her, sending her a message that said, "Don't push my buttons."

She shrank back, wondering why he was so irritable. *He must really hate parties.*

"Come here."

Odette made a face, "I'm right next to you."

"Come. Here." He was scary calm but his eyes were blazing.

She shuffled closer by two inches, her arm pressed against his chest. Grayson rolled his eyes and wove his arms around her waist. Her arms were pinned to her sides and she was immobilized. Grayson bent her back and planted a kiss on her lips. Her eyes were open the whole time, staring into his. She silently asked him what he was doing and why he was doing it in front of all of those people. He only held her tighter.

Grayson wasn't trying to crush her into him or suck her soul out—no, this was possessive. This was him telling the others to back off if they were even tempted to approach. He was staking his claim.

When the two finally broke apart, Odette could feel the blood rushing to her face. Him and his stupid possessiveness. Grayson stood her upright, stepping back. In the dim lights, she could see how flushed he got. Odette wasn't any better—if anything, she was worse. She also felt too sweaty but she wouldn't dare step foot in that pool.

"I'll never allow other guys to be around you," he said quietly. "Just get used to it."

Odette didn't think he had left her much of a choice,

Grayson wrapped his arms around her. "Do you want to go back inside? There isn't anyone I want to talk to."

"I don't know. I think I have to go home soon. I don't want my parents to worry too much," Odette said, holding him back.

He tensed beneath her fingers. "Don't leave me yet. Please. I don't want to give you up again."

She couldn't help it, she laughed. His words were stupidly childish. "Don't worry. We'll get together soon. I promise. It's just my parents are protective of me. Yeah, it can be stupid and annoying and frustrating at times, but they care. They want to make sure that I'm safe."

Grayson shook his head, the action shaking his whole body. "But what if one day they wanted us to break up? What if they tried to keep us apart again?"

"Grayson ... are you okay?" It was really obvious that he wasn't. "Why are you so scared I'm going to leave you?"

"Because that's all everyone does. They all leave. My parents, any ... any friends that I ever made. They all left me. If you were to leave me too, I don't know what I would do. I'm at my breaking point, Odette," he breathed, holding onto her for support.

Odette forced herself out of his arms, looking over his face. He didn't look well. He was a little too flushed and his eyes were heavily dilated. "Let's get you inside. I'll text my parents that I'll be here a few more minutes, okay? Come on."

Grayson seemed to relax a little more when she took him by the hand and led him to the door. She didn't exactly remember the way back to his room but she knew that he would help her. She had her hand on the door knob when she heard some shouts. Odette turned around and saw a group of people pointing in the same direction.

"There's a fire!" some girl screamed.

A fire? Had one of the tiki torches fallen over?

Odette whipped her head around and looked where everyone was pointing. Her heart caught in her throat. She didn't know how she could have missed it before. Some distance away the woods were on fire as orange flames licked the dusk sky and a smoke stack several stories tall towered over the trees.

"Oh my God!" Odette cried. She took off running without a second thought. Her home was over there. "Mom! Dad!"

She could hear people exclaiming in horror as she ran from the party and towards the raging fire. They grabbed at her but she shoved past them and sprinted down the street. The thong of her flip-flops dug between her toes painfully, so she threw them somewhere in the woods but she didn't look back.

The smell of the smoke got thicker the closer to her house she got. The brilliant light nearly blinded her. They had to have gotten out of the house. Their room was on the first floor and it wasn't like there would be anything to get in their way. It was still early in the night too, so they would have been awake. These thoughts comforted her as she sprinted. They would be waiting on the lawn or in the street for the fire department to show up. They might be a little dirty from escaping their burning house, but they would be fine. After all, they were her parents. They were always fine.

Trees around her were on fire. It was a bizarre version of the home she had come to know. Instead of the cool tones of the trees and the house itself, it was all oranges and reds, turning the white of the house brown. She could make out the side of the house that was supposed to hold her room, the glass shattering from her window and scattering onto the grass. The heat was nearly unbearable and she brought her hand up to protect her face.

"Mom! Dad!" Odette screamed again. They weren't on the lawn or on the street. "MOM! DAD!"

Glass shattered from an upstairs window, the sound startling her. If they weren't outside, where were they? Had they gone out for the evening? No. Both cars were in the driveway. Her throat constricted painfully and she huffed and wheezed as more smoke blew into her lungs. Odette ripped off her hoodie and used it to cover her head and her mouth as she raced for the front door. It was suicidal; the house was teetering on the edge and on the verge of collapsing.

She shoved her body against the door, the weakened hinges giving away instantly and smacking onto her burning living room floor. A large plume of the flames erupted from close to the kitchen, blowing towards her.

"MO—AHHH! NO! STOP! WHAT ARE YOU DOING?!" Odette beat against the person's arms.

They were wrapped tightly around her torso and had her hoisted up in the air. More smoke blew into her face and she coughed and sputtered but it didn't hinder her fighting.

"LET ME GO! I NEED TO FIND MY PARENTS!" Odette screeched, twisting and kicking wildly.

"Odette, stop it! I won't let you go in there!" It was Grayson. Of course it was him. He probably took off after her when she left him at the party.

"BUT THEY COULD BE STUCK INSIDE!" She was hysterical. She couldn't think straight or see clearly, all of the cells in her body were urging her to elbow Grayson in the stomach and run back inside.

"That isn't your problem! You go in there and you die too!" Grayson shook her for emphasis, to help her gain perspective.

You die *too*.

Odette sobbed loudly, her nails tearing at his bad arm in hopes of gaining some leverage. "SOMEONE NEEDS TO SAVE THEM! I NEED TO SAVE THEM! IF YOU DON'T LET ME GO, I'LL NEVER FORGIVE YOU!"

Grayson ignored her words. "Maybe they got out. Maybe they got to another house." But both of them knew that, had her parents gotten out, they would have gone to the Mages. They didn't know anyone else.

"MOM!" she screamed again, hoping that she might hear something from the inside. "DAD!"

The crackling fire taunted Odette as it flicked back and forth. The flames were reaching higher and higher into the night sky, creating stars that lasted for three seconds as they blew away. It was sweltering, even without the jacket.

Odette finally gave up fighting Grayson, so he sat her on her feet. She just sunk down to the ground and hugged her knees, watching the bonfire from hell along with forty other teenagers she didn't know. She could feel her heart fluttering erratically, and she probably should have been doing something about it, but she couldn't move. It just didn't seem important at that moment.

More glass shattered like fireworks, scattering onto the road. Odette thought to herself, maybe she should have one last ditch attempt at getting inside. Even if she didn't save her parents, she wouldn't have to live with the crippling emptiness that was already setting in inside her.

"Has someone called the police?" Odette whimpered.

"I don't know," he whispered.

This angered her, more tears bubbling to the surface. "WILL SOMEONE CALL THE POLICE?! PLEASE! *Don't just gawk!*"

She couldn't believe that she had to beg. She thought that someone would have done it by then ... but they didn't. They all just sat back and watched her house burn like it was a *freaking* campfire.

Grayson spoke again, softly. It was so soft she almost didn't hear him at first. "Odette, I don't think that you should stay here."

"I can't," she sniffed. "I have to be here when they arrive."

Grayson closed his eyes. "Do you know what they'll do? They'll bring you to the police station and then they will ask you about extended family. You will be sent away before we can have a proper goodbye."

Odette froze, her fingernails digging into her flesh. She couldn't let that happen. He was all she had left unless her parents were still alive in there somewhere. She didn't have any extended family, both of her parents were only children and her grandparents had all died. So, what would they do to her? Would they put her into foster care? That future seemed just as bleak. She continued to cry into her knees, the heat stinging her eyes horribly.

Grayson continued talking. "I think it will be best if you just come back to my house for the night. Rest up. We can figure everything else out in the morning. How does that sound?"

It sounded better than any other option that she was given.

"Please," she whimpered. "I don't want to be alone."

Grayson helped her stand up and they started to walk back to the Mages' mansion. It was a depressing walk with the fire crackling mercilessly behind them. The summer air felt like winter compared to what she had just been exposed to. It pinpricked against her face and her arms, the air too clean and breathable. She needed to be choked up; she needed to feel that same pain. It was only fair.

"Odette, you're shivering," he pointed out.

Was she? She didn't know. A cold bath might help. Or ... a plunge in the indoor pool. She could see her parents again that way.

What was the last thing she said to them? It was nice, right? All because they had allowed her to go to the stupid pool party to ensure that Grayson wouldn't cheat. How would her day have been different if she stayed with them? They were talking about going shopping after the pizza place, weren't they? Maybe all three of them would have missed the start of the fire. Maybe they all would have burned together.

Odette was still crying, the tears wouldn't stop. They just ... fell, silently. She hoped that her parents didn't feel like she abandoned them ... right now, or earlier. Most importantly, she hoped that they had somehow gotten out of the house and found a way to the hospital or somewhere safe.

"Odette ... stop." Grayson's hand was around her shoulder, the pads of his fingers dipping into her skin. She didn't know what he meant by "stop." "This wasn't your fault, okay? Don't blame yourself."

She didn't respond.

Grayson led her up the front steps to the door and pushed it open. The endless barrage of stairs didn't bother her, Odette just felt numb. There was a rotting feeling inside of her that was growing, though. The pain would get to be too much and she would break down again. She didn't know what was worse—feeling that numbness or feeling that the world was closing in on her.

Grayson went to his room first and grabbed a new set of clothing for her, then led her into the bathroom.

"Wash up," he said. "I'll be waiting nearby."

Odette closed the bathroom door and locked it. Her reflection showed nothing but a shell of a girl. She had a soot-covered face and tear tracks from her sobbing. Her brown eye looked sunken in but her blue one was overly bright with her tears.

She longed to punch the mirror and feel it shatter underneath her fist but she knew that, if she wasn't strong enough to save her parents, she wasn't strong enough to break a mirror.

Once she got the shower working, she sat in the corner and cried.

XXI

Odette stayed wrapped in Grayson's arms. They hadn't moved in hours. She was pretty sure that he was asleep and that she was serving as a human teddy bear. Every time she would shift her weight, he would only hold her tighter or pull her closer. She didn't care.

It was probably early morning when Odette saw his door opening. It was Thorn; she could recognize his molten silver hair anywhere.

"What are you doing in here?" Odette rasped. Behind her, Grayson shifted in his sleep, his hand seeking hers out.

Thorn's steps faltered. "W-well, this i-is a dream, m-miss!" He seemed almost cheerful, which was very strange for someone like Thorn.

Odette narrowed her eyes. "Why am I dreaming of you? I don't remember falling asleep."

"My m-master asked m-me to h-help y-you. H-he told me to make you ... make you dream of h-him." Thorn motioned to

Grayson, who seemed too solid to be a part of some dream. "He said ... he said it w-would make yo-you happy."

She would have sat up if the supposed "dream Grayson" wasn't holding her down. "You do understand that you can't just come here, tell me this, and expect me to be fine with it. You can control dreams? I thought you just helped with the show?"

Thorn played with his fingers. "Err ..."

Odette pushed him further. "How do I know that I'm not just making this all up in my head? Huh, Thorn? How can you prove it to me?"

She wasn't in the mood to be nice.

She was much too *numb* to be nice.

"D-do you remember ... the ... no, master would ... master wouldn't l-like me reminding you." Thorn started murmuring to himself. "M-master wasn't himself ... wasn't himself. He h-hurt the miss."

Odette squirmed forward as much as she could. "What are you whispering about?"

Thorn sputtered and spun back around. He went over to Grayson's wall and hit his head on it repeatedly.

"Hey! Don't do that! Just tell me what you're talking about. Remind me about what? By 'master,' you mean Grayson, right? Why wasn't he himself? What did he do?" Odette egged him on, straining to get closer to the end of the bed.

Thorn stopped his self-punishment and turned around. For the briefest of seconds, he forgot to lower his head and part of his face was visible. It was puckered and scarred horribly—but only on one side. She had to fight her instincts to not react. There was no telling what the man would do if she did.

"It's okay, Thorn," she said softer this time. "I want to know. Tell me, so I know that this isn't a dream."

"Do ... y-you remember th-the nightmare you had ... th-the night you c-came to m-mistress' sleepover?" he said slowly, inching closer to her side.

Odette paused to reflect. She remembered waking up. Whatever she dreamed about made her run home—she remembered that too. *Home*, her throat tightened. She pushed past that and furrowed her eyebrows.

Then it came to her. How she "woke up" and walked down the hallway, only to find a hallway that wasn't the same as the one as she had been in before. There was a door that led her to a dungeon ... and in the dungeon was Thorn, who was bloody and beaten. Grayson appeared and then ...

Odette clenched her jaw. "Yeah."

"It wasn't a—it wasn't a dream, miss."

Odette sat bolt upright, clutching the duvet to her chest. Where was she?

Grayson's room.

The blue walls and the smell of his sheets gave it away. But where was *he*? Hadn't he been right beside her? Maybe. The sheets were kind of wrinkled on the side that she wasn't occupying.

"What a strange dream," she muttered to herself, rubbing her forehead. It was daytime now, the light was shining through his blinds. Her head ached and it occurred to her that all of her medication had burned in the fire last night. *What a pain. Literally.*

There was a knock on the door. *"Princess?"* It was Grayson.

"Yeah?" The door opened soon after and he peeked inside. "You know you don't have to knock, this is your room."

He shrugged. "I wanted to make sure you were up. How did you sleep?"

"Fine," Odette said with a yawn. She laid her head on his shoulder. "I was confused when I woke up, though. I didn't know where you went."

"Sorry about that; I had to go deal with people," he grunted.

She shook her head. "This early in the morning?"

He ran his hand through his hair. "Unfortunately. But I'm back. I told Greer I wouldn't be going to practice today; I have to make sure that you're okay."

Odette hated the words that were about to come out of her mouth. She reached for his hands and played with his fingers to distract herself from the thickness forming in her throat. "What ... what about the police? Don't I have to go to them today?"

"Do you want to?" He scooted himself against the headboard and tucked Odette's head under his chin. His free hand played with the ends of her hair, waiting for her answer.

Odette didn't know herself. She knew that she should but the thought of never seeing Grayson again terrified her. "I don't know."

"We can put it off another day," Grayson suggested. "Wait until you've gathered your bearings."

"I like that idea," she muttered into his chest. She liked the shirt he was wearing—even though she was wearing one just like it. It was soft and it didn't hinder his warmth. "Just another day."

Despite Grayson's efforts, Odette felt worse as the day progressed. It wasn't anything he could help, though—at least, not readily. Missing her dose of medicine had brought on the mind-numbing headaches, and more than once had she nearly fainted on him. She was weak and it would only get worse the longer she was off her medicine.

"You don't look very well, sweetheart," Jethro commented that evening. He was in the library, looking for something that probably wasn't a book.

Grayson stopped reading aloud—*Jane Eyre*—and regarded his grandfather coldly. "Way to make her feel better. If you want to help, maybe you should go out and get her some medicine instead of hoarding your money."

Odette held up her hand weakly. "Grayson, its fine. He's just concerned."

Jethro rubbed his neck. He left the library—without a book—a quickly as he could.

"Don't excuse his actions, he's a miser. He should be helping you instead of hiding in his room and counting his money," Grayson spat. He pinched the bridge of his nose, massaging it softly. "I wish *I* could help you."

Odette closed her eyes in an attempt to quell the dizziness that she felt. "You are helping me. You're taking care of me and comforting me."

Grayson didn't reply. His lips were twisted up in a snarl as he stared into the empty fireplace, deep in thought. While the mansion was freezing cold—the library, especially—he was not about to light a fire and cause Odette to have a panic attack.

"My sister will not allow me to skip rehearsal again tomorrow," he said. "Or the show."

"That's okay—"

"So, you will be coming with me." His tone didn't leave room for her to question him. She simply had to smile and say yes. "I can't leave you alone in this house while you're in this condition."

Odette opened one of her eyes to look up at him. "I'll be fine. I don't want to be a distraction."

"I'll be more distracted if you aren't right there where I can see you." Even though he probably shouldn't have, he started to stroke her head. It added to the spinning sensations Odette felt but she didn't dare tell him. "This is the clearest I've been able to think in a while with you right next to me."

She hummed and held on to his pant leg, mentally willing herself to stop feeling everything. At least it was a distraction from the night before. Her hair still smelled like the smoke, something that wouldn't leave her no matter how many times she washed it with the shampoo.

The back of her eyes burned with more tears. Odette thought she would have run out by now. They were hot, contrasting with her frozen cheeks. She didn't know if Grayson felt them soaking his leg or not; she might be a little embarrassed if he did.

"Princess?"

Crap. Odette quickly wiped them away but it was a futile attempt. "Sorry."

Grayson shifted slightly as he reached for something but Odette didn't move. Something heavy covered her—a blanket in the Mages purple and blue color. "Try to rest. I promise you, you'll have good dreams."

That was doubtful. Every dream Odette seemed to have was a bad one. Even now, with everything that's been going on, it would surely seep into her subconscious and dictate her dreams. When was the last time she had had a truly good dream? It must have been before she came here to Maine. She couldn't think of one while she was living in Sunwick Grove.

Odette allowed herself to relax, ignoring the pain in her head. It felt like forever until she actually went to sleep. Maybe it was because Grayson kept staring at her.

"You're here again," Odette said.

She didn't know where she was, maybe on the grounds around the mansion. It was sunny, but it wasn't hot. Perhaps this was what it looked like in the spring time? She was sitting in the shade of a large tree with a white sundress on—which was a really bad idea because she could stain the dress if she wasn't careful. But it was a dream. Logic didn't matter.

"Y-yes, miss," Thorn stammered. He had hid himself behind a tree.

Suddenly, there was a weight on her legs. She looked down to see another "dream Grayson."

"I'm sorry, but I don't really remember the last time that we talked," Odette added, stroking "dream Grayson's" hair absentmindedly. "I just remember that we did. And you told me something."

Thorn's head bobbed as he nodded. "Th-that tends to h-happen. This i-is st-still ... still a dream, miss. Conversations w-will fade. Don't worry."

Odette could spy him through the branches. Why did he try and hide? What was so horrible that he couldn't come out and face her like a normal person? Hadn't she seen it all already? Maybe she hadn't. Maybe there was more to him that he wanted to keep hidden.

"So, why are you here?" she asked him. "I remember you said that you ... influenced dreams, right? Is that kind of like hypnotism?"

The scene shifted and, while they were still outdoors, they were now in a garden. Odette sat on a stone bench in front of a small pond with little swans floating inside. The shift made her head swirl uncomfortably but she shook it away. It was only a dream. She couldn't afford to be dizzy in her dreams like she did in her real life.

Thorn had his back to her. He inspected the flowers that grew on the lush green bushes before him with great interest. "N-not exactly. I-I must enter ... enter your mind. I c-can control th-them outside u-u-usually, but I-I must t-talk to-to you, miss."

She frowned. "I don't understand. Why not come talk to me in the real world instead of in my head? And how can you even do that? Are you magical like the twins?"

Thorn's shoulders went rigid. "N-not exactly. I-it is v-very c-complicated ... complicated, miss, this family that you have joined. They ... they participate in-in very d-dark things. Things that someone ... someone as p-p-pure as you sh-should not be n-near to."

Odette huffed and turned away from the man. Her irritation was reaching its very limit. These people ... they would never understand her. "You can't say cryptic things like that and not expect me to ask more. I'm not 'pure' either; no one is 'pure.' That means that someone is without sin and that is impossible because we are humans."

The girl wrapped her hand around the nearest rose and ripped it from its bush. The thorns instantly tore at her skin but the wound did not hurt and the blood dripped down onto the dress. Odette discarded the rose, not caring for it.

"M-miss, your hand!" Thorn whirled around—as though he sensed it—and rushed to her side. All thoughts of concealing his face flew out the window. Odette was left to see the full horror of it all.

He obviously wasn't born with it, they were man-made wounds carved into his flesh ... even worse, his eye. Memories of seeing it before poured into her head and she shuddered. She pulled her bloody hand from him and forced him to look up at her.

His hair fell away so she could examine the damage. His right eye had it worst—with a long scar running through it. It ran from the top of his forehead to the bottom of his nose. The left side of his face was horribly disfigured. His one good blue eye begged her to let go and filled to the brim with tears.

"Who did this to you?" she breathed, her eyes focused on his one good eye.

Thorn kept his lips sealed. He looked like he was waiting for something ... pain, maybe? Did he think she would hit him?

"I'm not going to hurt you, I want to help," Odette begged, "in any way I can."

The man shook his head. "You would ... would n-n-not understand."

"Then explain to me. I probably won't remember this anyway if that's what you're worried about. If I do, though, I want to help you." She wanted to let go of him but she knew that, as soon as she did, he would bolt.

Thorn was wailing, fat tear drops falling from his one good eye. It was pathetic but Odette felt bad for him. "I-I-I ... *I can't!*"

The girl released his chin with a huff. Her blood covered him like war paint; he, however, didn't seem to be in a hurry to wipe it away. She wasn't sure he even knew it was there.

"Fine. Don't tell me. Keep giving me vague bits of information in hopes that I somehow chain it all together. Do I have to come out and say that I'm a pretty dense person and need you to smack the information full force *in my face?*" Odette held up her hands. "But if you can't tell me, that's fine."

Thorn seemed so confused. His blubbering had begun to die down, but it became more like a confused crying. Odette wondered if she had actually gotten through him. She could kind of see why Grayson and Greer were so annoyed with him when she first met him. All he did was stutter and cry.

"O-okay ... I-I must, then, i-if you ... if you really n-need me to," Thorn murmured to himself. He reminded her of a child even though he had to have been in his twenties. "I-I am the source o-of m-my masters' powers."

Odette blinked rapidly. *What? Him? How?*

The man continued on. "S-Seven years ago ... Master Jethro f-found a book. A da-dangerous book that ... that should have not been given t-to humans at all. He l-learned a way to en-enslave a holy creature ... and that is what I am. An angel who must serve the Mages family until the e-end of time. B-But, because I am here, I am c-considered *fallen*." Large crocodile tears welled up in his good eye and spilled down his cheeks.

The hairs on Odette's arms stood on end. Thorn, the man whom she thought to be the world's largest crybaby, could not have been an angel. And Jethro? A dangerous book? The man was old, yes, but he didn't seem to be crazy enough to try occult things.

"That's impossible," she whispered.

"It's true!" Thorn insisted. "I-I can change my form but th-this is th-the one I am b-bound to. I-I helped m-master look over ... look over you at night. Even be-before you k-knew my masters, I-I was gi-given the task t-to see wh-who the new family was."

Her mouth tasted sour. Something *had* been watching her. It didn't make her feel better knowing that the thing that had been there was the stuttering angel. What good could that have done? Not that she believed his story.

"*Impossible*," she said to herself. She was on autopilot, feeling far too detached from this situation. She should be screaming or running. He thought he was an angel—that had to make him certifiable. And the part where he said Grayson was involved in something that he shouldn't be. Was this it? Was this slavery? Were angels technically an oppressed race? Her head hurt thinking about it.

"I-it isn't, though. Yo-you just need to ... need to be involved in some d-dark things," Thorn said. He looked like he was trying to be helpful with an almost dopey smile but it only served to creep her out more.

She could see her hands shaking before she felt it. "What kind of dark stuff?"

Did she really want to know? Oh, she really hoped that she would forget everything when she woke up. Her nerves were already shot, she didn't need this.

Thorn could see her apprehension and frowned. "Black m-magic. The occult."

Odette felt strangely relieved at this. For some reason, she believed that it would be something so much worse. The occult ... and then, the surreality of the situation hit her. She was actually considering what he said—no, not even him, but a dream version of him. Something her mind made up! She couldn't help but laugh. How could she believe anything that he said? How could she know that she wasn't making it all up in her mind, no matter how real the dream might have felt or the strange things that seemed like they might be true?

She closed her eyes. "This is just a dream."

Really, she wasn't sure anymore. It felt real but not at the same time. In her mind, she felt so disconnected from reality. The place, however, was too vivid and she couldn't control what came next. She was at the mercy of a dream-invading angel ... or was she? It was starting to hurt her head even worse, thinking about the endless possibilities of it.

"This is just a dream," she said again, firmly this time. "And I'm going to wake up now."

Thorn's figure swirled like it was being sucked through a whirlpool. The entire landscape drained through him and it was macabre. It was as though the world was being eaten or sucked of its life. Color went first, then all distinguishable shapes. Things were twisting and morphing; things that looked like faces of monsters or of nightmares surrounded her, and yet she stayed the same.

Odette was left floating in an endless twisting vortex. She clamped her hands over her head in an attempt to still it all but nothing worked. She wasn't in control. The spinning didn't even stop when she was in her own bed. The sheets were twisted up around her feet, restricting her movement, and sweat poured from every pore in her body.

Odette let out an involuntary moan of pain, clawing at the bed covers to get herself in a semi-comfortable position, but nothing was stopping the spinning. Her breaths came out in short, deep pants. She needed something—a doctor, preferably. Someone who could make it stop.

If it didn't stop, Odette was nearly positive that she would begin to retch.

In the midst of all the agonizing spinning, she could feel pain bubble up behind her eyes and in her chest. Her heart was fluttering uncomfortably, clenching up every few seconds. Her muscles weakened and, one by one, her fingers were forcibly relaxed. The ever familiar feeling of being trapped inside of her body was nothing short of terrifying. Seconds later, her eyes rolled back into her head and she lost consciousness.

☆☆☆

"NOT LEAVING HER!"

"YOU'LL HAVE TO AT SOME POINT! THERE'S NOTHING YOU CAN DO FOR THIS GIRL, GRAYS! ABSOLUTELY NOTHING!"

Something shattered violently. It was enough to wake Odette up from her episode, and she felt surprisingly normal aside from the crippling exhaustion that sank deep into her bones and the soreness of her muscles.

She opened one eye and peeked to see that she was still in that all white guest room. She must have been in the same position as when she fainted but she didn't really know.

At the foot of the bed were the fuming twins. Grayson must have been the one to throw the thing that shattered because there was a glass lamp in pieces on the wall by Greer. The female twin hadn't flinched.

"SHUT YOUR MOUTH, YOU GOOD-FOR-NOTHING! WHAT HAVE YOU EVER DONE TO HELP HER?! HOW AM I ANY WORSE THAN YOU WHO HAS TRIED TO KILL HER?!" Grayson roared. He looked like—at any second—he might throw something else.

He was terrifying. Odette had never seen him this angry, not even after both of her ER visits. He was emitting a raw power that made her want to hide underneath the covers. Or the bed. She was just glad his anger wasn't directed at *her*.

Greer scoffed, her voice lowering to an icy hiss. "Don't even get me started on that one, little brother."

Odette shuffled back on the bed to avoid any further fire but that only drew their attention to her. They looked so similar with their live-wire blue eyes and wild expressions. She felt like the defenseless lamb in the den of two lions.

Grayson was the first one to break. He rushed to her side and drew her into his arms.

"Oh princess," he muttered into her hair. His rough petting of her hair didn't bother her too much but she pulled away from him all the same.

"Grayson, be at practice *or else*." Greer tossed her hair over her shoulder and stormed out of the room.

Odette didn't miss how he glared at Greer. He seemed unstable, a little too unstable for her to deal with. Still, she laid a comforting hand on his.

"How are you feeling?" he asked quietly. It was a stark contrast to his mood a moment ago.

"I feel fine. I'm tired but I'm fine."

Grayson pursed his lips and shook his head. "I woke up because I knew something was wrong. I came in here and you were having a *seizure*? I didn't know that you even had those."

"I didn't know either." Odette felt like her mouth had gone dry. "It had always been a possibility but it's never happened until now."

"You're getting worse?"

Odette didn't know the answer to that. She shrugged her shoulders. The silence in the room seemed deafening.

He swore loudly, tugging on his hair. "I don't know what to do, I'm sorry. I can't leave you in this house by yourself, though. It's not safe. Are you—are you well enough to go out today?"

"I'll do whatever you need me to." Odette glanced down at the clothing she was wearing. It was all his—a regular shirt and flannel pants. Those weren't exactly something she would be comfortable going out in eighty-eight-degree weather. "Um ... do you have anything else I can wear?"

Odette wasn't certain where he got the dress—it was very possible that he could have raided his sister's closet but it didn't look like something that Greer would wear. Greer tended to stick to purples and blues and the dress was ivory and was not bold or flashy in any way.

Grayson pulled them into the parking lot of the Tent of Mystery a little too aggressively. Odette was thankful that he had loaned her a pair of his sunglasses to not only block out the sun but help hid her reactions to his angry driving.

The lot was empty aside from Greer's car and it seemed unnatural. The last time that she had been there it was packed. Seeing it so empty was unsettling. With all of the buzz and people gone, it felt less mystical and more haunted. The tent's pentagram was ever watchful on the grounds.

Grayson held back the tent's velvety fabric for Odette to pass through. "You don't have to do anything while we're here. You can just sit in the seats for the time being. Later, you can come back to my dressing room and rest if you need to."

She nodded, glancing back at him. "Okay, thanks."

"Just don't wander off," he added.

Greer was on the stage, the harsh white lights pointing directly at her as she threw knives at a target. They connected with several *thunks*, all of them circling around the bull's eye.

She turned her head briefly to show that she had indeed seen the pair come in while twirling the last knife in her fingers.

"Hello, Odette," she greeted. She pulled her arm back and flicked her wrist, letting the weapon whizz through the air and hit the center of the target. "How has my dear brother been treating you?"

Odette swallowed thickly, making sure that she kept a distance between the two of them. The girl descended from the stairs, her heels stomping on the floor with purpose. She was dressed for the show later that evening, minus her skirt. Grayson, however, was not.

"I wasn't certain you'd show," Greer said to her brother. Her tone was even but her eyes were icy.

He didn't react. "I'm here."

Odette held onto his arm, hiding half of herself behind his body. She didn't like the anger that was building up in between the two of them. It was as if, any second, a spark would be lit and they would explode, tearing one another to shreds. She almost couldn't believe it; she had never seen such animosity between either of them before.

"You're also *late*," she enunciated, jabbing her finger in his chest. "You can't use *her* as an excuse either. Just get up there."

Grayson waited until she was out of his face before he did anything else. He placed Odette in a seat towards the middle. He kissed her softly, slowly. Odette knew it was to anger his sister more.

"Grayson! Now!" Greer demanded.

The boy dragged himself back, keeping his lips connected with hers as long as he could. "This won't take long," he assured.

XXII

Odette wasn't bored. She found the practice extremely dull. It was painfully dull. In fact, coming up with ways to describe how boring watching the twins practice was actually somewhat entertaining.

They had moments when they would be very intriguing to watch when they were performing magic or when they would do a trick. Other than that, it was a lot of arguing between them and a lot of very colorful threats. Some of them she caught and some of them were too hushed for her to make out.

Greer, just as Grayson had said, spent most of the time directing what they would do. Most of their lines were already scripted apparently; it was just a matter of rearranging the tricks, so that they would not be always saying the same thing over and over again.

"If you don't stop it, I might just use your little girlfriend as target practice," Greer hissed. This was about the fifth time that she had dragged Odette into a threat. It had begun to lose its sting. "Just cooperate!"

"You wouldn't get within ten feet of her before you would be facedown, out cold," he responded coolly, twirling one of the knives in between his long fingers.

He must have done something that Odette couldn't have seen because Greer let out a screech of rage. "You know, all of this crap has been going downhill since Zeke left!"

This really caught Odette's attention. "Zeke left? When?"

As if the twins suddenly remembered she was there, they both shut up.

"I thought I saw him just the other day. This must have been really recent." Odette chewed on her lip. He didn't act unhappy but she didn't know him very well. It just seemed so sudden.

"It really isn't any of your business," Greer sniffed. "But he quit yesterday morning."

Odette shrank back. She didn't mean to get in their way. "Sorry."

"Greer," Grayson warned. He looked back at Odette, his face softer this time. "Don't worry about him, okay?"

Greer snorted and then found something else to gripe about.

By the time the afternoon came, the twins retreated into their dressing rooms. Odette went with Grayson—because he was afraid if he left her for a second, she could start seizing—and was again startled by the sheer size of the tent.

The dressing rooms were behind the stage, far back enough that fans couldn't get in if they tried. Even if it was a tent, it was heavily guarded. And then there was the whole "magic" thing, something that Grayson had neither confirmed nor denied, but Odette was a little more inclined to believe.

"You're so quiet," Grayson commented. He was fixing his hair in the mirror, his cape laid over the back of his chair at the ready. "Is there something wrong?"

Odette met his eyes in the mirror and shook her head. "No ... I guess I'm just in my own world."

"I hope I'm in there too," he said. "You're always on my mind. Always. I was thinking of you when I was with Greer and I'll be thinking of you when I'm on stage."

The girl tilted her head playfully. "What about your screaming fangirls? I'm sure you'll think of them."

"You're the only fangirl I *actually* care about." He used his hands to pat down his hair, smoothing it where the comb hadn't.

Odette snorted, imagining herself in a Grayson Mages T-shirt or waving around an "*I <3 Grayson*" sign in the front row. She remembered seeing those girls when she came for the first time ... with her mom.

Her heart began to thump loudly. Was she a horrible daughter for just assuming they were dead? For just leaving? No, Grayson was right. If they were ... *alive* ... they would have found some way to contact her even if they were in the hospital. They would have done something or sent someone. And no one had come. That thought pulled hot bile up and it rested on the back of her tongue. She was an orphan. That shouldn't be possible. How was it possible?

"Princess?" Grayson was knelt down in front of her. He searched her face but he knew better than to ask her if she was okay. "You know, it's unfair that you should be so pretty when you cry."

Odette recoiled from him. It didn't matter if he was trying to comfort her—that was a weird comment to make. She didn't like that he thought like that.

"Do you want to talk about it?" his voice was gentle, so gentle that she just wanted to have him hold her until the pain went away, pushing out his previously odd comment.

She sniffled, "Just remembering stuff about my parents."

They were both silent. The sound of the crowd filling up the tent reached all the way back there. Loud, excited patrons ready for the show.

"It's never going to go away ... the pain of it," Grayson said slowly. "But it will get easier each day. You'll find new things to enjoy and, soon, a new family. There's actually something I want to give you."

Grayson stood up and walked over to his dressing table. Among the many items that littered the top of it was a black box that he picked up. It was relatively small in size, larger in height than in width and length. He went back to where he was kneeling and handed the little box to her.

Odette furrowed her eyebrows, glancing between him and the box. It was heavy. She had seen similar boxes before. Never in her wildest dreams had she thought he, of all people, would be holding one.

With hesitant hands, she opened the box and her breath stopped. It was a ring. A huge one at that, one far too gaudy and expensive for her. The band was a silver color but the focus was drawn to the oval sapphire in the center, one that looked similar to the amulet he and his sister wore all the time.

"Grayson, I ..." *I really don't know what to say.* She didn't want to refuse him and the gift but she couldn't keep it. Just looking at it made her feel anxious that she would lose it or break it. "It's beautiful ... but why? It's too expensive."

Grayson licked his lips. "You've just lost your family, Odette .... What if you became mine?"

"It's—it's an *engagement* ring?" Her eyes widened to the size of saucers. "I'm only seventeen! We haven't even known each other for that long."

Oh God, she felt like she was going to pass out.

The boy took her hand, grinning. "Yes, but I'm all you have, aren't I? And I care deeply about you, Odette. I think I love you. Don't you love me?"

She wanted to shout at him. She wanted to get it through his head that they were not in a fairy tale or a movie. Her mouth had run dry from fright and he was only making this worse. Weren't they just talking about her *dead* parents a moment ago?

"Grayson ... I ... I don't know. I want to and I think I do. I'll know some more with more time, but marriage? This is too fast! I can't even think straight right now; my mind has gone haywire and my parents aren't even cold in their graves. I'm still a *minor*!" Odette was having trouble breathing. The room seemed too tight. Was this a panic attack?

"Then don't think of it as an engagement ring," Grayson rushed. He took the box from her hands and freed the ring. Still holding her hand—her left one, she realized—he slid the ring on the proper finger. "Think of it as a promise ring. I don't know what I was thinking, springing that on you."

The ring weighed heavily on her hand, winking vulgarly in the low light of the naked light bulbs. It took up most of her finger, the coldness causing a trail of goose bumps to rise up her arm.

It fit her perfectly. Did he guess her ring size or did he just know?

"You promising to be with me ... now or in the future, whenever you're ready, it makes me happy." Grayson wiped her tears with his thumb. He was smiling a genuine smile, not a cold smirk.

Odette hadn't answered him but she knew that there was only one way to. After all ... she didn't want to spend the rest of her life alone.

"Someday," she promised.

Grayson embraced her and Odette could see what she looked like in the mirror. She looked scared. She was careful not to wrinkle Grayson's shirt but her fingers started to dig into his back, burying her face in his neck to avoid seeing her pitiful and pathetic visage any longer.

Odette was half asleep on Grayson's couch when she realized that she was not alone anymore. In the corner of her eye, she could see something moving in the silver section of the drapes. Her head snapped over in that direction, her heart dropping into her stomach. She clutched Grayson's jacket over her like a defense, causing her knuckles to turn white from shock.

"Thorn?" she whispered, squinting in the dim light to see him well. "What are you doing here?"

He certainly looked more disheveled than he had any other time that she had seen him. His shirt was wrinkled and only halfway tucked. His brown pants had rips in them and were more worn the further down to the bottom. He looked exhausted.

"Thorn?" Odette asked again, sitting upright.

"You ... you had a-asked me t-to come an-and see you in rea-real life," the man stammered, rubbing the back of his neck.

Odette pursed her lips and tried to recall herself saying something so strange. "I'm sorry, I don't remember."

"Pr-probably my f-fault, miss. I wo-wouldn't want anything to happen ... to happen to y-you if you d-did."

There was a loud roar of applause coming from the stage area that drew both of their attention away.

"Shouldn't you be with the twins? I mean, you said that you helped with the shows."

Odette could see Thorn's lips twitch slightly. "I-I don't think th-that I'll be missed."

"You shouldn't say things like that," Odette said. "I'm sure that it's not true."

Thorn stared at his feet and shifted from side to side. Odette watched how he wrung his hands, how his fingers seemed to twitch every few seconds, like he might reach for the door handle.

"You said that I told you to come and see me in 'real life,' when did I say that?" Odette asked him.

His fingers began to tap against his thigh, flexing and curling uncomfortably while he turned his head to the side. "Um ... a-a dream, miss."

A dream? Odette's lip curled. The guy had a dream about her? Or was that supposed to be the other way around?

"I ... I suppose th-that I can p-prove it ..." Thorn murmured. He shuffled closer to the couch and hesitantly sat down on the edge close to her. His whole body seemed to suck the warmth out of the surrounding area, drawing Odette in closer. Thorn pressed the palm of his hand to her forehead and a silvery blue light lit up all the veins in his body. Odette's muscles seized up and she prepared to push away from him and scramble to safety, but the light had reached her before she could.

Odette's head flew back from the force of the energy, a collage of memories filling her mind—but they weren't memories. They were too hazy and too *uncertain* to be memories; they were snippets of a dream that she had experienced. She recognized them almost instantly, the images giving her the warm feeling of familiarity.

The words that were said, she knew them because she had heard them before. It was like rewatching a movie that she had only seen once before in her childhood.

Finally, Thorn pulled his hand away from her. He stood up from the couch and returned to his spot in the corner of the room. "That was jus-just the dream from l-last night."

"Yeah," Odette said, her body still buzzing from the power he used. "Are there others? More that I don't remember, I mean?"

Thorn pursed his lips. "Y-yes, but I-I will n-not give you an-any more. Wha-what I have given y-you is e-enough."

She was slightly nauseated from the angel's power, lightheaded from being forced back into her own mind. Her hands were all sweaty and they shook like she had been sucked of all her energy; her mouth tasted like metal. Odette would trust the angel on with what he said. What he had given her was most definitely enough.

"I-I must le-leave," he said abruptly.

Her eyes widened. There was still so much she needed to ask him. "Hey, hang on—"

Thorn didn't wait. He didn't even stand up from the couch. The angel vanished before her very eyes, like he hadn't been there at all.

The new information made Odette's head spiral. *Well*, Odette thought, *it wasn't technically new but newly remembered.* That man who wrote the journal, the one who had been so obsessed with the twins, his theories of their magic being real was … correct. Odette laid her head in her hands, desperately trying to squeeze more information out of her head, remember all that he had written? The journal was all burned up now thanks to Grayson, and her notes of her dreams and her books had all been claimed by the fire. But, the more she thought on it, the more she could come up with snippets of lines and flashes of previous dreams. None of it was good enough. Her memory couldn't be trusted, not with how strung out it had been the past few days. There was only one thing to do—ask Grayson herself.

She made a plan to do it as soon as he left the stage. Luckily, he was on the last show of the night and Odette knew that he would come back as soon as the curtains dropped.

Odette wasn't far off. She could hear the crowd from where she sat, accompanied by the twins' shouts of goodnight. It wasn't two seconds later when the door to the dressing room swung open. Grayson gave her no warning and swept her off the couch before she could speak. Odette could feel his body shake from adrenaline, muscles trembling from the high of the performance and the magic. His hair had become askew from one of the tricks, his forehead damp with sweat. None of it, however, made him any less attractive.

Grayson kissed her, no words being exchanged as he did so. His amulet burned cold against Odette's *décolletage*, cutting into her flesh through the thin lace of the dress. Odette made a noise of surprise, her hands pressed against his chest in an uncomfortable manner. She pried her face away from his, flustered by his sudden action. "Don't you have a meet-and-greet with your fans right now?" she asked through gasps of air.

"I'm not going to it. I have you to look after," he reminded her, his finger brushing against her cheekbone. "I think that we should get you home, you've been out for too long for today."

Odette licked her lips and shook her head. "No, I'll be fine. This is your job. I wouldn't want you to lose fans because of something like this. Plus, your car's out front. What will your fangirls think when they see you leaving with someone else?"

"I don't care," he snapped.

She jumped. He wasn't angry, no; she knew what he looked like when he was angry. It was more mildly annoyed. His eyebrows rose, daring her to protest.

"You know what," Odette said quietly. "I am feeling a little tired. Maybe ... maybe the two of us could go ahead and go home?"

His hands that rested on her hips flexed and he smiled kindly. It didn't match the rest of his face. "Of course, princess."

Grayson quickly pecked her on the lips, softly and sweetly. His nose nudged against her own coyly and he chuckled to himself, his eyes raking over her face. He kissed her again and, this time, she knew that he wanted it to be more than a simple, childish peck. She feigned a yawn and turned her head just as he was opening his mouth up. His breath fanned over her cheek with a dissatisfied sigh but he made up for it by kissing her temple.

"Come on," Grayson said finally, helping her stand up on her feet. "It's late. I'm sure that you're hungry."

Grayson pulled into his driveway, Odette had her arms crossed over her chest and her eyes trained on her lap. He had to take the road past her old house and she made the mistake of looking up at the charred remains. Police tape ran the length of the property but, as far as she could see, there were no officers present.

Just seeing it made her feel sick.

It also reminded her of her question but, with the way he was acting, she wasn't sure if she was willing to go down that path.

"Princess?"

Odette knew that everything that she was feeling was due to her high strung emotions at the moment. It had to have been. There was no way that she was actually afraid of her own boyfriend. He had only surprised her earlier with that ring and then his overprotectiveness. Her anxiety was just making her feel things tenfold, nothing more.

Odette got out of the car on her own, practically forcing herself to go and lean into Grayson's touch. She felt like she might be getting sick again.

"Hey, what do you say about watching a movie when we get inside?" he suggested, helping her up the front steps.

Odette eyed her sandals, "Yeah sure."

The summer breeze rustled the trees and brought with it a horrible rotting smell. Odette gagged, cupping her hand over her nose and her mouth, but it wormed its way through and got into her eyes.

"Ugh, do you smell that?" Odette asked, now holding her stomach as well. It was so thick that it was choking her, mingling with the humidity.

Grayson's face twisted up in disgust, which mirrored her own. "What is that? Maybe there's a dead animal nearby?" he suggested, stepping into the mansion.

Odette glanced behind her, squinting into the darkness. If anyone did the poor animal in, Odette didn't doubt that it would be Squiggles. Or Squiggles' mistress.

She was about to join Grayson inside of his frigid home when she caught sight of something just underneath of her shoe. It was a splotch of rusty brown, which marred the rest of the chalky white steps.

Odette was quick to jump back from the spot. She felt like it had attacked her, or that she had attacked it for stepping on it. It frightened her that there was something that looked like blood on their front steps but she couldn't think like that. She had to think positively or else ... or else she didn't know what she might do. But the more her eyes stayed focused on that spot, the more she could pick up the tinier spatters that led off to her left. There was another medium sized splotch of the rusted brown something just before the steps dropped off into nothing, leading into the bushes.

"Odette?" Grayson asked quietly.

The girl wasn't moving on her own accord, it was like her body was on autopilot. She was in the grass before she even realized it; the putrid smell finding its way through her hand and even in through her mouth.

Grayson leaned out of the door, frowning at her dreamlike movements. "Odette, what are you doing?"

She glanced back at him, silently begging him to come to her side and join her. He didn't. He stayed put, his eyebrows furrowed and his lips parted in confusion. Odette turned back around, walking the length of the house slowly. She was nearing the garden and she expected to see whatever it was laying there. She didn't know how bad it would be, the severity of the injury of whatever poor creature it was. She didn't really want to know either but she could feel her curiosity getting the better of her.

Even in the hot summer night, she felt a shiver go down her spine. Her first thought was, naturally, *Greer*. Somehow, the girl had beaten them home and done something horrible beyond imagination. Or, she let her pet do it while she watched from afar.

Odette rounded the corner and ... nothing. No poor dead animal or—God forbid—a person. The rusted splotch trail ran cold as well. It was just the garden. Her shoulders slumped down with relief; she didn't even realize how tense she was until then.

"Are you feeling okay?" asked Grayson who was unexpectedly close.

She jumped.

"You're looking pale."

Odette clutched her chest, feeling her heart beating erratically. He had really scared her. "I don't think I'm getting enough sleep," she said to herself, pressing the heel of her hands to her eyes.

Her paranoia was going to be the death of her. Nothing scary was going to just jump out at her. She didn't know what she was even doing.

Grayson moved out of her way and led her back along the path to the front door. "That is a horrible smell."

It only got worse the closer they walked to the house. The wind blew again and, even though it blew the stench away from them, the smell wouldn't leave them.

That was when Odette *saw it*.

At first, she couldn't believe exactly what she saw; it was only a glimpse in the bushes, foliage parted by the wind. A horrifying glimpse that made her jump backwards yet again.

She turned to Grayson with wide eyes. "Did you see that?"

"See what?" he asked.

Odette slipped away from him, her arms shaking by her side the closer she got to the hedges. The twigs and rough leaves scraped at her palms and she didn't even have to push them back all the way to see it again. She wanted to let out a scream. Quickly, she turned around to get Grayson's attention with a small cry leaving her mouth, but she fell to the ground and blacked out.

Odette woke up screaming, tearing at her high-collared dress. She felt like she couldn't breathe. She couldn't see anything around her; all she could think about was the fact that she had found Zeke's body lying in the bushes. In her mind, she was still in the yard, or—even worse—right next to *it*.

She could practically still see him in her mind's eye. Zeke's poor lifeless body. It was all too much for her. The room was too cold and too hot at the same time. She wanted to throw up but she had nothing in her stomach. All she knew was that she had to get the dress off of her or else she would die from contamination.

"*Odette!* Hey! Snap out of it!" Grayson demanded, his hands clutching both of her hands and forcing them away from her body.

"NO!" Odette cried, struggling against him. "I can't breathe! I can't breathe! Just let me go!"

For a brief second, Grayson was not his beautiful, youthful self. Instead, he was death himself. He was *Zeke*.

A garbled, horrid choke left her lips. The scent alone made her hair stand on end.

Odette shrieked again and thrashed against the dead weight. "NO! GET OFF!"

"You need to listen to me!" *Zeke* insisted. "If you don't calm down, you could trigger something and make yourself worse!"

She was hyperventilating; her heart pounding much too fast. There was a dead body on top of her, just like that time before, and it was talking. Her head swam with vicious dizziness and she felt like her limbs were being sucked into many different directions at once with the bed swirling as though it was on water.

Can't breathe!

Grayson forced his lips on hers but it wasn't a kiss. He was forcing air into her mouth. Odette jerked her head away, coughing and sputtering from the extra oxygen. She began to gasp and paw at the air, tears fell down her face. Her mind was still too hazy to be thinking rationally.

It took several minutes for her to truly calm down. The pressing weight on top of her was not a corpse but Grayson. She was in his room and it was probably the middle of the night seeing as it was still very dark outside even though his room was lit up by various candles all over and a lamp.

The flesh on her throat stung as her tears dribbled down onto it. She must have cut herself with her fingernails in the midst of her panic. Strangely, though, she didn't mind the pain. It was a welcome change as it reminded her that she was still somewhat alive … if this was what was called *living*.

"You saw him too, right?" Odette whimpered, her hands curling into fists. "Oh *God*, Grayson, what happened?!"

Even though he was right next to her, he seemed so far away. He pursed his lips. "I don't know. I was more concerned about you."

Anger and terror mingled inside of her, bubbling up into one uncontrollable mix. "There is a *dead body* in *your* front yard! I do not take first priority!" she shouted, shoving against Grayson and successfully pushing him off on top of her.

"When the police will be focused on taking you away from me, you are!" The boy snatched her left hand and forced it into Odette's face. "You promised to be mine and if you are shipped off to the other side of the country, then we have no chance!"

She groaned, "Grayson! Nothing is going to take me away from you, and even if I had to go away it would only be for less than six months! They release you from foster care when you turn eighteen—"

"Do you know what could happen to you in that time?" his voice had turned deeper, anger and sadness in his eyes. "Do you know what goes on in the foster care system? Huh, Odette? You couldn't handle it. It doesn't matter if they would try anyway, you're not leaving me." His words were final and left no room to be questioned.

She shook beneath him, her emotions getting the better of her. Everything that had happened in the past few days, all of the horror and the tension inside of her, strangling out the last bit of sanity she possessed. At first, Grayson only frowned at the trembling movements. It soon turned into full on jerking limbs and Odette's eyes rolled back into her head, her eyelids fluttering shut. That was when he began to panic.

Someone pounded on his bedroom door but he really didn't care. "LEAVE!" he roared, focusing his energy on keeping Odette's head propped up on his pillows. Small whimpers and grunts left her throat, followed by half choked sounds and twitching eyelids. Her leg would jerk and shake, and her back would arch up and off the bed; her arm twisting painfully beneath her.

Suddenly, Grayson became aware of the fact that he was not the only one in his bedroom anymore. His sister was kneeling down beside the bed, moving Odette onto her side while Odette seized. Greer didn't seem like she was there to cause harm but Grayson knew better than to trust a snake like her.

"*Get out,*" he hissed, wrapping a protective arm around Odette. Her violent shakes were beginning to calm down slightly but he held her with the same bruising strength.

Greer pouted. "I was only helping, brother. This might have saved you another screaming match with your little toy."

He glared at his twin, fighting himself on what he should do.

"Here's something that you should keep in mind," Greer said, standing up from the floor. "Stress can cause seizures."

She looked at her brother knowingly while Odette began to wake up. She looked like she was in a great amount of pain from the dimness in her eyes and the way she was squinting.

"Greer?" Odette whispered, drawing herself closer to Grayson for protection. Her limbs felt like they weighed a ton but she knew that the smart thing would be to stay in his arms.

Greer seemed mildly annoyed. "Your screaming brought me here."

"Well, you can leave now," Grayson replied. "We wouldn't want you to miss out on any beauty sleep."

Even though her thoughts were muddy and her body exhausted from whatever had just happened, Odette knew better than to dismiss the female twin. She just had to gather herself before she spoke again.

Odette squeezed her eyes shut. "No. Greer, don't go. Something bad has happened," she rasped. "Maybe you can convince him to call the police."

The girl quirked an eyebrow. "It must be bad if you're asking for me to stay. What happened?"

"Zeke—Zeke's body," Odette shuddered in revulsion. "He's dead, Greer."

Greer's reaction was reserved compared to what Odette had expected. She didn't scream or cry. Her eyes only widened a fraction and her lips parted. "Grays, is this true?"

His jaw clenched. "I saw him too."

"So, what now? Grandfather won't like this," the female twin muttered, her shoulders shaking lightly.

Grayson rolled his eyes. "Naturally, Greer."

"Are you kidding me?" Odette couldn't believe the both of them. "Call the police! Let them investigate this because I'm pretty sure that he didn't just lose his limbs on a whim!"

Greer tugged on the ends of her hair. "She's right. They need to be notified of this or else, when they do eventually discover it, they'll think we had something to do with it ... Odette, you're bleeding."

Odette didn't know where because she couldn't see but she figured that it must have been on her neck. The dress was sticking to her uncomfortably anyway, and the fabric of the collar was becoming unbearable.

"I'll help her," Grayson sneered. "Go ahead and call those pathetic policemen. Odette, you aren't allowed to be downstairs when they arrive. Don't even look out the window."

There was no use in arguing with him on the subject. His resolve was clear and Odette had no energy to fight him on it. She allowed him to help her up and onto her feet and tilt her head upwards to examine the damage that she had done to herself.

"What an obedient pet you are," Greer commented. Why she had not moved from her spot yet, Odette didn't know unless it was to torment her some more.

"Leave before I throw you out, Greer," Grayson ordered once again, his electric blue eyes glaring at her.

The girl held her hands up in defense, a sly smile on her face. "I know when I'm not wanted."

"*Obviously not.*" Grayson lightly touched one of Odette's wounds, a small smudge of her blood staining his finger. He frowned lightly before he licked it off. "Come, we'll have to clean that. I'll give you some new clothes too. And *you* better be downstairs by the time I have helped her," he shot a pointed look to his twin who still loitered by his door.

Grayson released her chin finally, taking her by the hand and leading her out of his room to the bathroom. The darkened hallway reminded her of some kind of dream that she had had before but she couldn't recall the details.

The wind outside howled, shaking the windows. At the end of the hall, lightning flashes caught Odette's attention. It was yet another storm but she couldn't bring herself to enjoy it. Every flash of light was sending her reeling back into her memories— memories of the deaths that she has had to deal with in her time in Sunwick Grove. She could see the young man dangling at the end of the hall—in her mind—and, while time had blurred some of his features, she could recall his bulging and bruised face vividly.

With another flash of lightning, that body was gone but replaced by that of the kindly Zeke. He lay in a heap in front of the window in a pool of his own rusted blood, his eyes open and begging for help. Odette couldn't help but recoil, wrapping her arms around Grayson's strong one.

"Are you frightened of the storm?" He stopped walking to look down at her. "Don't be, it can't hurt you."

Odette shook her head, burying her face in his shoulder. "It's not the storm. I'm scared of *them*."

"'Them'?"

"The dead bodies."

Grayson inhaled and pulled her into his chest. He pet the back of her hair gently, his fingers massaging her scalp lovingly. "Don't be scared of them. They can't hurt you anymore either."

Once in the bathroom, Grayson had Odette sit on the sink while he tended to the cuts she had made to herself. His face was neutral but focused as he cleaned her skin with soap and water. "Don't do this again," he whispered but it was loud enough for her to hear.

Odette winced in pain. The washcloth felt rough against her wounds. "It's not like I meant to."

"Doesn't matter. You don't do this again; I don't like seeing you in pain." He pulled out a bandage and wrapped it around her neck slowly and carefully, brushing her hair back out of his way.

"How can you be so calm?" Odette wondered out loud. "You've seen what I've seen and you act like it doesn't affect you? You act like you aren't going to be scarred for the rest of your life. How?"

His hands faltered but he continued a second later. "I've seen some pretty horrific things, princess. I've become ... numb, I guess. That would be the best way to describe it."

She frowned, letting go of the high neckline and fixing it back into its proper place. "You can't possibly be numb to *death*."

"You can be when you watched your parents die," he said casually. "I had a front-row seat to their gory end ... and Greer. It was the worst day of my life and it made me what I am today." He didn't even sound bitter about it, just numb, like he said. "Love and life are fleeting. You have to hold on to what you care for and fight for it tooth and nail, otherwise, there's no point in keeping it."

Odette knew that it was better to shut up. Grayson was getting into one of his moods. She swallowed hard, the bandages feeling more like hands constricting her airway.

So, she did the best thing that she could. She cupped his jaw and pushed his messy hair out of his face. The result was almost instant—Grayson's emotionless facade melting away and his face regaining color. Odette pecked his lips slowly, the thunder from the outside shaking the mansion at the same moment.

Odette pulled back while Grayson chased her lips but she didn't kiss him again. "Thank you for helping me."

When the police did arrive, it was nearing three forty-five in the morning. Odette had been moved to the guest bedroom once again—although she somewhat thought of it as her own—and she was given strict instructions to keep the lights off and make no noise. Under no circumstance was she to leave the room unless Grayson—and only Grayson—came to get her.

She had shed the white dress, which had lost its comfort long ago, and wore an old nightgown that looked like something a woman in Victorian London would have worn.

"Where on earth did you get this?" she asked Grayson.

He shrugged his shoulders. "It was one of Grandfather's strange buys. He either claimed that it belonged to a queen or that it was cursed."

Odette blanched.

"It's *fine*. Do you really think I would give you something dangerous?" Grayson chuckled, shaking his head. "We mainly used it as a prop for the shows around Halloween."

She remained skeptical about the garment but she didn't outwardly tell him. He left her not long after and she changed into it, marveling at how the lace wasn't irritating against her skin. Odette curled up on the bed and tried to close her eyes but she couldn't. Her body wouldn't let her. If it wasn't for the fear of what she might see in her dreams, it was the horrendous storm raging on out her window.

She huffed, kicking the sheets off of her legs and letting them pool at the bottom of the bed. She threw her arms up over her head to stretch out when the lightning caught the reflective glare of her ring. Odette had completely forgotten about that being on.

It had only belonged to her for a short number of hours but she found herself overly comfortable with the weight it held on her ring finger. In the dark, it looked black rather than blue and it didn't glitter at every single moment like Grayson's or Greer's. She began to twist it but found out that she couldn't turn it all the way around her finger—only half—because of how large the stone was. The ring simply refused to move.

Marriage, Odette thought with a grimace. *He wants to marry me. How strange.* And something that she most definitely wouldn't do ... not for several years at least. *Our emotions have been everywhere,* she reasoned with herself. *It isn't like he actually meant it. It was a spur of the moment kind of thing. He thought he was helping.*

The sound of her bedroom door opening made Odette sit upright. The lights came on and she saw ... Jethro.

"Oh hello," she greeted, her voice sounding scratchy from lack of sleep. And the screaming. "Have you ... do you know?"

Jethro furrowed his eyebrows, his face drawn. He looked ages older than he had when she first met him. "Yeah, I know, sweetheart. It's hard not to with the police swarming my front yard. How are you holding up?"

She figured he didn't just mean tonight. "I don't know .... One minute I'm screaming and trying to rip my throat to ribbons and the next I just feel nothing. Is this normal?"

He rubbed his face, a sad laugh filling the room. "I don't know, kid. With all you've been through, well, you're doing a lot better than I would be."

"I don't think so." Even in the bright white room, she felt nothing but darkness around her. "I think that it's driving me insane. I can't even do anything to make these ... these hallucinations stop. And the strange thing is, is that I have been miserable since ... *I* moved. I'm scared every time I go to sleep and I've never had a legitimate reason to be but I always am.

"Grayson ... Grayson's helping me. He can make them go away, I think. He's like a shield or something. Nothing bad ever happens when he's around and he's always there to help me pick up the pieces. He only wants what's best for me."

Odette hugged her knees, her eyes not focused on anything particular in the room.

"I'm sorry. About your parents, I mean." Jethro stepped further into the room and leaned against the dresser. "The police are investigating it right now but it was supposedly set by gas stove. A freak accident but it does happen. But the real messed up bit is that they're looking for you ... not only as a missing person but a person of interest."

Odette gasped. "You mean ... they think that I might have set it? But that's impossible!"

The older man hung his head tiredly. "I know. Grayson's convinced us all to keep our mouths shut about you, though; that we 'don't know where you are.' But, you have to admit, it does look sketchy that you just vanished after they died. I know that, if you go to the cops, they'll take you away but, sweetheart, don't you think that it would do you better to be away from here and all this death? At least they'll know you're innocent."

She flinched, gripping the bed sheets so hard her knuckles turned white. "I want to but I can't leave. I have no one. Grayson is the closest thing that I have to any family now and I'm scared what will happen to me if he's gone too."

"He doesn't take abandonment well," the man agreed with a sigh. "But, kid, you need to think about it. If he really cares about you then he'll have to understand. We'll help you as much as we can but, even with the powers we possess, they may not tell us enough concerning you."

Odette didn't want to do what he was telling her to do. Even if it did make sense, even if it was the responsible thing to do, being all alone was something she couldn't handle. What would happen to her if she went away? What would happen to Grayson?

She was beginning to feel very lightheaded just imagining the possibilities. All worst-case scenarios filled her mind along with the bone-crushing weakness that she had come to know. The room around her felt all too small and her breathing was shallower.

"I can't," she muttered, her shaking hands coming up to thread through her hair. "I can't be alone."

Her limbs tingled with numbness and dread pooled in her stomach. Odette was aware that Jethro was moving around in her peripheral vision. A large hand clamped down on her bicep and she could feel another on her knees.

Odette squirmed away but Jethro was much stronger than her. Her head was forced between her now propped-up knees and she grunted from discomfort.

"Just breathe," the man ordered.

He rubbed small circles into her back, repeating those words over and over again. Odette wanted to yell at him to *shut up and let her panic*, but found that the sick feeling started to recede after a few minutes like that. The metallic taste on her tongue started to vanish and she took several shuddery inhales before she moved again.

"How did you know what to do?" she asked him quietly, moving several strands of hair that had entered her mouth away.

She could feel a few tears fall from her eyes but she wasn't sad. She didn't think she was anyway.

Jethro pursed his lips. "You aren't the first kid I've known to have panic attacks." He rubbed his hands on his pants almost awkwardly. "I didn't mean to trigger one for you but you need to think about it, Odette."

She opened her mouth to respond when an imposing shadow fell across the bedroom floor. Grayson stood in the doorway, his eyes fixated on his grandfather.

"Why are you in here? What have you done to her?" He yanked Odette off of the bed and put her behind him protectively.

Jethro scoffed quietly. "No need to get defensive, Grayson. I figured I would check up on her to make sure that she was fine. But now that you're here, I think that I'll go back down to those officers and help however I can."

He smiled politely at Odette and left the room just as mysteriously as when he had come.

Grayson angrily closed the door, checking both ways to ensure none of the cops had come upstairs. "Why was he in here, Odette? That man only causes trouble wherever he goes. He knew better than to come in here, especially when they are just outside."

The light switch was flipped and they were in total darkness once more. It reminded Odette of the nights when he would sneak in through her window to come and see her, only with more anger and tears.

"Come on, Odette, tell me," Grayson demanded. "Or do I have to force it out of you?" He wasn't threatening her, rather, he sounded bored, like he was talking about school.

She bit her lip. "H-he wanted me to go to the police. He wanted me to go, so that I could prove that I wasn't involved in the fire and ... so that I could get away from here."

Odette could see the silhouette of Grayson, how his shoulders were tensed and the way his fists were clenched. Outside, the storm was receding but a flash of lightning illuminated his features. She didn't know what she expected. Anger? Sadness? No. He was blank and still as a statue. He wasn't looking at her but rather through her.

Odette reached out to him, "Grayson?"

As soon as her hand made contact with him, it was like he woke back up. "Princess, I love you. You should go to sleep."

What?

"I—" Odette was cut off by Grayson tugging her into him. He hugged her tightly, his fingers lacing into hers. "I ... care for you too."

Grayson kissed her forehead, long and sweet, and the next thing she knew she was asleep in his arms.

XXIII

O dette woke up and realized that she was standing up in her bedroom. That was far from the strangest part as the air around her was thrumming with some kind of energy. She could feel the energy's warmth in her teeth and the buzzing in her eyes.

Her hand reached out to the bedroom door and clasped the cool handle, the knob clicking mechanically. When the door opened, she came to understand that the hallway was not the same as it had been the night before. It wasn't a matter of a change in décor, but the doors were missing and so were the windows. It was just blank and grey.

Stepping further into the hall, her door shut behind her and promptly vanished as well. Odette swore under her breath, pressing her hands against the solid wall, pushing against it, but there was nothing that revealed that there was once a door on it. She was trapped.

"This is just a dream," she muttered to herself, punching the wall lightly.

She breathed out, frustrated, and turned around. The hallway seemed to stretch out forever in front of her but not behind her. If there was a way out, it would be down in the endless darkness. Odette kept a lookout for anything that resembled a door of some kind but there was absolutely nothing. Even more frustrating was that there were no turns or corners, and there was nothing that distinguished just how far she had come like a picture frame or something.

I'm so tired, Odette thought to herself. *Maybe I should just curl up on the floor and sleep. Can you sleep in dreams?*

And then she walked straight into a wall. Odette was more stunned than hurt; she hadn't seen a wall at all. It had just seemed like the corridor kept going but, apparently, it didn't. She rubbed her nose, which had taken the brunt of the hit and silently cursed the wall. She was about to turn around and go back to where she had started when a door just to her side caught her attention.

"*Déjà vu,*" Odette said to herself, reaching out to push open the door.

It revealed a set of steep, dimly lit stairs that went down and down for several floors. What was even worse was the nauseating, rotting smell that smacked her in the face as soon as the door was open. The air smelled like iron and it was bad enough to make Odette want to retch. She cupped her hand over her mouth and nostrils but the smell continued to break through her defenses. She found herself stumbling down the stairs, holding onto the walls for support.

The air was thicker down below and much warmer than what she was used to in the mansion. Sweat broke out along her hairline and she couldn't help but gag. It smelled like something had died. And then she came to the conclusion that this must be another nightmare. When she would reach the bottom of the stairs, she would be greeted by the sight of death and have to live through it until she scared herself awake.

I don't want to but I might as well get it over with.

The last few steps were the worst with Odette staggering and feeling faint. What greeted her was a prison or a dungeon of sorts. Bars lined the walls and the cages took up majority of the width of the room. It was dimly lit, only by one candle every few feet, and those candles did not cast a very powerful glow.

Odette, however, could make out movement further down in the cages. She could hear strange noises that went along with it, and the girl frowned. She began to walk as quietly as she could towards the sounds, clutching her skirt tightly in her hands.

The noises she heard became clearer the closer that she got to them—whimpers and quiet pleading, growling, and the sound of something sloshing and tearing. Odette furrowed her eyebrows, debating on whether or not to turn around, when something touched her foot.

It was warm and liquid-like and she jerked away instantly, gasping. The liquid looked black, but, upon further inspection, Odette realized exactly what it was. She couldn't scream, not even as more blood pooled at her feet and stained them a bright red. She watched the trail with wide eyes, following it until she saw exactly where it came from. The very last cell.

She couldn't run and she couldn't scream. Her body worked on autopilot, creeping slowly towards the end of the darkened room and to the very last cell. There was only one question on her mind—whose blood was it? Deep inside, Odette didn't want to find out but it was far too late to turn around.

She stood before the mouth of the prison and what she saw wiped her mind clean. For an entire ten seconds, her mind had completely shut down and she wasn't even frightened. She just felt numb to the macabre scene in front of her.

Jethro ... and Thorn ... and Bonnie ... and Nadia ... and Grayson ...

All in the same cell. All bloody.

Only... only some of them weren't dead.

Bonnie and Nadia—they were very dead. Whoever had done it to them did so without a single shred of remorse. Their faces were unrecognizable, and the rest of them ... Odette couldn't even look. There wasn't even a "rest of them." Everything was too scattered and bloody to pinpoint *what* belonged to *who*.

Jethro was still twitching. That made it even worse to bear. Odette clapped her hand over her mouth to keep herself from screaming. His eyes were downcast at his stomach and she couldn't help but look in that direction too. That was her worst mistake. Whoever had done it to him had given him no mercy. She didn't understand how he was still alive with his insides out.

Odette staggered back, her only saving grace was the stone wall behind her. The trembling in her knees wouldn't cease. There was so much blood ... so much carnage ... it had to be a dream!

But the worst of all was Grayson ... *Oh God!* He was drenched in blood from head to toe; his eyes as dull as his expression. His pale skin glistened under the lighting and she could see the last bits of sweat on his brow. The only sign he was still alive was the rapid rising and falling of his chest and the flushed color of his cheeks.

"What have you done?" Odette clutched the brick wall behind her for support. There was so much gore, too much for someone to have witnessed in their lifetime—let alone in a time span of a minute.

Thorn was trembling in the corner of the piles of bodies, his one good eye trying to tell her something. But he wasn't innocent, she could see the blood on his clothing and the knife and chain in his hand.

"M-Miss—"

"*Shut up, you stuttering idiot!*" Grayson roared. His fists clenched and two brilliant blue chains made of light wrapped themselves around Thorn's neck and wrists. The scent of singed hair and blood invaded her nose.

Thorn dropped his weapon and screamed like a wounded animal, his face becoming the picture of pure agony. He collapsed to his knees and tried to claw at his chains but it did him no good. He was powerless against his supposed master.

Grayson watched him with no expression, no pity or mercy in sight. He was only a cold shell. Odette cowered against the wall, her eyes darting towards the exit.

Every single bone in her body told her to run. That was no man she was dealing with but a cold-blooded killer—a beast.

Odette had pushed herself off the wall when Thorn stopped screaming. Grayson turned around to face her, all sympathies gone. Her blood ran cold the closer he came towards her and she stumbled back. The blood made the ground slippery and she nearly fell into it, but she caught herself by grabbing onto the bars of the cell closest to her. For a moment, she wasn't sure he would be merciful towards her. She feared for her life.

"Don't kill me, Grayson, please! I thought you loved me? Why would you do this?!" she cried, scrambling back.

Grayson scoffed, "Why would I kill you? I did this for you!" He reached out and quickly snatched her hand, pulling her off the ground. All of the blood that covered him smeared onto the once pristine gown she was wearing. "I did this for us."

Her skin crawled feeling the blood on her. It was still warm.

Odette struggled against him. "No! Don't you dare use *me* as an excuse for what you just did! Let me go!" *This has to be a dream. This has to be a dream. This has to be a dream. Thorn's here, yeah? Isn't he always here in dreams? And a "dream Grayson"? This is just a nightmare—!*

"Just listen to me! They had to go!" Grayson insisted, shaking Odette by the shoulders. "They all had to go because they were taking you away from me. Grandfather for—for trying to get you to go to the police behind my back; and those *skanks* that my sister associates with, they were just going to let you die, you know, when Greer tried to drown you.

"Then there was the noble and courageous Zeke who wanted to take you away forever! He said that you had to go to the police, that I couldn't keep you all to myself. He was always meddling in our relationship. What does *he* know about *our love*?!

"And then there was that stupid gangster who tried to shoot *you*. You weren't meant to find him—no, not until I was with you—but that pesky cat of yours got in the way. You understand why she had to go too, don't you? I hated seeing you so torn up about that rodent but she was a distraction. I must say its death gave me the perfect opportunity to comfort you, so something good did come of it. You are so pretty when you cry, it's unfair."

Grayson laughed bitterly, licking his pale, blood-smeared lips. "Then ... your parents tried to separate us. You were generous to warn me about them but my own past made me merciful. I should have listened to you. When they *kept you from me* for an entire two weeks, I was so angry. You don't even understand how much energy it took to stop myself from going over there and stealing you away in the middle of the night ... BUT ... you came back to me so willingly and I knew that you loved me then too."

"GRAYSON, STOP IT!" Odette screamed, crying harder than she had in her entire life. "*You're* the monster h-here! N-not Greer, no-not Jethro. You killed m-my parents! Y-you killed my c-cat! I *hate* you!"

He growled. "No, you *love* me. And I *love* you!"

Grayson threw Odette against the bars of one of the cells, the metal rattling with the sudden weight. Odette cried out, her head erupting with the splitting pain. She was too disoriented to fight against him when he pinned both of her hands beside her head and glared down at her.

"Tell me you love me," he demanded, squeezing her wrists with such a force she was certain he would break them.

"I hate you, Grayson! You've *ruined* my life!" she spat. She kicked at him, trying to nail any weak point, but he was very much in control of the situation.

Even though he had never shown true anger towards her before, Odette couldn't be certain that he wouldn't. It wasn't his face that displayed his true feelings but the strength of his hands that were making hers pop. Odette screamed in agony and begged him to stop. She knew that she provoked him but she didn't mean to. She just wanted him to stop.

"You know," he started, his grip loosening just a little. "I can always make you love me. You've come so far, you've already accepted to be mine. There's no way to escape this, Odette. The only way out is death and I can assure you that, when the time comes, it will be me that ends you."

Grayson smashed their mouths together. She was twisting and screaming against him but he wouldn't let her head move. There was something metallic that filled her mouth—no doubt from him—and the more she fought, the more frustrated he grew with her.

He slammed her head against the bars once more, sending her reeling. Her eyes opened but everything she saw was Grayson and he was all blurred. What she could make out, though, were his narrowed eyes, daring her to fight back more. It was all a game to him. He wanted to see how far they could push one another before they both broke.

He shoved her away with a huff, wiping his mouth off on his shoulder. When he turned back towards her, he had calmed down. It was only surface-deep; she had learned a long time ago that his true emotions were shown in his eyes.

Grayson licked his lips and sighed. "You know, Odette, I never really wanted you to find out about any of them. But you just had to go and be so nosy. Your curiosity is one of the things that just make you so beautiful, though. You can't help it, can you? Sheltered all your life and you just want to be free, so you let it get the best of you."

The boy took a lock of her hair between his fingers and twisted it around, as if he were enthralled by it. He then pushed it back and petted her, slowly and methodically.

"Please, Grayson, just let me go," she sobbed, turning her face away from him. She couldn't stand it, the fact that he had been a killer the whole time and tricked her into feeling things for him.

Grayson *cackled* like some kind of super villain. "And where will you go? No one will love you like I do, princess. No one. They'll all pity you, yes, but they'll never love you. I'm the only one you can ever trust. I can keep you safe!"

"Let me go!"

His grin slipped. "Is this—is this because I didn't kill Greer? I can't, she possesses the same powers as I do, thanks to that good-for-nothing *angel*, so we are evenly matched. But I could hurt her; I could torture her for you if that is what would make you feel better. You and I, we can hurt her together!"

Odette screamed, kicking her legs out again. From the corner of her eye, she could see more of the blood crawling out of the cell. It sickened her that he could stand the smell.

"No! Just leave me alone!" Odette didn't want anything more from him.

Grayson was ripped away from her by an invisible force and tossed against the wall roughly. He grunted and collapsed, not moving an inch. She held onto the bars behind her, her legs almost too weak to hold her weight.

"Run!" Thorn shouted. His arms were extended like he was holding something back.

Odette put two and two together, how Grayson couldn't move and the stance that the angel had taken. He was helping her. A large hole appeared in the cement wall across from her. The edges of it looked like silver wisps, like fire was surrounding it. What was outside of it, she couldn't tell.

"Through there!" Thorn urged her.

There was no time to hesitate. She just had to trust. Odette leapt through the hole and didn't look back. She was suddenly outside of the mansion, outside of its gates. The rough terrain scraped against her feet and dirt clung to her feet, mixing with the blood. Odette spared the mansion one last glance, the magical hole that she had jumped through sealing up instantly. She knew that she only had a limited amount of time as a head start, so she sprinted in the direction of the town.

Adrenaline pumped in her veins, a sudden burst of energy filling her body. The trees on either side of her were rocking and swaying in an archaic dance due to the hectic winds that blew against her. The sky was a muddy gray mess. There was a brief flash of lightning that illuminated her way. Odette wanted to scream. She wanted to tear her hair out and throw herself into the sea. Maybe that would purge her of the feeling of sickness that was plaguing her. The horrors that she had to see. She threw herself towards the trees, knowing that it was better to be hidden by them than out in the open should she be chased down. Branches and twigs scraped her face and pulled at her dress, tugging her and pulling her at every direction. She became scared with every pull, every time her hair would be yanked and tangled, because she believed that that mad man had caught up with her.

Odette threw her hands up to protect her face but it was useless. Nature was lashing out at her for not seeing it before, for not seeing how crazy in love he was. Normally, the stinging pain would have brought a kind of clarity to her but not this time. It only added to her agony as her skin felt like one open and raw nerve left to be tortured.

The faces of all of the dead were surrounding her in the forest. They were every branch that pulled her hair, every twig that scraped her face, every rock that cut her ankles. She wondered if they wanted Grayson to find her, as if Grayson was like a shark that could smell her blood and her torment.

Odette's foot was caught under a root and she splayed out onto the damp earthen floor. For several seconds, she didn't move and allowed her entire body to ache. That was when the entire world seemed to have gone abnormally silent, with no more wind and no more thunder. Alone in the dark, Odette found that she wasn't scared of the trees anymore, nor the monsters that she used to create.

She was only scared of him.

"ODETTE!" His voice was purely animalistic, chilling her down to her very core. "ODETTE!"

She couldn't tell where it was coming from; his voice echoed all throughout the woods, from the top of the trees to the floor where she laid down. What she knew was that she had spent enough time lying around and scrambled to her feet.

"ODETTE!"

She choked out a whimper; she refused to let him get to her. He was a horrible person ... not even a person but a monster. He was pure destruction. *Why?* Odette wanted to scream. *Why did you have to be like this?!*

He was too perfect ... so his flaw had to be horrendous. Worst of all was that Odette found that a tiny part of her still cared for him but she would smother that part out. She would destroy that part of her until it was nothing but a distant nightmare.

Odette tore through the police tape that sealed off her old house. It didn't matter to her that she was passing it; she didn't even think about what it was until she was already several yards past the charred remains and nearing the town.

Businesses dotted either side of the road but the whole place was abandoned. It must have been the middle of the night but Odette had no clock to check if she was correct. Not that it even mattered. She ran down the sidewalks, her legs burning with exhaustion. She wouldn't be able to keep it up much longer, her body would shut down soon and she would be left to the mercy of Grayson should he find her.

Odette couldn't bring herself to glance behind her. If she did, she was certain that she wouldn't like what she would see. He could be right there, ready to tackle her to the ground and drag her back to that prison by her hair. He'll claim it's for her own good. Odette stifled a sob.

In the corner of her eye, Odette spotted an abandoned church. She didn't think, she only did. Odette threw herself at the wooden doors and they burst open without much more shoving. Splinters poked at her through the thin material of her dress but she didn't care.

Odette slammed the doors shut, squinting into the darkness. Graffiti was all over the walls and many pews had been overturned, but, in the front, the altar stood relatively unscathed. The cloth that covered it was moth-bitten and torn in places, but it reached the floor and made for the perfect hiding spot.

Stumbling through the darkness, she slid underneath the altar as fast as she could. Odette pulled at the cloth, hoping that it was low enough to hide her away. Her hands were trembling with exhaustion but she was too afraid to close her eyes. Her breath came out fast and uneven; she couldn't hide it, and her heart was beating too fast.

Wind howled, whistling through the cracks in the walls and making the whole building sway. The thunder seemed to have no compassion for her nerves and picked up, going from low rumbles to loud, threatening crashes.

Through one of the many holes in the altar's cloth, Odette was given a view of Jesus on the cross. He, too, had been defiled by those who graffitied the holy building. The statue seemed to be looking down at her with a pitiful face.

"Please, God," Odette found herself whispering. "Don't let him find me."

Lightning flashed and illuminated the Son's face, the shadows casted making him seem like he was crying. Odette didn't take that as a good sign. She squeezed her knees to her chest, inhaling the scent of blood, sweat, and earth as fat tears rolled down her cheeks. When would this end? Could she hope to survive the night and maybe make it to the police department? What a sight she would be, coming out of the church? What would people think?

Odette hiccupped quietly, pressing her eyes on her knees. She wished that her parents were alive to help her but that wouldn't make much sense, would it? If they were alive and they tried to help her out of this situation, Grayson would wind up trying to kill them again. *I wish we never moved to this awful place!*

"Please," Odette repeated. "Please, don't let him find me."

And the doors of the church slammed open.

XXIV

Odette held in her gasp, her eyes flashing over to the front
door. She couldn't see anything but she knew she wasn't
alone. It was never just the wind. They must have been in a
blind spot.

"Hello?" the person called out. "I saw you run inside here ...
I'm not a cop or anything like that but are you in trouble?"

Odette didn't know if she should respond or not. This could
have been a trick by Grayson but he didn't seem like he was in
his right mind to be tricking anyone.

Please, go away, she begged.

The male walked forward, the sound of his shoes echoing
throughout the room. Each tap was like a gunshot and Odette
couldn't help but flinch the closer he got to her.

Why won't he just leave already?! Odette squeezed her eyes
shut, not seeing anything helped her feel more hidden. *Is he
going to search the whole church?*

"I promise that I don't mean you any harm," the guy continued. He was probably nearing the front two pews at that point. "I just thought that you looked like someone who needed help."

The scuffing of his shoes on the steps leading up to the altar made Odette's heart lurch. She could see his feet from where she was curled up, his shadow marring the cloth. Odette scrambled back as he lifted her last line of defense, tearing the altar cloth away. She yelped, cowering in front of him. The man was crouched down low, so he could see her hiding beneath it, and she didn't know if she should be frightened or relieved that the man looked nothing like Grayson.

"Oh my God, are you okay?" the man asked, his eyes darting all over her ripped, blood-covered nightgown. He was horrified by her, scooting back an inch in case she were to lash out.

"M-most of it is-isn't mine," Odette stammered. She looked behind him. If he saw another man cornering her .... It made her ill just thinking about it.

"Do you need a hospital? The police? Can you call your parents?" He held out his hand to her, which she took with great caution. She didn't want this innocent man to be Grayson's next victim; she needed to get away from him.

She tore her hand away from his and put some distance between them. She needed a new hiding place, this man had ruined hers. If Grayson was nearby, he would see the open doors of the church and hear their voices.

If I have to, I'll duck behind one of these pews, Odette thought. *And then I'll make a break for the door.*

Odette realized that she had been quiet for some time and that, if her plan was going to work, she needed to get rid of the man. She hadn't answered his question either, so she did so slowly. "No ..."

The man scratched the back of his head, looking around the abandoned church as well. "I guess that makes things easier on me."

Before Odette could ask him what he meant by that, something hard slammed into her head and she collapsed onto the stairs.

Even without opening her eyes, Odette was acutely aware that she was not where she had been last. Unlike the Mages' mansion, wherever she was now was warm. The thing she was laying on was rough and lumpy, and there was a breeze that ran across her bare legs and arms. She wasn't wearing what she had been wearing last.

That thought alone made her open her eyes.

She was in a prison cell ... or a room that had been converted into a prison cell. There were bars that gave her maybe fifteen feet of cell space before they stopped, the room beyond looked like it could have had more. She had a tiny window high up inside of her prison and there was a much larger one outside of the bars. White sheets that were two feet wide had been pinned up along the bars to give her the illusion of privacy, but they didn't go all the way through the length of the cell.

Her room was fairly simple—the bed which was chained to the wall, a table and two chairs, and a toilet. The girl frowned.

Odette obviously wasn't very happy about being locked up inside of a cage but she felt no need to panic. She was still groggy from just waking up and the back of her head throbbed from being hit with something. Whoever had kidnapped her was very strong.

Odette went to stand but was too weak. She collapsed onto the floor, her knees taking the brunt of the impact, scraping the skin even more what they already were. Her new white nightgown fluttered around her. It was thin like the "curtains" and it gave her no real source of warmth.

She narrowed her eyes, her skin crawling with disgust. Whoever her abductor was had not only changed her out of the horrendous nightgown she wore before, but had also cleaned and bandaged her injuries. The thought of some creep laying his hands on her made her shudder in disgust.

Well, Odette thought. *I'm already down here. Might as well look for something to defend myself.*

She spent a good ten minutes sweeping the cell. There were no loose nails or other pointed objects. The bars were very sturdy and seemed to be newly installed. They didn't give in at all when she shook them, and they were too thick and close together for her to try and slip through. The table and chairs were bolted to the floor and they wouldn't even come up. Same with the bed.

The room had been babyproofed. Whoever made it had done a thorough check of everything, making sure that nothing would be to Odette's advantage. Even the window was too high up for her to reach.

Odette eyed the gauzy curtains. She wondered if, she was careful enough, she could twist them up and strangle whoever it was that took her. Using the bars as leverage, she hulled herself upright and leaned against the painted wall. Sweat had already gathered along her hairline from the summer heat and also from how much energy she had to use.

Odette reached out and gathered the fabric into her hands and began twisting it up until it was almost as small as her arm. Luring the guy would be a little difficult, especially getting him close enough to the bars. He would have already seen her trap by the time he walked through the doors. It was pointless—no— it was hopeless.

He would never fall for it. Still, it was her best option.

"Trying to come up with a way to kill me? Not very nice of you."

Odette jumped, releasing the fabric. The man was there, leaning against the far wall. He looked pretty amused by her actions and far too casual for someone who just knocked out a minor and locked her up in a cage.

"Who are you? What do you want? Why—"

The man waved his hand, silencing her. "Why are you here? You need to be more creative with your questions, doll."

Odette recoiled. "Are you kidding me? I want answers! Now!" *I did not run away from one psycho to be taken by another.*

It was dark when she had first seen him, so she hadn't been able to see him all that well, but now, in the light of day, she could see him much better. He seemed tall but he might have only been a few inches taller than her. He had more of a broad build and he held himself in a way that made him seem arrogant. His blond hair was the only striking feature about him; his brown eyes far too dull and hidden under his thick eyebrows.

Odette saw that he was really nothing like Grayson.

"It hurts me that you don't remember me ... then again, I suppose I didn't leave a very lasting impression. We only talked the one time. Still, you'd think that you would remember talking to someone different than your mommy and daddy and the Mages." The man came closer but still not close enough for Odette to try and choke him. "Hmm, let's see if you remember. You wore a white dress and I had on a suit."

Odette recoiled. She didn't like where this was going.

"There were a lot of people around us. A lot of people talking and dancing and almost everyone knew each other except for you. The little girl that no one knew. You looked like a little princess or an angel dressed in your white and silver.

"Still don't know who I am, doll? How rude. Anyway, I came up to you so I could get to know you better. I wore a gold mask that night, shaped like a rabbit's face." He was forming a deranged grin on his face, one that was only used on cartoon characters.

Odette's lips parted and she gasped lightly. She did vaguely remember talking to someone. That guy who kept trying to learn her name and she couldn't remember his.

"It's coming back to you, isn't it?" the guy teased. "Good, otherwise I might have done something drastic."

"Why did you do this?" she croaked, still searching her mind for his name. "Why did you knock me out and ... and take me here ... Claude?" The name rolled off of her tongue easily. Claude. That was his name.

He laughed loudly, the sound echoing throughout the very small room. "That's the thing, isn't it? Why *you*? Why did it have to be *you*? I can tell you, Odette, that I am sorry it had to be you. If Grayson Mages had loved any other girl, it would have been her in your place."

The girl stepped back, furrowing her eyebrows. "What? You ... you did this because I was his girlfriend? That doesn't even make sense, you sicko!"

Claude clicked his tongue, "Oh no, no, no. Don't you know that you're supposed to flatter your captor, doll? Eh, it wouldn't matter anyway. I need you as ... bait. You can think of this as a hostage situation if you like."

"So, you think that Grayson will pay you money to get me back?" *Not unlikely.* "I'm sure that you don't care but I don't want to go back to him."

"Ah, so you found out about the killings?" Claude leaned against the opposite wall as her, his face smug and his eyes knowing. He was egging her on, she could tell.

Odette clenched her hands into fists. "How can you say it like that? He murdered my family; he murdered his own grandfather—"

"That's not what I meant, silly girl," Claude hissed. "I meant the ones before that. Surely, you must have known that the deaths in his past weren't just an accident. The deaths in his sinister past, such as Romy Bacheller and her family. When she rejected Grayson's advances, the poor boy didn't go home and whine about it. You can't be so stupid that you can't figure out the rest."

She clenched her hands into fists, her nails digging into her palms. "And why should I believe anything that you say? You did kidnap me."

The man's eyebrows shot upwards. "Are you defending him now? You change your mind a lot. Romy didn't just run away to kill herself, doll; she wasn't suicidal. Depressed, maybe, but not enough that she wanted to kill herself. That was your *beau's* doing. He offed the rest of her family too, saved the father for last and made it look like he did it himself."

Odette's mind flashed to the body that she had found in the woods. She had believed that the man killed himself too but it had been Grayson. How was he even capable of something like that?

"How do you know about all of this?" Odette inquired. She pressed her face against the bars to get a closer look at him.

Claude licked his lips, his eyes fixated on the window above her head. "I have been watching the Mages for a long time now. They have something I want and ... so do you." He motioned to the ring that was on Odette's finger.

Horrified that she hadn't lost it in the chase the night before, Odette tried to pry the jewelry from her finger. The dull blue stone didn't budge from its spot. It was like it had grown attached to her. She could wiggle it a little and move it up and down ever so slightly, but she could not get the band to go above her knuckle.

"I've already tried that. My next idea is to cut your finger off but I don't think that it will do me any good," Claude sighed dejectedly. "Yours is different from theirs. It doesn't have any of that supernatural power in it."

Her nostrils flared. "And how would *you* know?" she snapped.

"Because of your eye," Claude motioned towards her brown eye.

She raised her hand up to cover it.

"If you had the same powers as those twins, they both would have been blue."

"So, you're after their amulets? Is that what you're hoping to be paid with when *he* 'rescues' me?" Odette asked, smoothing her thumb over the jewel on her ring.

Her captor pointed his finger at her and winked. "*Bingo!* Maybe you aren't a silly girl after all, but a *clever* girl. Yes, Mages will give me his and his sister's amulets or you will sadly—" he imitated having his throat sliced with his finger, complete with noises and faces. "And you might think, 'There's no way he'd give up his power for someone like me!' but you would be wrong," he sang. "Grayson has it bad for you, doll; he's mad about you. If he had to choose between giving up his magical powers and being like the rest of us just to save li'l ol' you, he will."

Odette studied the crazy man in front of her carefully, her face twisted up in disgust. "You won't let us go, though."

"Hm?"

"You won't let us go; you'd have to be stupid to let the people you assaulted go. You'll kill us once you get what you want." Odette released the bars and stepped back. "I'll be dead either way."

It took the man a moment to think through everything that she had said. He was a rather dramatic fellow. Odette thought that he and Greer would get along well if the circumstances were different.

That was when Claude snorted, holding in his laugher. It grew and bubbled until he was cackling and wheezing, holding his sides from laughing so hard. His face was contorting into a gleeful expression but it looked painful with how his cheeks were stretched and eyes shut tight.

"Oh doll, I don't have to kill you! I'll have so much power that it won't matter what you kids try and do to me; I'll still be right on top with my magnificent magic."

Odette narrowed her eyes, challenging him. "The Mages are still famous even if you have power. It won't matter if they have to cancel their shows. They still have weight over the media and they can hunt you down and make your life as miserable as mine."

"Sounds to me like you want to die," Claude said. "Say, I do kill Grayson and Greer, what will you do? I won't kill you. You'll be all alone and the one person who still loves you will be dead."

Then I'll kill myself, she almost said, but she caught herself. "So, what if Grayson still loves me? He's a monster. He can rot for all I care," she rasped. Those words didn't really sit well with her.

"Oh, that's rich." Claude shook his head, his eyes sparkling with mirth. "You still love him. I'm not blaming you; he did condition you to the best of his ability. If he had a couple more months, you would have been the perfect housewife. The poster child for Stockholm Syndrome."

White hot rage flowed throughout Odette's body. In a matter of seconds she had crossed back over to the cell bars and she slammed her fist against them, the pain not registering with her. *"Shut up!"*

Claude snickered, shaking his head. "You're about as terrifying as a baby bunny, doll. I think I'll keep you after I finished with the Mages family; you can be my little pet. You're so amusing."

There was no way that she would allow herself to be held captive anywhere again. *"Shut up!"* she screamed, ready to break through the bars and kill him.

"Oooh, okay," he said in mock terror. "I'll come back later to bandage your hand. I hope you don't try to yell at me some more."

Odette's left hand was starting to turn purple in color. The ache from punching the metal had finally set it. She only glared at the door Claude had gone through a few hours before. She felt so insulted, his words stinging her even as she sat alone in the dimming cell. She wouldn't be anyone's pet.

There wasn't a whole lot to do besides imagine ways to escape and/or ignore her creeping paranoia the darker it got. Her leg had started to shake from the anxiety, tapping incessantly against the concrete floor.

The door swung open silently but the movement caught Odette's attention. Even though she had been waiting on it, it startled her enough to make her gasp and recoil further onto her bed.

Claude peeked through, his stupidly annoying smile in place. In his hands, he held a tray with an array of supplies and possibly food, but Odette couldn't see anything too well.

"Are you going to be a good bunny rabbit when I open your cage?" Claude teased, dangling the keys in front of her playfully.

Odette's stomach lurched but she relaxed against the cement walls. "I'm too tired to try anything." Not a complete lie.

"That would probably be the shock. Poor doll. This has been a rough summer, huh?" The cell's door swung open and she was half tempted to get up and headbutt him in the gut in order to escape. The chance of getting caught, however, by two—potentially three, if Greer got involved—psychos was too great. She stayed put.

Claude seemed pleased with how compliant she was being; she could see the light blush on his cheeks and the way he smiled haughtily. He sat the tray down on her table and motioned for Odette to come and join him.

"Hold out your hand for me," he instructed while grabbing something that looked like athletic tape.

Odette gave him her hand cautiously; worried that he would come through on the threat to cut off her finger. Thankfully, he only paid attention to her ring when he had to move her finger to bandage her hand.

"Um thanks," she said flatly. She felt like a mummy because she had so many cuts and abrasions that had been bandaged.

"Well, we don't want Grayson to think I'm mistreating you," Claude joked, wiggling his eyebrows.

Odette didn't laugh.

"I've brought you bread and water because you are my prisoner and some painkillers," he said and gestured to the other things on the tray.

He had indeed provided bread and water but the multicolored medicine tablets looked like the ones that burned in the fire. Did he think she was that much of an idiot?

She wet her lips and looked him in the eyes. "There is no way I am taking any medicine that you give me. That's, like, hostage survival one-o-one."

"Unless you want me to shove them down your throat and block your air passages until you swallow," he replied casually. "Then I would suggest you take them."

Odette sat up a little straighter, looking between him and the pills. "I don't want to."

"Oh well, that changes everything, doll," he said sarcastically. Claude shoved the tray forward and the water sloshed against its cup.

With a shaky hand, Odette tore her bread into smaller pieces and began to pop them in her mouth one by one. Claude wouldn't look away, he just watched it all with interest or a perverted fascination, Odette couldn't distinguish.

Soon, there was nothing more to eat. Her bottom lip trembled and she glared at the man. Her silent refusal irked him and his once playful expression darkened into something more deranged.

"Odette," he sang. "Are you testing me? Are you trying to see if I won't do what I said I would?" His fingers tapped out a haunting beat on the tin table, his nails scraping against it. The hair on the back of Odette's neck rose with the irritating and shrill sound, watching him carefully as he stood up from his spot.

Claude knelt down beside her, smiling kindly but it didn't meet his eyes. He looked scarier than Grayson in that moment. His hand was quick to shoot out from beside him and he gripped her jaw with a bruising force. His fingers dug into her cheeks and forced her mouth to open wide.

One by one, like the pieces of bread, he dropped the bitter pills into her mouth before he shut it. Odette tried to take a large breath of air through her nose but Claude cut it short by pinching her nostrils close with the same roughness he used before.

Odette's eyes bugged out and she fought against him, screaming and trying to force her mouth open. She didn't know what the medicine actually was; it could have been anything. Her throat contracted and she involuntarily swallowed all of the pills that he shoved into her mouth. Still, Claude did not let her breathe.

She was choking; she needed to cough. She needed *air*. Odette tried to convey to him just through her eyes that she was sorry and that she had done as he asked, but it didn't move him. Claude's eyes sparkled with delight seeing Odette suffer. He was smiling again but it was only a slight upturn of the lips. It was just as creepy as his other one.

Finally, he did rip his hands away from her face and made her fall onto the floor. Odette coughed violently, wheezing and panting loudly. Her head was pounding and the lack of oxygen had amplified all of her aches and pains.

Claude giggled from somewhere behind her. "That was fun. You must be a little masochist, doll, 'cause you need pain to motivate you to do things. This just makes you even more fun!"

Odette wanted to argue with him but she couldn't. He had won that round and done it far easier than Odette wanted to admit. What could she do about it now, though? Nothing but glare at him from the floor and curse at him.

"Yo-you're as bad as *him*," she rasped, her throat raw. The pills that she had swallowed dry were sitting uncomfortably inside her. "No, you're worse!"

"Aw, wouldn't that make him happy?" he cooed in a sickeningly sweet voice.

Odette wanted to just lay on the floor and fall asleep, but she wouldn't allow Claude to have the satisfaction of knowing he hurt her that much. She lifted herself up onto her hands and knees and crawled at an agonizingly slow pace to the bed chained to the wall. She could feel him watching from the door, enjoying her pain to the fullest extent. As soon as she was laying on the "mattress" the door slammed shut and she was finally alone again.

It was a hazy summer day in her dream. White butterflies fluttered past her eyes, dancing together in a small cloud. The garden that she was in was the same one that belonged to the Mages family, and the same one that she had visited before in a previous dream. There were many people there, all of them looking like death dressed up for a tea party.

Odette swallowed back a scream, pressing back against the stone bench she sat on. None of them paid attention to her; they just went about their business and talked or ate with each other. But they weren't normal people—they were *zombies*.

"It sure is a beautiful day, princess."

An icy tendril of dread ran down her back. Odette looked to the side only to see Grayson. He seemed cheerful, not bored or insane, and he most definitely was not dead. His face was bright and lively, his lips pink and in the shape of his gorgeous smile, but his attention was trained on the party.

He wore a white suit with a blue bow tie, his amulet sitting in the center of it. His hair had been slicked back nicely and there was a small blue rose in the breast pocket of his coat. What drew Odette's attention, however, was the silver ring he wore on his left hand.

"What's going on?" Odette cried, narrowly avoiding having someone's intestines fall onto her lap.

Grayson laughed at her, caressing her cheek. "Well, this is generally the part of the wedding during which the guests eat and wish us well."

"*Wedding?!*" It made sense why her dress was fancier than their "guests" now. "I don't want to be here."

"Are you not feeling well? Do you need to go inside?" His concern was stifling. It looked so genuine and she supposed that it would be if he claimed to love her as much as he did. "Is it just nerves? You're so cute, Odette. Greer told me that, sometimes, girls get cold feet before the wedding, but to still be nervous after ... it's endearing."

Odette's eyebrows twitched and she snarled. "This isn't 'cold feet' and I am not 'endearing'! I don't want to be here with *you*."

She sprung up from the bench and took off running, her skirts gathered in her fists. Strangely, she couldn't run. It was like she was the only one in slow motion and, every time she tried to push herself faster, she only got more tired and irritated. Odette still managed to put a good distance between her and the morbid wedding reception, but not enough.

Grayson's hand wrapped around her bicep and pulled her to his chest. "You were trying to run away from me. Why would you do something like that?" his voice was broken. She could feel his tears falling onto her face.

"I don't want to be near you, Grayson! Not after what you've done to me!" She was glued to him. "You've ruined my life—you and your sister! How can I ever love you after all of the killing you've done?"

She couldn't see his face at all, like she was physically incapable of looking at him. All she knew was that she could feel his emotions go through her and he felt angry.

"There are many ways I can make you. It doesn't even have to be done with magic; I can do it with my words and my actions. You are meant to be mine, Odette; all of those other girls in my past were nothing. The two of us have to be together for the world to make sense, and I promise if you just love me back, it won't hurt you."

"You mean you won't hurt me," Odette snapped. "You just want me to be a mindless doll. When I came to town, you saw someone you could easily manipulate and you lunged at the chance. I don't think you even love me for who I am."

"But you want me to."

In the corner of her eye, Odette spotted a splash of silver against the green landscape. Her head snapped in that direction but she didn't see anything or anyone. "Thorn?!" Odette called out.

Grayson's arms tightened around her. "How dare you yell for another man!"

"Thorn?!" she shouted again.

"How about I cut out your tongue, huh?" Grayson threatened. "How would you yell for your precious Thorn then?"

If he's really in here, maybe he can save me from Claude.

"He doesn't deserve you, Odette!" Grayson continued. "No one deserves you! No one can love you like I can!"

Odette ignored his words, twisting even more to find the angel. "Thorn, please! I need help!"

The world tilted and swirled, the scenery changing from the Mages' garden to an entirely blank room. It didn't even look like a room; it was just pure white as far as the eye could see—on the ground and in the sky and all around.

"Miss Odette, are—are you safe?" Thorn cried from behind her.

She turned around and sighed. It was an odd feeling of relief seeing him but he was her only hope. "No. Not even close. Some insane man has me locked up in a cell. He wants to use me as bait for Grayson; he's after the twins' amulets."

Thorn moaned, tearing at his hair. "Th-this isn't good!"

Odette nodded, her breathing ragged. "I figure that Grayson won't give up the amulet anyway—"

The angel shook his head. "N-not that, miss. The amulets ... the amulets will b-be useless to your c-captor. You b-being trapped is terrible! I-I would help you if I could b-but I-I-I *can't!*"

"Can't you track me down?"

Thorn shook his head, "N-no. I-it would be dif-different if yo-you had an amulet th-that worked. Un-unless, y-you kn-now where you are?"

"No ...." Even if she did, what would happen? She would tell Thorn and Grayson would come "rescue" her. She needed strength she didn't readily have if she was going to survive. She sighed, running her hand over her face. It wasn't like Claude would just spontaneously fall over dead.

Odette had an idea.

She took the angel by the hand. "Thorn, why don't we make a deal?"

XXV

"I have more pills for you!" Odette heard Claude before she saw him. When the door swung open, he had yet another tray in his hands. "Are we going to have more fun today or are you going to take them like a good girl?"

She glared at him, her rage burning hot in her chest. "I'll be good." Probably a lie.

"Ha! Okay then, I'll have to find some other way to punish you then," Claude said offhand. "Don't worry about that yet, though. Live in the moment."

The cell door opened up and he stepped in, going to the table like he had the day before. Odette got up and joined him, smoothing out her nightgown before she sat.

"Did you sleep well?" she whispered, picking at the bread that he brought her. He certainly looked better than he had the day before, his face cleaner and he smelled better too.

Claude crossed his arms over his chest. "Aw, are you developing a little bit of a crush on me so soon? Can't say I'm surprised, I am devastatingly handsome but I think that I'm a little out of your league, kiddo." He was egging her on again. It was working but she had wanted to punch him pretty much since the moment they met.

Odette couldn't help but wonder what he would do if she did. Maybe he would try to strangle her again, or maybe he would try something different like slap her or just hit her in general.

"No," she said finally. "I'm not. I was just curious."

Claude hummed, his foot tapping against the floor. He was watching and waiting to see if Odette would put up a fight about her pills again. She didn't. As soon as she finished her "meal," she took the medicine slowly, making eye contact with him the whole time.

Each pill that she dropped into her mouth felt like it weighed her down even more. Each pill that she dropped into her mouth made the madman smile larger.

"Happy?" Odette asked.

He chuckled. "Can't you tell?"

"So, tell me," she shifted forward in her seat. "Have you contacted Grayson or are you just running on faith that he'll miraculously find out where I am?"

There hadn't been anything that gave a hint to where she could be but she assumed that it was still somewhere in Sunwick Grove. *But would he be that bold? Keeping me right under their noses?* He seemed pretty narcissistic, so that gave her a good idea that he might try something like that.

"No, I'm relying on you to get in touch with his demon—or is it an angel? Those two are always so hard to tell apart ... especially when they're enslaved. Anyway, there is no way that your lover boy wouldn't leave you unprotected. Someway, somehow, it will happen." Claude's eyes were boring into her own, his bushy eyebrows raised and his tongue peeking between his lips.

How did he know? What does it matter?

Odette's eyes widened but she flexed her jaw and looked down. Tears pricked at the back of her eyelids. "Too bad for you. He can't help because I'm not family, so your plan just fell through."

Claude grinned, showing off his overly whitened teeth. "So, he has contacted you?"

She slammed her hand against the table, throwing the metal tray against the bars of her cell. The sudden outburst startled her captor. "What part of *'your plan just fell through'* do you not understand?! They aren't *coming* for me because Thorn can't *get* to me!"

"The whole bit, so explain it to me," Claude pressed. "Can't the slave tell Mages where you are? Surely it can do that much?"

"I don't even know where I am! How can I tell him where to find me if I don't know where I'm being held?"

"You're in the lighthouse, you stupid girl! Contact the thing right now and tell him! Tell him!" He slammed his hands on the table for emphasis. It reminded Odette of a child throwing a tantrum.

She hated that he was getting to see her so vulnerable, so weak. "I can't. Thorn is the one who controls when I see him; I can't summon him at will. And he only comes in dreams."

"Well then, I'll just put you right to sleep, huh?" He cracked his knuckles and Odette recoiled.

"It won't work! He's the one who has to enter my mind, why can't you understand that? He's not always waiting around for me; he's with the Mages during the day doing God knows what." It took all of her willpower not to cower any more than she already was.

The man gripped the table harshly, his knuckles turning white. Claude's composure was slipping right before her very eyes. It wasn't the same as the night before when he had turned dark and lashed out at her. Now, it was a raw and untamable anger that made his lip twitch and his eyes narrow. Long gone was his smile; now, he was snarling and seething, his face turning maroon.

"Tell me *exactly* what this creature told you," he ordered, his voice shaking with the effort to keep it even.

Odette sniffed, wiping away the tears from her cheeks. "He said that the amulets would be useless to you. He said that, unless you were a part of the Mages family, they would just be pendants. Think of them like an electric guitar, without the amp, it just makes a little noise. The amp would be Thorn, and if you had him and the amulets, only then would you be able to work it.

"I-I tried to make a deal with him ... I tried to give him whatever he wanted in order to power up my ring so I could escape from you ... but ... but he said that I wasn't family either..."

Claude screamed, tearing at his hair. It seemed that he finally understood. He ripped himself away from the table and kicked the metal tray repeatedly, hitting the bars with all his might.

"NO! NO, NO, NO, *NO!*" he roared. Quicker than Odette had anticipated, he turned to her and crossed the space between them. He threw her to the floor and began to strangle her. "NO! THIS WAS NOT SUPPOSED TO HAPPEN! I HAD EVERYTHING PLANNED OUT AND IT HAD TO BE RUINED BY YOU!"

Odette wheezed, feeling like her eyes were about to pop out of her skull. Something was popping under his grip and she wasn't sure what it was. She clawed at his hands, making them bleed but not making them loosen up from around her airway.

"S ... s ... t ... op!" she begged him, pressing her hand against his face. She pushed against him but it wasn't working. She was beginning to become lightheaded and weak but she had to get him off of her. She didn't want to die being strangled by a madman.

Claude released her neck, frowning. He wasn't looking at her but through her as he began to think. He pushed himself off the floor and began to pace back and forth, smoothing his now messy hair back with his hands.

"No, no. I can work with this. I'll just up the price for you. They'll have to give me their creature too, they will ... yes. I suppose making you look so beaten up will help me out after all, tug on ol' Graysie's heartstrings," he murmured to himself.

Odette scooted herself back towards the wall. Her heart was beating too fast and she wanted to scream but her throat hurt too much for that. She just wanted him to leave; she regretted ever provoking him.

Claude turned his head slightly, smirking at how she cowered. "Are you terrified of me now? Good. I like that expression on your face. It's nice and pathetic."

Her body shook with each step he took towards her and she winced, turning her face away and shutting her eyes. Two fingers were forced under her chin and turned her head back towards him. Odette's skin crawled just having him touch her, it was revolting.

Claude backhanded her, the pain exploding in her cheek. Inside her mouth, she could taste blood from where her teeth cut into the inner cheek. She whimpered softly, her hair serving as a curtain over her face.

"Hmph. Get some rest, doll. You look like crap." The man retreated from her cell, making sure that he had collected the battered tray and cup from the floor. He slammed the door hard, rattling the entire room.

Odette didn't want to cry anymore. She had done it so much and she didn't want to give that man the satisfaction of knowing that he had succeeded in breaking her. Her entire body just felt numb to the pain, like she had turned it off with her mind. She had her knees pressed against her chest, relishing in the warmth they provided. Her mind had been wiped clean of all thought and she just stared at the bars of her prison with dull eyes.

The day passed like that with her sitting absolutely still and doing nothing. She yearned to sleep but she was too tired to do that. The only thing that she had become aware of was the warmth in her stomach, the bubbling anger that she longed to unleash. It continued to climb throughout her body, spreading through her veins like liquid fire.

Odette didn't do anything about it, though. She only let it fester and mutate, thinking of ways that she could hurt Claude. Even if he tried to hurt her again, she would be able to sleep well knowing that she delivered a harsh blow to him. Watching him bleed would make her very happy.

The door handle jiggled once again and all thoughts of revenge left her mind, replaced by the cold fear for him.

"Hello, Odette." Claude's mood had not gotten any better either, it seemed. "You haven't moved since I left you."

Odette didn't respond to him.

"I would have hoped that you had done as I asked," he continued, unlocking her cell door. "But we've already established that pain is the best motivator for you. How about it?"

"I couldn't get in touch with him," she lied. Her voice was scratchy from his torment earlier. "Like I said ... he isn't always around."

Claude made a noise in the back of his throat. "So, he might be there tonight?"

"I hope so."

He motioned for her to join him again at the table. She ate. Took her pills. Drank her water. Stared at him.

"Tell me, Odette, between the two of us, who do you prefer?" Claude asked quietly.

Odette frowned, clutching her own hand for comfort. "Between who?"

"Grayson and myself." He wasn't annoyed that she had asked for clarification, thankfully, but that didn't mean she was in the clear yet.

"I don't like either of you," she rasped. "You're both abusive and crazy."

Claude waved his hand, like it didn't matter that he was certifiably insane. "You have to choose one of us, that's how you play the game, doll."

Odette wanted to snarl or roll her eyes but she stayed calm. "Right now, I would pick Grayson."

"Cute," he snickered. "Young love."

"No. I just don't want to be anywhere near *you*." She was walking on thin ice, insulting him again. Odette wondered if she had just become so suicidal that death-by-Claude had become her subconscious' favorite way to go.

Claude merely shrugged his shoulders. "Sorry to disappoint."

I'm sorry that I have to look at your face, Odette spat in her mind, staring down at her lap. She twisted her ring around, wishing that she was back in Oregon with her family.

"Hmm …. If I had to choose between you and Greer, well I just don't know. You've both got the same-ish looks, although she is a whole lot taller than you and I. Her sadistic side would be very compatible with mine, haha … I just don't know about what I would do if she became obsessed with me.

"But you're pretty fun too, doll. Well, I assume you can be when you aren't all mopey. That's what you get when you deal with angsty teens, though. But you … I think I would have to go with you, doll. At least, with you, I don't run the risk of being killed if I don't accept your feelings. HAHA!"

Odette hardly listened to him. She was more focused on not making any sudden movements that would gain his attention. That was when her ring did something strange. The jewel—

which was normally very dull in color—seemed to come to life and pulse with vibrant blue color. The flash only lasted for a second but she was positive that she hadn't imagined it.

"What is it?" Claude asked suddenly.

Odette blinked, shaking her head. "What is what?"

"You made a face," he narrowed his eyes. "I want to know why."

"I didn't know I made a face, I'm sorry. It was nothing," she lied while squeezing her fingers.

Claude's lips twitched, the second sign that he was about to lose it. "About ninety percent of what leaves your mouth is lie and I'm just about sick of it. I'm giving you a chance to redeem yourself here, Odette, and I think that you should take it."

Her stomach dropped. "I think that you're paranoid, Claude. I'm telling you, it was nothing." But, as soon as she said the words, she wished she could take them back.

Claude busted out laughing his raw, animalistic guffaw. Spit flew from his mouth and splattered on Odette's skin. "I'm the paranoid one? Oh no, no, no. Darling, you are the worst case of paranoia I have ever seen! Scared of the dark, scared that you're going to see some dead bodies. Scared that your boyfriend's always one step behind you. You're always *so scared*, it's ANNOYING!"

He leaned across the table and grabbed a fistful of her hair roughly, yanking her to the middle of the table to meet him.

"You want to be scared?! HUH?! I'll give you something to be scared of!" Using all his strength, he threw Odette by her hair across the cell until her back connected with the metal bars. "I'll make you terrified of me, you stupid girl!"

There was a streak of blood on the concrete from where it had scraped her shoulder, the wound stinging fiercely. Odette just wanted to pass out, that way, she wouldn't have to live through the pain. She would just deal with the repercussions when she woke up.

Unfortunately for her, she was going to stay wide awake for the whole thing.

His first kick to her gut was hesitant if she had to describe it, almost like he wasn't sure if that was the attack he wanted to use. It knocked the wind out of her and she grunted, reaching for his leg to stop the attack.

Claude kicked her again and it was much harder this time. "Let go of my leg, you child!" he shouted, trying to kick her and shake her off of him at the same time.

Odette's agony couldn't be hidden any longer. She cried out, digging her nails into his leg. She wanted him to hurt too.

Suddenly, everything grew quiet. It wasn't because Claude stopped his assault but because of a great energy sucking the spirit from Odette's surroundings. Then there was a great crack. The cell bars shook roughly, banging against the back of her head. Claude staggered back in shock.

Odette couldn't move—her ribs were surely broken—but a sick sense of dread filled her. She knew who it was.

"Step away from my girlfriend."

XXVI

I f she wasn't in so much pain or in danger of passing out, Odette might have felt a little more afraid. She would be lying if she wasn't somewhat grateful for Grayson's appearance. He was, at the moment, the lesser of two evils.

Claude regained composure and smiled. "Grayson Mages, as I live and breathe. I'm a big fan of yours, ya know? I hope you're here to make a trade ... for Odette's sake." He wrenched her upright by her hair and she screamed. The pain in her stomach was excruciating.

Her gaze locked on her "saviors." Grayson, Greer, and Thorn. A sick feeling of gratitude filled her. If they were there, they were willing to negotiate. She didn't want to think about what would happen after.

"Why shouldn't I kill you where you stand? You've put your hands on what is mine, I don't appreciate that." Grayson rivaled Claude's anger easily.

"Because, then, you'd really lose your princess. She was so *anxious* to be rescued, you wouldn't want her to turn right around and run away again." He pulled on her strands harder for emphasis, drawing a pained whimper from her.

Panic flashed across his eyes. "Stop hurting her or I swear—"

"Swear later, little boy. Give me your amulets and the monster and then you'll get your girl," he instructed. He grabbed Odette's left hand and waved around the ring playfully.

Odette yanked her hand away, cradling it against her ribs. "They won't," she hissed. "I'm not worth that much."

Grayson, however, grabbed his amulet in his hand. A blue bubble surrounded it and then *popped* as he ripped it off his shirt, tearing the fabric in the process. He was determined, staring Odette down the whole time. "Don't doubt me."

"Brother, don't—" Greer started but she was cut off when he snatched her headband off of her head. Instead of a soft popping, it was like shattering glass. The purple aura that surrounded Greer broke into thousands of pieces, raining down around her before vanishing. "NO!"

He snapped the headband and slid the amulet off of it. They both sparkled in the dimming room, even though there was no real source of light around. "Take them and give Odette to me."

Claude reached through the bars to accept the amulets, Odette pressing against them uncomfortably. She had silent tears pouring from her eyes and she looked at Thorn in the back of the room.

"Ha! Would you look at that, Odette? You apparently were worth it," Claude cooed in her ear, shoving the two amulets in her face. "You have been a true doll. Thank you. I could just kiss you."

"But you won't," Odette wheezed, her hands clenching into fists. "I would bite you."

"Oh-ho my! Confidence out of nowhere! See, this is why I want to keep you all for myself. You'd be such a fun toy to break." He spun her around to face him, taking her in.

His eyes aren't blue, Odette noted. *That's good. Thorn hasn't done anything yet.*

"We have a deal!" Grayson shouted. He reached through the bars and grasped the fabric of her skirt, pulling her towards him. "Give her to me now or face the consequences."

"Yeah, well, I kinda lied too. What can you do about it?" Claude shrugged. He motioned to Thorn. "You there, you're mine now. Do your thing and power the amulet up!"

"That wasn't part of the deal," Greer hissed. "Thorn, don't you dare."

Claude rolled his eyes. "What are you going to do about it, girly?"

Thorn shuffled forward towards the bars, sniffling as silently as he could. Silver tears streaked down his cheeks and he muttered a very quiet, "Y-yes, s-sir."

"Thorn!" Greer shouted. She lunged for him but Grayson pulled her back by her arm. "No, stop it! She isn't worth this much!"

The room was silent until a low hum could be heard from inside of the cell. Claude was ecstatic. "I can feel it, I can feel the power! Haha! It's addicting!" He shivered pleasantly, his eyes fluttering shut.

The hum grew louder until a blue and silver aura began to expand throughout the cage. It grew and grew, getting so bright that it was painful to look at. Then it sucked inwards silently, leaving everyone hanging on edge. They expected a big booming sound or an explosion but there was nothing of that sort, only the deafening silence, ringing louder in their ears than any bomb would have.

Claude opened his eyes. His entire demeanor had changed once more, something darker and scarier in place. "Okay, Mages, are you ready?"

"Are you?" Odette asked. She shoved Claude backwards and he went flying, connecting with the cement wall with a loud *crack.* "*Doll?*"

She lifted her hand and sucker punched him in the face. She kicked him in the gut a couple of times, feeling the anger inside of her going over the boiling point. All of her pent-up frustrations were taken out on him and she kicked him hard in the face for good measure.

Odette bent down to his level and snarled. "I want to repay you for everything that you've done to me. All of the pain. I think you've earned it."

Claude squirmed beneath her, crying out in surprise. He thrashed around but, for some reason he could not move. It wasn't because of Thorn. The angel would not help her—he knew that she had to do this on her own—but she realized that it was coming from her. That impressive silver light that pinned him—it was coming from her.

Odette didn't exactly know how the amulet worked, only that she was making it happen. Every thought, every emotion that passed through her, fueled the thing and amplified the magic until it could not stay contained any longer. She clenched her fist and felt his life force connect with her own for a small moment.

Claude convulsed as though he were seizing. He gaped at her, the way that fish did at humans in their fish bowls, and clawed at the cement floor. Every sound became amplified in her ears in that moment—his heartbeat, the blood rushing in his veins, his gasp for air—before it all stopped. He fell limp. The silver light receded back into her hand and Odette was left cold and exhausted despite the new energy that flowed through her veins.

"He deserved it," she whispered to herself, shaking her head. If she hadn't ... he would have killed her, *or worse.* "He deserved it."

Then why did she feel so bad? She shivered from her nerves but mentally scolded herself. It wasn't the time to be weak.

Odette knelt down and plucked the amulets from Claude's fingers. Their power sparked to life as soon as they made contact. It buzzed through her veins, new strength that she had never known in her possession. She could actually feel herself being sewed up, every little injury being fixed. Even her chest felt different. *Whole.*

"Odette?" asked Grayson in disbelief. She could feel his awe and anxiety slam into her like a brick wall. She gritted her teeth and forced herself to focus.

"What? Are you confused?" Odette exited the cell and nodded to Thorn in thanks.

The twins could see even in the light of dusk that she had changed. Where she had once been a small, sickly pale thing, she had now grown a couple of inches and earned more color to her skin. Her lips were fuller and had a pink tinge to them; her dark circles disappeared as well. All of the injuries on her body—ones that they had seen only minutes before—were gone. There were no bruises and no scars, but she was the same Odette.

Most startling of all—her two electric blue eyes.

Grayson began to approach her but Odette shot her hand out. Translucent silver chains wrapped themselves around the twins and dragged them back against the front of the cell bars. They both struggled against them but it was ultimately useless.

For the moment, she was the one with all of the power.

"Let me explain. I tried to make a deal with Thorn. I offered him my soul in exchange for powers. It didn't work but I was desperate. I needed him to give me power," she tapped the jewel of the ring, "so I could escape from Claude. From Sunwick Grove, actually. Thorn, however, told me that it was impossible. He couldn't give me his power because I was not a member of the Mages family. That is the same reason the amulets wouldn't work for Claude. He was just too thick-headed to listen."

Odette swallowed hard, walking closer to the twins. "I really needed a way out. Alive or not, with or without Thorn ... when I remembered why you gave me the ring, Grayson."

Grayson's eyes widened and Odette was shocked to see that they were also a different color—brown. He seemed like a different person, warmer, not as emotionless. "I gave you that ring ... so that ..."

"Grayson, you didn't," Greer spat. "How could you?!"

Odette glared at the girl and tightened her fist, making the chains warm up enough to threaten her. Greer squeaked and shut her mouth, writhing some more.

"So, I've accepted your proposal, Grayson." Her voice cracked, much to her displeasure. "I am technically your fiancée anyway."

It was the best compromise she and Thorn could come up with. Odette knew Grayson would hunt her to the ends of the earth if she ran. Thorn mentioned that, should she kill herself, he knew that Grayson would find a way to bring her back, human or not. There was no escaping him. Odette's stomach rolled just thinking of him trying such a thing.

At least, this way, she had protection from him.

Grayson leaned forward, mixed emotions coursing through him. "Then why are you acting like this?"

"Because I *hate you*," she hissed. "You have killed the people that I love. I am doing this so that I no longer have to be sick, and I'm doing this so that I can protect myself from the likes of you for the rest of my life.

"You aren't going to hurt Thorn anymore either. He is going to be treated with more respect, do you understand? He deserves it after having to put up with both of you for seven years." Odette glared at them both, standing up taller. "I'm not going to let you all go away unpunished, not for what you've put me through. So, until I deem you worthy, I'll be keeping your amulets."

Grayson's lips parted. Odette could hear the way his heart thumped faster from fear. "Odette, please ..."

The guilt inside of her grew but she squashed it. His pleas were false. "Don't try to make me sympathize with you! I'm not about to be your next victim, Mages. Understand?" she growled. "And Greer, I can assure you I will never be a victim of yours again."

Odette shouldn't have had to feel guilty. They were the ones who hurt her. They would always try and hurt her.

"You're trash," Greer spat. "I don't know what Grays sees in you."

Despite the overwhelming desire to make her take the words back, Odette couldn't help but laugh. It was bitter, and it hurt, and she was positive that she was just fighting to keep herself from crying at that point.

Greer stared at Odette with wide, disgusted eyes as she laughed.

"You know what? I don't know what he sees either."

EPILOGUE

December

G rayson fixed a glare at Thorn. It irked him that the angel not only got to be free of his room in the dungeons but that his wife had allowed him to have more of a position in the family. Even though he had now taken the job of the butler, Grayson and his sister were limited with just how much they could order him around.

All due to his wife, again.

"Master, would you like your breakfast now?" the angel asked him.

The male pursed his lips, looking down at what had been brought. French toast, fruit, and bacon. "I suppose. Make sure Odette's is ready as well; she'll be here any minute."

Grayson played with his amulet that was on the edge of his robe, finding its weight comforting. It had only been back on his person for about two months, which had caused quite the hiccup with the magic shows at the Tent.

"Thorn, Odette was sick last night. Make sure that whatever you made, you never make again," he snapped suddenly. Yelling at the creature always made him feel a little better but he really deserved it. He couldn't have *his* wife in any pain … not unless he caused it.

Before Thorn answered, Odette's form appeared through the arched doorway, her white robe fluttering behind her, making her look like an angel in Grayson's eyes. He smiled at her and she gave him a small smile back.

"Come here, princess." Grayson extended his hand to her and she put her smaller one in his hesitantly. He coaxed her down to press a kiss to her cheek, enjoying the light pink blush on her cheeks from it. "Do you feel better?"

Odette forced herself to answer, "Yes, I'll be fine." A lie.

Thorn laid out a plate of food in front of her and she thanked him quietly. The angel, much like herself, had changed over the course of the several months that they all lived together. His hair had begun to darken with the more confidence he gained, so it had become a light bronze color with streaks of silver. He looked more like an aging man than anything else despite his youthful outward appearance.

"Your birthday is coming up in a few more days," Grayson reminded her. "What would you like to do?"

Odette shrugged, "I don't know, I don't have anything special in mind."

"We can go somewhere," he suggested. "They are putting on *The Nutcracker* in the city and I know how much you enjoy ballets."

She didn't express an outward distaste for the idea. Everything had been cleared up with the police thanks to the magic of the amulets, but Odette was still wary about being out in public. "That could be fun."

Grayson frowned. He didn't like not knowing what was going on inside her head. He could tell that something was bothering her due to her body language, but he wouldn't force her to tell him.

Odette, on the other hand, loved not having him constantly analyzing her every thought.

"Princess, is something bothering you?" he asked, reaching for her hand. He gently stroked the back of her knuckles with his thumb, trying to pull an answer from her.

Yes, Odette thought to herself, eyeing their hands. Her stomach turned uncomfortably. "I'm actually not feeling good. I think I might have caught something."

Grayson glared at Thorn, the root of all evil in his eyes. "Can you fix her?" he snarled. He wanted to lash out at the thing so bad. Maybe call it a few names—he always cried when he called him "demon," thus demoting him from his angelic title.

Thorn looked up, allowing the two to see his horribly disfigured face. With his one good eye, he studied Odette and then spoke, "I think some tea will help the miss. Will you join me?"

"Yes."

"No," Grayson said at the same time. Odette frowned at him. "If you're sick you shouldn't be walking."

Odette's body language changed to a defensive one in a second. "Grayson," she warned, "Don't. I am going to go and drink my tea in the kitchen with Thorn watching over me and you are going to sit in here and finish your breakfast."

Her husband could hear the underlying fear in her voice, the slight warble of her tone when she told him to stay away. Even after everything that had happened over the five-month period of her stay, she still refused to let go of what he had done in order to be with her. She still didn't love him but he knew that she would eventually.

He didn't want to let her win but he sighed in defeat. "Fine. Come and find me after."

Odette nodded reluctantly and he released her hand. She walked with Thorn to the kitchen, both of them quiet. It wasn't a long walk, only a few corners turned and they were there.

Once they were in the kitchen, though, Thorn turned to her with a serious look. "When are you going to tell him?" he asked.

Odette shook her head. "I can't. Do you know how he would react?"

"Two months, Odette, you won't be able to hide it much longer. Robes and sweaters can only do so much." He glanced down at her stomach, which she was holding with shaking hands.

"I don't know if I can do this, Thorn. I can't bring a child, *his child*, into a world like this. It would give him even more of a reason to obsess over me, to constantly watch me at every hour of the day. I'm only seventeen, I can't," Odette reasoned, feeling a panic rise up inside of her.

Thorn raised an eyebrow, "You're about to be eighteen. You're married and you're wealthy. It isn't like your parents are going to disown you—*ow!*" he howled as Odette pulled his hair.

"Don't. EVER. Mention my parents like that," she hissed, her eyes like live wires.

"I-I'm sorry, Miss Odette," Thorn apologized. "But w-what I'm trying to say is that the situation is in your favor."

Odette scoffed, running a hand through her hair. "How is anything in my life in my favor? That man in there is attempting to *gaslight* me with every passing hour. One day, I may not be able to fight him anymore, do you understand that? I'm so terrified of this child being tortured by their father, or worse, turning out just like him!" she cried.

"Calm down, being upset isn't good for you or the child. Sit down, please," Thorn instructed. "I'll make you some tea now."

She wandered over to where a chair was off to the side and sat in it, her hands rubbing her stomach. It was slightly swollen and Thorn was right, she wouldn't be able to hide it from Grayson much longer. She pulled at her robe, wrapping it around her tighter for the warmth and to hide the tiny bump.

"You're going to have to start changing your diet, you know?" the angel said, handing her tea.

Odette pouted her lips. She brought the cup to her mouth and took a sip when the sound of someone approaching caught her attention.

"Oh my. What's going on in here?" Greer sauntered in the kitchen towards the duo, her eyes cold and calculating.

"Thorn is helping me," Odette informed the older girl. "I'm not feeling well."

"Oh? Well, you need to feel better because I have a guest coming over to the mansion in a few hours. Thorn, tea ... *please.*"

"A guest? Have you told Grayson?" Odette asked skeptically. They didn't have many guests on purpose; Grayson's possessiveness getting the better of him. He, however, didn't use that as the reason; he said that they would get in everyone's way.

Greer giggled. "He's going to find out next, silly girl. Our guest's name is Skylar Lucas and he is really cute. He actually approached me a few months back at the mall, during the summer. I was just too busy to get into anything at that time."

The girls glared at one another but Odette was the one to stop first. She didn't want to get into any unnecessary violence with the other girl.

"Okay, I'll make sure to stay out of your way then." Odette drank the rest of her tea and passed the cup to Thorn. "That is why you're telling me, right?"

"No, you have to meet him. You and Grayson. Don't worry, I'll talk some sense into him so that he doesn't act all crazy around our guest." Greer sighed dreamily, a strange smile on her face. "I just feel like he's '*the one*,' you know?"

No, I don't.

Odette was becoming more nauseous and it wasn't due to morning sickness. There would be more than one person trapped in the same godforsaken mansion with her soon. She didn't know if she would be able to handle that.

CPSIA information can be obtained
at www.ICGtesting.com
Printed in the USA
LVHW032327230919
631984LV00016B/736/P